HORIZONS
WITHOUT BOUNDARIES

HORIZONS
WITHOUT BOUNDARIES
ERIK FOGE

Deeds Publishing | Athens

Published by Deeds Publishing in Athens, GA
www.deedspublishing.com

Printed in The United States of America

Cover design by Mark Babcock.

ISBN 978-1-961505-30-8

Books are available in quantity for promotional or premium use. For information, email info@deedspublishing.com.

First Edition, 2024

10 9 8 7 6 5 4 3 2 1

This book is dedicated to all those individuals who made the ultimate sacrifice to defend my freedoms so I could write this book.

"Everything I write has a precedent in truth." —Ian Fleming

This is a work of fiction. Names, characters, government agencies, places, projects, events, and incidents either are the products of the author's imagination or used in a fictitious manner. Any resemblance to actual persons, living or dead, or actual events is purely coincidental.

PARALLEL MIRRORS WITHIN A DANGEROUS MATRIX

"The fact was, all that stuff was back in our past, and we were dealing with a very, very different present."

— T. Torrest, *Remember When 2: The Sequel*

CLASSIFIED LOCATION, JULY 30, 2012

During the last few days of summer, there had been little rain in the capital, and temperatures were mild and dry. A black Lincoln MKZ with dark-tinted windows and government plates pulled up alongside the entrance of an unmarked executive building. Admiral Bonesteiner and Jacques leaped from the car and ran up the steps toward the doors as fast as they could. As soon as they reached the top of the stairs, Alan pivoted and followed them. The admiral gestured to a security guard, who permitted Alan and Jacques to follow him past the checkpoint. Secretaries, suits, and uniforms from every branch of the US armed forces filled the hallways, all quietly keeping to themselves and spending the day as though it were just like any other. As Jacques and Alan proceeded down the hallway, they did their best to keep up with Bonesteiner as he headed for an elevator.

"Admiral, why are we here?" Alan asked.

Bonesteiner did not reply for several moments, though he could see Alan and Jacques' eyes were becoming increasingly impatient as they waited for an answer. With a deep sigh, he narrowed his eyes and turned to them. "Havoc, destruction, and death." He stepped into the elevator, inserted a brass key, turned it, and pressed the button that would take them to sublevel four of the building.

With his eyes fixed on Alan, Bonesteiner continued. "Are you certain he is alive?"

He was referring to Dr. Erik Függer. Alan nodded.

The elevator dinged as the doors slid open to reveal a subterranean corridor. The admiral once again steamed ahead with long, hurried strides, leading Jacques and Alan to a conference room. Bonesteiner raised his hand and turned around to emphasize the next point. "We are at DEFCON 2[1]. They are liable to ask some direct questions. Give them direct answers." Before Alan or Jacques could ask a question, Bonesteiner lowered his eyes and looked at them. Neither of them said anything, waiting for the rest of the orders. "Don't mention his name until I give the okay. Understood?" They both nodded.

As he proceeded toward the sublevel security checkpoint, he advised Alan and Jacques that they should pull out their ID cards so they could be verified. Several agents of the Secret Service stood guard, and one of them signed them in. A Marine guard held the door open for them as they entered. The soundproofed complex engulfed them, occupying 5,525 square feet and dominated by a conference room in the center, in which they stood. It seemed small and somewhat cramped, however. Even though the subterranean complex was enormous, every square foot was put

____

1. A state of high readiness, with armed forces ready to deploy within six hours.

to effective use, the surrounding offices filled with a full range of workstations, computers, technical equipment, and communications equipment, all of it the most recent technology.

A massive, polished conference table occupied the center of the room. There were approximately thirty people gathered around it. These included the National Security Council, the national security adviser, the Joint Chiefs of Staff, and the directors of the CIA, DIA, NSA, and ONE. Attendees greeted and introduced each other as they made their way to their seats and sat down. As part of the generic Watch Team, three duty officers, a communications assistant, and an intelligence analyst were assigned to monitor the situation. Five Watch Teams monitored international events around the globe twenty-four hours a day, seven days a week.

Jacques, Alan, and Bonesteiner took their seats and waited for the meeting to begin. The muffled chatter suddenly ceased as the Marine guards outside the room snapped to attention with the sound of wooden heels clicking in unison. Everyone around the table stood, then there was almost complete silence; the only sound was the squashing of carpet under the shoes of the President of the United States as he entered the room. Everyone stood at attention with their eyes forward and postures straightened. The president took his seat in a black leather chair with a higher back than the other chairs around the table, then everyone followed suit. A monumental wooden disc adorned with the presidential seal filled the wall behind him at the head of the room, lending an undeniable gravitas to the slender man sitting in the oversized chair.

He greeted everyone at once while emphasizing the extreme sensitivity of the matter at hand and that it should not leave the room. He looked into the eyes of the directors of the CIA and DIA as his temples throbbed with rage, but he controlled himself. Then he asked, his voice intense but apprehensive, "Gentlemen, have you found any more on Israel's intentions?"

Lieutenant General Burgess gave a subtle nod to General David Petraeus, directing the question toward him.

General Petraeus said, "Mr. President, both General Burgess and I believe Israel is planning airstrikes on several targets in Iran." He got up and walked over to one of several screens lining the side walls of the room, this one displaying a map of Eastern Europe. "Gentlemen, the last twenty-four hours have seen some extraordinary ground and naval activity in Europe, the Middle East, and the Pacific." Petraeus pointed at Russian's western border against Ukraine, Belarus, and the Baltic States. "Russia's total ground forces included sixty-nine divisions: seventeen armored, forty-seven motorized infantry, and five airborne." He looked around the room, then continued. "In April, NATO deployed another five divisions, including two tank divisions, to Poland and the Baltic states to reassure those members against Russian aggression."

Everyone knew Russia had an advantage, but General Burgess made sure they all knew the numbers involved. "NATO and American total ground forces included forty-seven divisions: thirteen armored, thirty motorized infantry, and four airborne."

"What's the situation in the Middle East?" The President asked as a yeoman tended a computer terminal to one side of the conference room, putting a map of the Middle East up on one of the larger screens.

Petraeus stepped back to the conference table, took a sip of water, then walked over to the larger screen. "Moscow announced in May that it was heightening its military posture in Europe and the Middle East. They fielded an additional ten divisions, including three tank divisions and new divisions in the western and southern military districts along the borders of Europe. They fielded seven divisions, including four tank divisions, along their southern border." He dragged a laser pointer across the borders of Georgia and Azerbaijan. "Tensions are rising sharply between Russia and the US over ships stationed in the Atlantic, the Mediterranean, and the Black Sea. We have played out a variety of attack strategies and find that a lightning thrust by the Russians from the north and south through Ukraine would lead to total victory in seven days against any defense scenario. However, this will probably only take place if Israel launches their airstrikes against Iran." The yeoman enlarged the map of the Middle East on the screen.

"If the Israeli air force attacks the Bushehr reactor, they may kill Russian personnel at the Russian-built facility. This would infuriate Moscow and could lead to them declaring war on Israel, and then the dominos will start falling, just like the assassination of Archduke Ferdinand in 1914."

"What targets would an Israeli first strike include?" the president asked.

"There would be four primary targets," Petraeus explained as he pointed at each target within Iran. "The Natanz and Fordo nuclear enrichment plants, the Esfahan uranium conversion facility, and the Arak nuclear complex."

"Do you believe the Israeli air force has the capability of carrying this off?"

The yeoman changed the display to show four different approaches the Israeli air force could use when attacking Iran.

The general used his laser pointer as he addressed the room again. "Bombing Iranian nuclear facilities is a complicated task." The President gave a gesture to explain further. "Compared to the operation carried out in Iraq thirty-one years ago," he looked directly at the President, "it would be a very large-scale operation."

Lieutenant General Burgess stood up as Petraeus took his seat. He pointed with a laser pointer. "The Israelis have six Dolphin-class 2 diesel-electric submarines. Each of them can launch four submarine-launched cruise missiles." He took a sip of water between each thought. "Each cruise missiles have a range of at least nine hundred and thirty miles." He took a deep sigh and emphasized his next point.

"Our sources have confirmed each SLCM has a two-hundred-kiloton nuclear warhead containing up to thirteen pounds of plutonium." Dead silence fell upon the room as Burgess continued. "According to our Directorate for Analysis, Israel has four squadrons of F-16Is[2], also known as the Suefa or Storm, and one squadron—about twenty-five planes—of F-15I[3] jets, also known as the Raam or Thunder. Bombing Iranian nuclear installations, as General Petraeus pointed out, would be exceedingly difficult for two important reasons.

"One, Israeli fighters lack the range to reach most of the likely targets in Iran, so Israel would also need to put tanker aircraft into the sky. Israel has at least seven KC-707 tankers that it could use for airborne refueling. Second, S-200 and Hawk surface-to-air missile batteries defend all four targets." He looked into everyone's eyes. "Israel would have at least two secondary targets as well, the Tabriz and Imam Ali missile bases in the west."

"What's the significance of those two targets?" The President interrupted.

"Mr. President, this is to prevent a retaliatory missile attack."

The president sat motionless and erect, like a Doberman on guard duty. He propped his elbows on the table and clenched his fists together in disdain. Under his broad, bulging brow, slanting black eyes looked down with deadly calm as he surveyed the room. The president got out of the chair with authority, pushing himself up with his arms, holding his breath as he rose. He slowly

---

2. Israeli version of the US F-16 Fighting Falcon.

3. Israeli version of the US F-15 Eagle.

tilted back his head, gazed into the nothingness of the ceiling in the conference room, then lowered eyes which hid his inner rage at the news. His voice was calm, but it held an authority that commanded close attention. "Can anyone in this room tell me how we can prevent World War Three from happening?"

"Sir, we still have time to prevent a global conflict. We know Israel is planning their strike at the end of August."

The President slammed his fists to the table. "That doesn't answer my question." He scowled as he looked around the table. "Anyone?"

The Director of the NSA, General Keith Alexander, his eyes bloodshot with strain and lack of sleep, stared across the table into the eyes of the President. "Mr. President, a few months ago, our Directorate S33 intercepted a cryptic message between Amir Kane, Director of Security of the Defense Establishment, and Tamir Pardo, Director of Mossad. It said, 'Fall daylight saving time succeeded and proceeding. Change their finest hour to allow sea lions in and the isolationist will come to our aid.'"

"Okay, what does that mean?" The president lowered his head and looked into the general's eyes.

The general shrugged as he replied. "We don't quite know what to make of it."

Order in the room had broken down. Generals, admirals, and directors argued vehemently about the coded message and what it could mean. Both Alan and Jacques pondered together as they tried to break down the message. It was like trying to solve a complex Sudoku puzzle.

A thought went off in Jacques's mind, and he explained it in a half-whisper to Alan. "'Fall daylight saving time succeeded and proceeding' means that in the fall, the clocks go back." Alan motioned him to continue as they both realized the Israelis must have a time machine.

Bonesteiner glanced over as they worked out the second part of the message. "What are you two talking about?"

Alan ran his fingers through his hair and a moment later, without realizing his tone and volume, said, "Oh my fucking God."

"You've something to add to the discussion, Mr. James?" the president asked.

"The Israelis went back to 1940 to change an event in the past, and that is causing this situation."

"Do you mean to suggest…" one of the joint chiefs bristled.

"They have a time machine?" Alan asked. "Yes, I do."

The President lowered his eyes and looked at Alan; he said nothing, waiting for the rest of the explanation.

Alan drew in a deep breath before explaining. "First, 'their finest hour' refers to England in the Battle of Britain. Second, to 'allow sea lions in' refers to Operation Sealion, the German invasion of England. Third, 'and the isolationist will come to our aid' refers to America getting involved in the war in 1940, a year before Pearl Harbor."

CHAPTER 1

MYSTERIOUS SEMBLANCE WITH A STRAND OF HOPE

"They say no plan survives first contact with implementation. I'd have to agree."
— Andy Weir, *The Martian*

The president studied Alan as Bonesteiner nodded, suggesting he agreed with him. In a commanding tone, the president ordered everyone out of the room except for Bonesteiner, Jacques, Alan, and Greg, the representative from ONE. The silence was unnerving as everyone waited to hear what the president had to say. Then he narrowed his eyes, turned sharply, and addressed Greg. "I thought we were the only country that has that capability."

"Mr. President, we believe Jonathan Pollard gave this information to Lekem, the Israeli agency responsible for obtaining and securing secret technology." He took a sip of water and continued. "The Israelis dissolved Lekem in 1986, and its director, Rafi Eitan, resigned over the exposure of Jonathan Pollard, whom a United States court convicted of spying for Israel in 1987."

"And we are just finding out this now?" The president was not looking for excuses or explanations. He wanted answers.

"Mr. President, I can assure you my agency and other agencies in the Intelligence Community are eliminating any threats, including the one in Israel."

"That still hasn't answered my question." The president's look was cold, hard, and scornful, and everyone in the situation room felt his eyes scrutinizing them. "I would like an answer and a solution to our problem. We are running out of time."

"Mr. President, I believe I know someone that could help," Jacques said.

Bonesteiner pivoted his head and, after a moment, gave a subtle nod to continue.

The president turned his attention. "Who are you?"

"I'm Senior Intelligence Officer Jacques Yves. I work under Admiral Bonesteiner."

"Mr. President, he is referring to Dr. Erik Függer," Bonesteiner explained. "We believe he is in Washington, DC in the year 1948."

The President raised his hand as he shook his head. "Did I hear you correctly, 1948?"

The admiral nodded. "Yes, sir."

"Admiral Bonesteiner, what in the hell can someone from 1948 do to help us?"

"Because he worked under me as the paramilitary operations officer of O.G.D.S. Team 42. I will put my career on the line and know he can do it." He looked at Greg to back his story up. "Greg and I have worked together on a similar project. Dr. Függer is the most capable of fixing this problem."

Greg added. "He was the individual that prevented the Nazis from obtaining and using an atomic bomb."

Jacques elaborated, holding up one finger. "Not just that, but he is familiar with the Wehrmacht. He knows their regulations and strategies, and can anticipate their every move well before they do." He raised a second finger to emphasize his last point. "Dr. Függer can blend in."

"I was his control officer," Alan added. "There is no other better candidate to send back in time. Dr. Függer has conviction, willpower, and the capability to plan and execute complex projects through to the end to right a wrong, no matter how large or small." Alan stood by Bonesteiner. "I will leave things on this last note: All paramilitary operations officers are creative and think outside the box." He paused for a moment. "However, Dr. Függer won't even see a box."

CHAPTER 2

SECRETS FROM DIFFERENT POINTS OF TIME

"Understanding is not absolutely final. What's now right could be wrong later."

— Toba Beta, *My Ancestor Was an Ancient Astronaut*

KENNEDY WARREN APARTMENTS, WASHINGTON DC, AUGUST 1, 1948

The Second World War was over, and the Cold War between the United States and the Soviet Union was in its third year. Erik's life as a CIA operative was behind him, and he was happy that he could experience civilian life and have free will. That was something he could never have when he was working for the agency. He, Jamie, and Max could start a new life in 1948.

Erik felt a measure of inner peace after changing his last name. He was a freelance writer under the name Erik Foge and had done consulting work for several national museums. He wrote and published many articles in historical and political journals. To ensure a comfortable life, Erik invested the money Bonesteiner gave Jamie in secure investments that brought in good returns. He gave some money to the Tucker Corporation and became good friends with Preston Tucker, who gave Erik one of the Tucker

48s he produced. Also, he introduced Preston Tucker to Howard Hughes, another of Erik's friends, who helped Preston find sheet metal for his cars.

Lastly, Erik bought a place at the Kennedy-Warren. Even though ONE would send an operative back, Erik made reliable connections with the local Mafia family in Washington DC. He gained their trust by providing incriminating information about J. Edgar Hoover and ways to beat local and federal law enforcement agencies. In time, the Capofamiglia, or boss, made Erik a Giovane D'Onore—an associate member usually not of Italian ancestry—and offered to put him on their payroll. Erik declined, but suggested another form of payment. He asked for round-the-clock protection for himself and his family, and that if they did give him money, that it would be sent to a Zurich bank account. Finally, he told them never to ask questions about his sources or anything about his past.

Jamie, four months pregnant, was Erik's executive assistant when he consulted for the museums. Jamie loved her job as Erik's assistant, and she hadn't forgotten her duty to assist Erik in his needs, even if they were small things.

Most importantly, they both kept a low profile.

Erik took a deep breath.

"Is there anything wrong?" Jamie asked as she pulled out of their embrace.

Erik placed Max down. "No. I'm just trying to get some things done for the National Air Museum."

"President Truman and the director of the museum are pleased with your work." Jamie opened Erik's appointment book, which was full. "He wants to meet you next week."

"Yeah, I know. I've been told that my work is excellent, but that's attention I don't want to draw to myself."

"Are you worried they'll come back for you?"

"No one can be too certain, but if they do, I'll be ready for them."

"Babe, if they were going to send someone, I'm sure they would have done it by now."

"Maybe you're right." Erik kissed Jamie on the lips.

"Good. You know we have dinner invitations tonight."

"We do? With who?"

"John and Bobby. Remember? John called a few weeks ago and said he was going to be in town and wanted to go out to dinner."

Erik grinned and nodded. "Let me grab my coat while you get the diaper bag. I'll meet you in the living room."

"How do you know John and Bobby?"

Erik shrugged. "I don't know. Maybe they saw me give a lecture."

"He said you had served together."

"I was never in 1943, so I don't see how that's possible. I guess I'll wing it."

They smiled at each other, and Jamie left the room. Erik grabbed his coat off the coat rack and strolled to the window that overlooked Connecticut Avenue.

"Babe, are you coming?" Jamie yelled from the living room.

"Yes." Erik peered out the window. A man wearing a black suit and sunglasses was loitering outside and caught Erik's attention. He nodded at Erik with a haughty expression, then walked on down the sidewalk. A bald eagle landed in a nearby tree, and as he watched, Erik evaluated his situation.

With a vast knowledge of history comes great responsibility to preserve it. His gift was to know future historical events, both good and bad. But it was also a curse since he couldn't interfere or change them. Protecting Jamie and Max came first, though. Without hesitation, Erik walked to his desk, opened a drawer, pulled out a Luger, and loaded a magazine.

As Erik strolled into the living room, Jamie gave him a quick glance over and felt the bulge under his left arm. "Do you think that is necessary?"

What Jamie still didn't realize was that once one was in covert ops, they would always have enemies. Oddly enough, those enemies could be from the future or government agencies of the present. Those enemies would want Erik for different reasons. Some might seek information, hoping to question him. Others might simply wish to kill him.

"I trust your judgment," Jamie said, patting the bulge before heading to the door.

They had been living their new life since late 1944, and had been in Washington DC since the spring of 1945. Every day, Erik still needed to be aware of his surroundings and apply everything he learned. He often recited a quote from training in his mind: *Remember, you don't hide in the darkness. You are the darkness.* However, Erik knew that wasn't always about sticking to the shadows; it was about hiding in plain sight. In fact, his enemies stood out in 1948 society because they don't know the mannerisms. Even if they did, Erik could pick them out. With that in mind, there was no better place to be than in the open where they could find him. If they could find him, he could find them and set traps for them.

The elevator arrived at the lobby of the Kennedy Warren Apartments. As Erik and Jamie stepped out, the steward held the door opened and said, "Have a good evening, sir." Erik nodded with just the right amount of disdain, as most people of high-society would. By post-war standards, Erik looked like a badass. He was dashing in his brown, three-piece, herringbone tweed suit, polished wingtips, fedora, crisp white oxford shirt, and an Art Deco tie. Jamie looked stunning yet conservative in her outfit. She wore a green two-piece ensemble with a small collar, puffed shoulders, and short sleeves. She accessorized with a tiny hat, large handbag, nylon stockings, and matching pumps with thick, high heels. They looked the part of the typical 1940s American family, although from the upper crust of society, and no one would think they were from sixty years in the future.

An average crowd filled the lobby, upper-middle-class families, and couples, getting ready to go out to dinner or social parties. Erik and Jamie mainly kept to themselves, careful of everyone who they contacted.

One thing Erik liked about the Kennedy-Warren was the doorman named Jerry Greene, a World War One Veteran who was a part of the 369th Infantry Regiment. Jerry was a fifty-eight-year-old black man with a strong, robust face, a round nose, and a firm jaw, standing the same head height as Erik. He wore a charcoal doorman's jacket over his broad shoulders, perfectly fitted, with polished buttons, matching slacks, and freshly shined shoes. On duty, Jerry walked straight, his face held forward in a steady gaze, bearing an air of authority and purpose.

Erik loved talking to Jerry about history and his service in Europe. The 369th arrived in France in 1917 and was lent to the French 4th Army. They wore US uniforms and bore French weapons when sent to the frontline for 191 days. They made a name for themselves and were victorious against the Germans, who gave them the nickname the "Hell Fighters"; however, the 369th proclaimed themselves the "Black Rattlers".

Every time Erik stared into Jerry's eyes, it was like looking through a window at an unknowable soul. Those hardened, dark brown eyes hid horrors the man never shared. However, his peppered hair softened his eyes, and his thin mouth offered a warm smile for whomever he greeted. Erik had the same eyes, so Jerry shared stories from time to time. Sadly, most people didn't care about his well-being, or they treated him as if he were invisible, but not to Erik or Jamie.

"Good evening, Erik," Jerry said, then he turned to Jamie and offered a slight bow. "Jamie." He paused for a moment as they nodded in response. "How are we this evening?"

"We are well. How are you, Jerry? Your family?"

The smile didn't leave his face. "I'm well, and so is the missus." Jerry stepped closer to Max, cradled in Jamie's arms, as others stared, as if that wasn't socially acceptable. He felt their presence and stared down at them. Once the crowd seemed inclined to focus their attention elsewhere, he then turned back to Jamie and glanced under her arms, to her slightly swollen belly. "Oh, it seems to grow every day." He and Jamie exchanged smiles. "How many months are you?"

"Four," Jamie replied.

"Oh, a December baby. How exciting." Jerry said as he walked them to their car and opened the door. As Erik placed Max in a baby seat, Jerry asked, "Where are we going this evening?"

Jamie replied, "Martin's Tavern."

He thought for a moment. then raised a finger. "That's on Wisconsin Avenue, right?"

Closing the door and facing Jerry, Erik nodded. "We have never been. Have you?"

"No, Erik, they don't allow us colored folks in."

Erik sometimes forgot there was still segregation in the country. Even though both he and Jamie didn't like it, it was a reality they could not change. "Well, I think they should. Especially because you are a veteran."

Jerry stepped closer, and his reply was hoarse, flat, and without emotion. "They don't care." He looked at the affluent crowd exiting the building, all of them white, and back at Erik. "They never will."

Erik knew it was pointless to argue and even give insight into the future.

"You're a veteran, aren't you?" Jerry asked.

Erik nodded.

"All places will treat you like a hero. But not for us colored folks." Jerry pointed to Erik to get his next point clear. "There's something different about you from all the other white folks I met before. I don't know what it is, but you are different, and I respect and like you." Jerry had a gleam of satisfaction in his eye. "Did you fight in Europe?"

Erik nodded.

"I know you were no grunt. So, what did you do?"

Erik shook his head.

"Secret stuff?"

Erik offered no clues, merely looking Jerry in the eye and remaining silent.

The doorman flashed a slight grin. "You were one of those guys."

"Sorry, I don't follow what you are talking about."

Jerry squinted and rubbed his chin, his thoughts turned inwards. "How do you think the Germans could have lost the Battle of Britain?"

Erik paused, almost carried away by the moment as he helped Jamie in the car. He caught himself, turned to Jerry, and shrugged. "They lost."

Jerry looked with confusion at Erik's blank expression. "Are we talking about the same war?"

Erik felt Jerry's eyes scrutinizing him. The CIA trained Erik to act dumb. The trick wasn't only not giving anything away, but also to learn something valuable in return. So, he shrugged again.

The doorman's face twisted into a mask of confusion. "Are you telling me you forgot that the King and Queen of England, and even Churchill, left England in the fall of 1940?"

"I forgot," Erik lied. He gestured, suggesting it must have

slipped his mind, then looked at his pocket watch. "Jerry, we'll have to talk about this later. We're running late."

Jerry nodded and laughed. "You are too young to be losing your memory. Have a good night, Erik."

"You too, Jerry."

Jamie's sweet, calming voice broke in on Erik's thoughts as he focused on the road and Jerry's crazy story. "Babe, you seem troubled. Are you okay?"

Erik had become tense, whiteness appearing around his lips. His intense, blue eyes stared blankly at Jamie. His words sounded severe, as if forced to speak before he lost his sanity. "What in the hell…" Jamie glanced at him while looking at Max in the rear-view mirror, and he knew he had to watch what he was saying. "Did you hear what Jerry said?"

Jamie nodded as replied. "Perhaps he is uncertain, or read it in the book or something."

"But he actually believed it. That's the scary part."

"We'll talk to him tomorrow."

As Erik parked on Wisconsin Avenue near Martin's Tavern, he started analyzing his surroundings. He recognized the license plate numbers of all nine cars on Wisconsin Avenue, including a member plate from the 80th Congress, meaning John Kennedy was there. Upon entering, Erik instinctively checked the exits, seeing several men with ties that had themed hobbies and interests, like fishing or hunting. Bobby and John Kennedy wore Western and tropical-themed ties, which seemed to be everywhere. The fashion was the crazier the tie, the better, though Erik disagreed. The tavern was a single story and had a humble atmosphere, with odd columns, and dark wood, and walls stained by decades of cigarette smoke covered in fox-hunting prints and black-and-white baseball photos. Several people sat at cramped seats, around the bar, and in the rear "Dugout" room. Tiffany-style lamps dangled overhead, which cast a soft glow throughout the establishment. It was a warm, friendly environment, and no threats seemed to be present.

"Good evening and welcome to Martin's Tavern." A young man in his twenties approached Erik. "How many for this evening?" Erik nodded in John's direction, and the man gestured to follow him. As they neared the Kennedys, Erik asked if they could sit in the corner booth.

The young man replied, "Of course, sir. It will just take a minute for me to get it ready for you."

"That'll be great, thank you," Erik said.

As the young man hurried off, John approached Erik, shook his hand cordially, and said in a heavy Bostonian accent, "Erik, it's been a long time. How have you been?"

Erik recalled his training at the Farm about re-establishing an old cover identity. He would have to remember the name used, which thankfully was his name, the cover story he had created, and be consistent down to the smallest detail. "Never better. Seems like forever."

John looked at Jamie. "He told me so much about you when we were stranded, before we were rescued." Erik let John take the lead and fill in all the blanks from their past. He nodded along and added vague, yet convincing affirmations.

"I never thought we would be rescued," John said, staring at Erik. "Did you?"

"No, I thought things were hopeless."

"I also remember when—"

"Congressman, your table is ready." The young man, holding a highchair, gestured to the booth in the corner. Erik controlled his emotions. He knew it wasn't easy to get information on something he knew nothing about without revealing as much. That untimely interruption would probably lead to John forgetting his train of thought.

"I'm starving," John said as he turned toward the table.

Erik placed a hand in front of John. "You don't mind if my back is against the wall, do you?" John shook his head as Jamie placed Max in the highchair. The high-backed hardwood booths creaked and groaned as everyone took their seats, and the young man handed out menus.

Erik tried to recover the dangling thread of the covert interrogation. "So, John, what were you saying before?"

John waved it off like a fly as he looked over the menu.

Bobby asked, looking up over the top of the menu, "Have you guys been here before?" At the same time, Erik and Jamie shook their heads. "John and I have been here several times. The food is amazing."

A server came over, took the orders, and left, then came back in minutes with everyone's drinks and left again.

"I can't believe the last time I saw you was…" John's eyes turned inwards, remembering, "five years ago." He took a gulp of beer. "So, what have you been doing?"

"Working at the Aerospace Museum and finishing my novel. That's about it. What about you?"

"Well, I'm sure you can imagine being in the House of Representatives keeps me pretty busy."

Bobby jumped in the conversation, leaning forward. "John is preparing to run for the Senate in 1952 against…" He snapped his fingers several times, then pointed to Erik as he remembered the name. "Lodge. Henry Lodge. He's a Republican and a three-term incumbent."

"Have you heard of him?" John asked. Erik shook his head. "Bobby is helping with the campaign, and he came up with the slogan 'Kennedy Will Do More for Massachusetts'."

"Catchy, huh?" Bobby asked. Erik smiled in agreement. "You guys served together?" He glanced between Erik and John.

Erik took a sip of his wine while John lowered his eyes, but said nothing, waiting for the congressman to complete the rest of the story.

"Erik was a lieutenant commander assigned to my boat for some secret mission. Since the war is over, am sure you can share."

Erik sometimes was in a unique position like then. He needed a believable story and a lot of confidence, but there were details he did not know. "No."

John turned to Jamie with a frustrated smile. "Is he always this secretive?"

She nodded and said, "And mysterious."

"Exactly." John pointed at Erik with a cunning grin. "He knows what we are talking about."

Bobby jumped in. "Erik, what did you do in the war?"

No matter where he was, in a restaurant with friends or in the field, Erik knew people would question what he did and his cover would be tested. He felt John and Bobby's eyes scrutinizing him. "Naval Intelligence. I prevented bad things from happening." Erik believed that a certain amount of deception in social relationships was necessary, especially since he could alter history or a person's life with something as simple as saying the wrong thing or making too lasting of an impression.

"Like?" Bobby motioned Erik to continue.

Erik took a sip of his wine. "Things."

"You know what you remind me of?" Bobby tilted his head to back him up. "A buddy in college told me about this covert agency. The OSS, Office of Strategic Services. Tell me, am I right?" Bobby lowered his eyes, studying Erik.

Erik stared the man in the eye with a blank expression, revealing nothing, not even a blink, to confirm or deny the accusation.

Erik didn't know that the Kennedy brothers, with their father's connections, did a background check on him. They found nothing on Erik before 1944. Their sources said Erik claimed to be a major in the OSS, but John remembered him as a lieutenant commander in the Navy in 1943. However, they found no military, OSS, or CIA record of Erik. It seemed his background was so secret that he didn't even exist on any government database. John's father told him not to trust Erik, but the man saved his life, and his secrets and mysterious past were intriguing.

After a long pause, Erik still said nothing, revealed nothing.

"I knew I was right." Bobby smiled as he patted the table.

"Bobby, you have a vivid imagination," Erik said. "Maybe you should write spy novels." He needed a distraction to kill the suspicion about who he really was.

A man approached the table, breaking the tension, and said in a thick Irish accent, "Congressman, it's so nice to see you again." He turned to Bobby. "And your brother."

"William, how is your family?" John asked.

"Great, thank you."

"I would like to introduce you to a good friend of mine, Dr. Erik Foge. We served together."

Erik stood up and shook hands as the man introduced himself. "William Martin, nice to meet you, sir."

"Mr. Martin, this is my wife, Jamie." William did a slight bow. "And this is my son, Max."

The server approached again, and the savory, flavorful, and wholesome aromas of grilled lamb loin chops, slow-roasted prime rib, and New York strip got stronger and intoxicated everyone at the table. Their heads craned back, their mouths watering and eyes enlarged with delight. After the food arrived, William excused himself.

Bobby was still probing. "Erik, can I ask what you did, or is that top secret?"

Erik knew he needed to stop the man's curiosity. He leaned

forward, his eyes narrowing, and replied in a firm tone, "I prevented certain things from happening."

Bobby realized he went too far as he looked at Erik's disdainful expression.

"Done?"

Bobby nodded.

"Good."

Jamie had seen that stare from Erik before whenever someone questioned him about being with the CIA. Even though Erik had been out of the agency for nearly four years, she wondered if he could adjust and if he would ever get to say what was on his mind and who he actually was.

Bobby, realizing he would not get anything out of the man, quickly changed the topic. "You said you are writing a book."

Erik nodded. "Yes, I'm writing a book."

"What's your book about?"

"It is set in the future, about a curator and a tour guide at the National Museum of American History, living in a condominium in Washington, DC, or so everybody thinks. He actually works for a government agency. He is with a newly developed task force within the agency, assigned to a separate division known as O.G.D.S., Orbital Group Destination Services. His missions take him to the underground hallways of a Russian nuclear submarine base, to a warehouse containing secrets of the Third Reich in Berlin, and back to DC. He is caught in an accelerating tempest of secrecy and lies, but hides it from the girlfriend. Things get even more complicated when his close friend, who works for another government agency, gets murdered, initiating threats that could expose him to his enemies. He must then risk not only his career, but also his life, to find the truth behind the most significant secrets from World War Two. In the end, he battles for what he believes in while feeling betrayed on all sides, but if he falters, he will become a star on the agency's memorial wall."

Both John and Bobby are speechless and cannot come up with the words that express how they feel, visibly trying to collect their thoughts. While pondering the story, John momentarily glanced up at the ceiling, then back at Erik. "Wow." He looked at Bobby, Jamie, and again at Erik, "Where in the hell did you come up with that?"

Bobby comprehended what he just heard, focused, and replied, "Well, you certainly have a vivid imagination."

"Do you have a name for your book?" John asked.

Erik nodded. "*We Know Your Name.*"

After dinner, they continued to talk about history, politics, and a wide range of other topics. John said he would eventually like to run for president. Bobby was going to get his law degree. It was hard for Erik to sit in front of the two brothers, knowing both would be assassinated within two decades. Not only that, but knowing of other events, such as the Korean and Vietnam War, that would shape American society and foreign policy.

Bobby's voice broke Erik from his thoughts. "John, I believe you should have Erik in your cabinet when you win the presidency, with all the knowledge he possesses."

Erik paused from drinking his wine, almost carried away by what Bobby said.

"What about it, Erik? Would you do it?" John asked, taking a sip of his coffee. "You know more about the Soviet Union than anyone I know."

Bobby nodded in agreement as Jamie stared at Erik.

John pressed on. "We would make a talented team."

Erik kept his eyes and expression neutral, but his pulse beat in his right temple, as it always did when he tried to hide his tension building up. "I'm honored, but I would have to turn it down."

John was dumbfounded. "Why?"

"I have my reasons."

John motioned him to continue.

Erik's eyes locked on the congressman's as he said in a low, even voice, "What did I do during the war? Sometimes, the lines between right and wrong got blurry. So much so that after a while, I didn't want to fight anymore and wanted a quiet life." Erik looked at Jamie and clasped her hand, then turned back to John. "I would like it to stay that way."

John knew when to quit while he was ahead. "Maybe you could give me advice if I come to ask."

Erik nodded.

Bobby broke the gloomy mood. "Anyone hear about fortune cookies?" He pulled a few of the plastic-wrapped novelty deserts from his coat pocket. "I got these while I was in California." He motioned everyone to grab one and read their fortune as John paid the bill.

Erik, like the others, opened his cookie. He let out a deep sigh and shook his head. One by one, they read their fortunes out loud.

Jamie said, "You will have to remain strong in the coming months with the challenge that lies ahead."

Bobby was next. "When you are in the kitchen; watch where you step."

John laughed, adding that Bobby was a lousy cook, but Erik knew it would come true, because he would be killed in the Ambassador Hotel's kitchen in Los Angeles. John then read his. "You will be an eternal light to future generations." John laughed it off, saying that's why he got into politics. Erik knew all too well that when John will be buried in 1963, there will be an eternal flame.

Finally, Erik read his. "Before you travel, ask 'Am I doing the right thing?' When you arrive, ask, 'Am I prepared to put things right?'"

He just shook his head as Bobby added, "Looks like you are going on a mysterious trip."

"I hope not."

With dinner taken care of, it was time to go. Erik and John shook hands, gave each other a brotherly hug, and agreed to meet again soon. They parted ways, and Erik excused himself from Jamie. He went to the restroom and stared in the mirror. His intense eyes revealed his thoughts as he reread his fortune. He pondered each facet of his life. There could be an untraveled road or an untold secret anywhere. Through each passing day, there were tomorrows with hidden paths. He freshened up and met up with Jamie in the lobby. Beside her were several Secret Service agents, President Harry S. Truman, and his wife, Bess.

"Erik, how are you doing?" Truman asked with a wide smile.

"Good, Mr. President." Then Erik looks at Bess. "Mrs. Truman."

The president gestured for Erik to follow him away from the others. "I now see things differently than others. My campaign manager says Dewey is gaining popularity in some states. You think I should be worried?"

Erik shook his head.

"Are you sure?"

"Yes, Mr. President. Just stay the course." Erik rubbed his chin, then raised his finger. "When you win the election, hold up the Chicago Daily Tribune from the third of November."

Truman looked puzzled.

"That paper sometimes has their facts wrong. Better yet, when you hold it up, make sure people are there to take your photograph."

"Are you sure?"

Erik nodded.

"Okay, I will. I hope I won't look like a fool."

"You won't. Trust me, the Tribune will be the only fool in that photo."

"I would like to say thank you for all your help with the National Air Museum. Do you think we should put Nazi planes on display?"

Erik nodded.

"Why?"

"Because it will show people how lucky we were defeating the Nazis with all their advanced weapons."

"I like your thinking." Truman removed his glasses. "Do you remember how lucky we were defeating the Germans? Especially when we stopped Rommel in the Middle East."

Erik was suddenly bewildered and struggled to maintain his composure. He didn't know what to say or how to ask for an explanation. He looked at Jamie, then back at Truman. He couldn't believe what he was hearing. He gathered his thoughts and asked with care, "Mr. President, are you referring to Operation Theseus and Aida, the invasion of Egypt and the Suez Canal from Libya, or Plan Orient, the projected invasion of the Middle East by the Afrika Korps?"

Truman nodded as he pointed at Erik. "That's why I like you." Then he tapped his temple. "I would like you to come see me at Camp Shangri-La."

"I would like that, Mr. President."

Truman cupped Erik's shoulder. "Good." He looked at Bess and back at Erik. "She thinks I talk too much, and she wants dinner." They walked back to their wives, and Truman addressed Jamie.

"Your husband is a gentleman and a scholar." He then faced Erik. "We will talk soon."

The couples parted, Erik leading Jamie toward the exit, with Max in her arms.

"What is it?" she asked, knowing something was troubling him.

Erik's reply was hoarse and emotionless. "History has changed."

As they stepped out, Erik took a deep breath. As his mind cleared in that moment, he noticed a car across the street with a man he couldn't identify behind the steering wheel. The car was running.

Jamie placed Max in the back seat. Erik opened her door and, once she got in, closed it. He then walked around to the driver's side, keeping his eyes on the man across the street. He took a deep breath before getting into the car and turning on the engine.

He was glad strategic driving was an essential part of his training. He'd also learned what his car could do: the speed, power, and handling. He was confident with the machine. It also didn't hurt to have over a hundred and fifty horsepower under his hood, while most cars only had ninety.

Erik turned on the high beams, penetrating the night and blinding the mysterious driver, even if just momentarily, then popped the car into reverse and slammed the accelerator to the floor. The Tucker screamed back through the tight spaces between cars going in opposite direction, then made a tight ninety-degree turn on Wisconsin Avenue. He dropped into drive, and the Tucker's wheels squealing as they gripped the asphalt like an eagle's claws on a salmon. Erik's pursuer swerved around a slower car, its engine roaring.

Jamie turned her head, knowing they were being followed, her heart pounding in her chest.

Erik pulled out the Lugar and handed it to her.

CHAPTER 3

FROM HERE TO A MYSTERY

"Compliments make me feel uncomfortable cause I feel like I fooled someone into believing I'm this special person that I'm not."

— facebook.com/infjrohit

Erik knew when being chased in traffic, there were two things he would need to focus on: speed and maneuverability. He needed speed to create distance. Maneuverability, on the other hand, could put him in a position where the other driver could not follow. In the best-case scenario, he could make them crash.

Erik sailed through traffic, the Tucker gaining speed down Wisconsin Avenue. Despite the velocity of the getaway, Erik remained calm at the wheel, weaving around vehicles like the Millennium Falcon going through an asteroid field. The Tucker 48 had three fundamental characteristics Erik appreciated while being pursued: speed, maneuverability, and stability, especially as he neared the intersection of Wisconsin Avenue and P Street NW.

Erik reached fifty miles per hour, then sixty, running parallel to a city bus. As he came up to the intersection, he eased off the accelerator, braked, and pulled hard on the wheel to make a sudden right. The smell of rubber filled the cabin as Jamie lay low in her seat, bracing herself. Erik looked in the rear mirror to see what the other driver was doing. From that, he would know who he was dealing with. If the man tried to pull the same maneuver and failed, Erik was dealing with an amateur. If he continued down Wisconsin Avenue, he had enough experience and confidence to find another way to catch up. However, the car flew over the sidewalk to make the turn with great precision and skill, which was bad news. The driver not only knew what he was doing—this wasn't his first time at it.

Erik's worst enemy was traffic. Although he was trained for just such a situation, racing through midtown traffic resembled playing chess with twenty beginners who don't have the foggiest idea how to play. That was also a benefit, because the other driver would feel the same frustration. So, Erik changed tactics from out-running to out-smarting his pursuer.

He knew he was nearing the end of P Street because there was a buildup of cars, meaning they were nearing the roundabout of Dupont Circle Northwest. Normally with a roundabout, drivers must slow down or stop to yield to traffic already in the circle, wait for a gap, then carefully proceed. Instead, Erik plowed through it, trying to ignore a shrill cry from Jamie, forcing all other traffic to brake hard and aggressively maneuver to avoid collisions. Erik used speed and maneuverability to avoid crashing and left the ensuing chaos to test his pursuer's skills.

They barreled down Massachusetts Avenue into aggressive evening traffic. Erik crossed the double line and tore past oncoming vehicles, then revved through several traffic lights as he tried to disappear.

A glance in the review mirror showed his pursuer still hot on their trail, nearing the last intersection they passed through. Moments after the light changed to red, a large box truck entered the intersection. The follower braked and swerved, missing the truck by inches, then accelerated with a burst of speed.

As Massachusetts Avenue dipped into a tunnel under Thomas Circle Park, the pursuer was closing the distance between them. He entered the tunnel, avoiding two other cars by inches, and continued to gain ground. Exiting the tunnel, the car's tires gripped the incline like a spider climbing a wall, and the vehicle blasted through an intersection with perfect timing and precision.

Eventually, Massachusetts Avenue turned into New York Avenue NE, and the roaring car was almost on top of them. Erik realized he would not shake their tail and would have to stop the man.

Erik swerved to the left lane and shouted for Jamie to brace herself. The pursuer got closer, staying in the right-hand lane, coming alongside them.

Erik slammed on the brakes.

The tires gripped the asphalt as smoke from burning rubber engulfed the car. As the man surged past, Erik stepped on the accelerator and lined up the front end of his car with the rear of the pursuer—who had just become the pursued. As soon as he felt the telltale bump he was hoping for, he spun the wheel to steer into his target. Erik pushed the gas all the way to the floor, forcing the other vehicle's tires to lose traction. The mystery man's car skidded out of control, spinning across the middle of the road.

Erik steered away from the uncontrolled vehicle, straightened his car, and continued toward his destination.

He turned about on Morse Street NE and parked near A. Litteri, Inc. In front were several well-dressed men in designer suits and fedoras, some with large diamond pinky rings. Late model Cadillacs were parked along the curb, owned by those gentlemen. Historians would say Washington, DC didn't have an organized crime problem, but there were two reasons for that. First was that most of their legitimate and illegal businesses were outside the DC area, where they could bribe local law enforcement. Second, and the most important reason, was they could bribe members of

Congress to pass legislation that would benefit them by setting up legal lobbyist groups.

Erik ignored them as he got Jamie and Max out. However, their eyes were fixed on Erik, and one glanced up and down the street looking for anything out of place—particularly the feds. Erik approached two of the men and ordered them to bring Jamie and their son inside and protect them at all costs. The men nodded and did as they were told. The others stepped aside for a large man, standing six-feet tall with cold, brown eyes that could turn medusa to stone and a hard-hearted face. His name was Paulie Bongiovanni, but everyone knew him as Ice. Ice earned his nom de guerre because he solved problems by having problematic people killed. He also showed no emotion outside his inner circle, which Erik was part of.

Ice approached Erik with open arms and gave him a brotherly welcome. "What's the problem?" he asked.

Erik pointed at the intersection. "In around two minutes, there will be a car coming around that corner which has been following—"

"Feds?"

Erik shook his head.

"Who?"

Erik flashed an expression only Ice understood to mean *don't ask questions.* He made Ice and his organization lots of money, but it was a no-questions-asked arrangement.

Ice looked over his shoulder, and his men knew what they had to do. They didn't even hesitate to consider asking things like 'who' or 'why'. He gave simple orders, and if someone questioned his authority, they got hit so badly they never asked questions again. One didn't even think about questioning Ice's reasons or orders.

Tires screeched against the pavement as the pursuing car

skidded around the corner. Ice's men met him, maneuvering to encircle the car.

Ice and Erik walked inside, marching through the Deli toward the restaurant, which was closed. Jamie, looking worried, stared at Erik to make sure everything was under control. When he gave her a subtle nod, she flashed a grin.

"I want him alive. He will be packing." Erik ordered Ice, and with a snap of his fingers, Ice passed on the order. One of his men ran outside to pass on the belated stipulation.

Ice pulled Erik away so Jamie wouldn't hear. "I will make this fed talk." Ice raised a finger to emphasize his point.

Erik said nothing.

Ice flashed a psychotic smile and nodded. "Or would you rather make the piggy squeal? Don't let me get in the way of your fun."

Again, Erik ignored him. Government agencies, like the CIA and other dark ones, used different method interrogation techniques than police and the mob. Cops used psychological intimidation and threats of prison time. The mob used physical intimidation, often delivered with brute force. Erik preferred a more subtle approach. He started his interrogations without saying a word, then calmly asked questions, and maybe graduated to waterboarding, then repeated the process as needed.

Ice's son, Paulie Jr., approached them with a pistol and handed it over. Ice looked it over and pulled the clip out. He was trying to make out the model, but gave up and handed it to Erik. "Seen anything like this?"

Erik knew instantly it was a Glock 23. He removed a bullet and recognized a Fancier Hollow Point. The sidearm was police or government issue, and from the future.

"What kind of bullet is that?"

Erik ignored Ice and questioned Paulie. "Did they put up a fight?"

Paulie shook his head.

Erik loaded a round into the chamber of the Glock, then handed the gun to Jamie.

She looked into his eyes and asked, "Friend or foe?"

"To be determined." He gave her a wink.

One of Ice's men walked the captured driver into the restaurant, sat him down, and secured his hands behind the chair. Ice stepped over and slapped him across the face. The man grunted. Again, Ice's man slapped the man.

"That's enough," Erik said. leaning in to stare at the driver after Ice stepped aside.

The man slowly raised his head, met his inquisitive eyes, and said, "1940 was a good year."

"It's good to see you, too." Erik smirked. One of the toughest parts of adjusting to civilian life, especially in 1948, was he didn't know who to trust. He had to be careful about what he said and choose his friends wisely. Of course, there wasn't much choice involved when he was staring into the eyes of his best friend from 2008, Jacques.

***

Upon entering the residence, Jamie headed to one of the bedrooms to put Max to bed, and Erik gave Jacques the grand tour, rambling on about Jamie's home design quirks. Linoleum was in style, especially in bold geometric patterns and people loved talking about. However, Jamie knew it required lots of regular maintenance to keep clean and shiny, so she only wanted dark, hardwood floors, which some would say was outdated. Nor was she of a fan of floral patterns in the bedrooms and living areas, or wallpapered bathrooms. Jamie kept their design concept simple with understated surfaces and open spaces. Even though most homes had a bright look, suiting the shift from wartime to peace-time, she kept to the style she felt comfortable with from 2008. It was also a clutter-free look, applying to every room, including Erik's office. She insisted everything had its place.

Jacques stopped in the living room, looked at a painting by Victor Gabriel Gilbert called the Scène de Bal, and turned to Erik, "Didn't you have that print in your apartment in 2008?"

Erik nodded and whispered, "Yes, but that one is the original."

Jacques looked bewildered.

"It was a gift."

They walked into Erik's office as their conversation continued. The room, which Erik used both as a library and for meeting clients, was a decent size. The bookcases and furniture were hand-crafted from mahogany, the former flush against the wall from floor to ten-foot ceiling. Erik had filled each with volumes dealing with both World Wars, covering every aspect, and novels dealing with political science and foreign policy. The light fixtures around the office were made from brass and kept their luster. The smell of old books and newspapers hovered in the room like fog in the San Francisco Bay. Mixed in between the books was World War Two memorabilia. One was the Knight's Cross of the Iron Cross with golden oak leaves, swords, and diamonds.

"How did you come by that?" Jacques asked, pointing at the German medal.

"I got it for saving Hitler's life."

"From whom?"

Erik simply smiled.

Jacques had seen that smile on his friend's face, and sometimes, like then, it was out of place. "You had the mob steal it?"

Erik shook his head.

"Is that your day job?"

"Hell, no. I just provide them with information. In return, they offer me protection and place money in my societe generale account in Geneva."

Jacques tilted his head with a you've-got-to-be-kidding expression.

Erik shrugged. "They offer a full range of products. Wealth management, investment advice, financial engineering, alternative investment, and estate advisory, all tailored to their clients, like me."

"What kind of information do you provide?" Jacques asked as he took a seat and placed several folders and a book on Erik's desk.

"Crimes that are already going to happen," Erik flashed a cunning grin, "and I also told them about J. Edgar Hoover's little secret." He poured two glasses of cognac.

"You didn't."

Erik handed a glass to Jacques, then walked around his desk and took a seat.

"In God's name, why?"

"I was told about it by a credible source." Erik took a sip of his cognac. "That's what the Mob had over him, so I took the liberty to tell them."

"You're crazy," Jacques tilted his head and the cognac slowly trickled down his throat. "What are we drinking?"

"A cognac bottled in 1783."

"Should that year mean anything?"

Erik nodded.

"Care to share?"

Erik ignored the question as he took another sip and leaned forward. "Why are you here?"

They stared at one another and contemplated what the other was thinking. Jamie strolled in, breaking their concentration. She glanced over at the several folders with orange borders and the words TOP SECRET. She gave Erik a peck on his cheek as she gave a haughty stare at Jacques. Then she left. Jacques knew, as did Erik, that when operatives showed up unannounced, there was a situation and they needed help. However, Jacques knew it may take more than a stern lecture to convince Erik.

Jacques adjusted himself in his chair and cleared his throat. "I learned in history class the RAF defeated the Luftwaffe." Erik nodded. "However..."

Erik leaned forward. "However, what?"

Jacques took a sip. "However, we are going to need your help."

"Who is we?" Erik stood up. "Need my help?" He pointed to himself, and Jacques nodded. "You haven't gone crazy on me, have you?"

"It will not be like before."

Erik let out a long, thoughtful sigh. He'd finally made a life for himself and was starting a family. He never expected to get dragged back into service. However, Erik knew it was a matter of doing his duty for his country, even if it meant he might die, and he took an oath.

Jacques broke the extended silence. "It involves you going back to 1940 and infiltrating the Luftwaffe."

"I'm no pilot."

"I know that," Jacques finished his drink as Erik sipped the last of his. "They said you would be a bombardier on an He-111 bomber."

Erik's eye enlarged as the blood drained from his face.

"I'm sure you won't go up every day."

Erik stared down at Jacques as he walked over to a bookcase, pulled a book, and flipped through the pages until he found an entry on the bomber in question, complete with a photograph, then walked back to his desk, glaring at Jacques. "Well, you know more about the Luftwaffe than me." Erik dropped the book in front of him as he took a seat. "The bomber doesn't look so bad."

"Not so bad? Hmm?"

Erik looked at the ceiling and then met Jacques' eyes. "The Heinkel bomber had weak defensive armament." Erik rubbed his chin as Jacques continued to analyze the photograph.

"To top that off, you want me to go back to 1940?" Erik leaned forward. "It's not a no or a hell no." He pounded his palms against the desk. "It's a fuck no!"

Jacques had similar training to Erik. Their work was like playing chess. He knew what each piece could do and he knew his opponent. He just had to find a maneuver to checkmate him. Perhaps he could kill him with kindness. He hadn't actually asked yet, so it was no surprise the answer was no. He had to find out how far Erik would go. Jacques took a deep breath as he tried to find the right words. "I know you don't want to get involved again, but we need your help."

Erik glared back with an intensity that scrutinized every single word Jacques said as he walked from around his desk.

"We all hesitated to even consider you, but you're the best there is," Jacques stood to face Erik.

"Did you volunteer me?" Erik pointed at Jacques with an accusing finger.

Jacques nodded.

"Find someone else."

"We need your help."

Erik walked away and pivoted to face Jacques with his arms crossed around his chest.

Jacques pressed on, sensing he was wearing down his friend's defenses. "I remember when you believed in doing the right thing, and you would do anything for the agency and your country." He let those words sink in. "If we don't change the past, it will engulf the world of 2012 with war."

"I don't care!" Erik jabbed a finger at Jacques to get his next point clear. "I've been out of the game for four years." He shook his head and rubbed his temple. Then he leaned forward. "To be honest, I'm tired of it. I'm tired of the endless, mindless conflict of those who want to control the past for their benefit."

In a cold, level tone, Jacques replied, "You can't quit, turn your back, and act like you don't give a damn about what happens in the future."

"I didn't ask for your fucking permission, Jacques," Erik turned his back on the man and poured himself another cognac.

"Max dies in 1965, in Vietnam," Jacques stated, handing over a KIA list from July of 1965 to Erik. "Maybe going back will save his life."

Erik's eyes narrowed as he took a gulp, then he slammed his glass down. "You bastard!" He then snatched the paper out of Jacques' hand.

Jacques' voice became firm. "You can't stay out of the game, Erik." He walked over to a bookcase and pulled out a book dealing with World War Two. "Everything in this book will be…" Jacques tilted his head as he tapped the book and stressed his next word, "altered."

"Damn it, Jacques!" Erik tossed the paper and immediately clutched the book from Jacques' hand and tossed it across the room. "I want nothing to do with the game!" He pointed at himself. "I want to live as a civilian, and I already started a new life."

Jacques remained calm as he picked up the book and flipped to the chapter dealing with the Battle of Britain. "Somewhere in the timeline it was skewed into this tangent, creating an alternate 1948 and 2012. Have you noticed anything different?"

Erik rubbed his chin as he pondered and shook his head.

"Come on. Think, Erik. You are the historian. Has anyone possibly said something that made little sense?"

Erik let out a long breath. Since he spoke to Jerry, he knew something was wrong. He knew something like a visit from Jacques was coming, but he didn't want to believe it. Finally, he relented to the inevitable. Without looking up to meet Jacques' eyes, he said, "Yes."

"What is it?"

"Jerry said he remembered—"

"Who?" Jacques asked.

Erik waved a hand to dismiss the question. "He asked if I remembered when the royal family and Churchill left England before the German's occupation."

Jacques gave a puzzled look.

Erik walked around the room as he tried to piece it all together. "Also, after dinner, Truman said something about us stopping Rommel in the Middle East."

"Very odd that history is alternate to you and me, but reality for everyone else." Jacques collected his thoughts. "Rommel was stopped at the Battle of El Alamein?" Erik nodded in agreement.

Erik nodded, then took a step closer and looked into Jacques' eyes. "I bet Cole and Plackett are behind it."

Jacques shook his head.

"How can you say that after what they planned last time, when they sent me back?"

"Because they are dead."

Erik tilted his head inquisitively.

"They both died in a jet crash."

Erik let slip a satisfied grin, and one word came to his mind: Karma. He then said, "Well, we have two questions we need to answer. First, why was history changed? Then, who would benefit if England was defeated? Who also has a time machine?"

Jacques shook his head as both men sat back down at the desk.

"What is it like going back to World War Two?" Jacques asked between his sips of cognac.

Erik pondered a moment before replying. "Going back to World War Two and correcting the past is strange."

"Do you like it?" Jacques placed his glass down. "I mean, correcting it."

"I'm good at it."

"But do you like it?"

Erik shook his head, "No." Erik placed his elbows on his desk and his face on his hands. "Only because it takes me away from Jamie and I hate cleaning up people's messes. Otherwise, I'd enjoy it. Ironically, sometimes I'm more comfortable in the past than in the present. Our present. The future. Whatever you want to call it."

"Why?" Jacques was mystified.

"In my time, I cannot alter future events, so I take it as it comes and there is no stability." Erik leaned back in his chair. "However, when I travel in the past, things are simpler, and I have a certain objective. Black and white. Right and wrong." He leaned forward. "I'm the one correcting history, and there are others who want to change the timeline. However, someone is always trying to kill me." Erik reached over the desk, showing he wanted to help and go back in time, and Jacques slid over the folders and a book titled *US Army in World War II: Reader's Guide: The Middle East Theater.*

Both Erik and Jacques stood and shook hands.

Jacques turned to leave, calling over his shoulder as he showed himself out, "See you in a week."

CHAPTER 4

DEEPER THAN THE UNKNOWN

"This all sounds like a great idea with no chance of catastrophic failure. That was sarcasm, by the way."

— Andy Weir, *The Martian*

Erik walked to the kitchen to give his eyes and mind a rest from digesting the manual on the He-111's bombsight and the MG 15 machine gun, both of which Erik would have to use on the He-111. He would also have to serve as navigator en route to a target and gunner in front of the aircraft. His mind spun with details, like magnetic declination requiring an adjustment of ten degrees and eight minutes when charting a course. He was thankful he didn't have to pilot the aircraft, since he only knew the basics from getting an aviation merit badge in the Boy Scouts. Most people would have information overload and walk away. However, Erik needed to learn and apply the information, or he would suffer severe physical disturbance, otherwise known as death. That also applied to the pilots in the Spitfires and Hurricanes whose mission it was to shoot down German bombers. Bomber crews went up every other day, meaning he only had three, maybe four times if he could solve their temporal crisis within a week. However, it only took one bad day to get shot down and killed.

Jamie was at the dining room table, taking care of Erik's upcoming appointments. She glanced up for a second, then went back to working.

"You want to talk?" he asked.

"If I wanted to talk," she got up and scowled as she stood in front of him, "I suppose I'd be talking." She shook her head. "I was told I have a great imagination, but who could imagine the CIA coming back in time to talk to you?" She got closer to him and rubbed his arms. "Erik, I want to leave."

Almost caught speechless, Erik replied. "You want to leave me?"

She crossed her arms and stepped back. "You'd think a person who worked for the CIA would learn how to listen."

"But that's what you said."

"I meant I want to leave, not you, but this place. Here. All three of us." She hugged him tight. "We could be in Paris by tomorrow. Valensky could hide us until this passes over, and prevent Max from enlisting."

"Jamie, I know what *should* happen. But now, there is no way we can know what *will* happen since the past has changed. I didn't know they would come back for me."

"Well, it's going to be like how it was when we were dating." Jamie did an impression of a younger Erik. "Sorry, darling, I have to go on a secret mission. I can't tell you when I will be back." Tears came to Jamie's eyes as her anger built up. "Damn you! Damn the CIA! Damn your mission!"

Erik embraced her to comfort her. "I'm not your enemy, you know." He stared into her eyes. "I have to go out for a little while." Erik caressed Jamie's face to wipe her tears away.

"Erik, does anyone, especially you, know why you always volunteer for these types of missions?"

Erik shrugged.

"After these four years, is it that simple for you to get up and disappear?"

"Of course not." Erik's voice got firm. "But I didn't know they would come back and ask me."

"It will happen again."

Erik shook his head.

"How do you know?"

"Maybe we will do what you suggested."

Jamie motioned for him to continue.

"We can move and disappear."

***

Erik got in his car and headed to an isolated farm outside Washington, DC. He was going to meet Delon Stojanović, who went by Deks to his friends, of which Erik was one. They met under unusual circumstances, in late 1945, when a group of men heard Deks speak German and thought he was German. Deks was Serbian, but that didn't matter to them, so they ganged up on him. Erik helped Deks, and over time, their trust grew. They became good friends and training partners in martial arts. They met secretly, on Deks' farm, and Deks introduced Erik to naša nauka—our science. It was also known by a stylized name—Nauka.

Delon Stojanović, a successful wine trader, created Nauka in the early twentieth century on the Balkan Peninsula. One day, bandits and assassins attacked Delon's business, wounding him and killing many of his workers. They left him for dead, but he survived. After healing from his injuries, he researched hand-to-hand combat and applied the hajduk culture of asymmetric warfare and survival tactics used during the occupation by the Ottoman Empire and in combat, such as during the Battle of Čegar in 1809.

After fighting in the First World War, Delon began to develop his defensive methods. He leaned on his passion for old Slavic folk martial arts, the tactics of the hajduk resistance fighters, his experiences from the war, and his travel adventures. What made Nauka effective was that it worked against multiple opponents, in all positions, under any circumstances, with or without weapons.

Between the wars, Delon continued his business with his wife and two sons. Once his sons were old enough to fight, he passed on the skills of Nauka to them, which they used during the German occupation of 1941 to 1944. During the war, Delon joined the Yugoslav partisans fighting against the Nazis. When they formed Tamni Medvedi, The Dark Bears, they commissioned him as a major. Their motto was "Walk in shadows… Strike Hard". They demolished railroads and bridges, wore disguises to infiltrate German strongholds, and did anything that would disrupt the German army.

During this time, Nauka was constantly evolving and was notorious for its effectiveness. Delon and his men were very successful against the Germans. However, the SS eventually suspected him and his family of crimes against the state. He got his family out of harm's way and remained in hiding until the end of the war.

The communists slowly transitioned Prime Minister Šubašić's government to a Communist Regime by 1945. Within that short period, the NKGB, or People's Commissariat for State Security, replaced the SS with similar arrests, horrors, and interrogations. The new communist government placed a strict ban on martial arts. The only individuals who could practice and train in martial arts were the military and police. Delon and others like him either went against the government, were killed, or fled the country. Delon and his family crossed the border into Greece and took a steamship to America to start a new life. Once he arrived, he and his family kept to themselves and continued to practice Nauka secretly, trusting no one until he met Erik.

Erik pulled up to a long, low-profile ranch house with varying roof lines that made it stand out. The building was pale yellow with green shutters. Meticulous landscaping surrounded the house. Erik got out of his car and headed to the front door. After a moment, a man in his late fifties with broad shoulders, the trim physique of a much younger man, and dark, mysterious eyes emerged. Although he was dressed casually, he exuded both confidence and power, likely stemming from his mysterious past. As Deks opened the door, soft swing music, possible Benny Goodman, drifted into the yard. Deks strode across the driveway toward Erik.

"I trust your trip down was comfortable, Erik." They shook hands and gave each other a brotherly hug. "It's good to see you again."

"How have you been?" Erik asked as they made their way to a structure next to the house.

Deks just grinned, which was a good thing considering everything he had been through. He pulled out an embossed, stainless-steel hip flask and handed it to Erik, motioning for him to take a sip.

"This will put hairs on your chest."

Erik sniffed. The aroma was so strong it made his eyes water. "What is it?"

"Serbian water. A strong man like you shouldn't be afraid of a little water." It was actually Manastirka Slivovitz, brandy made from a plum called Pozegaca, from western Serbia.

Erik took a gulp, the liquor burning as it flowed down his throat.

"Do you really think I'm trying to poison you or abstract information?"

Erik shrugged as he took another sip, then handed over the flask. "I think you're crazy."

"What made you come see me without calling?"

"I need to get some practice in."

Deks raised an eyebrow. "We usually practice on Thursday."

Erik gave a blank expression.

"Relax, Erik. We're not enemies, and I know we hold the secrets of our pasts deep inside so no one can find them."

Erik shook his head.

"There is more to you than meets the eye, Erik. I sense you can't trust anyone, wherever you go."

Erik nodded. "It's because of the things I've done and who I've worked for."

Deks respected him for that because he was in similar shoes during the Second World War. He pulled out a set of keys and unlocked the door. Stepping in, the darkness transformed to a blinding light, to which their eyes quickly adjusted. Inside was a training room. This was where Deks introduced Erik to Nauka. Like any other martial art, Erik knew there was much more than merely learning and applying combat techniques and skills. It also dealt with intellectual and moral education. Nauka has its own culture, heritage, and traditions. Every Nauka training session started with a traditional greeting ritual.

Erik and Deks stood facing each other and performed the ritual. Deks needed him to present the significance of each progression, which he did. He clenched a hand over his heart, signifying he was prepared to give kinship and love. His left hand was set on his left hip, as if grasping a blade, implying he was ready to defend himself. Standing in that position, they bowed to each other while maintaining eye contact. That meant they were ready to serve and help, but saw everything.

With the ritual out of the way, training began. They reached for each other's arms in a controlled wrestling drill. Both were trying to grasp their opponent's wrist or the upper arm, to keep him controlled, in an endless circle of grabs and dodges. The purpose of the drill was to move from a defensive state to an offensive one quickly, because the defense of being grabbed is to grab the attacker. As they went on, they moved around the room, augmenting their handwork with footwork and body alignment. It was a good warm-up drill. Erik remembered standing no chance against Deks in drills like that, but he got better with Nauka over time.

Deks grabbed a blunted knife from an old wooden box in the corner and attacked Erik with slashes and stabs from different angles. He wasn't too fast, but the attacks were intense enough to keep his opponent on the defensive.

Erik moved out of the way, using similar movements from the wrestling drill. He added Nauka strikes to his defense and attacked Deks' arms while evading. Erik did very well until Deks distracted him by kicking a leather bag from the ground toward him. Deks exploited the distraction and nearly stabbed Erik with the knife. He stopped and said, "Take care, boy! Anything can happen in a fight, and anything can be used as a distraction. Fights are never fair."

After several hours of training, Deks and Erik sat on the porch. As Deks took a sip of lemonade, his face hardened. His eyes then settled on Erik as he gave the man a thorough look over. "What are you thinking about?"

Erik shook his head.

"Where are you going?" Deks studied Erik for a long time, reading his emotions in the lines of his face. "I just want you to know you if you want to talk about it, I am here for you." Deks placed his cupped hand on Erik's shoulder.

Erik let out a deep sigh. "I've been on countless missions and buried more friends than I can count. Death is a part of my life. I'm wondering when it will be my time."

Deks nodded in understanding. "Some things are best left

unknown, but every time we meet, things get very clear. There's one thing I know, Erik, and that is we are here for a reason. My reason is fighting for my beliefs, for Serbia, and passing my knowledge of Nauka to my sons." Deks put his arm around Erik. "I don't know your reason, but whatever it is, I am sure you will make a difference in this world." A soft smile appeared on Deks' face. "They say one man can make a difference."

***

Erik came home to Perry Como's "Till the End of Time." Like in 2008, Jamie kept the house warm and welcoming. She was sitting in Erik's office, going through his calendar, when he walked in. Her large, puffy, brown eyes were buried in her work, with her shoulders slumped, before she turned to Erik and clutched her body with folded arms. She looked up with down-turned lips. Her eyes were red from rubbing them, or maybe crying, or both. She furrowed her brow, revealing nervousness and frustration. Erik walked around his desk and massaged her shoulders.

"What are you doing?"

She flipped through the pages and picked up a pen. "Calling to cancel your meetings. You'll be leaving soon." She paused with tears running down her face. "You have to fix the past, but I still have the present to deal with."

"This will be the last time."

Jamie looked as if she didn't believe him.

"I promise."

She nuzzled his cheek. "Sometimes I wish I was an operative."

Erik shook his head and tilted it forward.

"It would simplify things, wouldn't it?" she asked.

Erik shrugged.

"We could share things, like work and places we have been."

Erik shook his head.

"You still couldn't share."

Erik nodded. "No one can choose what they are. Not you. Not me." Erik kissed her. "We are what we are."

"That's why I will let you go, my wandering knight, charging off to right all the wrongs of the world." Jamie got up and headed out of the office.

Erik took her place at the desk and flipped open a book.

1940

16 JULY	Adolf Hitler issued Directive No. 16, Operation Sealion, the invasion of Britain, preparations to begin.
21 JULY	Adolf Hitler declares that the 15th September 1940 is the latest date for Operation Sealion to take place. Adolf Hitler issued Directive No. 17, conduct of air and sea warfare against England. "The Luftwaffe is to overcome the Royal Air Force with all means at its disposal, and as soon as possible.
7 AUGUST	The Luftwaffe raid several areas across the United Kingdom including Aberdeen, Poole and Liverpool.
8 AUGUST	The Luftwaffe starts to target British ports and harbors.
11 AUGUST	Kanalkampf (Channel Battle) ends.
13 AUGUST	"Eagle Day". The Luftwaffe launched its offensive against Britain, with 1,485 sorties.
15 AUGUST	A day of intense attacks. The Luftwaffe launched a total of 1,790 sorties
17 AUGUST	Adolf Hitler orders on 25 August 1940 Operation Sealion to take place, Directive No. 16.
25 AUGUST	The Germans invasion force, Army Group C (von Leeb) drawn from the 6th Army and Army Group A (von Rundstedt) drawn from the 9th Army and the 16th Army and two airborne divisions and the special forces of the Brandenburg Regiment land and successfully set up beachheads.
27 AUGUST	George VI, Queen Elizabeth, and Winston Churchill leave England and head for Canada. England surrenders to German.
7 SEPTEMBER	Adolf Hitler issued Directive No. 18, Operation Felix, the invasion of Gibraltar and Africa (Rommel), preparations to begin.
21 SEPTEMBER	British Army and royal Navy surrenders Gibraltar to German Army and Navy.
25 SEPTEMBER	The Germans invasion forces (Rommel) 15th Panzer Division, 21st Panzer Division, and 90th Light Division, land in Tripoli.
12 OCTOBER	Germans occupy Alexandria and on the Suez Canal and plan their attack for the Middle East.
15 OCTOBER	Roosevelt sends U.S. troops to Middle East.

Erik rubbed his fingers through his hair and pulled it as he racked his brain to find out what went wrong. The folders and the book Jacques gave him were a gigantic jigsaw puzzle of information that would require months of research and analysis, but he only had two days to find the answer. It was like finding a needle in a haystack. The information was right in front of him, but where was the needle? Jamie said he was very smart. He denied it. He simply remembered things in history: dates, events, people, causes, and effects. Smart people in 2012 had been analyzing the same information and couldn't find where things went wrong. He was searching for an answer in the past to become a hero for the future. No pressure.

He looked out the window at the hustle and bustle of the city. Going back in time was an incredibly emotional experience. Sometimes it was amazing, being a part of history, but it was also downright frightening because someone was always trying to kill him.

Outside the window, two children played with paper airplanes, attempting to fly them into a trashcan. One boy's plane was on a perfect approach, but as it neared the trashcan, a gust of wind sent it off course.

A lightbulb lit up in Erik's head, and he ran back to his desk and dragged his finger down the timeline, stopping on August twenty-fifth. He found the needle. That was where the timeline was skewed. As Erik recalled, on August twenty-fourth of 1940, German night-time bombers aiming for RAF airfields drifted off course and bombed London, which was a forbidden target. Thus, Churchill ordered the Royal Air Force to bomb Berlin on August twenty-fifth in retaliation. This resulted in Hitler ordering the Luftwaffe to bomb London again, along with other major British cities. That allowed the British to rebuild their airfields and aircraft to defeat the Luftwaffe. Erik grinned. He found the problem, and he made it look easy, yet people didn't know how his mind worked. Still, he needed a plan to put the timeline back, which would be more complicated.

CHAPTER 5

LOVELY TO SEE YOU AGAIN, MY FRIEND

"One of the most beautiful qualities of true friendship is to understand and to be understood."   — Lucius Annaeus Seneca

AUGUST 8, 1948

Erik stood in front of a full-length mirror and adjusted his tailor-made, gray, worsted wool, double-breasted jacket. It complemented the matching, neatly pressed trousers, and white cotton Oxford shirt. He also wore a brown silk tie, polished black wing-tips, and finished the wardrobe with a brown fedora. Like so many times before, Jamie stood before him to make sure he looked his best as her eyes began to water and tears slowly rolled down her cheeks.

"Jamie, there are instructions in the desk drawer. I want you to follow them if I don't come back." She tried to get a word in, but he pressed on. "There's a power of attorney for you. You'll have everything you need."

"You're coming back. Do what you need to do, then you're coming back. You are the air I breathe... I cannot live without you."

They embraced each other and kissed gently. Jamie composed

herself as they made their way to the living room, where Jacques was waiting.

He placed his tea cup in the sink and thanked Jamie.

She nodded while taking bagged lunches out of the refrigerator, then handed one to Jacques. She was about to hand the other to Erik, then stopped as something clicked in her mind. Jamie then ran back to Erik's office, returned, jotted a quick note, placed it in Erik's bag, and handed it to him. They kissed again as a solid, rhythmic knock sounded on the front door.

"Hey Doc, you ready?" Paulie Bongiovanni Jr. asked. Erik nodded while Jacques stepped out. "Is he coming with us?" Paulie asked with hesitation.

Erik glared at the man. "You have a problem with that?"

A stress line appeared on Paulie's brow as he shook his head.

"You take care of my family while I am away," Erik said just under a whisper. Then he turned to Jamie, who was holding Max, one last time, and they blew each other a kiss and caught it with their hands. Once outside, Erik said goodbye to Jerry before Paulie led the way to a 1948 Cadillac Series 62 four-door sedan. As they approached the car, a young, impeccably dressed, lean, and handsome man, part of Ice's mafia gang, opened the rear door. Once in the car, they headed to Bridgewater Air Park, in Bridgewater, Virginia, nearly four hours away.

Erik took a deep breath and closed his eyes. He felt Jacques' and turned to face him, as if to ask what he was thinking.

"I hope you'll forgive me," Jacques began as Erik slowly opened his eyes and glared. "You know Jamie showed me your book. From what I've read, your manuscript is very good. I mean, really very good."

Paulie turned around. "What are you writing about?"

"History," Erik replied vaguely.

"You a historian, Doc?" Paulie's head bobbed like a confused dog. "Is this what you are going to be doing on this trip?"

"I guess," Erik turned back to Jacques as he continued. "I'm a little bit of everything."

Paulie's questions were like a jackhammer on concrete. "What exactly does that mean?"

Erik took a deep breath and composed his thoughts. One of the toughest parts of adjusting to talking to civilians was making his job sound extremely boring, or make it extremely exciting but vague, so they would stop asking questions. "Very simply, I look at the way people did things in history, and if I can think of any alternatives, I write it up and submit a report to the Department of Defense."

"Doc, do you think you'll find some?"

Erik nodded. "I always find alternatives." Again, he tilted his head toward Jacques, then he closed his eyes for the remainder of the drive.

Jacques gently nudged Erik as they pulled into Bridgewater Air Park's parking lot. "Did you enjoy your nap?" The car was parked, and the driver was already out and holding the door open for Erik.

Jacques asked as they got out of the car, "So, which one is our ride?"

Erik pointed to a plane taxiing off the runway. The aircraft's sleek, shiny, aluminum alloy fuselage could be compared to an elongated fish, or a whale, with smooth curves. It had a circular cross-section, a snub nose, and a triple-fin tail. On each wing were a pair of low-mounted, powerful-looking propeller engines, the roar of which came to a sputtering halt as the plane stopped.

"We are flying in that?"

Erik nodded as they walked toward the runway.

"What kind of aircraft is that?"

"Constellation."

"And you can fly that?"

Erik shot Jacques a side-eyed glance. "You know as well as anybody, the CIA prepared me for almost anything before sending me back here."

Flight crews placed a gangway at the rear hatch of the aircraft for departing passengers while a tanker truck prepared to refuel the aircraft. Appearing first at the hatch was a man in his fifties. His neatly pressed suit gave the impression of a straightforward businessman. However, he had a tall stature, broad shoulders, a solid frame, and carried himself like a prizefighter. The imposing figure, Noah Dietrich, was the chief executive officer of the Howard Hughes business empire.

Next, was Glenn Odenkirk, or Ode to his friends, a thin man with a small frame. He was dressed casually, as if he were taking a stroll in a park. To Howard Hughes, he was a brilliant engineer with an innovative imagination. In addition, he was one of the few people Howard saw as a friend, not as an employee.

Once off the gangway, the two men approached Erik with warm eyes and smiles, extending their hands to greet him.

"Erik, how you been?" Noah asked as he offered a firm handshake. "Last time we saw you was when the Hercules flew."

"Been busy and with the National Air Museum."

Ode seemed to perk up at the mention of the museum. "Howard is talking about getting started on jet technology for commercial airliners. It's a fascinating idea, but I'm not sure if it would be practical."

"Sounds expensive to me," Noah added, sharing a glance with Ode before turning back to Erik. "He wanted me to contact Bob Gross. What do you know about them?"

"Jets?"

They both nodded.

"Well, the Germans used them in the war."

"The Messerschmitt 262," Ode added. "That's the one I know of."

Noah shrugged.

Erik nodded. "There were others." Both men seemed intrigued, so he continued. "There was the Arado-234, Arado-234 V21, Heinkel He 162, and the Horten Ho 229." Erik raised his hands and moved them apart to dismiss the subject. "What I can tell you is yes, the military is using them, and eventually commercial airliners will use them too."

Howard approached from the plane, saying nothing, but certainly close enough to hear them.

"That's a lot of jets," Ode replied as he swallowed a lump in his throat. "How do you know about all of them?"

"What did you do during the war again?" Noah asked with a sly grin.

Erik said nothing.

"Jet aviation will be the way of the future," Howard declared, like a shell fired from a warship across the enemy bow. "Don't you agree, Erik?"

Erik nodded.

Howard wore the distinctive fashion in the post-World-War-Two cultural boom. He had on a white cotton shirt with a long, pointed collar, plain front, breast pocket, and button cuffs. Over this was a tweed, bronze-colored plaid, four-button loafer jacket with brown gabardine camp collar and sleeves, single-button cuffs, welted breast pocket, and patch hip pockets. His slacks, also known as "Hollywood trousers," were camel tan and double-reverse-pleated, with a high-rise design, dropped belt loops, slanted side pockets, and cuffs. A brown woven leather belt with a brass double-ring buckle held up the slacks, resting over brown leather lace-up shoes. A dark brown felt fedora with a dark brown ribbed grosgrain band finished up his wardrobe.

Howard motioned for Erik and Noah to follow him. "Walk with me." Then, turning to Ode, he added, "Ode, make sure we are good to go. We leave in ten minutes." As if the prior conversation hadn't been interrupted, he turned back to Erik and Noah and continued, "Jet aviation will be the way of the future. The way of the future. The way of the future." Howard's face turned pale. Fear consumed his expression. Then panic. He seemed defenseless.

Noah looked around to make sure no one was staring as Erik got Howard's attention. "Howard, relax. Focus on my voice." Howard stared at Erik. "Howard, everything is okay. I have everything set up for Noah to meet investors in jet aviation." Erik slowly nodded his head.

Howard did the same, then asked, "Erik, who are those fellas?" He was referring to Jacques, Paulie, and the driver, all waiting by the car. "Do they work for me?"

Erik shook his head.

"Do you trust them?"

"I do, and they're going to take Noah to the investors."

Howard nodded.

"The taller one," Erik gestured to Jacques, "is my best friend, and he is coming with me to Colorado Springs."

"Okay." Howard started back to the Constellation. "Erik, I will be on board."

"He is having panic attacks," Noah whispered, staring at Howard. "When he does, Ode and I make sure no one is staring at him."

Erik nodded and waved Paulie and Jacques to come over.

"Paulie, this is Noah Dietrich." They shake hands. "He is the man that I told your father about."

Paulie smiled.

"Jacques, are you ready?" Erik asked.

He nodded.

With Noah in Paulie's capable hands, Erik and Jacques boarded the plane and took their seats by the cockpit. Ode, acting as flight engineer, was already at a complex instrument panel. He would check systems before flight, help develop flight plans, and continue to perform checks while the aircraft was airborne. Ode's job was to ensure that there were no mechanical concerns, monitoring the engines, other systems, and fuel levels during the flight.

Howard looked back and made a hand gesture. "Erik, why don't you come on up front here?" Erik gazed around at everything in the cockpit. The complexity was overwhelming, yet gleaming and elegant. Howard settled into the pilot's seat as Erik glanced out one of the forward windows. "Why don't you strap yourself in right over there?" Howard pointed to the co-pilot station. "You should be able to see great." Howard made a quick visual check of the complex instrument panel before him, a beautiful anarchy of dials, instruments, and gauges. There was a series of four throttle levers to his right. Howard took a deep, focused breath and touched the sacred, elegantly designed wheel ahead of him. He smiled and nodded, because it felt right. He glanced over his shoulder. "Okay, Ode, let's power her up."

Ode flipped a switch. "One's good." Engine one came alive, belching thick, choking black smoke from the exhaust. He did this three more times, with the same results. Eventually, all four propellers were spinning and humming in perfect harmony. The roar of the massive engines and the thrum of the propellers hummed in the cockpit, though not so loud the men couldn't easily communicate.

Ode called out, "Howard, she's gotta hit two-twelve before takeoff."

"I know, I know," Howard mumbled. Then, he spoke clearly, "Advancing master throttles." Howard reached to his side and pressed the four large throttle levers forward while his other hand gripped the yoke.

"Lower flaps fifteen degrees," Ode said.

"Understood. Lower flaps fifteen degrees." Howard flipped the switch for the flaps to the appropriate setting, then folded his fingers around the throttles and applied more pressure. The Constellation rumbled forward, picking up speed at an impressive rate for the large aircraft. The terrible bouncing and vibrations from the runway abruptly ended. There was silence but for the distant roar of the engines still echoing in the cockpit. Once they reached their assigned altitude, Howard leveled the plane off and let up on the throttle, bringing them to a cruising speed. He then looked over and said, "Erik, I never got to say thank you for your help against Brewster in the Senate Hearings."

"You are welcome, Howard." Erik knew it was not always easy to be Howard's friend—he demanded a lot—but the man paid a great deal of attention to their friendship. He looked almost robotic and focused as he gestured for Erik to grab the co-pilot's yoke. "How did you know all those things about Juan Trippe? And that he donated twenty-thousand dollars to Senator Brewster's last campaign, and that the senator got free tickets from Pan Am so he could circle the globe in support of his CAB bill?"

Normally, Erik would offer the silent treatment to such questions, but that wouldn't work on Howard. "All I can tell you is that I am very informed about certain subjects."

"Sort of like when you informed me that over sixty other airplanes ordered from Boeing, Lockheed, Douglas, and Northrop never saw action either?"

He nodded as Howard moved to the rear of the plane to search for a bottle of milk, leaving Erik to fly the plane. He was absolutely terrified, knowing he might do the same soon in a German bomber, so he focused on every detail, his knuckles white as he gripped the yoke tighter.

"Keep us at 5,700 feet," Ode called out from his station.

Erik's face paled as he frantically looked for the altitude indicator. It read five thousand feet.

Howard said, completely calm, "You're doing fine." He took his seat as he opened his milk and a package of cookies. "Pull back on the yoke a smidge."

Pulling back on the yoke, and the plane nosed up, then Erik leveled off at their assigned altitude.

"See, I can make you an expert pilot," Howard said with a grin.

He shook his head.

"Do you like chocolate chip cookies?" Erik nodded, but remained focused on the plane as Howard continued. "I like mine with medium chips, none too close to the outside. I hate chocolate on my hands. You?"

Erik nodded again.

"So, were you a spy during the war?"

He straightened his posture and spoke in a serious tone as he stared Howard down. "No."

"You sure act like one."

Erik was used to people being suspicious about him. It was like being in high school. But, when people talked to him, they tried to confirm their suspicions, digging into his secrets or determining if he could help them with something. Erik and Howard's personalities were like a magnetized pair because they were similar enough to understand each other and different enough to create a spark. However, despite those differences, they shared a strong connection because they understood and respected each other's values and needs. For example, Erik resonated with Howard's passions and convictions. That's why he displayed fierce loyalty and devotion.

Erik finally noticed cellophane wrap on the yoke in front of Howard and nodded toward it.

Howard just sighed.

"Howard," Erik made sure he could hear him before he continued, "people have no idea what crap they carry around on their hands."

Howard's eyes brightened up in agreement, then turned his attention to the yoke in front of Erik, still locked in a white-knuckled grip. "Erik, you don't have to squeeze it. Get a feel for it. Don't worry, you got this. You are gripping too hard. Relax your hands."

Erik loosened his grip, trying to relax.

"You want to feel the vibration of the engine through your fingertips." He paused for a moment to let Erik focus. "You feel that?"

Erik nodded as his confidence grew.

Howard explained, "Flying requires mastery of the four basic flight maneuvers, upon which all aeronautics are based on: straight-and-level flight, turns, climbs, and descents. Just keep us steady. Focus on the horizon without boundaries. Pull back on the yoke a smidge."

Erik pulled back on the yoke and regained altitude. After that, they were content in silence, as Erik focused as they skimmed above the clouds.

"Maybe one day" Howard said, "you will take what I taught you and will rise to an important position." Erik was about to respond, but Howard raised a finger to stop him and squeezed his headset, as if engrossed in what was coming through. He motioned to Erik that he needed to take over. "Colorado Springs Tower, Constellation 8121K, ten miles southwest at 5,500, inbound for landing with four passengers."

"Constellation 8121K, Colorado Springs Tower, report entering left downwind Runway thirty-one."

"Report entering left downwind, Constellation 8121K."

"Constellation 8121K entering left downwind Runway thirty-one."

"Constellation 8121K, cleared to land Runway thirty-one."

"Cleared to land Runway thirty-one, Constellation 8121K."

Howard did a textbook landing with a sudden bump as the tires grabbed onto the tarmac. The landing was otherwise smooth as the day the runway was paved. Once he reached the correct speed, he taxied the aircraft to its assigned location. As the Constellation came to a halt, the ground crews wheeled up a gangway so anyone who wanted to exit could.

Nearby was an olive drab Ford sedan bearing government plates with a uniformed driver inside and a person of authority standing by the car. Jacques, Erik, and Howard proceeded to the car, their footsteps crunching small grains of sand and pebbles as they moved off the tarmac. Erik focused on the individual who approached them, who stopped beside Erik and addressed each man by their names. Erik motioned for Jacques to continue as he and Howard finished their conversation.

Howard looked at Erik and spoke quietly, his brown moustache lifting slowly from the spread of his upper lip. "Erik, do the impossible. Almost everyone has told me my ideas are merely fantasies but look what I've accomplished."

Erik leaned in toward Howard's good right ear and whispered, "I'm not judged by efforts; I'm judged by my results."

Howard looked into Erik's eyes as he considered what to say next. He took a deep breath, pointed to Erik's chest, and replied, "Erik, I don't know what you do with the government. Even though what you go through might be difficult and complicated," his finger touched Erik's chest, "you know you have what it takes to get it done." Howard smirked, and Erik replied only with a thankful nod for the kind words.

Before Erik stepped into the Ford, Howard got his attention one last time. "Erik, I believe in you and stand firmly by your convictions. Remember, meeting adversity well is the source of your strength."

Once inside, the driver got to his seat, and the car accelerated, pressing Jacques and Erik into the seat. The vehicle moved like a snake through the traffic, which thickened as they reached the outskirts of town. Jacques' curiosity grew as they continued, while Erik was more focused on preparing for his mission and what to expect once he got to 1940. The driver followed the road that led up to a gate and a sign that read *Hidden Meadow Apartments*. He brought the car to a halt and rolled down his window as sentries approached the vehicle.

"Dr. Foge and Mr. Yves," the driver stated as a sentry scrutinized the men in the back seat. Once he recognized Erik, he snapped a salute, which Erik returned.

Once through the gate, the car accelerated within the compound. Jacques peered around the compound in a cleared area of forest outlined by towered fencing with razor wire, watchtowers, and armed soldiers strategically placed around the perimeter. In addition, soldiers with submachine guns, guard dogs, and jeeps patrolled the grounds. There were cookie-cutter prefabricated buildings of varying sizes identified only by two-letter prefixes and a four-digit suffixes, surrounded by postage-stamp yards, lining unnamed streets. Individuals came and went in every direction.

The driver parked in front of a pre-fab building marked UW6766. After disembarking, Erik and Jacques walked into a large, open area with several fitting rooms to the left, a desk with several individuals behind it to the rear, and several multi-plan, double-deck automated garment feeding conveyors to the right, with more than five thousand military uniforms from a wide range of countries and military branches, including the United States. Erik approached the desk, stated his name, and requested the uniform he needed while Jacques took a seat.

A woman stepped around and motioned him to get on the

platform. Within moments, she took a montage of his measurements while others obtained everything he needed for the uniform.

Following that, Erik took a seat, and Jacques glanced over. "You know, I've been thinking, as long as I can remember knowing you…"

Erik rolled his eyes. "Oh, not again."

"Excuse me?" Jacques paused for a moment. "You don't know what I'm going to say."

Erik gave him a glance of ironic inquiry.

"As long as I remember knowing you, you've not had the best cards dealt to you, but you play the cards you hold well."

The tailor approached Erik with her arm extended. "The dressing room is over here."

Once inside, he took a deep breath and analyzed the uniform. It was not a replica, which was a good thing. The blue-gray tunic was single-breasted, with four silver buttons down the front and an open collar. In addition, it had two upper pockets with box pleats and two lower-button flap pockets. Jacques's voice got his attention as his hand appeared through the curtain, holding a pair of jackboots and a pair of flight boots. Both fit. Then, Erik adjusted the tunic and checked himself in the mirror. After he put on the belt, he exited with a commanding presence and the tailor handed him a peaked, blue-gray cap, the German Cross in gold.

On his right upper pocket, an operations flight bomber badge… for the upper left breast, ribbons for the Iron Cross and the Wehrmacht Long Service Award. On top of the upper left pocket, an Iron Cross First Class, and finally, an aviator badge that went below his left pocket.

Erik took a deep sigh as he walked to the counter, with Jacques hovering over him. "I am not wearing this." He placed the German Cross in gold down. "Or this." The Wehrmacht Long Service

Award was next. "And especially not this." He tossed the operations flight bomber badge onto the counter.

"Sir, your objective is to blend in."

Erik sneered and dismissed the suggestion with a sideways jerk of his hand as he replied, "Infiltrating a Luftwaffe bomber base and acting as if you belong there is all about blending in, which means I don't need to wear any awards or ribbons that would bring attention to myself." The tailor nodded as she handed him a garment bag and a duffle bag, which contained a week's worth of clothes. With a motion of her left hand, she advised Erik to go to the building next door.

Jacques helped Erik with his bags as they returned to the waiting car, and the driver assisted in loading them in. They drove to their next stop, with Jacques mentioning the uniform looked good on him. As before, Erik gave his name to the clerk, and they looked him up and asked what he needed. There were other individuals in different uniforms waiting as well. In the background, there were individuals carrying files, doors opening and shutting, muted telephone bells, and the flash of photography—a normal, routine day. Erik was called back. The setup was very similar to the DMV. It was a three-step-process. First, Erik's picture was taken, then he filled out identification papers in a Soldbuch, or pay book. Following that, he was instructed to wait in the lobby while they completed the documentation.

Moments later, Erik was called to the desk and received his completed Soldbuch. He was ready to go back to the height of the Battle of Britain.

Their last stop was an unmarked, weathered, brick, two-story building with a lieutenant waiting for them. Jacques and Erik followed the officer inside to a desk, where they signed in, received visitor IDs, and were told to sit in a chair and wait.

"Here you go," Jacques gave Erik a small parcel.

"What is it?"

"A book. I figured during the slow times you could read."

"Thanks."

The sound of hard rubber heels on dress shoes echoed through-out the lobby, magnifying as their owner drew closer. Then, the noise stopped. "Gentlemen, follow me," a man in a three-piece-suit said in a neutral tone.

CHAPTER 6
CLOSE YOUR EYES AND SEE ANALOGICAL

Bilbo: "Can you promise that I will come back?"
Gandalf: "No. And if you do… you will not be the same."
— *The Hobbit: An Unexpected Journey*

"Gentlemen, my name is Captain Burrows. I will escort you while you are on campus." Burrows gestured for them to follow him. He was slim, but with a solid build with broad shoulders. He towered over Erik and would need to look down to meet his eyes. Burrows' eyes were fixed, which presented an apathetic expression; however, he was focused on his surroundings and those he escorted. One could say he was ruggedly handsome, yet he cultivated the look of a leader and acted distinctively tough, exceptional, and intimidating.

They walked across the room toward the elevator flanked by two armed sentries. The elevator doors let off a metallic sound as they opened, as if it were expecting them. Once inside, the doors closed, and Burrows inserted a brass key, turned it counter-clockwise, and pushed an unmarked button.

As the elevator descended rapidly, the lieutenant instructed them to grab their noses and blow gently to make their ears pop, which is similar to a diver's equalization technique. Once the elevator came to a halt and opened, they were greeting by two armed guards carrying high caliber weapons.

The temperature was comfortable, and the lighting was dim, but they could see where they were going as their eyes adjusted. They continued down a rough-hewn stone corridor, nearly fifteen feet high, with numerous electrical conduits and water pipes attached to the ceiling—everything needed to run an underground installation. Three painted lines in different colors ran along the floor. Erik recalled the last time he was there, in 2008, and that they had the same color-coded system to prevent staff from getting lost. Eventually, they came upon more sentries and two wooden doors. Jacques was led to one room and Erik to the other. Once inside, Erik took several deep breaths, straightened his posture, and waited for whomever may come through the door. Moments later, the solid wooden door opened, and a major general stepped inside.

He shut the door behind him, strolled over to a table in the center of the room, and tossed an envelope on it before sitting down. Erik followed suit as the general scrutinized him. Both men had deadpan, professional faces that hid each other's stories. They revealed nothing with their eyes as they studied one another. Both men had looked into such faces many times before.

"I am Major General Cochran Ethan Lane," the officer said in an authoritarian tone. His eyes analyzed Erik as he continued. "I tried to run your jacket, but nothing comes up. It isn't even flagged top-secret." Lane gestured for Erik to explain himself.

Erik said nothing. His eyes wandered over the table, trying to get information at the same time as the general was doing the same, and noticed an envelope addressed to Lane from the White House.

"Were you born fully grown, or is your background so secret only the President of the United States knows who you are?" Lane took a letter out of the envelope and looked it over. "I was told you were sent here because of a national emergency."

"Yes, sir. I was."

"I heard we are in a race against time, so the Nazis won't win the war."

Erik nodded.

"Would you like to see this?" Lane motioned to the letter. "Maybe you can clear some things up."

September 20, 1947
Major General Cochran E. Lane
Director of ONE
GRID 8

My dear General Lane,

I very much appreciate the work you and your staff undertook prior to the Japanese Surrender, to liquidate the wartime activities of the Office of Strategic Services which will not be needed in peacetime. As my predecessor advised me, another agency will hold something more sensitive to national security than the Manhattan Project. That is why ONE was formed: to protect the United States from enemies using time travel.

In 1944, Roosevelt advised me that in the years to come, if there are individuals who come to Hidden Meadow Apartments, they are to be treated with the utmost respect because they are serving their country by traveling back in time to correct the timeline in history. These time travelers will help preserve those resources and skills within your organization which are vital to our peacetime purposes. Consistent with the foregoing, the attached executive order compels your agency to continue without interrupting other

services of a military nature, the need for which will continue
for some time.

I want to take this occasion to thank you for the
capable leadership you will bring to activities that are not
conceivable at this time. I hope you will find satisfaction
in the achievements of ONE and take pride in your own
contribution to them. These are, in themselves, large rewards.
Rest assured that all peacetime services of the government are
the foundation of your agency, which will be given any and
all resources we are capable of providing without interference
from Congress or future presidents.

Sincerely yours,

Harry S. Truman

As Erik handed the letter back, Lane cleared his throat, relaxed, and said, "I believe you are like William Stephenson." Lane lit a cigarette and sat back in his chair, resting his elbows on the arms and interlacing his fingers before continuing. "Codenamed: *Intrepid?*"

Erik nodded and answered flatly, "Stephenson was charged with establishing and running a vast, worldwide intelligence network across Nazi-controlled Europe."

"I was told by President Roosevelt that you have the ability to infiltrate into any walk of life, to literally become anyone." Lane paused to study Erik, who sat motionless. "Is this true?"

Still, Erik did not move or speak.

"Are you going to answer me?"

Erik's answer was flat and without emotion. "No."

Lane pressed on, calm but with authority. "Simulation Sixteen, Simulation Twenty-Seven, Simulation Forty-Two, and Simulation One-Eighteen. Care to explain?"

"I'm a man from a strange and distant time. I travel in time and sometimes am left without a hope of going home."

"So, are you a time traveler?"

Erik nodded.

"You become a chameleon when you travel back."

Erik nodded again.

"I don't know if you are aware that with help from Nikola Tesla's research, we've achieved time travel." Lane paused for a moment, searching for a reaction that never materialized, then continued. "According to George Scherff, who used to be Nikola Tesla's assistant, they were able to make it work in 1940, three years before Project Rainbow."

Lane leaned forward, lowered his eyes, and looked at Erik. "I meet President Roosevelt in December of 1940. That's when I met Scherff, with all of Tesla's research, including a box with folders on this technology. Neither the president nor I understood it, but Scherff assured us we needed to invest in it because if people could travel in the past, it could have devastating effects in the future. Thus, as much of America's industrial might and scientific innovation was applied to this as was to the Manhattan Project. FDR wasn't convinced at first, but Scherff explained in no uncertain terms that he saw New York City devastated by a single weapon in 1960." Lane pointed at Erik, "So, there's a chance you will succeed when you travel back in time?"

"It is my abilities that will determine if I am successful."

"Are you saying that there's a chance you will fail?"

"There's a chance, yes."

Lane raised his voice. "Have you ever done this sort of thing before?"

Erik nodded.

"Do you care to elaborate?"

"Were you ever told of any conversations between Robert Oppenheimer and General Groves?"

Lane shook his head.

"General Groves told Oppenheimer that we were ahead by twelve-months over the Nazis in developing the atomic bomb. Oppenheimer corrected him and said eighteen months. However, they were both were wrong."

Lane's stoic mask slipped, revealing a hint of confusion.

"The Nazis had the atomic bomb in 1944."

"Then why didn't they use it?"

"Because I stopped them from using it. That's all you need to know."

A knock came to the door, and Lane replied without turning around for the individual to come in. The man who entered appeared to be a scientist from his white overcoat. He looked much younger than his thirty-eight years, with a youthful face shadowed by eyes revealing a lack of sleep.

"General, temporal insertion is in six minutes." he said with an arrogant tone.

"It seems like it's time to clean up someone's mess in the past," Erik said, not waiting to be dismissed as he got up to follow the scientist out of the office.

Lane, visibly flustered at the breach of protocol, had to jog after them to catch up.

As the scientist walked down the corridor, he paused to look at Erik closely. He gave Erik a once over and rubbed his chin.

"Have we ever met before?" The scientist asked.

"No. I am sure of it."

The scientist looked at Erik intently, then shook himself out of what he was thinking and just nodded as he walked to a control panel.

"Who is that?" Erik asked Lane, jerking a thumb at the unusually gruff scientist.

"That's George Scherff."

"Nikola Tesla's assistant."

Lane nodded.

Another scientist approached Erik. He was tall, handsome, and charismatic with German facial features.

"You have to be fucking kidding me," Erik muttered.

"Do you recognize him?" Lane asked.

"He was an SS-Obergruppenführer, equivalent to a lieutenant general. He was in command of the Nazi civil engineering projects, the V-weapons program, and the Emergency Fighter Programs."

Lane was left speechless. It became clear to him Erik could retain knowledge like no one he had ever met.

Erik continued, "However, in May 1945, Kammler and his research disappeared. There was much conjecture regarding his fate." Erik smirked and shook his head. "Now I know the answer."

Kammler approached Erik with an ingratiating smile with his hand extended. "Major, it's so nice to see a familiar face." As he squeezed Erik's hand, he took in the uniform the man was wearing. "Interesting. The uniform you are wearing is quite the contrast to the uniform you wore last time."

Scherff yelled, "We got three minutes."

Kammler accompanied Erik to the entrance of the time machine, explaining as they walked. "We're going to put you within a three-block radius where the pilots are housed." Erik nodded as he absorbed the information. "We can get you in the ballpark. We don't know exactly where, but rest assured, you won't be fused to parts of buildings, vehicles, or other things."

"I sure hope not." Erik stared at Scherff, who was tapping his watch. Technicians stood by their workstations as they stared at him. Erik remembered from 2008 the first time he walked past the foot-wide, bright red line on the floor adorned with the words, *DANGER: RADIATION. ONLY TRAVELERS AND AUTHORIZED PERSONNEL BEYOND THIS POINT.* Nearby, Erik saw Jacques, whose hand was raised with two fingers crossed. Erik then stepped over the red line and through a large, black blast door, then proceeded down a stark white hallway that led to a circular room.

Scherff turned to Jacques. "He's going to be stuck in 1940 during the height of the Battle of Britain, and he'll be totally alone with no way home, but he just looked like he was walking down the hall to take a shit. He's either the bravest man I've ever seen or the craziest. What kind of effect does time travel have on one's psychology that he'd volunteer to do this for the *second* time?"

Jacques simply shrugged.

"I wonder what he's thinking right now."

Erik stood perfectly still as the walls emitted an electronic humming, sounding like a million bees. It consumed the room and grew louder by the second, assaulting Erik's eardrums. A blinding, bluish-white light filled the room. Erik took a deep breath. A chill suddenly ate through his body, and he had the sensation of being pulled back. His eyes bulged, he felt as if he were falling, and his last thought before he was ripped through time and space was a quote from Alan Shepard: "Dear Lord, please don't let me fuck up."

CHAPTER 7

DISAPPEARING INTO THE NOW

"I already knew that, of course. But there's a difference between knowing it and really experiencing it."

— Andy Weir, *The Martian*

SOMEWHERE IN FRANCE, AUGUST 14, 1940

Leaves rustled as the wind danced with tree branches, carrying the sweet vapor of flowers kissed by the rising sun over a small village. Suddenly, a terrifying boom broke the tranquility of the morning, followed by black smoke, with twirls of silver-blue puffs, rising over the horizon.

Erik opened his eyes to a blur and a feeling the world had flipped upside down, something he hated about time travel. Being in France would thrill most people, but Erik was not one of them. He blinked, trying to clear his blurry vision to take in the unfamiliar surroundings. He was between two walls with an open sky overhead. The pavement below his feet ran past the edge of the blur, parallel to the walls. He pressed a hand against one wall as he struggled to stay upright and could almost touch the other one. An alley. He was in an alley.

The first few minutes after the time jump always felt like

waking up from a dream; it was hard to tell what was real. Erik knew he wasn't dreaming. He ran over the mission in his mind, using it to center himself and shake off the mental fog of the trip. Erik was in 1940 at the height of the Battle of Britain. An Israeli agent changed something in the past, allowing the Germans to execute Operation Sealion, invading the British Isles. He was to pose as a bombardier on an He-111 bomber. Every step he took could lead to being discovered and killed by the Mossad agent.

With heart pounding and adrenaline surging through his veins, Erik set out to find the airfield. He stumbled through a few steps, pausing to ensure no one saw him, then proceeded down the alley.

Like any op, he had to blend in and not seem desperate for answers to things he should know. He carefully navigated the treacherous streets of a once quiet French town enslaved under the iron grip of German occupation, blending in with German soldiers and Luftwaffe personnel. Anyone could wear the uniform, but there was more to fitting in than looking the part. To really blend in, he would need to incorporate things like posture, gestures, facial expressions, mannerisms, and odor. The Mossad agent could use even that last aspect to figure out who Erik was. If he wore the wrong deodorant or cologne, that would be a red flag. Erik had to act like he belonged, displaying nothing but confidence.

He relied on his sense of direction to guide him through the labyrinthine streets, vigilantly avoiding the gaze of the enemy soldiers patrolling the area. An unexpected turn of events, however, soon plunged him into a realm of even greater peril. A sleek black car pulled up beside him. "You seem lost," the driver said.

It would be most effective for him to lean into it and act like he *was* lost, in place rather than time, when confronted as such. Humor would break the ice. That was one of many skills Erik had to work with. "Actually, I was looking for a bar to have a drink and calm my nerves before I meet the base commander." He stared the stranger in the eyes, selling the lie with a friendly face, if nothing else.

The driver, a pilot judging from his badges on his uniform, gestured for him to get in. "We have better stuff at the hotel." As Erik climbed into the car, the driver extended his hand. "I'm Gunther."

Erik introduced himself and shook the man's hand. With a mix of relief and anxiety, Erik settled into the vehicle, unsure of what awaited him at the hotel.

Gunther glanced at Erik with a curious expression, "Replacement?"

Erik nodded. "Navigator-bombardier."

Gunther explained his last navigator-bombardier suffered from kanalkrankheit, or channel sickness, a form of combat fatigue leading some to go AWOL or become deserters.

They approached the main entrance of the Luftwaffe bomber base. Gunther had one hand barely draped over the steering wheel and his free arm resting on the door as if out for a Sunday drive. Meanwhile, Erik's heart raced with trepidation as he pared to get into character. The pilot seemed to enjoy the morning air flowing in the open window, while every breath Erik took was laden with uncertainty. They drew nearer the gate, where armed guards stood watch, their stern faces a sign of their vigilance. The guards had their fingers poised just over the triggers of their MP 40s, ready to react to any potential threat.

As the sleek, black car glided to a halt, three formidable guards emerged from the watch shack, their penetrating gazes locking onto Erik and Gunther with an unnerving intensity. The air crackled with tension as Erik's instincts warned him of the imminent danger lurking in those scrutinizing eyes. With a purposeful stride, a hulking guard with a face chiseled from stone advanced toward the vehicle, demanding their identification with a voice as cold as steel.

Gunther smiled and handed over his papers, making some comment about the weather that Erik could barely make out over his pulse pounding in his ears as he focused and passed his own documents to the driver to relay to the guard. The statue-like soldier inspected the papers with a meticulous eye, his silence amplifying the palpable anxiety that hung in the air. Time seemed to stretch into an agonizing eternity as the guard absorbed every detail, every nuance captured on those pages. Finally, with a subtle nod that cut through the heavy silence like a blade, he signaled their clearance, a silent acknowledgement that their identities had passed the most rigorous scrutiny. With a gesture, the guard permitted them to proceed, but the weight of his gaze lingered, a constant reminder that they were being watched, their every move carefully monitored.

Gunther skillfully maneuvered the car, his steely gaze focused on the road ahead. Erik's eyes were inexplicably drawn to the main building of Generalmajor Angerstein's office. Before it, standing in an imposing formation, rows upon rows of He-111 bombers loomed, their metallic bodies glistening under the unforgiving sun. It was a sight that sent shivers down Erik's spine, a chilling display of power and devastation. The He-111s exuded an eerie sense of quiet authority, like a haunting melody that foretold the impending chaos they were capable of unleashing. Erik couldn't help but imagine the lives that would be shattered and the mayhem that would ensue once these war birds took to the skies. The formidable machines, poised and ready, were like a sinister lullaby, silently waiting to unleash their wrath upon unsuspecting targets in England the following day.

Gunther must have sensed Erik's unease but interpreted it as pre-combat anxiety. "Don't worry. There aren't many Spitfires in the air, so there's no need to panic when you go up. Are you still wanting to get that drink afterward?"

Erik shook his head. "I'm here now. I might as well report in."

"I'm headed to his office as well. I'll join you," Gunther said as he brought the car to a stop outside Generalmajor Angerstein's office. As they entered the building, Erik shook off the unease gnawing at him from within and was prepared with false cover and legend.

The sound of their footsteps on the creaking floorboards echoed through the main room. Angerstein's assistant was on the phone and gestured for them to wait. Soon, he hung up the receiver and addressed Gunther. "How can I help you, Captain Buchheim?"

"I want to know if the replacements have arrived."

"The generalmajor has been trying to find out that information." He picked up the phone again. "Herr Generalmajor, I have Captain Buchheim here asking about replacements, and…" He cupped the receiver and stared at Erik. "Who are you?"

"Lieutenant Erik Függer, replacement navigator-bombardier."

The assistant went back on the phone for a few seconds, then waved Erik and Gunther in.

The atmosphere was tense in Generalmajor Angerstein's office, a room lit mainly by large, open windows behind a large desk. Bomber status charts and maps of southern England adorned the walls, flapping slightly as a breeze blew under them. Behind the imposing desk, cluttered with mission reports and weather up-dates, sat Generalmajor Angerstein himself, a man known for his strict demeanor and attention to detail.

Angerstein stood up from behind his desk, his gaze cold and calculating as he stared at both men. "Lieutenant Erik Függer," he barked, his piercing gaze fixed on the young navigator-bombar-dier standing before him, "where are your transfer papers?"

Erik straightened his uniform and met the generalmajor's gaze with a calm disposition. "Sir, I have recently been assigned to this jagdgeshwader. The Ministry of Aviation should have sent my transfer papers to you."

Angerstein shook his head, but more in resignation than denial, a gesture that spoke volumes. It seemed missing transfer papers wasn't an uncommon issue for him. He let out a deep sigh and glanced toward Gunther, who had been silently observing the exchange. "Very well. Captain Buchheim, Lieutenant Függer will be your replacement navigator-bombardier. He will report to you from now on."

Both men nodded their understanding.

"You are dismissed."

Erik and Gunther saluted and left the office.

As they left the headquarters, Gunther explained that the bomber crews were billeted in a nearby hotel. "I'll be happy to drive you there, and we can get that drink you were looking for."

"That sounds like a plan, Captain."

As they made their way to the hotel, Erik and Gunther started getting to know each other in the short time they had before the imminent danger of their upcoming mission. Over a quiet dinner, they formed an unexpected camaraderie. They exchanged stories of their families and shared their hopes and fears about the future. Despite Erik's initial apprehension, he found solace in Gunther's amiable company. The man had a natural charm that was hard to resist.

Gunther seemed to feel the same. Their shared passion for serving the Fatherland forged an instant bond, though the captain was not aware that everything passing through Erik's lips, other than dinner and drinks, were lies. He bought into Erik's cover so much, in fact, that he suggested they bunk together. "I could stick you with the other boys and keep the room to myself, but I think we're getting along well, so I'd rather give you the space than risk the general dumping somebody I can't stand in my lap."

As the night wore on, the conversation shifted from light-hearted banter to the daunting mission that awaited them the next morning. Gunther explained that Generalmajor Angerstein had strict orders not to divulge details to anyone about the mission until the last possible moment, so they wouldn't get a full briefing until just before they boarded their plane.

After dinner, Gunther showed Erik to their dimly lit room. Gunther stared at the ceiling, thoughts of the mission entangling his mind. He knew, and kept to himself, the chances of success were uncertain, but his dedication to his duty propelled him forward.

Erik sat at a small desk, staring at a photograph of Jamie and Max. His palms were sweaty and his heart raced, but he reminded himself of the reason he was there. He turned off the light before he went to bed. The darkness amplified the dread of the dangers that lay ahead, but the promise of the morning sun to come was hope that illuminated his path. As Erik laid in bed, his heart pounded with a mixture of anticipation and dread, but he steeled his nerves with his unwavering commitment to correcting the timeline.

Erik closed his eyes in the darkest of times, determined to secure a brighter future.

CHAPTER 8

WHERE SWALLOWS AND EAGLES GATHER

"Nature taking its course—hunter and prey, the endless circle of life and death."
—Stephenie Meyer

AUGUST 15, 1940

The room lay cloaked in darkness, its stillness broken by approaching footsteps. Erik and Gunther slumbered, unaware of the impending intrusion. Suddenly, the door swung open, and a blinding beam of light pierced through the blackness, targeting Gunther's face. "Captain Buchheim, mission today. Breakfast at zero-six-hundred, briefing at zero-six-forty-five," a sergeant declared, his voice laced with urgency.

Gunther glanced at his wristwatch, the hands indicating five am. He grumbled as he roused himself from sleep. "Thanks, sergeant," he replied, his tone tinged with weariness.

The sergeant shifted his flashlight, its glow now directed toward Erik. "Lieutenant Függer," he called out.

Erik, already stirring, responded promptly. "I'm up."

Before departing the room, the sergeant turned back to Gunther and Erik, his words filled with a mix of encouragement and determination. "Sirs, give them hell today."

"Will do," Gunther answered, a steely resolve gleaming in his eyes.

Erik offered a thumbs up in agreement.

Gunther rose from his bed, stretching his limbs, and began to sing, his voice echoing through the room. "Oh, how I hate to get up in the morning…"

Erik rose and couldn't help but voice his irritation. "Do you have to sing this early in the morning?"

Gunther nodded mischievously, a playful grin on his face. They both gathered their toiletries and made their way to the bathroom.

The other crewmen moved with urgency; their words kept to a minimum as they swiftly donned their flight suits. The tantalizing aroma of freshly baked bread wafted through the air of the hotel, igniting a primal hunger within each of them.

In the dining room downstairs, tables were meticulously arranged with delicate China and sparkling crystal, beckoning them to partake in a traditional German breakfast. A steaming cup of tea warmed Erik's hands as he savored the first bite of a warm bread roll. His appetite whetted, he placed an order for scrambled eggs, eagerly anticipating the arrival of his chosen dish. Butter, an assortment of jams and preserves, and golden honey adorned the table, tempting the pilots with their sweet and savory offerings. Before the eggs could be served, the stewards placed quark, a velvety curd cheese, alongside succulent sausages and an array of other cheeses. Erik, desiring a refreshing accompaniment to his meal, requested a glass of apple juice. The atmosphere was tense, and conversation was sparse, as they all anticipated the imminent arrival of the trucks that would transport them to the airfield. As if on cue, an enlisted man materialized at the hotel's front door, his silent nod conveying the message they had been waiting for.

"Gentleman, the trucks are here. Don't forget your gear."

Outside the hotel, darkness enveloped everything, casting an eerie atmosphere. Erik and his comrades moved cautiously, as if they were descending into the depths of a bottomless well. The biting cold seeped through their flight gear, causing them to shiver. A few of them nervously lit up cigarettes, while others remained silent, attempting to steady their trembling nerves.

In a hushed tone, Gunther leaned toward Erik, whispering words that only he could hear, seeking reassurance of his well-being.

Erik nodded in response, his face reflecting a mix of determination and underlying fear.

The Opel Blitz trucks came to a quiet halt, and once loaded, resumed their journey. The trucks stopped at the airfield, and the men disembarked and quickly congregated in front of a board concealed by a heavy curtain. Forming a semi-circle, they gathered around, their eyes focused on the mysterious object. Erik and the other navigators retrieved their maps and pencils, ready to record with diligence every crucial detail that would guide them on their perilous mission.

"Achtung!"

Everyone stood at attention as the flight officer walked in front of them and prepared to give his briefing. Erik thought there was something regal about how he carried himself and the way he walked.

Lieutenant Colonel Evander Arioch was a tall, broad-shouldered man in a neatly pressed Luftwaffe uniform. He had a square jaw, thinning blonde hair, and piercing blue eyes that demanded attention. His physique was trim and muscular, appearing able to handle any confrontation.

"At ease, gentlemen."

The assembled flight crews shuffled and sat as Arioch pulled back the curtain to reveal a map of southern England. All eyes anxiously looked for the target—was it far? A bold red arrow reached from France across the channel, a black arrow turned sharply and penetrated over land, and a green arrow extended from England back to France.

Arioch looked into everyone's eyes. "This is it. Gentlemen…" He paused. "We will continue the destruction of the Royal Air Force on the ground. Zero hour for takeoff will be zero-eight-one-five." He stepped to the side of the map and traced the arrows with a metal pointer, tapping points of interest on the map as he spoke. "Our targets today in southern England are the following airfields: Manston, Biggin, Kenley, Dover, and Hawkinge. Your target is the airfield at Kenley."

The mood among the crews was enthusiastic. Everyone assembled knew that the Royal Air Force was struggling and were confident the Luftwaffe was on the verge of winning the campaign. Their strategic objectives were no longer aircraft factories, airfields, or transportation centers. Destroying the Royal Air Force was a necessary prelude to a successful Axis invasion of England.

Arioch continued with the briefing. He pointed at the coast, where antiaircraft batteries were marked in red. The Stuka staffel's job was to knock out the coastal radar. Command assigned two staffels of Bf-109 fighters to protect the formation Erik would be in. Arioch emphasized to the navigator-bombardiers, "You'll have nil to low cloud cover at takeoff with visibility of one to two miles." Then, he focused on the pilots. "Pilots, you are to assemble over the field at 14,500 feet." Then Arioch concluded the meeting with one word and single clap of his hands. "Dismissed!"

At that moment, a dozen Opel Blitzes dropped off the enlisted men, the rest of the crews of the He-111s. Two men approached Gunther, who introduced them to Erik as Alexander and Matthias.

"Sir, where are we headed?" Alexander asked.

"Kenley." Gunther motioned for the men to turn around and head to the aircraft.

The first rays of sunlight broke over the horizon, illuminating sixteen colossal Heinkel He-111 bombers, which loomed in the distance. Their distinctive, extensively glazed greenhouse-like nose and top glass dorsal gun positions reflected the first rays of the rising sun. Each bomber stood resolute on its hardstand, concealed beneath a meticulously arranged camouflage netting. Adorned in early-war German splinter camouflage, the He-111s sported a mesmerizing combination of dark green and black-green patterns over a light blue underbelly. Boldly displayed beneath the glass, on the pilot's side, were the squadron markings, accompanied by an imposing black swastika outlined in white on the vertical stabilizer. With its forward landing gear providing a wide stance and its nose pointed skyward, the aircraft seemed to possess an insatiable eagerness to take flight.

The sheer magnitude of the plane was spell bounding to Erik. It was a behemoth, defying all expectations that it could ever ascend into the sky. Its sheer weight cast a shadow of awe and trepidation upon the onlookers.

A hive of activity surrounded the aircraft as ground crews swarmed around them like ants, their movements feverish and purposeful. They scrutinized every detail with unwavering diligence, leaving no stone unturned in their meticulous preparations. The weight of responsibility hung heavily in the air as the crew members double-checked their tasks, their minds filled with a sense of urgency and anticipation. The ordinance crews, having dutifully loaded the bombs into the bellies of the planes, made their way back, their departure signaling the final stages of readiness. Meanwhile, armament crews busied themselves with the finishing touches, placing saddle drums of ammunition within the planes. Their expert hands moved with precision, leaving no room for error. In the belly of each aircraft, the three MG 15 machine-guns stood as formidable sentinels, ready to unleash their deadly fury upon the enemy. A-stand in the nose, B-stand on the dorsal, and C-stand on the ventral were carefully inspected, ensuring each gun was primed and prepared to fulfill its purpose.

Amidst the fear and uncertainty, underlying all the frenetic activity of the ground crews, a steadfast determination burned within the hearts of the airmen. They were prepared to face whatever lay ahead; their minds focused on the mission at hand. As the sun continued its ascent, casting a golden glow upon the scene, the stage was set and the players were ready. The time for action was drawing near, and the world held its breath, awaiting the outcome of the high-stakes game.

Matthias grasped a camera tightly, his fingers trembling with anticipation. With each click, he captured the essence of the moment, immortalizing the armament crew and their mighty aircraft. As the lens focused on the determined faces of the bomber crew, Erik couldn't help but give a thumbs up and a smile, a reflexive gesture that betrayed his excitement.

It was only later, in 2003, when he would stumble upon that very photograph, that the weight of his actions would truly strike him. He was captured in that frozen frame, forever bound to that moment in time.

The crew swiftly made their way toward the gondola hatch, their hearts pounding in sync with the rhythm of their steps. Meanwhile, the ground crew scurried around the plane, meticulously performing their final checks. One of them, a rag in hand, wiped the glass of the greenhouse nose, erasing any smudges that dared to obscure their vision. Gunther nudged Erik, directing his attention toward the glass. With a knowing nod, he explained the pilots' disdain for this particular windscreen design. Its distance from the pilot's reach made it nearly impossible to clean, leaving it vulnerable to the deceptive tricks of dirt and grime, often masquerading as enemy aircraft.

Stepping inside the aircraft, Erik found himself engulfed by the sea of dials and switches adorning the instrument panel. An array of mysterious gadgets adorned the left wall, their purpose known only to those who had dedicated their lives to mastering the art of flight. Directly in front of the pilot and co-pilot seats stood the formidable A-stand, housing the bombsight and a fearsome MG-15 machine gun. Just below, another box lay in wait, its switches and wheels controlling the trim tabs, elevators, and rudders, granting the pilot the power to maneuver through the treacherous skies. Erik settled into the navigator-bombardier seat, feeling a surge of electricity pulsating through his veins. He plugged in his intercom, ensuring clear communication with his comrades.

"As soon as you're ready, call in," Gunther commanded, his voice steady and resolute as he took his rightful place beside Erik, ready to face whatever lay ahead. The stage was set, the players assembled, and the fate of nations hung in the balance.

"B-stand, checking in," Alexander answered.

"C-stand, checking in," Matthias replied.

Erik meticulously arranged his tools of the trade—pencils, compasses, rulers, map, and logbook—on the small table in front of him. The weight of his responsibilities bore heavily on his shoulders, just as it did for every member of his He-111 crew. That they had downed countless enemy planes only added to the tension and apprehension that hung in the air. Gunther's voice echoed in Erik's mind, reminding him of the importance of keeping the crew occupied. It was their only refuge from the haunting thoughts that plagued them. Each crew had devised their own routines, carefully crafted to keep their minds and bodies engaged. Erik tapped Gunther on the shoulder, directing his attention to a man waving a red flag, signaling for the bombers to take flight. Gunther adjusted a small slip of paper tucked next to the compass, and Erik studied it closely. The paper, labeled as a *Compass Correction Card*, was a vital tool for their navigation. Updated before every takeoff, it bore the date and signature of the person responsible for its accuracy.

N	30°	60°	E	120°	150°
001°	029°	060°	089°	120°	152°
S	210°	240°	W	300°	330°
181°	212°	240°	268°	301°	330°

Kompass Korrektur Karte

Positioned near the magnetic compass, it contained valuable information about the deviations between the compass readings and the true geomagnetic directions. Those variances were recorded for the four cardinal points, ensuring the crew had accurate bearings to follow.

Gunther, his fun-loving demeanor not dimmed by their situation, quipped, "Without the card, we would be forever lost. I could use a vacation. Think I should get rid of it?"

Erik couldn't help but appreciate Gunther's attempt to lighten the mood. In the midst of the chaos and uncertainty, their routines and tools offered a semblance of control, and the humor, a sense of normalcy. It was a small comfort, but one that allowed them to face the challenges that lay ahead with a glimmer of hope.

"Crew, assume positions for takeoff," Gunther said over the intercom.

The two 1,200 horsepower, Junkers Jumo 211D-2, twelve-cylinder engines produced an explosion of sound as they roared to life. Erik and Gunther's eyes scanned the many instruments to make sure that engine performance was satisfactory as a strong shudder shook the big spade—the nickname given to the plane by the He-111 crews—like a duck shaking water off its back. Gunther and Erik closed the hatches as the engines' roar eventually became a smooth, soft purr.

"Good thing we are leaving now," Gunther said to Erik, "before the sun bakes us to death in our glass house." He smiled and chuckled at his joke.

Erik grinned and shook his head.

The two aircraft of them left the Earth as they swung into position on the grassy runway. Gunther did a quick, last-minute mental checklist: tail wheel locked… check, mix and propeller set… check, fuel… check, auto-pilot off… check, and so on.

Erik looked over his left shoulder to check on the other two members of the crew, only to be surprised by a sudden flash as Matthias took a picture. They seemed to be in positive spirits and waved back. Erik turned around and looked to his right and saw the pilot of another He-111 giving a quick hand gesture to let them roll on first.

Erik waved an acknowledgement and tapped Gunther to proceed.

Gunther pushed the throttle. With the engines barely three feet away through thin steel and glass, they sounded like roaring monsters from the depths of hell. The explosion of exhaust and the beating sound of blades penetrated Erik's body. As they headed down the runway, whistling air joined the unholy chorus of the engines. Erik took several deep breaths. Strange motions and jolts assaulted his body. Then, the He-111 transformed from a lumbering, ungainly ox to a graceful bird as it lifted off the ground.

The plane soon reached cruising altitude and settled into formation with the rest of its brothers over the English Channel. Erik glanced at his map and measured their course, his hand shaking as he traced the line on the map out across the English Channel to the airfield in Kenley. Twenty-five minutes. He glanced to his right and left at the formation, spread out in perfect Vs across the sky.

Gunther tapped Erik's shoulder and pointed. Erik craned his neck upward and saw a dozen Messerschmitt Bf-109's, looking like Steller's jay birds with sky blue underbodies, streaking across the sky above the formation. They flew in plain view of the formation to show the black swastika on the vertical stabilizer and avoid being mistaken for enemy aircraft. The one-seat fighters had a single propeller with an engine mounted cannon and a 7.9 millimeter machine gun on each wing. They zoomed effortlessly through the air at around three hundred and fifty miles per hour, capable of performing dazzling acrobatics in the sky.

"Captain, permission to arm my bombs?" Erik asked.

"Go ahead." Gunther responded, then he gave the order everyone hated to hear. "Everybody, Action Stations."

Erik laid on his stomach and located the Reihenabwurfautomat FI. 50943. He made sure the switch to the correct kilograms bomb setting, then set the bombs to be released every five seconds. Moments later, he went back to his position. Bombers filled the sky from horizon to horizon, with Bf-109s strategically placed to provide protection. The German planes soared through the tranquil sky, their engines roaring with an ominous intensity, as they made their way toward their target.

Little did they know that danger was lurking just beneath the clouds. Sleek and deadly Spitfires suddenly appeared out of nowhere, their slender silhouettes cutting through the sky like knives as they swooped down from their hiding places among in the clouds.

Alexander yelled out. "Spitfires!"

Gunther barked, "Hold your fire till they're in range! Don't waste ammunition!"

Bf-109s peeled off to chase the Spitfires, which skillfully maneuvered through the air, unleashing a barrage of bullets targeting the bombers with precision and accuracy. The bombers struggled to maintain their formation.

Erik wrestled with the grip of the MG 15, his hands trembling with anticipation while his eyes darted across the expanse of the sky, searching for any Spitfires. The thumping of his heart reverberated through his chest, each beat fueling the surge of perspiration that soaked his palms, forehead, and armpits. A dryness spread in his mouth, and his whole body shook uncontrollably. The sound of machine gun fire echoed within the bomber, piercing Erik's eardrums. Gunther's knuckles turned white as he gripped the yoke.

The Spitfires, with their superior agility and speed, darted in and out of the German formation, unleashing deadly bursts of machine gun fire upon their targets. The roar of the British engines and the deafening thunder of their guns echoed even within the bomber.

Erik took a deep breath as he looked down the barrel of his weapon and focused on the crosshairs. Suddenly, a Spitfire flew directly in front of the main canopy. Erik muttered under his breath as he squeezed the trigger, "Not today." A barrage of bullets erupted from the machine gun, tearing through the fighter's fuselage. Fire and thick, black smoke blossomed from the plane as its fuel reserves lit off. The trail of smoke plummeted until the Spitfire plunged into the channel.

An icy chill gripped Erik's chest as he watched the British plane spin out of control. He knew if he weren't pulling the trigger, someone else would be, but that did little to assuage his conscience. He reminded himself that this was a necessary part of his deception, and that every life he took there could lead him to saving thousands or millions in the future.

A frenzied ballet of death unfolded in the skies as the Spitfires relentlessly pursued the advancing bombers. The Bf-109s engaged them while attempting to not become victims themselves. It was a game of cat and mouse like no other, with each pilot testing the limits of their skills and daring while hoping that they might bring down their opponent.

A pair of aircraft hurtled toward each other at more than three hundred miles per hour. Each aircraft fired, filling the air with tracers. It looked as though a collision was inevitable, but at the last moment, the Bf-109 swerved away, disappearing into the vastness of the sky.

As their adversary retreated, the Spitfire pilot zeroed in on another target: the head bomber. Other Spitfires joined it, ready to unleash their fury. They moved into formation and fired at the bomber, soared past, and maneuvered for a second attack, their guns blazing as they assaulted the lead bomber again.

Flames erupted from the He-111, and it plummeted toward the English Channel, leaving behind a trail of smoke. As the battle raged on, the bombers fought back with unwavering determination, knowing that victory hinged on their every move.

As quickly as it began, the skies were clear of Spitfires. The German fighter escort returned to France; their fuel supplies exhausted. The sun continued to rise over the English countryside as the bombers made their way toward the RAF airfield. Inside each, the bombardiers prepared to drop their payloads.

On the ground, the roar of the bombers' engines interrupted an otherwise peaceful morning as the Germans flew low over the fields, their targets in sight. The airfield at Kenley was a hive of activity, with aircraft being rearmed, refueled, and prepared to take off. Ground crew scurried about, preparing the Spitfires for the next wave. Over the horizon, dark silhouettes grew larger and more ominous with each passing second.

The tension reached its zenith as the bombers approached. The Spitfires scrambled to take to the skies, lining up on and near the runway, but they were too late. The He-111s gracefully glided over the airfield with chilling precision, dropping their bombs without mercy. Explosions erupted across the airfield as planes, hangers, and runways were reduced to heaps of smoldering wreckage and engulfed in flames. The runways were reduced to rubble, making it impossible for the RAF to launch any more planes. Secondary explosions filled the airfield as fuel and ordnance cooked off from the fires. Across southern England, similar scenes played out at other airfields as the coordinated attack was carried out.

The sun danced between the clouds as the bombers began their return journey to France. Even though the relentless assault on the airfields had been a success, everyone kept alert for fighters. There could still be Spitfires hiding among the clouds and the sun, and the bombers were vulnerable with no escort.

Erik excused himself and headed to the compartment behind Gunther to retrieve ammunition for the MG 15. He felt trapped inside the belly of the bomber, and a wave of acid welled up from his belly. Glancing out the front canopy, he was relieved to see the vast expanse of the English Channel below them. Gunther motioned for Erik to hurry up. Despite being over the water, they weren't safe yet.

"Spitfires!" Alexander screamed.

The deep, loud reverberation of the MG 15 penetrated Erik's eardrums. He headed to the front, but tripped over his own feet and crashed to the floor of the cockpit.

The burning smell of powder filled Erik's nose. A deafening whine pierced his ears. He froze, struggling to remember to breathe. His head pounded as if he'd been struck, and he realized he must have hit it when he fell.

Abruptly, the world erupted into chaos as Spitfires pounced on their prey. Machine gun fire echoed from both within and without the bomber, sounding dull under the persistent ringing in Erik's ears. Bullets rained down upon the bomber, plunging its interior into a maelstrom of chaos. The impact of the projectiles was cataclysmic, tearing through the metallic hull with a ferocity that seemed almost supernatural. Erik's eyes widened in horror as his comrades, once united, succumbed to the relentless assault. Both gunners met a tragic demise, their bodies dismembered by the merciless barrage. The cabin became a grotesque tableau of carnage, adorned with a macabre tapestry of entrails and brush-strokes of blood.

It was a nightmarish scene that would haunt Erik's dreams for years to come. The air was thick with the acrid stench of death and burning fuel, an unholy blend that assaulted his senses. He made it to the front and the battered cockpit welcomed him; its acrylic-glass riddled with bullet holes that whispered of imminent death as wind whistled through them. Erik's heart pounded with a volatile mix of adrenaline and fear as he glanced at Gunther, who was barely conscious. His face was sickly pale and smeared with blood, a cruel reminder of the brutality of their situation. The wounded aircraft coughed and sputtered, spewing black smoke like a wounded creature gasping for air.

CHAPTER 9

GALVANIC RESPONSE

"You're on your own now. You are not helpless. You will find your way."
— Robert Ludlum, *The Bourne Identity*

Erik's heart raced, his survival instincts surging to the forefront of his consciousness as he grabbed the yoke. He frantically scanned the surroundings, desperately seeking an escape route, his mind ablaze with thoughts of survival. The relentless onslaught had mangled the bomber's controls, complicating any attempts to regain control of the wounded aircraft. Time slipped through Erik's fingers like sand in an hourglass, every passing second bringing them closer to the edge of oblivion. However, surrender was not in his nature.

His mind raced, desperately searching for a glimmer of hope in the vast sky that enveloped him. His grip on the yoke tightened, his knuckles white with determination, as he scanned the horizon for any sign, any sliver of salvation, but the situation grew more dire. Erik understood that his only hope of survival lay in evading the relentless Spitfires and finding his way back to friendly territory. The odds seemed insurmountable, a mountain of impossibility threatening to crush his spirit. Even in the face of unimaginable horror, Erik's determination burned bright. He refused to succumb to the suffocating grip of fear. With unwavering resolve, he clung to the flickering flame of hope, determined to navigate through the tempest of bullets, even with the grim reaper hovering over him.

Amid the chaos that swirled around him, Erik's spirit remained unyielding. He stood firm, ready to confront any challenges that lay in his path. He took a deep breath as he tried to comfort Gunther, remembering what he was taught at the Farm.

You will eventually experience an op that's a complete cluster fuck, at which time you'll think, 'This is it… I'm going to live, die, or be captured.' Since rule number one is never to be captured and dying is not an option, there is only one choice left. Once you choose to live, you can work on making it happen. It's that simple. Just get started. It is a puzzle. After you solve one issue, you move on to the next, and so on. And you get to go home if you solve all the issues.

In the heart-pounding tale unfolding amidst the tumultuous skies, the menacing silhouette of a Bf-109 emerged, daringly challenging the very fabric of destiny just out of sight of the Spitfires. The Bf-109 waggled its wings, indicated it would fly over the bomber. Erik pushed the yoke forward, causing the bomber to descend. The Bf-109 pilot clenched his fists with his senses heightened, as he tightened his grip on the control stick, and maneuvered his aircraft toward the beleaguered bomber. As the Bf-109 roared over the bullet-shaped canopy of the bomber, Erik was engulfed in a symphony of roaring engines and the crackling static of radio transmissions from other bombers, but the stage was set for a breathtaking confrontation between the formidable Luftwaffe pilot and the valiant RAF pilots of the skies.

A Spitfire squadron soon came into view ahead of them, but with unwavering determination, the Bf-109 pilot locked his sights on the first Spitfire, his eyes ablaze with a fierce resolve. As the distance closed between them, time seemed to slow, each heartbeat echoing like a thunderous drumroll. In a daring display of skill and audacity, the adversaries clashed head-on, their machines trembling under the strain of the deadly dance. The Bf-109 pilot did a flurry of calculated aerobic moves and skillfully maneuvered his aircraft, defying the laws of gravity. Muzzle flashes from the German machine guns and cannon were the last thing the Spitfire pilot saw.

Bolstered by his recent triumph, the Bf-109 pilot veered sharply to the left, relentlessly pursuing another Spitfire that dared to challenge his dominance. With every twist and turn, the tension mounted, the atmosphere electric with anticipation. The dance of death continued, each pilot's fate hanging in the balance as the skies became a battlefield of warring spirits. As the sun cast its golden rays upon the aerial arena, the Bf-109 pilot unleashed a torrent of firepower upon his prey, his aim unwavering, his resolve unyielding. With nerves of steel, he seized the opportune moment, striking like a falcon diving upon its prey. The sound of gunfire filled the air, shattering the tranquility of the heavens, as victory was wrested from the clutches of uncertainty. In a mesmerizing display of aerial acrobatics, the Spitfire succumbed to the relentless onslaught, spiraling toward the earth in a graceful descent, its wings clipped by the merciless hand of fate.

With only one adversary remaining, the Bf-109 pilot's heart raced, his senses heightened to a fever pitch. The final duel commenced, a desperate struggle for survival, as the heavens bore witness to a battle that would be etched in the annals of history. In a final, defiant act of courage, the Bf-109 pilot unleashed a devastating barrage of gunfire, tearing through the air with an unstoppable force. The last Spitfire, once a symbol of invincibility, succumbed to the inevitable, its wings shattered, its spirit defeated. As the echoes of the battle faded into the distance, the Bf-109 pilot emerged triumphant, his path strewn with the wreckage of fallen adversaries. In the aftermath of this breathtaking encounter, the skies stood silent, bearing witness to the indomitable spirit of a lone warrior who dared to defy the odds and shape the destiny of the heavens.

With a thunderous roar, the He-111 bomber plummeted from the sky, its wings trembling in desperation as it fought against the unyielding forces of gravity. The once majestic aircraft, now a twisted mass of metal, tore through the air, leaving a trail of black smoke in its wake. The ground below seemed to tremble in anticipation, as if aware of the impending chaos about to unfold. As the bomber hurtled toward the earth, the grassy field below seemed to hold its breath, its green expanse transforming into a makeshift landing strip. Erik's heart raced, his hands gripping the controls with a desperate determination. With every passing second, the ground grew closer, its unforgiving embrace waiting to devour the fallen war machine. In a final act of defiance, the bomber's wheels touched the ground, sending sparks flying in a fiery display of resistance.

The once smooth field transformed into a battlefield, its serene facade shattered by the violent arrival of the desperate aircraft. The earth groaned beneath the weight, as if protesting the intrusion of man-made destruction. Silence enveloped the crash site, broken only by the crackling flames that licked at the bomber's broken frame. Smoke billowed into the sky, mingling with the remnants of the aircraft's former glory. The grass, trampled and scarred, seemed to mourn the loss of its untouched beauty. From a distance, onlookers emerged cautiously, their eyes wide with awe and terror. They watched as the wreckage smoldered, uncertain of what lay within. The He-111 bomber had become a monument to both human ingenuity and the mercilessness of war.

Rescue crews, their faces etched with determination, raced toward the wreckage of the He-111. They knew that time was of the essence in their mission to save lives. With bated breath, they pried open the twisted metal canopy, revealing the harrowing aftermath of the crash.

Amidst the wreckage, Erik grieved for his fallen comrades. The weight of their loss pressed heavily upon him, his heart heavy with sorrow. But from the darkness, a glimmer of solace emerged. The pilot of the Bf-109, a figure of strength and resilience, approached Erik with a comforting presence. His voice, laced with empathy and understanding, offered a ray of hope amidst the despair. Together, they left the wreckage behind, a symbol of the indomitable spirit that can rise even from the ashes of tragedy. In this tale of suspense and bravery, the skies witnessed both the horrors of war and the resilience of the human spirit. It was a reminder that even in the darkest times, there is always a glimmer of light, a hand reaching out to guide us through the chaos.

CHAPTER 10

LOOKING FOR A GHOST IN THE SHADOWS

"A man with remarkable survival abilities, and an alias, must seek to discover who has the same skills before they're found out and killed."
— Erik Foge

As an operative, Erik had encountered numerous brushes with death, each one leaving an indelible mark on his psyche. No matter how seasoned or battle-hardened, those near-death experiences possessed an uncanny ability to rattle even the most hardened of souls. Like a tapestry woven with countless threads, each encounter was as distinct as a snowflake, etching itself into Erik's memory with chilling clarity.

He stared at the empty bed in the silent room. He pulled out a book, *War of the Worlds*, desperately seeking solace within its pages. Just the day before, the room had been filled with Gunther's singing, laughing, and joking. They had exchanged stories of their families. But he was gone. Erik's entire crew were gone, fallen, having sacrificed their lives for their country. A heavy burden of survivor's guilt weighed upon him, threatening to crush his spirit. He knew he shouldn't get too attached—that those men were not only the enemy, but already long dead as far as his 2008 perspective was concerned—but it was difficult after getting to know them, especially Gunther, on such a personal level.

A solid knock drew Erik's attention from his book. The door opened as he stuck the book in a desk drawer, and a tall figure entered the room.

It was Lieutenant Colonel Arioch. "May I come in?"

Erik motioned for him to take a seat on Gunther's bed.

Arioch sat across from Erik, his serious expression softened with empathy. "I understand your pain, Erik," Arioch said quietly. "Losing your crew is never easy, but you must remember that their sacrifices were not in vain."

Erik lowered his gaze, his voice barely a whisper. "I felt helpless, sir. I fought alongside them, but there was nothing I could do."

Arioch stood up and placed a hand on Erik's shoulder, offering a reassuring squeeze.

He motioned Erik to join him, and they walked to his car to head to the base. Seated beside Erik, Arioch's serious expression softened as he spoke in a voice that carried the weight of experience. "Lieutenant, there'll be no disgrace. Those Spitfires tailing you, shooting with everything they had, would have shaken me up." As they approached the main gate, Arioch and Erik retrieved their soldbuchs and handed them over to the stoic sentry. When the guard handed them back, Arioch casually glanced over Erik's documentation before returning it. When they reached the headquarters building, the lieutenant colonel parked his car and stared directly into Erik's eyes. "A good pilot, navigator, or any crew member of a bomber is compelled to evaluate what's happened and apply what he's learned."

Arioch and Erik strolled through the darkened airfield, surrounded by the imposing He-111 bombers, watching Luftwaffe mechanics apply surgical precision as they dissected each intricate piece, scrubbed away the grime of battle, replaced worn-out fragments, and reassembling engines with unwavering precision. This meticulous dance of restoration was the lifeblood that sustained the bombers' optimal performance. There were other individuals, inside the bombers, ensuring the proper functioning of weapon systems such as machine guns and bomb racks. They conducted regular inspections, cleaned, and lubricated the mechanisms, as well as performing test firings to verify their reliability. As Arioch spoke, Erik kept engaged with the conversation. However, at the same time, he observed the base's inhabitants, meticulously studying their behaviors and mannerisms.

Erik understood the gravity of his task. One false move could lead to catastrophic consequences, both for himself and the delicate balance of the timeline. He had only eight days, and time was running out to unmask the enigmatic Mossad agent hidden within the base. The operative wouldn't hide in the shadows, but in plain sight, so danger lurked at every turn.

Mossad would have sent a special kind of operative back. Like him, possibly better. Mossad had a special unit called Metsada. They were known for assassinations and sabotage. That was how they would alter the timeline. An assassin would be a part of the kidon, Mossad's elite assassins, who received two years of training at Mossad's facility near Herzliya. They could handle anyone who stood in the path of their objective. The Mossad operative would be an unlikely suspect, a low-ranking soldier whose unassuming demeanor masked a dangerous intellect.

An individual emerged from one aircraft and headed to another. Erik's senses sharpened to a razor's edge as he observed the suspicious figure, his mind racing to decipher their true intentions.

Arioch followed Erik's gaze. "That is Technical Sergeant Eckhard Ritter, in charge of putting the compass correction cards in each aircraft."

"Is he the only one who has the authority to do so?"

"Yes," Arioch replied with a curious raise of an eyebrow.

Erik recalled the two boys trying to fly paper airplanes into a trash can, which always veered off course. If the Mossad operative altered the compass cards, they could put an aircraft off course. It couldn't be a high-ranking officer or the lowest rank. They would need to be undetected. Ritter would be the perfect cover if he needed to linger without being bothered. The position also gave him a pretext for talking to almost anyone. Erik had to navigate a labyrinth of deception and misdirection. He knew that the Mossad agent, operating under layers of subterfuge, would not reveal themselves easily. Ritter was his only suspect so far, but he was worth checking out.

Erik had to unravel an intricate web of lies and deceit. Each encounter would be a potential minefield, every interaction a test of his wit and intuition. Erik would play his role with precision, blending seamlessly into the backdrop of the base's daily operations. He was a master of his craft. With the spirit of a cunning operative and the mind of an analyst, he would venture further into the heart of the Mossad agent's game, ready to face whatever challenges lay ahead. The hunt for the Mossad agent had begun, and Erik was determined to emerge victorious, no matter the cost.

They continued walking until they reached the headquarters building. Arioch stopped in the parking area and turned to Erik. "I am going to speak to Generalmajor Angerstein and tell him I think you should have a few days off before sending you back up."

"Thank you, sir."

What Erik didn't know was that both Angerstein and Arioch feared Erik might suffer from Kanalkrankheit and not return. "Lieutenant, there is a chaplain from the army on the base today. Do you want to speak to him?"

Erik hesitated. It wouldn't get him any closer to accomplishing his mission, and he couldn't exactly pour out his soul about what he was really dealing with, but even he had to avoid burnout. Time with a chaplain would at least offer a break from the game, a chance to collect his thoughts and prepare for the next steps. Eventually, he nodded his acceptance.

As luck would have it, Arioch spotted the chaplain a few cars over, waved the man down, and briefed him on Erik's situation. The chaplain was about to head to town for lunch and offered to bring Erik with him. Arioch advised Erik he would check up on him later as they parted ways.

Erik climbed into the car with the chaplain. Arioch stared until Erik was out of sight before he walked into Angerstein's office.

"How you doing, son?" The chaplain asked as the car moved.

"Sir, I am alive."

"Lieutenant Colonel Arioch said I should keep you company," the chaplain said, glancing at Erik. "He told me what happened."

Erik nodded.

"How are you feeling, lieutenant?"

"I'm alive, at least for now, sir."

"Son, I can see you are alive, but am asking how you are *feeling*."

"What do you want to know? I couldn't save my crew, but now I have to get over what happened."

"You feel responsible for your crew, and you have a confidence problem?"

"Confidence problem?" Erik barely suppressed a chuckle. If only the man knew what he'd volunteered to accomplish, knowing he was the most qualified person to take it on. "No, I might have regrets, but not a confidence problem. It just seems that God has a wicked sense of humor."

"That's not the answer, blaming God, son. There is a reason for his actions."

"Are you sure, sir? Man has a knack for fucking with God's plan," Erik let out the chuckle and shook his head. "I'm sure you've heard that nothing ever goes according to plan. I think that applies to the big guy, too."

As the sun beat down on the cobblestone streets of Montreuil, the chaplain made his way toward the heart of the town in search of a place to eat, eventually parking by a tavern and heading in. The place was bustling, on the verge of uproarious. The air vibrated with a symphony of clinking glasses and animated conversations. Luftwaffe and Wehrmacht personnel mingled with the boisterous locals.

Erik looked for a vantage point and secured a table strategically positioned in the corner, affording him an unobstructed view of the eclectic mix of patrons. As they settled into their seats, Erik's penetrating gaze swept across the expanse, his astute eyes meticulously dissecting the essence of each individual within his line of sight. A waitress smiled and greeted them, took their orders, and disappeared, leaving the chaplain and Erik to enjoy the warm ambiance of the tavern.

As they waited for their food to arrive, the chaplain turned to face Erik. "I'm interested to know what you're thinking and try to shed light on it."

Erik tilted his head. "It's a little more complicated than you might imagine."

"I'm a chaplain. Try me. That's what I do." He smiled and cupped Erik's shoulder. "I have heard a lot of things. I can assure there is nothing I haven't already heard."

"Not this time," Erik smirked.

"Are you religious, son? I'm a Catholic."

"I'm a Lutheran."

"We can still talk, can't we?"

"What I have seen, experienced, and need to do would challenge your understanding of reality, boggle your mind, and test even your faith, Father."

The chaplain gulped, "Completely honest, yet avoiding the

heart of the matter?" At that moment, the food arrived, and the chaplain ended his inquiries. They ate in relative silence, exchanging nothing more than small talk after that.

Later that evening, Erik lay in his bed, his mind still buzzing with the events of the day. As an operative, he was used to the constant vigilance and careful observation of every detail. In his line of work, there was no room for mistakes. He possessed an extraordinary talent to absorb and remember every encounter, every conversation, and every nuance. His analytical mind was a blessing, a valuable asset in the world of espionage, but it was also a curse with no off switch. That meant that he could never forget the look in Gunther's eyes as he drew his last breath.

Erik shook his head, trying to shake away the past so he could focus on the future. His fate lay along one of three uncertain paths. In the first, he would successfully fix the timeline and return home, ending the treacherous game. However, the second path involved him changing the wrong thing, leading to a cascade of disastrous events and altering the timeline beyond recognition. The third path, the most sinister of all, involved the Mossad operative. If they were to uncover Erik's true identity, it would only mean one thing: death.

With only eight days left to fix the timeline, time was not on his side. Death loomed close, and other than a tenuous hunch about the course correction cards, he'd made no progress at all. But for an operative like Erik, failure was fuel. He rose from his bed, resolved to face whatever lay ahead. Erik moved with purpose, his mind racing with strategies and possibilities. He knew he couldn't afford a single misstep. As he opened the desk drawer, his eyes were transfixed with dismay as a sickening wave of terror welled up from his belly. The novel was missing.

CHAPTER 11

UNFOLDING THE MYSTERIES OF SKIES

"A risk is a chance you take; if it fails you can recover. A gamble is a chance taken; if it fails, recovery is impossible."

— Erwin Rommel

AUGUST 24, 1940

Erik and Major Maier, his new pilot and commander, stood in amazement, riveted by the sight before them. The Kübelwagen parked nearby seemed insignificant compared to the magnificent He-111s, each standing proudly on their individual hardstands. Ground crews swarmed around the bombers, their movements purposeful and urgent, as they meticulously prepared the aircraft for their impending flight. Opel Blitz petrol trucks and bomb carts whizzed past, their presence fleeting as they swiftly completed their assigned tasks. The air was thick with anticipation, a palpable sense of urgency lingering in every moment. Ordinance crews meticulously loaded fat, drab, black bombs into the bellies of the bombers, their movements precise and deliberate. Meanwhile, armament crews diligently armed the planes, ensuring that each of the MG 15 machine guns were equipped with seventy-five-round, double drum magazines of ammunition. The scene was a symphony of activity, a ballet of preparation and readiness.

Erik and Major Maier couldn't help but feel a surge of unease as they observed the meticulous attention to detail. It was as if every action, every movement, was a piece of a larger puzzle, a puzzle that held the fate of their mission. Little did they know, the impending flight would take them into the heart of danger, where their skills and courage would be tested like never before. The suspense was palpable, a silent warning of the perils that awaited them.

They noticed Arioch between the bombers, inspecting the preparations. Once he noticed he was being watched, he waved and approached them. "Lieutenant Függer, I'm glad I found you." He handed over a piece of paper. "Here is tonight's weather report." Then he looked at Maier. "Major, you will be first gruppen and the lead bomber. We have made some modifications for night flying. Each aircraft will be equipped with navigation lights on the tip of the wings."

Maier appeared confused.

"Major, have you been on a steamer?"

Maier nodded.

"Like a steamer, port will have a red light and starboard will have a green one."

"Sir, wouldn't the lights give away our position and make us vulnerable to anti-aircraft guns?"

Arioch shook his head and dismissed the thought with a wave of his hand. "You will be too high for them to see it." Arioch pointed to the bombers. "Each aircraft will be following your lead."

Maier nodded again but wasn't comfortable with the navigational lights.

"Major, they are collision avoidance lights. They cast a beam of light in an oblique forward angle to avoid a head-on collision course situation and so you can maintain formation."

"Do the other pilots know about this?" Maier asked.

"They will at the mission briefing." Arioch glanced at his watch. "That's in one hour."

In the dimly lit briefing room, anticipation hung heavy in the air. A small stage stood at the front, where Arioch would deliver his mission briefing. It was adorned with a mysterious curtain, its fabric concealing a map that held the secrets of their current mission. A taut, red spool of yarn rested on the right side of the board, its thread disappearing behind the curtain, hinting at a web of unknown dangers. As the room filled with a cacophony of pilots and navigators and swirling smoke, the tension grew. Erik, armed with determination, retrieved a couple of pencils from his pocket. With a sense of purpose, he handed one to Maier, their eyes meeting briefly, silently acknowledging the gravity of the task ahead. Turning to a fresh sheet in his notebook, Erik prepared himself to capture every vital detail that would be shared. Suddenly, a chilling silence fell upon the room, as if the very air had been sucked out. Just as the room buzzed with activity, a sudden hush fell over the crowd as a sharp, commanding voice pierced through the air, demanding attention and igniting a sense of urgency.

"Achtung!"

The room fell into a hushed silence as everyone snapped to attention. Arioch strode confidently onto the stage, commanding the attention of all present. His voice rang out with an air of authority, cutting through the murmurs and shuffling as the men settled into their seats. "As you were, gentlemen," he declared, his words laced with a mix of urgency and suspense. A collective sigh of relief swept through the room as the tension dissipated.

"I hope you're all well-rested, because it's time to get back to business." With a swift gesture, he pulled back the curtain, revealing a meticulously crafted map of Southeastern England. Gasps and murmurs filled the room as eyes widened in disbelief. Arioch traced a red yarn that stretched across the English Channel and sharply penetrated into England. "The target for today is the oil refinery at Thames Haven."

The room erupted into a cacophony of disbelief, with a mix of gasps, groans, and nervous laughter. Erik watched as pilots and navigators exchanged bewildered glances, their eyes then darting toward their comrades and finally settling on the map before them. The realization of the challenge ahead washed over them like a tidal wave.

They won't be expecting this, Erik thought, his heart pounding in his chest. He didn't remember this. It was not part of the timeline. The night raid of August 24, 1940, was famously a night raid on London itself, not the refinery.

As Arioch lowered a screen, the room plunged into darkness. A large black-and-white photograph was projected onto the screen, displaying an aerial view of the oil refinery and its surrounding infrastructure. Arioch tapped his pointer on several clusters of white circles, representing crude oil tanks, at the center of the photo. "Gentlemen, this is our target," he declared, his voice filled with a mix of determination and a hint of desperation. "The round circles, so you can't miss it. The ships along the coast and these roads will be dealt with at another time. We need to focus on the crude oil tanks. If we can knock those out, it will cripple the RAF and keep them grounded."

Erik scanned the room, observing the mix of confusion and determination etched on the faces of his comrades.

Arioch's gaze fell upon him and Maier, the weight of the mission evident in his eyes. "Lieutenant Függer has the weather report," Arioch announced, his voice cutting through the silence. "We're dealing with windshear and other challenges, but we have a plan to avoid error in flight. Each aircraft will have navigational lights on the tips of your wings, a new addition that will enhance the effectiveness of our bombing."

Confusion lingered in the air, but Arioch's explanations seemed to resonate with the men. He emphasized the importance of their mission, outlining the formation and strategy for the attack. Gruppen I would lead, followed by Gruppen II, with Gruppen III assembling over the channel at five thousand feet. As the lights flickered back on, Arioch stood tall on the stage, the room enveloped in a heavy silence. His voice carried with force, infused with both determination and suppressed anxiety. "Tonight, we have the opportunity to truly make a difference in defeating the RAF," he concluded, his words hanging in the air. "Let's execute this mission to the best of our abilities and leave the rest in the hands of fate."

The room remained still, the gravity of the situation sinking in. Each man knew the risks that lay ahead, but they also understood the importance of their mission. With a shared sense of purpose, they prepared themselves for the daunting task that awaited them.

***

The German bombers sliced through the ominous night sky, hurtling toward their target. Inside the cockpit of the lead bomber, an overwhelming sense of suspense filled the men as they approached the English coast, uncertain of what awaited them. Erik's eyes darted between the compass correction card and the weather report given to him by Arioch. With each beat of his heart, a mix of trepidation and determination coursed through his veins.

Major Maier skillfully maneuvered the aircraft, battling against the relentless wind that whipped in from the English Channel. Frustration etched across his face as he muttered, "This damn wind shear."

Erik turned around, his gaze falling upon the gunner at B-Stand, who held out a photo of Jamie and a folded piece of paper. Gratefulness washed over him as he accepted the items, relieved that he hadn't lost the precious picture of Jamie that had served as his source of strength. However, upon closer inspection, he noticed that the paper bore Jamie's handwriting.

I still believe in you. My love will always be with you everywhere you go. Standing so strong and true, Erik, I still believe in you and what you are doing.

He grinned and sighed, then a knot tightened in Erik's stomach as he unfolded the paper, his mind racing as he realized he was holding a weather report for August 24, 1940, which he had in 1948. He compared that to the weather report Arioch handed him, looking for any differences. The cloud cover was off, as well as the wind speed.

This was it. The pivotal moment was upon him. Things weren't adding up, so Erik knew this was the night he had to correct the timeline and prevent World War Three from breaking out in 2012. With a deep breath, he prepared himself for whatever lay ahead, knowing that their fate and the future of the world hung in the balance. Maier inquired about Erik's well-being, and Erik nodded, his expression tense. Beads of sweat trickled down his forehead as he scrutinized the two weather reports, his eyes scanning the information with urgency. Excusing himself for a moment, Erik felt the urgency conveyed by Maier's silent gesture, knowing they had only twenty-two minutes until they became the target. Flicking on a flashlight, Erik discovered a discrepancy in the weather report provided by Arioch. The minor error would not deter the bombers from their course toward London. He furrowed his brow, contemplating how he could subtly alter the aircraft's trajectory, leaving no trace of interference.

"Lieutenant, nineteen minutes until target," Maier reminded him.

"On my way, sir," Erik replied, his mind racing.

The gunner interjected, catching Erik's attention. "Sir, did you know that nineteen is a karmic debt?"

Erik shook his head, intrigued by the gunner's statement. "Explain."

"Sir, it signifies situations where you are compelled to defend yourself," the gunner elaborated.

Erik grinned, acknowledging the observation. As he glanced around, he noticed a small scrap of paper lying on the floor. Picking it up, his pulse quickened, drowning out all other sounds. It was a compass correction card, but not just any card—it was that day's card, signed by Sergeant Ritter. Gunther had mentioned, the first time Erik went up, that they were always dated and signed. Erik hurriedly made his way to the cockpit, his eyes fixated on the card beside the compass. Several irregularities caught his attention: no date, no signature, and the degrees were off by several digits, which would divert them from London. Returning to his seat, Erik deftly swapped the card while Maier was distracted by the view outside.

As Erik studied his map, Maier's gaze turned to him. "Lieutenant, is everything alright?"

Erik's voice was tinged with concern. "Yes, sir, but it seems you are slightly off course." Erik gestured toward the compass correction card.

"Damn it," Maier muttered, gripping the yoke tightly as he made the necessary adjustments. "Thank you, Lieutenant." He shook his head, rubbing his eyes, and examined the card once more. "I could have sworn those numbers were different when we took off."

"Major, it's possible that you misread them," Erik reassured him, placing a comforting hand on his shoulder. "We've rectified the error, and the problem has been averted."

The weight of his mission bore heavily upon him, but with the final piece of the puzzle in place, they were back on the original timeline. He just had to see the night through to its end.

"Permission to arm the bombs," Erik requested. Maier nodded in approval. Once Erik completed his task, he assumed his position for the bombing run.

"Ten minutes until target," Maier announced, his voice filled with caution. "Remain vigilant and alert. Report any enemy fighters immediately."

Erik was over the bombsight, making careful adjustments. He worked with great concentration, ignoring all outside factors. "Major," Erik said, his voice trembling ever so slightly, "I think there's been a mistake in the weather forecast."

Maier questioned. "What do you mean?"

Erik manipulated the course knobs on either side of the bombsight, but the ground was covered with low-lying clouds. "There is more cloud cover than we expected."

Maier furrowed his brow and adjusted his grip on the controls. "Erik, let me know when the target is clear."

The words hung in the air, an electric current charging the atmosphere within the confined cockpit. The crew members exchanged nervous glances, their eyes reflecting hope, fear, and a morsel of faith in Erik's judgment. Maier hesitated, his gaze darting between Erik and the instrument panel. Erik had to remain calm and delay. Looking at his map, either the oil refinery at Thames Haven or downtown London were directly below them, depending on if he made the right decision about the course card, but he couldn't see to confirm it. He had to delay long enough to be sure.

"Major, I must wait for the target to be clear. I cannot confirm until I have a visual."

In that eternal moment, uncertainty played on Maier's face, battling with just dropping the bombs and going home or waiting to be sure they would hit the target. Finally, Maier sighed, his voice laced with resignation.

"Alright, I trust you. Just let me know when we are over the target."

Relief washed over Erik as he configured the navigation equipment. The crew within the bomber, along with the other crews, huddled closer, awaiting further instructions. Erik got up and took his position by Maier and looked at his map. Even if he had been wrong about the card, delaying a few more minutes could take them over London as well, but in the dark expanse, the cloud cover made difficult to determine their location.

Maier and Erik frantically scanned the map and instruments before them, beads of sweat dotting their foreheads.

"I don't understand, Erik. Do you see any landmarks?" Maier asked.

Erik shook his head. "We should have been there by now." Erik continued looking at his map and out the window.

Maier agreed. "We should have been over the target nine minutes ago."

Erik looked at the weather report, then lied, "Sir, the wind has slowed us down."

"So, where are we? Where is the refinery?"

The bombers, unbeknownst to their crews, were over a new destination. Erik took an educated guess that London sprawled beneath them under blackout conditions, with windows covered and streetlights disabled. An eerie silence settled over the cramped cockpit, broken only by the sound of the engines roaring with determination.

"Are you sure you don't see any landmarks?" Maier asked again as Erik shook his head.

Erik continued looking at his map and out the window. "Sir, the wind has veered our location."

"So where are we? Where is London?"

"Far back in the south-west."

"Good. Then get rid of the bombs and let's go home." Maier turned the communication channel to alert the rest of the bombers. "Everybody listen. Pilots advise your bombardiers to drop their bombs and get the hell out of here and head home."

Erik opened the bomb bay doors with a mechanical creak, his knuckles turning white as he gripped the bomb release lever. The weight of the night bore down on Erik, knowing how many civilian lives were going to be lost. However, it was necessary to correct the timeline, so he pulled the bomb release lever. A surge of adrenaline coursed through his veins and he let out a sigh of relief. The bomber shuddered as it released the payload that would determine the course of history.

Bombs descended from the belly of the aircraft, hurtling toward the unsuspecting city below. Time seemed to stand still as the fate of nations hung in the balance. As they struck their targets, the deafening roar of the bombs filled the air, shaking buildings to their foundations. Windows shattered, buildings crumbled, and chaos erupted in the streets as the rain of destruction swept through the city.

"Erik," Maier said, his voice barely audible over the rumble of the engines. "We may be lost in the skies, but we're on our way home."

Erik gave a faint smile, tugging at the corners of his lips. The bomber continued to fly, heading into the inky night, and the tension in the cockpit eased as they flew out over the English Channel. Hope surged within their chests as they reorientated their course toward the familiar shores of France.

"We made it through, Erik," Maier said, his voice tinged with a mix of exhaustion and relief. "We'll make sure this mistake never happens again."

Erik nodded, his eyes never leaving the horizon. "Indeed,

Major. We'll rise above this setback and continue to fulfill our duty."

The He-111 sailed through the skies, the drone of the engines providing a rhythmic backdrop to their thoughts. In the face of adversity, they found strength in each other's presence. Time passed slowly, the minutes ticking away until the runway of their home base came into view. The bomber descended gracefully, gliding toward the tarmac like a tired bird finding solace in its nest. As the wheels touched down, the reality of their journey sunk in. They were back, the weight of their mission still hanging heavy upon them, but optimism kindling within their hearts.

"Well, Erik," Maier said with a weary smile, "the debriefing will be after breakfast, and we need to have our stories straight about what happened."

Erik nodded, unbuckling his seatbelt as relief washed over him. "Yes, Major. We'll learn from this and become better. Failure won't define us."

And so, Major Maier and Lieutenant Függer stepped out of the cockpit and headed to the vehicles to take them back. Maier knew they may have been lost in the skies, but their determination to fly again remained unwavering. He was willing to have Erik as his navigator.

However, Erik had to do one more thing. The pieces fell together in his mind. The unsigned course card ruled out Sergeant Ritter, who had signed the original one, meaning somebody else planted the false card. Nobody else would have access to the cockpit except the officer in charge of the final inspection of the bombers. That same officer had handed Erik a false weather report: Lieutenant Colonel Arioch. Erik's talents would be put to the test when he faced Arioch, the Mossad agent, and he knew their confrontation would have a deadly outcome.

CHAPTER 12

SUSPICIOUS MINDS IN THE SHADOWS

"One of the things covert operatives have to give up is the idea of a fair fight. Spies aren't trained to fight fair. Spies are trained to win."
— Michael Weston, *Burn Notice*, "Friends and Family"

Tension filled the air As Erik, armed with a Luger, entered the dingy hangar that housed three He-111 bombers and made his way through the shadows. Industrial lighting fixtures cast eerie shadows over the three aircraft that provided a stark backdrop for the dangerous encounter that lay ahead.

Arioch stood over a table, looking at a map, when the sound of wooden heels grinding grains of dirt and sand revealed Erik's approach behind him. He turned around slowly, his pupils narrowing and a thin smile forming as he focused on his next target. He assumed a Krav Maga stance, moving with calculated precision.

Erik gripped the gun and locked his eyes on Arioch, daring him to act. He recognized the Israeli martial arts stance and knew a physical fight with the man would be a deadly proposition.

"You are fighting for the honor of and your duty to your country, like me," Arioch said.

"I'm fighting to preserve the timeline." Erik paused for a

moment. "I avoid confrontations, but I will never stop putting right what went wrong."

The distance between Arioch and Erik eroded in a swift and fluid motion. Arioch's body moved like a coiled spring, every muscle in his body engaging. His fingers tightened around the gun, wresting it from his adversary. Arioch spun the weapon around, stared down the barrel, and squeezed off several rounds.

With lightning reflexes, Erik dove between the towering bombers, seeking cover. The Lugar roared as bullets whizzed through the air. Screaming metal, torn asunder by the impacts, echoed through the hanger. Arioch tracked Erik's movements, predicting where he would emerge from between the bombers. With Erik again in his sights, he squeezed the trigger. He missed again, and the bullets embedded themselves in the hangar's walls and machinery. More hollow echoes reverberated throughout the vast hangar.

Despite the ensuing chaos, Erik enjoyed a momentary respite in the cover of the cluttered hanger. Ten feet from where he ducked behind some machinery, he emerged and found Arioch's back facing him. He tried to approach quietly, but his foot kicked a wrench, sending it skidding across the floor with reverberations of metal screeching over concrete.

Arioch spun around. There was a moment of silence between them, their breaths labored, their survival instincts in overdrive. It was a short but potent standoff, marked by a collision of powerful purposes and ideologies.

Arioch raised the gun without hesitation, unwavering in his gaze.

Out of options, Erik charged forward, hoping to take the gun out of the equation. The gap closed, and the space around them seemed to shrink. Erik was mere steps from his foe as the energy of the moment crackled between them.

Arioch's finger tightened on the trigger; the weight of their encounter held in that singular action. In the moment's stillness, the sound of their heartbeats echoed through the air as their breaths mingled together. Arioch grinned as he squeezed the trigger, only to be rewarded with a dull metallic click. He pulled the trigger again with the same results.

A devious grin appeared on Erik's face as he said, "Oops."

Arioch's gaze only intensified, brows knitted in determination, as he tossed the Lugar aside. His left hand wrapped around a dark orange grip at his side, and he drew a Luftwaffe officer's dagger. The blade glistened under the overhead lights. Arioch smiled in contempt and said, "Oops."

Erik presented an unconcerned air, an outward calm, that belied the storm of thoughts and emotions raging within him. His stance was fluid, his eyes locked onto Arioch's with unwavering focus.

"I've killed just about everything that has breathed at one time or another, and I'm here to kill you," Arioch purred.

Without a further word, the duel began. Arioch lunged forward with a speed that spoke of his Mossad training. The dagger's double edges and point gleamed in the room's dim light. Erik's reflexes were equally sharp as he sidestepped Arioch's attack with a dancer's grace, his empty hands moving in deft arcs to redirect Arioch's momentum. Arioch stepped back, then lunged again, this time with a feint to the right. Erik anticipated the move, countering it with a powerful kick to Arioch's midsection. Arioch, doubled over in pain, stepped away to recover.

The deadly interplay of strikes, evasions, and counters continued as they tried to outmaneuver each other. Erik landed a few quick jabs before his foe evaded further punishment. Arioch then countered with a powerful uppercut, cutting Erik's left arm and sending him staggering back a few steps.

Erik quickly recovered and repositioned himself. Arioch's dagger was like an extension of himself, fluid and precise. He pressed forward with ferocity, testing Erik's reactions and defenses with a relentless barrage of slashes and thrusts. Erik deflected the attacks, barely matching his speed and accuracy. He was eventually forced to give ground and retreat.

Arioch followed close behind, pressing to his advantage. Erik used his agility and improvised tactics to create distance, his eyes constantly assessing Arioch's movements. He ducked under a high swipe, his training allowing him to avoid the blade's deadly arc. Sensing an opening, he closed the distance and grabbed Arioch's wrist, his fingers applying pressure to force him to drop the dagger.

Arioch's training kicked in, and he pivoted sharply, breaking free from Erik's grasp, keeping hold of the dagger, and gaining some distance. The fight continued, the hanger echoing with their crashing blows. Arioch feigned a forward thrust, prompting Erik to lean away from the attack, then pivoted at the last moment and swept his leg across the floor to knock Erik off balance. In the momentary advantage, he lunged forward again, his blade aimed at his opponent's chest. Erik twisted to the side, the blade grazing his shoulder instead of piercing his heart. He used the momentum of his twist to redirect Arioch's attack and reached for the dagger's blade.

The two operatives locked eyes, both gripping the weapon. The room seemed to hold its breath as they struggled for control of it. Arioch's strength was formidable, but Erik's determination was unyielding. With a sudden surge of adrenaline, Erik wrenched the dagger from Arioch's grip. In one swift motion, he twisted his body, spun the blade into a downward thrust, and drove it through Arioch's thigh.

The Mossad agent's eyes widened in surprise as the blade

found its mark. He stumbled and collapsed to the floor with blood gushing from his leg like a broken water main. The blade had severed the man's femoral artery, and he had only moments to live. Arioch grasped the wound, trying to staunch the flow, but soon went limp as his life faded away.

Erik stood over him, chest heaving, still gripping the dagger. The hanger felt colder, the air heavy with the weight of what had transpired. His gaze remained fixed on Arioch's lifeless form, a mixture of respect and disdain etching his features. He took a deep breath, closed his eyes, breathed out the tension of the confrontation. Erik then picked up the body and tossed it in a dumpster behind the hanger. He then sprayed the floor down with a hose meant for cleaning the bombers, erasing that sign of the battle. Only the bullet holes in the hangar walls betrayed that anything had transpired. Erik then recovered his Luger, and as he left the hanger, he disposed of the dagger. When he got to his quarters, he fell into a restless sleep.

CHAPTER 13

THE PROCESS OF BEING UNKNOWN

"Friends? I don't have any of those."

— Andy Weir, *The Martian*

AUGUST 25, 1940

Erik sighed as he sat down next to Major Maier in the dining room, his thoughts clouded by the prior night's events. He hoped no one would ask about the missing officer. Unlike in the movies, where killing the enemy solves all the problems, it generally creates more of them. However, there was another issue looming.

Normally, Erik would enjoy their breakfast, but that morning, his appetite was gone because there was something in the air. The whole dining room seemed silent. The other pilots and flight officers gave steely glances to each other and everyone was strangely muted. Something didn't feel right. As they ate their breakfast, the commandant headed in their direction. They stood when he was directly in front of them.

"Major Maier and Lieutenant Függer, report to Generalmajor Angerstein at once. A car is waiting for you and will take you there."

They both nodded that they understood the order. As they

headed out, Erik's mind was racing. Did they already find Arioch? Had they connected the body to him? Or, was it about the raid?

They climbed into the idling, purring staff car as the driver held the door open.

Once inside, Maier whispered under his breath, "What the hell is going on?"

Erik shrugged. "If it's about last night's raid, I will take full responsibility."

"What else…?" Maier shook his head. "Never mind. They will hold us both responsible."

"But you were going by my direction."

The driver looked back in the rearview mirror. Erik motioned for Maier to stop talking since the driver could be eavesdropping.

The driver parked in front of headquarters, opened the rear passenger door, and escorted Maier and Erik inside before leaving. Via phone, the secretary advised the generalmajor they had arrived, hung up the receiver, and advised them to go in.

Maier and Erik stood at attention, tense, shifting a bit on their feet in Angerstein's office. Weather reports, maps, and bomber status charts covered the walls. The cold light of morning filtering through the curtained windows bathed the office. More maps, military reports, and mission plans cluttered the desk. Angerstein sat behind that, his expression stern and unyielding. He started at Erik, then at Maier. The air in the room grew heavier with each passing second.

Angerstein leaned forward, his gaze unwavering, and cut straight to the heart of the matter. "Major Maier, explain yourself. What in the hell happened on last night's raid."

A wave of relief flowed over Erik. At least it wasn't about the dead body. He spoke up, "Sir, it was my fault."

Angerstein stared at him.

"We encountered a strong windshear, causing us to fly off course. Major Maier was just flowing my navigation. Sir, I will take full responsibility."

Angerstein gave Erik a scornful look, then immediately glared at Maier. "That does not excuse the fact that you and your squadron engaged in a bombing run over London. What the hell were you thinking?"

"Sir," Erik continued to explain, "there was also unexpected cloud cover. I was unable to visually confirm the target, but predicted that we were over the refinery. I was wrong."

"I was in command and gave the order to release," Major Maier cut in. "It is my responsibility."

Angerstein glared at the major. "Both you and Lieutenant Függer will be reprimanded. Do you understand?"

Erik replied, "Sir, I will take full responsibility. Major Maier is not at fault."

Angerstein pointed at Erik to get his point across. "Lieutenant, I don't care. Attacking London is forbidden!" He walked out from behind his desk, circling them like a predator stalking its prey. "Both of you know the order as well as I do: Attacks may only be made on the personal order of the Führer!"

Erik's mind raced as he searched for another explanation. He knew he had to choose his words carefully.

However, Angerstein raised his hand before he could speak. "I regret, gentlemen, the matter is now out of my hands. By order of Reichsmarschall Göring, you are to report to Berlin." He paused for a moment before concluding. "The car will take you back so you can get your belongings, and you will be on a transport within the hour. Dismissed."

Maier and Erik clicked their heels in unison and did an about-face. Within the hour, they were on board a Ju-52 and headed to Berlin.

The pilot performed a textbook landing and taxied the aircraft to the nearest hanger. Once the Ju-52 stopped, one of the crew hopped out and placed steps by the door so Erik and Maier could exit.

A rather unusual figure stood by an Opel Kadett. He had a stern expression with an unwelcoming scowl. The man wore a Luftwaffe officer's uniform with a lieutenant colonel's rank insignia. His posture was rigid, his back straight and shoulders squared, which complimented his impeccably tailored uniform, reflecting his discipline. His neatly combed hair peeked out from under his officer's cap, but not a single strand was astray. Everything about the man was by the book. Behind his glasses, his eyes stared at Maier and Erik as if they were a disgrace in the uniform; dogs that needed to be disciplined. He took a few steps forward and said, "Major Maier, Lieutenant Függer, follow me." As they did, the lieutenant colonel opened the rear passenger door. "A car will pick you up at oh-eight-thirty hours, outside the lobby of your hotel. You are to report to Colonel Schultheiss at oh-nine-hundred hours at the Ministry of Aviation. This car will take you to your quarters, where you will remain until then."

Before Erik got in, he turned to the lieutenant colonel. "Is there a restaurant in the hotel?"

"Yes." He motioned for Erik to get in the car.

AUGUST 26, 1940

In the morning, Maier and Erik waited outside the hotel. The presence of swastika-adorned flags was ubiquitous, fluttering in the wind, casting a shadow over the city. The flags, with their bold red and black colors, served as a constant reminder of the ideology that dominated the era. Amidst the bustling streets, people of all ages went about their daily lives, engaged in various activities. Civilians mixed with soldiers of all three branches. The SS, in their distinctive black uniforms, stood out among the crowd, a symbol of the Nazi regime's authority. The streets of Berlin also teemed with traffic. Vehicles of all kinds, from cars and trams to trucks, filled the roads, creating a constant buzz of activity. The flow was a testament to the bustling nature of the city, despite the underlying tension and uncertainty of the times. People conversed in hushed tones, aware that political discussions could have serious consequences, which were a part of daily life.

A car pulled up to the curb and the same officer from the night before opened the door. His demeanor was stern, reflecting the rigid discipline enforced by the Nazi regime. Erik noticed the interior was simple, lacking the comfort and luxury of his Tucker 48.

Berlin was a mixture of grand architecture that represented the Neoclassical style. Strategically placed propaganda billboards and posters promoted the Nazi ideology in a positive light and glorified the German military. The roads were meticulously maintained, showcasing the regime's commitment to order and control. The air was filled with a mixture of tension and anticipation as the specter of war loomed over the city since the RAF bombing campaign. There were loudspeakers installed on street corners, blaring out speeches and propaganda messages, further reinforcing the Nazi narrative.

As the car neared its destination, Maier got Erik's attention, pointing out the grandeur of the Ministry of Aviation. The imposing building reflected the might and ambition of the Nazi regime, probably designed with suggestions from Reich Marshal Göring. Armed guards, dressed in crisp uniforms, stood at attention, ensuring that only authorized personnel entered the premises.

Walking into the Ministry of Aviation, Maier and Erik were immediately struck by the grandeur and imposing nature of the building. The massive structure, that took eighteen months to complete, was adorned with intricate neoclassical details, exuding a sense of power and authority. It had a bustling atmosphere, as officials and personnel went about their duties with purpose and efficiency. The air was filled with a sense of anticipation and tension, flowing through a maze of corridors and hallways, guided by stern-faced guards who maintained a watchful eye.

As Erik and Maier were led through the labyrinthine passages of the ministry, the hushed conversations and the clicking of heels on polished floors created an eerie ambiance. The gravity of the situation was palpable, as each step took them deeper into the heart of the building. Eventually, the journey led to a dimly lit room, devoid of any windows and furnished with a single table and three chairs. The coldness of the room sent a shiver down Erik's spine, heightening the feeling of unease, but he was trained for situations like that. He had expected the regime would try to find out what happened and make sure it never happened again.

The starkness of the surroundings amplified the weight of the impending interrogation. Maier shifted in his seat while they awaited the arrival of the interrogator. However, Erik was un-phased. The silence was deafening, broken only by the sound of their heartbeats, which seemed to reverberate through the room. Time seemed to stand still as they contemplated the gravity of the situation. To Maier, the room felt like a prison, with its bare walls and the sense of confinement closing in on him.

The anticipation of what lay ahead gnawed at their nerves as they braced themselves for the grueling interrogation that await-ed. In that moment, under the full weight of the Ministry of Avi-ation and Göring's authority, the two men realized the power the ministry held over their fate. The interrogation room was a symbol of control, and they were left to wonder what their careers would be like after the ordeal—or at least, Maier had that to ponder. Erik had other considerations, such as escaping and finding his way to friendly territory.

An older colonel, flushed with anger, stormed in. Maier and Erik stood at attention. He motioned them to take a seat and did the same, slamming a stack of folders on the desk. The man introduced himself as Colonel Schultheiss, the Inspector of Bombers. Erik remembered that position had an administrative role within the High Command of the German Luftwaffe. They were responsible for the readiness, training, and tactics of the German bomber force.

Then, the interrogation began with softness as a sledgehammer hitting a kneecap. "Major Maier, Lieutenant Függer," the Colonel nearly shouted, "how in the hell did your command accidentally bomb London?" He pointed at them to express his next point. "I want answers, gentlemen, and I want them now!"

Erik leaped into the conversation. "Sir, as I explained to Generalmajor Angerstein, our flight over the channel faced a strong windshear which caused us to be guided off course. Unexpected cloud cover obscured the ground. I estimated our location to Major Maier, assuring him we were over the refinery. Sir, I will take full responsibility."

"Mistakes won't suffice, Lieutenant. You have a map and a compass so you wouldn't make mistakes! London has suffered significant damage and casualties. The Allies will respond like hornets from a kicked nest." Schultheiss turned his attention to Maier. "How could this happen?"

"Lieutenant Függer's assessment was correct. Due to poor weather conditions, we lost our bearings and not knowing London was below us without the ability to obtain visual confirmation of the target," Maier replied.

A spasm of irritation crossed Schultheiss's face. "I don't want excuses, I want answers! This is an inexcusable error, and Reich Marschall Göring is demanding an explanation!"

"Sir, we never intended to bomb London. We were meant to target the oil refinery at—"

"Don't waste my time telling me what I already know!" Schultheiss yelled.

"It was a mistake. A tragic mistake," Erik explained.

"A tragic mistake, you say?" Schultheiss hissed. "Both of you showed a complete lack of competence and failed to follow protocol!"

"Sir, I will take full responsibility. Major Maier only trusted my calculations."

Schultheiss calmed down slightly and shook his head. "Major Maier, Lieutenant Függer, I hope you understand the severity of this situation. There will be a thorough investigation to determine the appropriate actions to be taken." Schultheiss stood up and looked down to meet their eyes. "Gentlemen, you will have to face the consequences of your actions, both personally and professionally. This incident would forever be a dark stain on your careers." Schultheiss motioned for them to remain where they were as he turned to leave.

They sat there, not knowing what was going to happen next. Maier was going to have to accept whatever that was. Erik, on the other hand, had to find a way to the USA so he could return to 1948.

Suddenly, the door swung open again, and Reich Marshal Göring walked through it, accompanied by two heavily armed guards. His imposing figure commanded attention as he strode into the room. Erik and Maier stood and snapped to attention. Göring motioned the guards to wait outside, then gestured for the men to take a seat. A disdainful scowl shadowed his face as he said, "Major Maier, Lieutenant Függer, I trust you're aware of the gravity of your situation." They replied in unison that they did, then Göring continued. "Your mistakes will not and cannot be overlooked. Last night, the RAF bombed Berlin. Are you aware of that?"

Maier and Erik shook their heads, although Erik had known that was coming. Maier, on the other hand, seemed visibly shaken. "Bombed Berlin, sir? Last night? But we were here last night."

"You mean to tell me you slept through the whole thing?" Göring asked. "Maybe we should not have provided you with such comfortable accommodations. Tell me, did you enjoy your beauty sleep, Major? Lieutenant?"

Maier glanced at Erik, who shrugged and said, "Herr Field Marshal, we didn't land until 2050 hours."

Göring took a seat, shaking his head. "Your astounding abilities made you miss the air raid. The Führer is furious. He has made it very clear that if the RAF dared attack our cities again, we will wipe theirs out. We shall show them the full force of the Luftwaffe!" He gave a chuckle of amusement as he read the body language of Maier and Erik. "Indeed. The Führer understands the gravity of the situation. He knows that drastic measures are necessary to ensure our victory."

Erik asked, "Sir, what happens to us? Are we to be court martialed?

Göring leaned in closer, his voice filled with intensity. "Gentlemen, you two are lucky. I've received a message from the Führer himself. He understands the demands placed on you both, and in light of recent events and our need of experienced air crews, has decided to give you another chance."

Maier replied in a surprised tone. "Another chance, sir?"

Göring nodded and smiled. "The Führer believes that our country is under threat, and we need all our capable soldiers ready for battle. So, you are free to go. Consider yourselves fortunate, gentlemen."

Erik grinned and said, "Thank you, sir. We'll fight with everything we have."

Göring stood up, with Maier and Erik following in action. "Remember, every action you take from this point forward must be with an unyielding dedication to defeat England." He mustered a fist in the air. "We will crush England under our boot heels."

In harmony, Maier and Erik replied, "Yes, sir! We will not falter."

Göring nodded and smiled. "Very well. You are dismissed. Get back to your duties and prepare for the battle that lies ahead. Show the RAF what happens when they dare to challenge Germany!"

Maier and Erik snapped a salute as Göring turned and left the room. Once he was gone, they gave a sigh of relief and exchanged glances.

Maier had been given a second chance to prove his worth, and vowed to make the most of it. With renewed determination, he thanked God, and was ready to face the challenges that awaited him.

Erik was simply relieved he would be planning his escape from an airfield instead of a prison.

The door banged open and the officer who had been escorting them gave the order to follow him to the car. He informed Maier and Erik they would be driven back to their hotel. From there, a car would pick them up outside at thirteen-hundred hours, and they would fly back to their base.

As Maier and Erik walked out of the Ministry of Aviation, a sense of relief washed over them. The day had been long and arduous, but they were free to go. However, their moment of respite was interrupted by the sound of approaching footsteps. Startled,

Erik noticed two SS men in intimidating black uniforms headed straight for them.

"Lieutenant Függer, you are being summoned to SS Headquarters. You are to come with us immediately." One of the SS men stated in a commanding tone.

Erik replied cautiously, "SS Headquarters? But why?"

"It is a matter of state business. You will find out soon enough. Now, Lieutenant, please follow us."

Maier spun on the men. "I'm sure there's a mistake. What did Lieutenant Függer do?

"Major, as I said, it is a matter of state business and does not involve you."

Maier stepped in front of Erik. "Sergeant, I am his commanding officer. I want to know the reason for this."

"Major, stand down or you will be arrested for interfering with state business."

Erik cupped Maier's shoulder and shook his head. Maier leaned close and whispered, "Something feels off."

The SS sergeant continued impatiently. "Enough whispering. Lieutenant Függer, come with us now."

Maier scowled at the SS men. He'd only known Erik for two days, but the man was still under his command and was his responsibility. "Lieutenant, I'll do everything I can to find out what's going on."

The SS sergeant grew impatient, his voice said in a demanding tone. "Lieutenant Függer, it's time to go."

CHAPTER 14

CHEATING THE POLYGRAPH

"I suppose I'll think of something. Or die."

— Andy Weir, *The Martian*

AUGUST 26, 1940

Erik found himself in a dimly lit interrogation room, face to face with Captain Von Stetten, a formidable and ruthless SS officer. He was a perfect example of what an SS officer should be. His uniform was impeccably maintained, he smelled of German cologne, and he had striking ultramarine-blue eyes and neatly trimmed blond hair. His emotionless eyes and stern expression were serious and threatening. Von Stetten considered everyone to be an enemy of the state if they spoke ill or disapproved of the Third Reich, the Nazi party, and Hitler.

Erik was used to being in uncomfortable situations. He knew the SS wouldn't ask questions directly. They always hid what they knew and didn't know. He wasn't going to speak first, and he knew the SS would try to get into his mind before really asking questions. The captain might paint a picture of the world outside. He might search whatever Erik was holding on to and take it away. Of course, everything he was holding on to was in 1948. Failing the above, the captain might break small bones, like the ones in Erik's fingers, to make him talk. Once the captain tired of his resistance, Erik would be shot or sent to a work camp. It was like Erik and the captain would be playing poker, neither knowing what cards the other held.

Von Stetten was used to seeing beads of sweat on individuals' foreheads, but Erik was calm and collected, considering the weight of this predicament pressing upon him. "So, Lieutenant Függer," the captain began, his icy tone cutting through the silence. "I heard you have a particular taste in literature." Von Stetten placed a black leather attaché case on the table and removed a book from inside, placing it in front of Erik. The copy of *War of the Worlds*, from telltale wear marks on the cover, was Erik's book.

"Thank you for finding my book." As Erik reached for, Von Stetten slammed his hand down preventing that.

"So, you admit it is your book?"

Erik nodded.

"Where did you get this book?"

"It was a gift, captain."

Von Stetten remained emotionless as he absorbed what Erik was saying, then motioned Erik to continue.

"It was a gift from a friend from the United States."

"A gift?"

Erik nodded.

"Are you also from the United States? Your German is good, but there is something about you?" He held up the banned book. "This work is by an enemy from a foreign country who believes they can attack and denigrate the Third Reich and our Führer!"

Erik carefully chose his words. "Yes, I am from the United States, but I am a loyal German. Our Führer said all Germans should follow his orders, no matter where they are. So, I left the

United States and enlisted. I assure you; I am nothing more than a German patriot.”

Von Stetten’s cold eyes narrowed, skepticism etched across his face. “A German patriot without a Wehrpass, Lieutenant? That is quite unusual, don’t you think?”

After receiving registration notices, men were supposed to report to a recruitment center, where they would be issued a Wehrpass, or military pass, until they were inducted into active duty. Then the Wehrpass would be exchanged at the recruitment office for their Soldbuch.

Erik grinned, knowing the trap the captain was setting him up for. From his rear pocket, Erik pulled out his Soldbuch and placed it on the table. “I think you should be looking for this instead.”

The SS captain leaned back, an almost sinister smile appearing on his lips. He gave a light chuckle out as he rubbed his chin and replied. “You’re right.” He tapped the palm of his hand to his forehead. “My momentary forgetfulness must seem like a deliberate act to trick you.”

Erik flashed a smile back and chuckled.

“Where was your recruitment center?”

“Bremerhaven.”

“Bremerhaven?” the captain asked.

Erik nodded, a glimmer of hope fluttering in his chest.

The captain made his next words sink in. “Lieutenant Függer, if you would just hear me out. There is something you should know…” He stood up and stepped back from the table and drew his Luger. “I checked with the recruitment center, and they have no record of you.” He knocked on the door behind him, alerting the guards outside to come in.

Erik took a deep breath, choosing his words carefully. “Captain, I have knowledge that can help Germany win the war.” The captain motioned to the guards to escort him out. “If you want to win this war, captain, you are going have to cripple the northeastern rail network, effectively stop roughly eighty percent of troop and materiel traffic."

"What are you saying, Lieutenant Függer? That it holds the key to our ultimate victory?"

"Yes."

A moment of silence passed, the gravity of Erik's revelation sinking in. Von Stetten's expression shifted from curiosity to disbelief again as he shook his head again. "Get him out of here."

"The place is called M42, a basement under Grand Central Terminal." Erik replied with urgency in his voice. He knew they were already aware of M42, so he wasn't telling them anything they didn't already know, but it might still open a door for him.

Captain Von Stetten's face hardened, his eyes narrowing as he considered whether Erik's claim was true. "Even if you speak the truth, which you're not, it won't save your life." Captain Von Stetten stared at Erik closer, his cold eyes focused. "You appear to know more than you should, American," he sneered, his voice dripping with malice. "To bad it won't help you out of this situation."

Erik's heart pounded in his chest as he met Von Stetten's gaze. Fear that normally threatened and consumed most people rolled off his back. Erik knew the risk of going back, and he was willing to give his life to correct the timeline. His mission was already accomplished, so as long as he did nothing to further damage history, nothing he did from that point on really mattered. Still, he wanted to get home. "I assure you, Captain Von Stetten, I only know what I know," he replied, his voice steady despite the adrenaline coursing through his veins. "Do your worst……"

"Let me guess, because you will do yours?" The captain asked with a superior attitude.

"Wrong." Erik paused and said in Latin, "Flectere si nequeo superos, Acheronta movebo."

The captain looked baffled.

"It is a quote from Virgil: If I cannot sway the heavens, I will raise hell."

Suddenly, the heavy wooden door swung open, and in walked Reichsführer Heinrich Himmler and Reinhard Heydrich, their mere presence commanding respect and instilling fear. Von Stetten snapped to attention, saluting the high-ranking officers. Himmler's icy blue eyes scanned the room, settling on Erik, and he motioned him to sit down. Then he addressed Von Stetten. "Captain, leave, and take your men."

Von Stetten hesitated for a moment before obediently exiting. Erik sat alone with the two intimidating figures. Himmler took a seat as Erik recalled meeting the man in 1944, after he saved Hitler's life. At that meeting, Himmler asked Erik if they had ever met before. Erik truthfully said no at the time, but it seemed he had been mistaken.

Heydrich towered nearly six foot three inches, standing over Himmler as his gaze bore into Erik's soul, making him feel as though every secret he held was being laid bare. Erik stared into Himmler's pinched, pale face with a modest mustache above thin lips, and behind his thick, steel-rimmed glasses to his blue, inquisitive eyes.

Himmler took a deep breath and exhaled. "What brings an American like you into our midst, Lieutenant Függer?" he asked, his tone laced with suspicion.

Erik took a calm breath, considering his words as he faced two of the most powerful men in the Nazi regime. "I was born in the United States, in New Jersey," he began, his voice unwavering as he studied their body language. "I used to work at Grand Central Terminal, and once war broke out, I wanted to serve the Fath—"

Himmler held up a hand, interrupting Erik mid-sentence. "I care not about your origins. What intrigues me is your knowledge of M42," he said, his voice low and dangerous. "Tell me, how did you come upon this information?"

Erik's mind raced, searching for a plausible explanation. "When I worked there, I heard rumors, whispers among my co-workers. They spoke of a deep basement that was heavily guarded, and said anyone not authorized down there would be shot with no questions asked." Erik chose his words carefully, exchanging glances between Himmler and Heydrich.

Himmler leaned forward, his face mere inches from Erik's. "Do you think you can disable the generators if we train you on them and get you to New York City? You seem to know a lot about M42, and you would be doing a great service to the Fatherland."

Erik swallowed hard, suppressing his excitement and surprise at having a free ticket back to the United States handed to him by the Nazis. Was he really that lucky, or were they playing him? He had to keep playing the part and convince Himmler that he could be an asset. "Reichsführer, if I may?…" he began, his voice projecting confidence and determination in every word he spoke.

Himmler nodded.

"I know I could be of great service to the Fatherland."

Heydrich scoffed, his voice dripping with skepticism as he approached Erik. "You expect us to believe that a mere American could be of any value to the Third Reich?" he spat, his lip curling into a disdainful sneer.

Himmler held up a hand, silencing Heydrich. "Let him speak, Generalmajor," he commanded, his tone firm, yet tinged with a hint of curiosity. "I want to hear what Lieutenant Függer has to say."

Erik cleared his throat and continued. "If I understand correctly, The Führer intends to disable the generators that power M42," he began, his voice growing stronger with each word. "Since I have firsthand knowledge of those generators, I could disable them before the United States enters the war, not to mention slowing down or even halting the war materials and equipment being shipped over to England."

It was a plan they already had, since for Erik, it had already played out, and they failed. Volunteering for the mission wouldn't endanger the timeline. If anything, he could ensure it failed. Had he already caused it to fail? The intricacies of time travel made it hard to be sure. Himmler recognized him in 1944 even though, to Erik, they'd never met. Perhaps this was another mission he was destined to undertake.

Heydrich pulled Himmler aside, speaking in hushed tones. Erik strained to catch their conversation, his heart pounding in his ears.

"I do not trust him," Heydrich muttered, his voice barely audible. Himmler and Heydrich conversed, their gazes occasionally flicking in Erik's direction.

Himmler turned his attention back to Erik, his eyes narrowing, then looked at Heydrich. "If he is captured by the Americans, he will be shot as a spy."

Heydrich shot back, "If he fails his mission and survives, we can shoot him as a traitor."

Himmler grinned.

Erik stood and his posture hardened, his eyes locking with Himmler's. "If I succeed, I trust the Reichsführer will ensure my safety and provide me with the resources I need to return to the Fatherland?" He asked, adding a crack of false concern to his voice to sell the loyal German soldier act. Coming back to Germany before the war was over was the last thing he planned to do.

Himmler's lips curled into a slight smile, a glimmer of respect shining in his eyes. "Very well, Lieutenant Függer," he conceded. "But know this: if you survive, you will be walking a thin line between heroism and treason." With a final nod, Himmler signaled his approval. "You will be recruited into the Abwehr and given three weeks of intensive sabotage training in the German High Command school on the estate at Quenzsee."

Relief flooded through Erik's veins as he realized his life had taken an unexpected and dangerous turn. He had to keep up the ploy for three weeks, but then he could get back to America and go back to 1948. It was worth the risk. Hell, it was a gift horse, so he wasn't about to worry over the details.

Heydrich stepped forward, his gaze cold and calculating. "Do not disappoint us, American. Sic vis pacem para bellum. If you want peace, prepare for war."

With that, the two officers turned and left, leaving Erik to contemplate the magnitude of the task before him. As he stood alone in the room, he couldn't help but feel a strange mix of uncertainty and exhilaration. The climax of his mission was behind him, and now he was taking the first steps on the long road home. Three weeks of intense training, and then one to two weeks of travel to America. All he had to do then was infiltrate the German saboteurs in New York and make sure a mission that had failed according to history was indeed unsuccessful. Then, back to 1948, Jamie, and Max.

CHAPTER 15

WHISPERS FROM THE PAST

"There is so much to say… I cannot find the words. Except for these: I love you."   — Elise McKenna, *Somewhere in Time*

With Max securely strapped into his car seat, Jamie navigated down Morse Street NE, scanning the area for a suitable parking spot near A. Litteri, Inc. The street was lined with late model Cadillacs, a familiar sight, with a familiar group of impeccably dressed men, their designer suits and fedoras exuding an air of authority. Paulie, always alert, noticed Jamie's approach from a distance. He snapped his fingers, commanding his entourage to clear a path for her. Two men swiftly made their way to her, their presence both intimidating and reassuring. They guided her toward the entrance, their movements calculated and precise. As she reached the door, Paulie emerged, his face breaking into a warm smile. He embraced Jamie tightly, planting a gentle kiss on her cheek, a gesture that conveyed both familiarity and respect.

As he escorted her inside, he struck up a conversation. "How are you doing?"

Jamie offered a causal smile, hiding her true feelings, but her eyes were haunted by something.

"Is it Erik?"

She nodded.

He'd never seen her so shook up. "I'll straighten this out." He placed his arm around her. "I know just what to say to him."

Jamie shook her head.

"It'll be like when you first got married."

"That's not it, Paulie."

They took a seat, and Paulie grabbed a napkin to wipe her tears. "Let's get some food in you and that baby." Jamie shook her head, but Paulie insisted, and she gave in. "What's bothering you?"

"I miss him, and I don't know if he is alive." Paulie flashed a confused look, inviting her to explain.

Before she could, Paulie Junior approached the table. He looked sharp in his polished black wingtips, dark blue pinstriped trousers, white oxford shirt with a convertible collar, yellow silk tie, and double-breasted jacket. He smiled, clutching a massive book in his hands, its weight and presence demanding attention. Its robust construction safeguarded its priceless knowledge, preserving it for generations to come. Junior set the book down in front of Jamie.

With bated breath, she leaned over it, her eyes fixated on the gilded lettering that adorned its cover, a sight both captivating and refined. The meticulously crafted uppercase letters, emblazoned with gold, proudly proclaimed the title: *The Third Reich's Military Might: Unmasking the Dominant Forces of World War II.* Each stroke of the lettering exuded an air of magnificence, elevating the book's overall allure to the realm of grandeur.

Jamie's demand for the book was unwavering, her mind consumed by Erik's mention of the Battle of Britain and the infamous He-111 bomber. As a devoted wife, she embarked on a relentless quest through the pages' collection of black-and-white photos, her eyes darting from one frame to another in search of the familiar face she yearned to see. She nearly forgot to breathe as she scanned every detail, her heart racing with anticipation. And then, as if God himself had intervened, she stumbled upon a few pictures of the He-111 bomber.

One image seized Jamie's attention. She froze, completely spellbound, as her eyes locked onto the photograph. There, proudly standing beside the bomber, was Erik himself. His aviator cap perched upon his head, he exuded an air of confidence and purpose. The sleek design and menacing appearance of the aircraft mirrored the intensity of his role as a Luftwaffe bombardier. She froze, spellbound and captivated as she stared at the photograph's caption: *He-111 crew on August 15, 1940. Two days after Adlertag (Eagle Day).*

That had been a pivotal moment in history, and Erik had been right in the thick of it. Her admiration for him soared to new heights. However, the journey through the photographs was not yet complete. In another image, Erik was in the cockpit of the bomber, his eyes fixed on the instrument panel before him. The gleam in his intense eyes and the determined set of his jaw conveyed a sense of unwavering courage and unyielding determination. Jamie couldn't tear her gaze away from this captivating sight. In that moment, she knew her quest had been worthwhile. The pieces of the puzzle were falling into place, and she found herself on the brink of uncovering the truth. With renewed determination, Jamie vowed to delve deeper into Erik's mission to correct the timeline to unravel the mysteries that lay hidden within those photographs. She knew he was doing what he had to do to correct the past.

Paulie gestured for Jamie to follow him, and once they were away from everyone, he asked, "Did I see what I think I saw?"

Jamie nodded.

"Why is he wearing a nazi uniform by a Nazi bomber?"

"Do you recall when Erik said he worked for the government?"

He nodded.

"Well, he was a spy during the war."

Paulie blinked in surprise. He peered around the corner to make sure no one was hearing the conversation, then motioned for her to continue.

"He did a lot of top-secret work to defeat the Nazis. For example, he made sure they lost the Battle of Britain, among other things."

Paulie paused and blinked in quiet amazement at Erik's secret past. For the first time, he realized how truly dangerous his friend was and what he was capable of doing.

"So, did he contact the War Department about becoming a spy?"

"I don't know who contacted him about becoming a spy. I know there are women who would have left the minute their husbands became spies, or even a cop." Tears ran down her face as she continued. "He was going save the world. When I asked why it had to be him, he said somebody has to do it."

Jamie smiled as she wiped the tears from her eyes. After she composed herself, she made Paulie swear never to repeat anything in front of Erik or anyone.

Moments later, they approached the table. Paulie and his son sat to either side of Jamie so they could see the book. Jamie delved back into the collection of photos, flipping through them with a rhythmic precision. Suddenly, her attention was captured by a series of images depicting the German Navy, the Kriegsmarine. Those photos inexplicably drew Jamie, compelling her to study each image with a sense of urgency.

She searched for Erik's unmistakable intensity, the piercing gaze that transcended time and revealed a storm within. It was a look she would recognize in an instant, even amidst a sea of faces. With a pounding heart, she continued to flip through the pages. She couldn't shake the feeling that somewhere within those photos, she would find the person she was searching for. With every turn of the page, her determination grew, her pulse quickening.

Paulie Junior discovered something of interest, putting a pause to her search. His eyes widened as he pointed to a group of pictures showcasing U-boats. These formidable submarines were utilized by Germany during World War II, manned by brave volunteers who dedicated their lives to the war effort. Paulie Jr. informed Jamie that out of the staggering forty thousand men who served in the U-boats, a heartbreaking thirty thousand would never return home. The sight of these pictures stirred a whirlwind of emotions within Jamie. She was awestruck by the sheer sacrifice made by those who served during that era. The weight of their selflessness bore down on her, evoking a mixture of respect and sorrow. As the gravity of the situation sank in, Jamie couldn't help but be reminded of the countless lives lost.

The number thirty thousand reverberated in her mind, symbolizing the multitude of individuals who left behind shattered families and grieving loved ones. It served as a stark reminder of the exorbitant price paid for the sake of duty, if even to an evil regime such as the one those men served.

The weight settled heavily in Jamie's heart, causing her to lean against the table for support. The staggering losses of the Kriegsmarine made her think of all the Allied soldiers who lost their lives in the war to stop the machinations of fascism, whose sacrifices would never be forgotten, their presence forever felt in the lives of those they left behind. In that moment of profound reflection, Jamie's gaze returned to the images of U-boats and the brave men who manned them. The memories encapsulated within those photographs served as a testament to the enduring legacy of the past. They were a poignant reminder that even amidst a sea of faces, one could always summon the strength to acknowledge and pay tribute to those who came before.

Jamie's eyes moved deliberately across the worn pages, her breath catching in anticipation as she immersed herself in the forgotten snapshots of the past. As her gaze fell upon the faded images, a sudden hush settled upon her, captivating her senses and drawing her in with an inexplicable force. With narrowed eyes, Jamie's focus intensified, dissecting every minute detail of the photograph before her. Horizontal wrinkles etched her forehead, evidence of the unwavering concentration and intensity with which she studied the image. It was as if time had stilled within the confines of the photograph, leaving Jamie entangled in the frozen moment, oblivious to the world around her.

The image depicted a group of rugged, unshaven officers seated inside a U-boat. Amidst the hazy contours, one man stood out, his identity shrouded by the passage of years and the absence of light. However, Jamie recognized Erik instantly, despite the fact he had a wild-looking beard, and her heart shattering under the weight of resurfacing emotions. The photograph unleashed a torrent of happiness and elation, overwhelming her senses. Tears welled in her eyes, blurring her vision. Her trembling lips fought to contain the storm of emotions that threatened to consume her.

Paulie enveloped her in a comforting embrace, silently assuring her that everything was alright. Yet, the anguish proved insurmountable, and tears spilled down her cheeks, leaving trails of both joy and sorrow in their wake. Amidst the tumultuous sea of emotions, Jamie's unwavering gaze remained fixed upon the central figure, the one holding a sign. In that moment of chaos, a beacon of clarity emerged, offering a glimmer of hope amidst her uncertainty. With bated breath, she deciphered the words etched upon the sign, their significance resonating deep within her soul.

JAMIE 8-14 + 47 -> NYC 1437

She found the answers she so desperately sought in the coded message: *Arrived on August 14, 1940. It's been 47 days. I'm headed to New York City. I love you forever.*

She closed her eyes and said a prayer. *Erik, where are you now? Come back to me.*

CHAPTER 16

ARRIVING SOMEWHERE BUT WHY HERE

"I'm pretty much fucked. That's my considered opinion. Fucked."
— Andy Weir, *The Martian*

SOMEWHERE IN FRANCE

Along with Erik in the Kübelwagen was Fregattenkapitän Heinrich Lehmann-Willenbrock, who was behind the wheel, the captain of the U-boat, and the chief engineer who never went by his name, Klaus. Everyone called him Chief. Traveling down one of two unnamed roads to the harbor, Erik peered out to both sides, scratching at the new five o'clock shadow begun growing since his training started, part his disguise as a cast-away for his infiltration of New York City.

On one, the sun broke the gray mist blanketing the harbor. On the other, the mist concealed the silhouettes of several two-centimeter Flakvierling 38s on a structure. In addition, there were all kinds of buildings, from administrative offices to workshops. Cargo trucks congest the roads, with both army and navy personnel doing their duties. If one were audacious, they might believe the Germans were still considering Operation Sealion.

As they neared the waterfront, the smell of saltwater thickened and security became more apparent. Eventually, they couldn't travel any closer, so Heinrich parked the car. Erik and the others grabbed their belongings and proceeded the rest of the way by foot to the U-boat pens. Erik took in his surroundings, and impressed by how efficiently the base ran with so many moving parts, each with its own purpose in the harbor, like cogs in a machine.

As they walked, Heinrich explained to Erik that U-boats were prepared for three days prior to departure. On the third day, which was the day their boat was on, the diesel engines and electric motors were tested, the U-boat was fueled up, the rubber-covered hull was inspected, fresh and canned provisions were loaded, and its screws were tested. On the two prior days, the crew loaded the boat with fourteen G7a torpedoes and rounds for the eighty-eight millimeter deck gun and twenty millimeter anti-aircraft gun. Heinrich assured Erik he would eat well during the voyage, as U-boat crews were given the best provisions.

The massive structure of the U-boat bunker took Erik's breath away, with its slanted iron posts hammered into the concrete and armed with thick, twisted barbed wire that flanked the outer perimeter. As with entering any military installation, there was a guardhouse, its sentries armed with MP-40s, at the entrance. That reminded Erik of when he was doing ops in Russia.

After they passed through, they entered the bunker through a massive, armored, galvanized steel door. Inside, electric lights far overhead dimly lit a space echoing with an ear-piercing metallic clattering and nauseating smells, such as putrid acids for shaping rubber, benzine, and rotten fish, just to name a few. The acrid bouquet of aromas penetrated Erik's nasal passages and left a horrid taste in his mouth.

As they pressed on, Erik felt as if he were walking in a minefield, stepping carefully to avoid loose material scattered about and snakelike metal and rubber cables slithering around his feet.

To make it even more dangerous, small hand-pushed railway cars carried a wide-range of equipment, such as new machine parts, torpedoes, and ammunition for the cannons and anti-aircraft guns. If the physical obstacles weren't enough, dust and oil fumes were as thick as a London fog. Workers within workshops and machine shops wielded acetylene welding torches that hissed, sputtered, crackled, and howled, shooting sparks everywhere. Rather than simply a fortified dock, the U-boat pen was more like an entire shipyard squeezed into the confined space.

Eventually, the three men arrived at the basin of pen eight, which was flooded. They stopped to stare at the vessel in the pen, grins wide on Heinrich and the Chief's faces.

The captain turned toward Erik. "That's our boat."

"Fantastic, isn't it?" the Chief asked with a prideful smirk. "She's a VII-C boat. Designed specifically for fighting in the Atlantic. She can dive quickly and is nimble as a minnow. The operational range is 7,900 nautical miles on the surface, cruising at ten knots, with a maximum speed of just over seventeen knots."

Erik took a moment to absorb the view. Within the semi-darkness of the bunker, an untrained eye would have difficulty distinguishing the hull from the water. The weathered, pale white wall outlined the U-boat slightly rising above the pier, more clearly defining it. The oily, brackish water surrounded the deck, its hatches still open. The entire length of the boat had a flat, uninterrupted wooden deck. The conning tower gently sloped to the stern with steel cables forming net-guards interlaced with olive-drab porcelain insulators slanting to the bow and stern, all enhanced by reflections in the water. The blood-red Nazi naval flag flapped in the near-gale blowing through the open end of the bunker, the wind drowning out the cacophony from the workshop area.

As they neared the boat, the wharf crew made way for the captain, the Chief, and Erik, their heavy gloved hands standing ready with the hawsers. The crew lined up on the deck, eighteen to twenty-year-old boys behind officers and petty officers who were a few years older. An officer ordered, "Stand by for inspection! Attention! Eyes forward!"

The first officer, also known as the political officer, snapped to attention as he greeted the captain. "All hands presented and accounted for except control-room assistant Backer. Engine room ready, upper and lower decks cleared for departure."

The captain and the others followed across the gangway as the first officer barked, "At ease!"

As Erik, the Chief, and the first officer stood by the conning tower, the captain gave the crew a hard stare, offered a subtle, pleased nod, and waited until the shuffling had subsided to address the crew.

"It is an honor to speak to you today, and I'm honored to be sailing with you on the maiden voyage of our fatherland's most recent achievement. The Royal Navy doesn't know our full potential. They will try to sink us, but they will embarrass themselves as we leave their sinking ships behind. We have a guest on board, Lieutenant. Függer. He is a war correspondent writing about war heroes. He has even brought his camera, so you might to be in the papers." His voice grew firm. "See that you remember your manners."

"Aye-aye, sir!" the assembled crew shouted in unison.

"Harbor stations, men," the first officer commanded.

The crew disappeared from the deck and went to their stations. Erik took a deep breath and climbed down the narrow ladder into the cramped submarine. The metal walls closed in around him as he made his way to his bunk. Disorder reigned within the tight corridors. Nobody could move anywhere without pushing and shoving. Hammocks bulging with loaves of bread swung to and fro, even in the calm waters of the pen. The passages were filled with boxes of provisions, piles of canned food, and sacks. After getting situated and stowing his gear, Erik joined the captain and the first watch on the bridge atop the conning tower. The smell of diesel fuel filled Erik's nostrils as the engines turned over, omitting a noise that reverberated throughout the ship.

"Increase speed to one-third," the captain said. The navigator repeated the order over the bridge speaking tube.

As the U-boat glided smoothly out of the U-boat pen, Erik felt a sense of unease wash over him. He had never been on a U-boat during a war before, and the thought of being trapped beneath the Atlantic if depth charged was daunting. The mid-morning sun cast a golden glow over the harbor, buzzing with activity as the U-boat steamed through the main channel toward its escorts, S-Boats, which lined up on either side of the U-boat.

"There's our escort, S 24 and S 11," the captain said to the navigator as he looked through his binoculars and pointed to the S-Boats that would escort them to the Atlantic. The escorts were a smaller, more agile vessel that would provide protection from enemy aircraft until the U-boat reached the open ocean and could submerge.

Thick clouds blanketed the skies, adding an eerie ambiance to the already suspenseful atmosphere. Erik felt warm, the west wind blowing against his face, which made it a perfect day for late autumn. The S-boats soon peeled off, the bridge crew on the U-boat and crews on the S-boats waving goodbye. Erik focused and closed his eyes, taking a deep breath, and listened to the waves crashing against the hull, gulls crying overhead, and the wind whistling through the superstructure of the boat, creating a symphony of sound.

The U-boat's official mission was to patrol shipping lanes and hunt for prey such as enemy cargo ships, and the crew was filled with a sense of purpose and determination. What only the captain and Erik knew was they were actually on a highly classified mission direct from High Command to drop Erik off near the coast of New York City.

Minutes turned to hours, then days, as the U-boat journeyed across the Atlantic. The voyage was a long and arduous one. The ship's sleek hull cut through the water as Erik stood on the bridge, his eyes fixed on the endless blue that stretched out as far as the eye could see. It was a lonely and monotonous sight, with no signs of life or activity. He couldn't help but feel a sense of uncertainty about what lay over the horizon. The captain and his crew were ever vigilant, but to Erik, it all felt like a never-ending game of hide-and-seek.

Within the U-boat, the crew went about their duties, but not without some grumblings. The small space and the monotony of the journey took a toll on everyone's mood. As time passed, the crew's boredom would give way to frustration. They all yearned for something more, some sort of excitement. They weren't used to going so long without prey to hunt, and were already circulating rumors, in hushed whispers, that the captain was lost or going in circles.

Erik knew better, and the prospect of returning home to New York kept his spirits up. Still, the boredom was persistent, a constant reminder of the monotony of life at sea. Erik's mind wandered, imagining the endless possibilities that lie beyond the endless ocean, but most of all about returning home to Jamie.

CHAPTER 17

IMPENDING BOREDOM AND DEATH

"Hours and hours of boredom sprinkled with a few seconds of
sheer terror."   — Gregory "Pappy" Boyington

SOMEWHERE IN THE ATLANTIC OCEAN.

For the past four days, Erik had been confined to the claustro-
phobic confines of the petty officers' quarters, or U-room, while
sleeping. Wood paneling enclosed his white lacquer bunk on one
side and a drab green curtain on the other. The sounds of the boat
seeped through, reducing life on board to a cacophony of voices
and clattering. The room was cramped with ten men in two sleeping shifts, though it normally held twelve. Their narrow bunks,
three on the right and three on the left, offered little respite from
the constant activity. As a guest on board, Erik had his own bunk.
Every morning, he was jolted back to consciousness by the pun-
gent odor of eggs, sweat, bilge, and wet clothing that permeated
the air and assaulted his nostrils, causing his eyes to water.

Drawing back the curtain, Erik was met with the sight of another shift change—eight hours on, eight hours off. While half
slept, the others performed regular duties and tasks, a never-ending cycle of men trading places, each burdened by the stench left

behind by the previous occupant. Life aboard the U-boat was a perpetual barrage of odors and noises. Erik quickly learned the U-room was a thoroughfare for the boat's traffic, a narrow corridor through which everyone had to travel, including stewards passing with trays of food and clattering pots. The constant commotion made it nearly impossible to find uninterrupted sleep.

As Erik slid down to a lower bunk to join the newly relieved petty officers for breakfast, tables with folding leaves were already set up in the passage. A meager meal consisting of an egg, a slice of hard bread with butter, and coffee was served.

One of the petty officers approached Erik, informing him the captain wished to speak with him, further adding to the suspense and intrigue of the confined and bustling world within the boat. As Erik got up, another petty officer grabbed his camera and suggested taking a quick picture. Erik hesitated, quickly scanning the area. This was an opportunity to send a message. Unable to find what he was looking for, he made his way to the galley, grabbed an empty cardboard box, tore off a side, and scrawled a message with a grease pencil: *JAMIE 8-14 + 47 -> NYC 1437*

Returning to the group, Erik sat among the petty officers, grinning through his now-bushy beard, and the picture was taken. As they looked at the sign, a question arose. "Hey, lieutenant, what does that mean?"

With a sly grin, Erik turned and replied, "My wife will know," before exiting the compartment.

Erik emerged from the forward hatch and stepped into the control room of the U-boat, where the crew was diligently going about their tasks. The Chief approached Erik, checking to make sure he was all right, let him know the captain had invited him to have his meals in the officers' mess, also known as the wardroom. The section of the submarine served as living quarters for the Chief, the apprentice engineer, and the First and Second Watch Officers.

A compact table was bolted to the floor, designed to accommodate four diners, but with the captain and Erik joining, it was set for six. Taking a cursory glance around, Erik noticed the captain was not fulfilling his usual morning duties. The Chief indicated that the captain was on the bridge with the navigator, gesturing upward with his finger, before heading off in the direction of the U-room.

Erik made his way to the ladder leading to the bridge and, upon reaching it, announced, "Permission to come onto the bridge?"

"Granted!" came the response from the second watch officer.

Not wanting to interrupt the concentration of those on the bridge, Erik silently pushed his head over the rim, taking a moment for his eyes to adjust to the darkness of the early morning. He gazed upward at the scattering of pale stars faintly shimmering in the sky. On the eastern horizon, a red band of sunlight slowly emerged, heralding the approaching dawn.

The navigator and captain were having a private conversation in the wintergarten, which was positioned just aft of the bridge on a slightly lowered platform. As the sun rose, the ocean transformed from a mysterious inky blackness to a deep, dark blue. Erik was captivated by the sight and eagerly looked ahead to the bow. To his surprise, he saw thin white streaks of foam running irregularly along the U-boat's hull, traversing the blue surface like veins in marble. The streaks created a broad path of milky water that extended as far as the eye could see. The foam captivated Erik, as they seemed to be dancing along the surface of the ocean. The sight was both mesmerizing and serene, reminding Erik of a dance between two opposing forces.

Large groups of cumulus clouds appeared overhead, characterized by their flat bases and menacing, puffy, multi-level peaks extending high into the sky. Each had its own distinct shape and color, ranging from shades of gray to white. They seemed to move swiftly across the sky, presenting a dynamic and ever-changing landscape.

Erik's gaze shifted from the bow to the stern, where his attention was once again captured by the thin white streaks of foam. They continued to form a path of water that seemed to stretch endlessly. The sight was captivating, as it formed a stark contrast to the deep blue ocean.

The captain's eyes met Erik's, and he motioned for him to come over. Erik hesitated for a moment, but curiosity won over, and he made his way toward the captain.

The captain's urgent voice cut through the tense atmosphere on the wintergarten. "Lieutenant, we are two to three days out." He passed a concealed envelope to the Navigator, marked with bold, black letters that read *OPERATIONS DIVISION OF U-BOAT HEADQUARTERS*, and in bold, red letters, *Ü2 CLEARANCE*[4]. "This is for your eyes only," the captain emphasized.

The Navigator nodded, taking the envelope and pulling up a gridded map. The grid covered the eastern coast of the United States from Portsmouth, Hampshire to Cape Fright, North Carolina. It was divided into multiple squares, each designed to facilitate the exchange of location information. Erik focused on the map as the captain spoke, feeling the weight of their mission. "I believe that squares twenty-nine or fifty-two would be your best bet," the captain pointed out, seeking the Navigator's opinion.

The navigator, Kriechbaum chose square fifty-two with a skeptical air, explaining, "We will be away from major shipping lanes and can head into the Atlantic faster using the Gulf Stream, avoiding patrol boats." Erik understood Kriechbaum's skepticism. Even under ideal conditions, the mission was beyond risky.

The captain, noticing the men on bridge watch trying to

---

4. Secret Clearance

eavesdrop, snapped at them, demanding their focus. "Focus on your duties! If you don't, when we get back, I will replace you!"

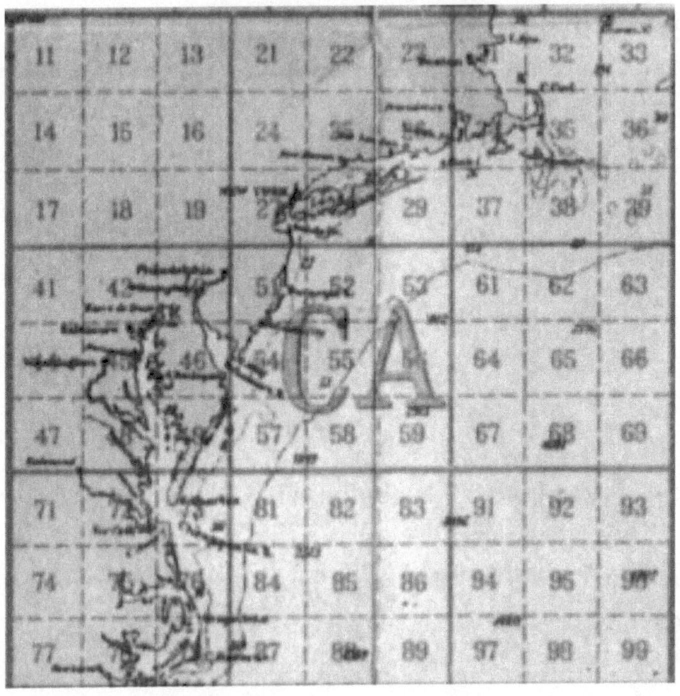

Erik proposed dropping off at square twenty-nine just before daybreak, suggesting it might increase his odds. The navigator was thinking about the risk to the U-boat, but it gave Erik a long distance to travel over land to reach the city. Kriechbaum shook his head, but Erik reassured the captain that the Americans wouldn't expect their boat to be so close.

"Can you pull it off?" the captain asked.

"It's possible," Kriechbaum said, "but it's not the safest choice."

The second watch officer granted permission for someone to come on the bridge. The first watch officer appeared on the bridge and approached the captain with a piece of paper. "Sir, this just came in." He then disappeared from the bridge. Both watch officers' primary duties involved decoding messages from base using the Enigma code machine.

Kriechbaum was in suspense as the captain read the message. "Convoy spotted at square CB 46,54. Heading: East. Course: 85 degrees. Speed: 8 knots. U-boat: 99."

Kriechbaum muttered to himself, drawing attention, and looked at the captain. "That's Kretschmer's boat."

The captain nodded and ordered Kriechbaum to calculate their distance and the potential time of arrival at Kretschmer's location.

As the navigator disappeared from the bridge, the captain addressed the bridge crew with a steely determination. "Stay alert," he commanded. Then he locked eyes with Erik. "Looks like you're about to see some action."

Erik followed the captain to the control room, his heart pounding with anticipation as he observed the intense focus of the crew. Kriechbaum hunched over a navigational chart, plotting their course with meticulous precision, while the first watch officer grappled with decoding another urgent message. The tension in the room was thick with anticipation, a stark contrast to the usual monotony of their mission. As Erik made his way through different compartments, he couldn't help but notice the array of emotions among the crew.

In the forward torpedo bay, excitement crackled in the air as men eagerly prepared the torpedoes for the impending attack. Meanwhile, the petty officers and engine room crew maintained a detached focus on their duties, their unwavering dedication underscoring the seriousness of their mission. Yet, amidst the intense atmosphere, some men sought refuge in much-needed rest, attempting to steal a few moments of sleep before the impending engagement. Returning to the control room, Erik took a seat beside the first watch officer, who was still engrossed in deciphering the message from the Enigma machine.

"These messages are our lifeline," the officer explained, his voice reflecting the gravity of the situation. "Sent from command headquarters in Kernével, they provide vital updates on the convoy's position, course, escort, and essential intelligence to guide our strategy." He stressed the importance of restraint, cautioning against premature attacks until more boats were positioned to maximize their impact. "Any captain who defies these orders will face severe consequences, such as a court martial," he warned, his tone conveying the gravity of the situation.

In the tense silence that followed, the crew braced themselves for the impending showdown, knowing that their every action could determine the fate of the mission. Kriechbaum made a subtle motion toward the captain and the chief engineer; their conversation barely audible above the hum of the U-boat's engines. The Chief quietly slipped out of the control room, leaving the captain bent over the chart with intense focus. His left hand gripped a pencil, while his right hand deftly manipulated a slide rule and divider. The first watch officer discreetly handed the decoded message to Kriechbaum, who read it with furrowed brows before passing it to the captain. The captain snatched the paper, scanned its contents, and flung it onto the table. He then directed Kriechbaum to his side, where quiet words were exchanged as the first watch officer diligently tapped out another coded message. As the message exchanged hands once more, the chief engineer reappeared, engaging in a hushed conversation with the captain before the crew was summoned over the loudspeaker.

"Now hear this. We're tracking a convoy sighted by U99. We anticipate interception around twenty-hundred hours. That's all," the captain announced, prompting unrestrained cheers and excitement that seemed to reverberate throughout the entire boat. As the captain ascended the ladder, he motioned for Erik to follow, a silent understanding passing between the two men as they ascended to the bridge.

Once on the bridge, Erik looked up again in the vast expanse of the sky. A multitude of cumulus clouds loomed, casting their ominous shadows over the endless ocean. The captain, seemingly at ease despite the surrounding chaos, signaled for Erik to approach. A beastly wave crashed over all those on watch, the strong Atlantic assaulting their bodies and tongues with its icy, salty embrace. With the U-boat hurtling through the water, Erik clung to the bridge railings, fixating on the bow cleaving through each crest, sending plumes of water cascading over the bridge.

With the wind howling and the waves roaring, the captain leaned in to speak. "U99 has sighted a convoy of forty ships," he shouted to be heard over the tumult. "Headquarters has ordered Kretschmer to hold his fire. We must maintain contact until our reinforcements arrive."

"How many more boats are on their way?" Erik shouted back, bracing himself against the thrashing of the sea.

"Two, besides Kretschmer and us," the captain replied, his eyes scanning the horizon.

Erik nodded, maintaining a stoic mask to hide his concern. The grid coordinates indicated the convoy was moving through or just leaving Delaware Bay. Most likely, they were filled with vehicles and weapons produced in Philadelphia and bound for England. Losing any number of those ships would be a blow for the English war effort, not to mention the loss of American sailors on board. Erik asked the captain if he felt four U-boats would be enough against such a large convoy.

The captain nodded and briefed Erik on the convoy's limitations, explaining how the U-boats could exploit the convoy because all the ships had to travel the same speed as the slowest steamer, even the escort ships and destroyers. As they drew near, each U-boat would deploy its loop antenna, sending out directional signals to coordinate the wolfpack's strike. The navigator would determine when the moon would descend, allowing the U-boat to slip into the cloak of darkness. Billowing clouds would also shield the U-boat from vigilant eyes. The crew would remain on high alert, their senses finely tuned, as they awaited their next move in the game of stealth and survival.

The captain then instructed him to aid any officer or petty officer in need before the engagement. If unoccupied, he could capture photographs—provided the crew consented. With nothing to do but wait until then, Erik decided to get some rest. As he passed through the control room, his eyes lingered on the Enigma machine, curious to see the decryption device in use. The first officer shot him a wary glare, protective of the machine's secrets even among fellow officers. Erik offered the man a smile and moved on, suppressing a chuckle since he already knew everything about its inner workings from reading about it in the future, and headed toward his bunk.

***

The steady drone of the diesel engines echoing through the U-room awoke Erik from his restless sleep. The steady thrum was a relentless reminder of the ship's powerful heart. As he made his way through the bulkhead doorway to the control room, the heightened tension among the crew struck him. They stood like statues, frozen in anticipation, their eyes fixed on the conning tower above, straining to catch any hint of imminent danger. The room was bathed in an eerie red glow, casting elongated shadows that danced in rhythm with the ship's movements. The red light, aside from providing visibility, also served to preserve the crew's night vision, a vital advantage in the unforgiving darkness of the open sea. Kriechbaum called out, "Ten minutes to contact!"

As he met the determined gaze of Kriechbaum, binoculars were pressed into his hand, a silent command to join the others on the bridge. With purposeful urgency, Erik climbed up, his every step imbued with a sense of impending peril as they ascended the ladder to the bridge. A commanding voice granted them passage, and they emerged onto the exposed deck. The moon cast a ghostly sheen over the roiling clouds, painting a dramatic scene that heightened the stakes of their clandestine mission.

In the midst of this ethereal spectacle, the second watch officer told Erik of the gravity of the situation. The simmering tension on the bridge was palpable, each officer locked in silent communion with the horizon, their collective focus unwavering. Raising the binoculars to his eyes, Erik sighted the convoy, a formidable sight comprising five columns, each with eight vessels. As he adjusted the lenses to focus on the distant flotilla, he marveled at the orderly array of silhouetted ships, each steaming proudly over the treacherous expanse of the open sea.

In a hushed tone, the captain leaned in toward Kriechbaum. "Do you see any escorts or destroyers?" he asked, his words barely audible.

"No screen. They have no protection. Nothing, sir," Kriechbaum replied, never taking his eyes off the horizon, where danger could be lurking.

"They could be chasing one of our..." The captain's voice trailed off as he lowered his binoculars, his eyes scanning the sky to ensure the moon wouldn't reveal their position. Bringing the binoculars back to his eyes, he surveyed the convoy once more before turning to the first watch officer. "How many boats have we deployed?"

"Three, including us, sir," the officer responded, his gaze fixed on the enemy vessels ahead.

The moon's reflection fragmented into a shattered mosaic on

the ocean's surface, its glow revealing the U-boat's stealthy approach. The captain motioned to the first watch officer, signaling that it was almost time to act. As the enemy convoy remained oblivious to the impending danger, Erik felt a rush of adrenaline and trepidation mix within him, knowing the unexpected was about to unfold. In the dim light, the first watch officer squinted through the uboot zieloptik his gaze fixed on the enemy ships. The UZO was a surface target-aiming scope with a luminous graticule attached to a bridge post that automatically fed target line-of-sight bearing and range to the vorhaltrechner. The vorhaltrechner was a Siemens-made electromechanical deflection calculator in the U-boat conning tower that fed attack headings into the gyrocompass steering mechanism of the torpedoes in their tubes. Each vessel was sharply defined in his view, from the forecastles to the smokestacks, laying bare their vulnerabilities. Erik's heart quickened with anticipation and uncertainty. A speaking tube connected the bridge to the bow compartment, allowing precise coordination for the torpedoes' launch. The first watch officer orchestrated the action with precision, impressing Erik with the efficiency of the operation.

"Tubes one to four, stand by for surface firing!" the First Watch Officer ordered, his voice carrying a sense of urgency.

Moments later, a voice confirmed, "Tubes one to four ready for surface firing."

Addressing the petty officer, the first watch officer relayed the intricate details of the enemy's position. "Enemy position, bow right. Angle, five-two right. Speed, ten knots. Range, three thousand meters. Torpedo speed, three-zero. Depth, three meters. Follow for bearing."

The First Watch Officer didn't need to worry about the proper lead angle for the torpedoes. The position calculator computed that. The calculator was connected directly to the gyrocompass and the target bearing transmitter, along with the torpedoes, whose steering mechanism was continuously adjusted. Every change in the U-boat's course was automatically translated for the torpedoes. All the First Watch Officer had to do was keep the target in the crosshairs of the scope.

"Commence attack! Full ahead both! Hard to starboard!" The captain commanded, his voice cutting through the tense air on the bridge. The U-boat roared to life, charging toward the convoy with a powerful surge, the waves crashing around the bridge as it sliced through the ocean's surface. Everyone felt the raw power and anticipation as the pivotal moment approached.

Adrenaline pumped through their veins and the engines roared as the U-boat glided through the ocean.

"Target identification!" The captain told the first watch officer.

"All freighters," the officer responded. He then nodded for the petty officer and the navigator to disappear off the bridge. After this, he shouted into the communication tube, "Bow angle now bearing zero-six-five. Lock on tube one."

The response from below came a moment later. "Locked on!"

"Range twenty-five-hundred meters."

"Check."

"New bow angle, now bearing zero-six-seven. Lock on tube two."

"Locked on."

"Range, twenty-five-hundred meters."

"Check."

"New bow angle, now bearing zero-seven-three. Lock on tube three."

"Locked on."

"Range, twenty-five-hundred meters."

"Check."

"New bow angle, now bearing zero-seven-five. Lock on tube four."

"Locked on."

"Range, twenty-five-hundred meters."

"Check."

"Open the torpedo doors," the captain ordered. "Tubes one and two, fire when matched."

"Tube one and two ready!" came the voice from below.

"Tube one, fire!" the watch officer ordered, then paused for a second before adding, "Tube two, fire!"

Again, the captain ordered, "Tubes three and four, fire when matched."

"Tube three, ready!"

"Tube three, fire!"

"Tube four, ready!"

"Tube four, fire!"

Beneath the unforgiving depths, the torpedoes slithered silently on their unyielding hunt for prey. The captain's eyes swept the vast expanse before him, a restless anticipation gnawing at his gut. Then, out of the murky shadows emerged a vessel, its slender form homing in on the U-boat. With keen scrutiny, the captain analyzed the ship's features: the forecastle, the bridge, the smokestacks, each detail etching itself into his mind. As the ship drew nearer, its silhouette sharpened, revealing its elongated frame, low profile, and distinctive bow. However, before the captain could process the implications, a blinding orange-red burst shattered the darkness, followed by another searing flash. In an instant, immense geysers erupted from the ocean's depths, casting a maelstrom into the air and unleashing shockwaves that pierced through the U-boat's bridge.

"Destroyer ahead! *Alarm!*" the captain's voice thundered with terror, sending a chilling cascade of fear through the crew.

Erik and the others pivoted toward the destroyer, their faces draining of color. With swift urgency, they descended into the control room, jostling for space as they maneuvered through the confines of the hatch. The captain descended last, barking orders. "Close torpedo doors. Dive to one hundred meters! Fast!"

Chaos swirled around Erik, a cacophony of urgent voices and frenetic activity. He pressed himself to the side as the crew surged around him in a flurry of motion, battling their way through the circular doors leading to the bow. The Chief yelled, "Hard down both. Both engines full ahead! All hands forward!"

Outside, the menacing silhouette of the destroyer loomed closer, its hydroplanes forcing the U-boat into a precarious imbalance. Meanwhile, within the engine room, the crew frantically switched from diesel engines to electric motors, their movements a symphony of urgency and expertise.

"Depth charges dropped!" the signal operator's voice rang out with unbridled terror, a grim proclamation that sent shivers down the crew's spines.

Then, without warning, all those inside the U-boat heard a muted thump as jarring explosions and dazzling flashes tore through the ocean's depths. The U-boat lurched violently, its compartments and occupants thrown into a disorienting dance of chaos. Plates clattered, glasses shattered, and light bulbs burst into showers of glass shards, leaving the boat in an eerie half-light. Amidst the turmoil, the captain and second watch officer sought to calm the crew, their voices cutting through the tumultuous panic that gripped the vessel. Throughout the U-boat, heavy breaths and the haunting drip of water into the bilge filled the air, a relentless reminder of the perilous dance between survival and annihilation.

Two dull explosions, these more distant, reverberating through the U-boat. The captain's eyes sparkled, and a satisfied grin spread across his face. The signal operator's voice pierced the tense atmosphere. "Destroyer making a second round. Propellers bearing one-two-zero, closing fast." Synchronously, two more torpedoes found their targets, igniting colossal explosions that reverberated throughout the ocean's depths.

Gritting his teeth, the captain barked, "Full ahead." The electric motors in the engine room roared to life, drowning out all other sounds. The relentless onslaught continued as more torpedoes struck, sending violent detonations rippling through the water. "Deeper, Chief. Quick!" the captain commanded, urgency lacing his voice.

Erik and the others listened in horrified silence as the haunting sounds of metal being rent asunder echoed through the hull. The depth gauge crept into the red, the Chief and the control room crew fixated on it, knowing the U-boat was being pushed to its limits one hundred meters. They dove another ten meters, then twenty.

"Deeper," the captain insisted as the creaking of the hull intensified under the extreme pressure. They plunged deeper into the abyss, the captain's order to level off offering a momentary reprieve from the impending danger. Erik uttered a silent prayer, knowing they were approaching crush depth. The second watch officer checked on him, silently seeking to reassure him in the face of imminent peril.

"Destroyer bearing thirty degrees to port. Getting louder fast!" the signal operator's urgent report shattered the eerie silence, prompting the captain to motion for silence. He directed the Chief to plot a new course, his eyes intent on the operator's lips for any shred of vital information. Everyone looked upward, hearing depth charges exploding above them. It seemed to last indefinitely. Then, the signal operator's hesitant pause heightened the tension before he announced, "Sound receding astern!"

Nervous whispers filled the air from wary faces drenched in sweat and grime, mingling with the hissing and spurting of leaks throughout the compartment. Over by the hatch, the Chief hurried back and forth from the engine room, delivering hushed updates to the captain.

"When?" the captain demanded, his voice laced with urgency.

The Chief ran his fingers through his hair, removing his cap. "Four to seven hours, give or take."

The captain nodded, his eyes reflecting the gravity of the situation. "Will the oxygen hold out?"

The Chief's hopeless expression spoke volumes. "No, sir."

The captain's gaze swept the room before locking onto the Chief's, conveying the severity of the predicament. "In that case, potash cartridges for everyone who's not working." He paused for a moment and looked at the clock. "All hands off-watch, turn in."

As the second watch officer distributed the cartridges, Erik received his and staggered back toward the stern, well aware of the dire straits of the U-boat. The crew geared up with the mouthpiece and rubber nozzle of the potash cartridges, preparing for the hours of despair ahead. Surfacing was out of the question. With no choice but to ride the situation out, Erik made his way to his bunk, adjusting the bulky metal case against his chest. The bunk was far from comfortable, yet at that moment, it felt like a sanctuary. He lay there, taking in the musty smell of the mattress and the worn-out pillow as he prepared to close his eyes. Drawing in breath through the cartridge, he tasted the rubber and foul stench, but thoughts of Jamie and her soft brown eyes momentarily distracted him from his reality.

***

Erik jolted awake in his cramped bunk aboard the U-boat. The sudden movement caused the metal walls to creak, and he could hear the hum of the engines vibrating through the submarine.

Rubbing his eyes, he tried to shake off the residual drowsiness. As he stumbled out of his bunk, he found the Bosun's Mate staring at him.

In a terse voice, the man said, "Lieutenant, the captain wants to see you on the bridge."

Confusion and curiosity mingled in Erik's mind with relief. If the captain was on the bridge, that meant they'd surfaced. He pulled the fowl-smelling mask off his face, dropped it on the bunk, and hastened through the dimly lit corridors. He wondered why the captain would summon him so urgently. What could be so important? When he finally reached the bridge, he found the captain standing at the far end of the wintergarten, his hands clasping a pair of binoculars. The captain lowered the binoculars and his steely gaze met Erik's.

"Lieutenant," he began, his voice serious and low. "We've come to the crucial part of our journey. New York is hours away. You need to prepare yourself and what lies ahead."

"Sir, I'm ready."

The prospect of reaching New York, of setting foot on friendly soil, filled him with a sense of both excitement and trepidation. Anticipation tingled in his soul. His fraught journey home was nearing its end.

The U-boat soon reached its destination, CA 29, looming just a few miles away from the majestic skyline of the city that never sleeps.

The captain, appearing sterner and more stoic than usual, approached Erik and said in a surprisingly soft tone, "I wish you good fortune and safety in your endeavors."

Erik nodded as he handed over his camera. "Captain, I was hoping you could get these pictures developed, especially the one where I was holding up a sign for my wife."

The captain nodded.

"Maybe it can get published in Signal," Erik suggested, referring to the German army magazine.

The captain nodded again.

After changing out of his German uniform and dressing in a threadbare outfit of British-made civilian clothing, part of his cast-away costume complemented by his unkempt beard, Erik climbed down to the deck and embarked on a raft, his only companion in the vast, unforgiving ocean. As the U-boat slowly submerged into the depths, Erik watched the silhouette of the vessel fade away, leaving him completely alone. The city lights of New York sparkled in the distance, just out of reach. With every passing minute, he paddled painstakingly, doing his best to stay on course. Erik's heart pounded in his chest as he clung to the raft, gliding through the dark, frigid waters of the Atlantic Ocean. The haunting echo of his own breath mingled with the crashing of ocean waves against his raft. Above him, the vast expanse of the night sky sparkled with stars, seeming ready to guide him home.

Driven by eagerness to finally reach the safety of friendly shores, Erik paddled even harder. Minutes turned to hours as Erik battled fatigue and the relentless currents. The raft bobbed up and down as the waves crashed against it, threatening to swallow him whole. The cold sea mist battered his resolve, yet thoughts of Jamie spurred him on.

Eventually, Erik collapsed into the bottom of the raft, exhausted. For every ten meters he paddled toward shore, the current pushed him out nearly as far or further. The glittering lights of the city receded into the distance as he was driven out to sea. Cursing the irony of coming so far just to be foiled by the current, he lay in a fetal position under the stars to keep warm, hoping a ship would spot him in the vast ocean.

CHAPTER 18

THE PERCEPTION OF SIGNALS AND CODES BETWEEN FRIENDS AND ENEMIES

"In the CIA, they recruit you to be an officer, an ops officer, in part due to how well you cope with stress and how well you adapt to new situations."
                                                  — Valerie Plame

Erik drifted aimlessly in the ocean, hoping to be picked up by a trawler or a ship before he drifted further away from shore and became shark food. His chances of being picked up grew slimmer by the hour. If he were found, he would act like a sailor who was lucky enough to be alive after a torpedo hit his ship. Until then, all he could do was wait, so he curled up to save his body heat and get some sleep before sunrise.

***

Sometime later, Erik was still asleep as the sun crept over the horizon, painting the sky violet and brushing the clouds with pink. A sea-worn, rusted-hull trawler plunged forward in the black waters of the Atlantic on its way back to New York City, its crew awaiting their reward for the trove of fish stored below deck on ice. As the trawler bobbed over the small swells, its wooden deck creaked, sounding like a wounded animal crying out in pain. Ropes twisted above the deck, holding worn nets smelling of rotted fish and dripping seawater onto the deck. Below, the orange illumination of cigarettes transitioned from dim to radiant and back. As the sun spread its light upon the ocean like a baker spreading icing on a cake, it repelled the blanket of the night and revealed a lone raft among the waves.

"Look! Over there!" A man shouted as he pointed in the distance.

"What is it?" Another man yelled.

"Port bow! There's a man in the water! He's in a raft!"

The skipper took the wheel, angling the boat to the right of the figure in the water, cutting the engines to reduce their wake. The men on the deck yelled at the bridge to stop as they gathered gear for the rescue attempt.

Erik, awoken by the shouting, looked up and assessed his situation as the trawler continued to break through the small swells. He rose to his knees and balanced himself on the rubber raft like a tightrope walker on a wire, ready to catch a rope.

As the ship neared, men yelled words of encouragement and did everything in their power to make things easier for the castaway.

Erik's eyes narrowed as he focused on the rope, knowing timing was everything. He raised his hands above his head with his fingers spread out, like a lizard's claws grasping a wall, and leaped for the rope, catching it on the first try. His knuckles were white as he gripped the lifeline, then cold water enveloped him, twisting him in circles like a piece of clothing in a washing machine. He lost his grip and gasped a single breath of air before the cold waters of the Atlantic engulfed him.

He had an urge to panic and struggle, yet he remained focused. There was a subtle thump from the side of the ship, and Erik instinctively grabbed where it came from and felt a net. He kicked furiously and clawed at the hull of the ship, which was slippery as ice. He mustered all his strength to hold the net as he tried to position his feet so he wouldn't fall. Finally, he broke the surface and took a deep breath of air.

"Easy now! Pull gently!" a crew member said, then his next words were focused on Erik. "Hang on there. We got you." The crew gave all their strength, as Erik clung to the net for dear life. "Almost there. Men, keep pulling!"

Erik climbed a few rungs of netting as the crew pulled him up the hull of the ship. "Lift him up. Grab his shoulders and pull him over. Easy, now!" After agonizing minutes of struggle, Erik finally made it to the deck.

The crew stood over him with rope-burned, gorilla-like hands and bloodshot eyes. Every exhalation of their breath engulfed Erik in a truly putrid smell, only outdone by their body odor, a powerful bouquet of sweat, seawater, and fish.

Erik had to get into character as a man whose ship was sunk by a U-boat. He was exhausted from the night's ordeal though, and simply blabbered unintelligible thanks, which seemed to be enough to sell the story.

The fishermen didn't ask questions, simply getting him some dry clothes, hot coffee, and then ushering him to a warm bed.

Erik rested, considering his next challenge would be the FBI agents watching the New York and New Jersey coastlines for German operatives. The captain would likely radio in that he found Erik, and the FBI might be waiting for him. If that happened, he would have to decide how committed he was to the castaway cover story. He might have to come up with a snap cover, which was something he could adopt on the spur of the moment if an opportunity presented itself.

He still had to infiltrate the German safe house while avoiding being compromised by the FBI. The layers of lies were so thick, even he had trouble keeping it all straight. He was a man from the future pretending to be a German officer who was pretending to be a castaway merchant sailor, all under the pretense of being on a German sabotage mission he was actually trying to thwart. Even the smallest mistake could get him detained or killed, and failing to stop the sabotage mission could jeopardize the timeline yet again.

Intermittent whistles of fishing boats and other ocean vessels and the incessant screeching of gulls, the sounds of the waterfront of New York City in 1940, woke Erik. The Manhattan waterfront was a kaleidoscope of individuals working on the docks and in-numerable types of ships in the harbor, from the most modern to picturesque, four-masted schooners from the nineteenth century. The ships came from across the seven seas to rest and exchange their goods before sailing away on further voyages.

The early morning sun lit the streets, penetrating every inch of the city and warming the cool, damp air. The Manhattan skyline rose above the harbor, the buildings looming over the bay like mountain peaks, with the Empire State and Chrysler buildings towering over the horizon.

Erik shuffled to the bridge and oriented himself as the ship pulled up to a dock with a large sign over it that read *Fulton Fish Market*. The familiar outline of the Brooklyn Bridge nearby was a welcoming sight. The skipper carefully docked alongside other fishermen unloading their catches while cooks from local restau-rants and other patrons filled the docks looking for bargains.

"How ya feeling?" The skipper spoke as if there were marbles in his mouth.

Erik just nodded.

"Yer lucky to be alive. The Atlantic is not very forgiving. She usually don't give up her dead."

"Thank you," Erik said, his breath catching as he realized that was the first genuine thing he'd said to anybody in weeks, maybe months. Then, he started towards the lower deck to disembark.

"Hey, you got a name?" the captain called after him.

Erik nodded as he continued walking, but said nothing.

"Well? What is it?"

"Jude Thaddeus," Erik lied, slipping easily back into the old habit. "I was named after the saint of hopeless causes."

The skipper kept asking questions like a kid picking at a scab. "You got family in New York?"

Erik shook his head.

The skipper stared with scrutinizing eyes. "Where are you from, boy?"

"I was born in New Jersey, but now I live in Washington, DC."

"A city boy?"

Erik nodded.

"What were you doing out there?"

"I believe I already told you." As Erik excused himself, he felt the skipper was hiding something. Just like in Berlin, when he had to save Hitler, time was of the essence. Since the boat was docked, he had at most five minutes to get off and disappear in the chaos of downtown Manhattan before whomever the weathered sailor had called came looking for him.

Erik tore along the deck, looking over the rail to find several men who appeared to be FBI agents from their tell-tale gun bulges walking toward the gangway. He turned and flew down the stairs to the lower decks, dashed down the corridors, and started around a corner. Suddenly, he threw himself backwards into a side corridor, out of the view of three crew members clustered near a cabin door. Erik stepped backwards and faded into the maze of the ship while checking each cabin door to see if was open. Finding one, he barged into a cabin with two beds, pictures of pin-up girls, end tables that need dusting, floors that need cleaning, and two locked footlockers. He quickly searched around the tables for keys, found one, and opened one of the footlockers. He headed to a small closet and took an empty duffle bag. Next, he filled the bag with items he might need until he got to the German safe house. Finally, he headed to the stern.

From there, he climbed onto the upper deck as the crew unloaded their catch. The skipper was talking to the agents, one who was glancing around. From the ship to the dock wasn't far, so Erik took a deep breath, leaped over the gunnel, and soared to the dock. Erik then got into character and disappeared into the crowd. He knew the first few hours on the run, he was most likely to get caught.

However, he has one advantage in that the skipper and crew might not give an accurate description of him. That would give him a few hours to find the safe house. The downside of going to the safe house was that there could be FBI agents watching it and making notes of who came and went from the building. Also, he didn't know if or when the FBI might raid it. In short, no matter what he did would be a gamble.

Immediately after leaving the dock, Erik scouted the parking lot for individuals who were leaving. Of course, he could easily steal a car, but there was the problem that he didn't know how to get to Henry Street without a map. He pulled a ten-dollar bill from his wallet, made himself more presentable, took a breath, and proceeded. The first several people completely ignored him and uttered things under their breath. So, he tried a different approach by asking if they would like to make some money first.

Not having any luck even then in the parking lot, Erik proceeded under the bridge, paying close attention to people walking to cars. It was like fishing—lots of trying and waiting. Within a couple of minutes, he was able to get the attention of a gentleman with inquisitive eyes, yet he was suspicious as Erik walked toward him. He assured he was a man of his offer by flashing the money. The man was like Pavlov's dog as he reached for it. Like a lion tamer, Erik calmed the man down and told him his desired destination.

Once in the car, the man drove down South Street. Driving in New York in 1940 was a new experience for Erik, quite different from traffic in 2010. There were less cars on the roads, no lines on the pavement separating the lanes, no clear signs of crosswalks, and most striking, there were horses and carts sharing the road. It was like driving in a NASCAR race while avoiding horses and jay walkers. To make matters worse, the car had no seatbelts.

"Traffic is horrible," the man said between yelling at the other drivers as if they could hear them. "Someone needs to come up with a plan to deal with the traffic."

"I don't see that's going to happen any time soon," Erik said.

"Di mi!" The man shook his fist at a car that had just cut him off. He then took a hard left, and once he got to a corner with a light, Erik motioned for him to pull over. Once stopped, Erik gave the man his money, thanked him, and grabbed his things before exiting the car.

Erik took in the crowd to make sure he spotted any FBI agents before they spotted him. Even though America and Germany were not at war, the FBI still looked for German spies and would arrest them. To make things worse, the German safe houses were not that safe, as they were being watched. It was hard to spot FBI agents in the 1940s without knowing what to look for. What Erik needed was contrast.

FBI agents were white and wore fedoras and suits, but that could describe most men in that part of New York at the time. They would likely be in their early- to mid-thirties, wearing almost identical suits, drinking coffee, and probably have a paper bag lunch and be in a car that was one to three years old. It would be tough, but not impossible, to spot them, though anybody sitting in a parked car in front of a building full of German spies would be a likely candidate. Thus, a good way to not be spotted would be to use a back entrance.

The sweltering grip of the fall heat assailed Erik as he emerged onto a side street buzzing with activity. Throngs of people from diverse backgrounds bustled about, each striving to leave their mark on the world while grappling with their own personal struggles. He gazed up at a decrepit apartment building, its weathered brick exterior standing in remembrance of the bygone century. Once proud, the façade was faded by the ravages of weather, neglect, and pollution. Concrete stairs leading to the entrance bore the unmistakable stains of neglect and grime. The drab gray window frames, peeling and open, offered a breather to the forgotten lives within, some propped with a piece of wood to latch onto the cool urban breeze. Iron fire escapes clung to the side of the building, their eerie creaks echoing ominously in the wind.

Stepping into the worn entrance, Erik was met with the musty odor of mold and mildew as his eyes adjusted to the dimly lit hallway illuminated by flickering lightbulbs. The cascading light revealed peeling wallpaper, once vibrant with life and color, now blending into a muted backdrop that cast long shadows across the cracked floor tiles.

The dilapidated wood of a creaky stairwell groaned beneath his every step as Erik ascended. Each landing offered a new panorama of neglect and desolation. To most, the conditions would seem deplorable, but to a slumlord, they were tolerable. If the tenants didn't like it, they could always leave. Upon reaching the floor of the safe house, Erik looked for the door to apartment 3B. It was one of many doors in the desolate hallway, distinguished only by a nameplate with a blank piece of paper, slightly askew from years of neglect. He paused for a heartbeat before rapping on the door, pondering the enigmatic secrets lurking beyond the flimsy barrier. Seconds ticked by as Erik waited, anticipation taut in the air. A deadbolt turned with a scrape of metal on metal, and a door chain rattled. Then, the door parted just a crack, revealing an intense pair of piercing blue eyes that locked with Erik's.

"Can I help you?" the man behind the door asked.

"I heard this is the New York Yankees fan club," Erik answered, following the script for the German spies' challenge and response.

"Who is your favorite baseball player?"

"Lou Gehrig."

"Because he hit the most home runs?"

"No. Babe Ruth hit the most home runs, sixty in 1927."

The door creaked as the blue-eyed man pulled it open.

CHAPTER 19

MUSINGS OF DENIAL AND DECEPTION

"Sigh…okay. I've had my tantrum and now I have to figure out how to stay alive."

— Andy Weir, *The Martian*

The brass doorknob, once shiny and regal, had succumbed to the wear of time, its luster replaced by a mournful, muted appearance. As Erik crossed the threshold, the old wooden floors groaned beneath his feet, like each step was transporting him back to the Victorian era. A frayed carpet revealed bare wood beneath, while the walls, once vibrant, lacked their former luster. Laughter and music seeped through the walls, adding to the mysterious atmosphere.

The furniture, though worn, still exuded a certain charm with intricate carvings and patterns, a testament to a bygone era. In the kitchen, stains adorned the once-pristine porcelain of the sink, a faucet dripped with persistence, and a stove was coated in layers of grease and grime. Yet, amidst the squalor, an unexpected sense of warmth and comfort enveloped the apartment. It was as if the very walls held secrets, whispering tales of a past that refused to be forgotten.

Erik glanced around the room to see eight shady characters,

each recruited by the Abwehr, and each with some importance. Like Erik, they were given three weeks of intensive sabotage training in the manufacture and use of explosives, incendiaries, primers, and various forms of mechanical, chemical, and electrical delayed-timing devices. Erik learned all that on the Farm.

The spies had spent considerable time developing their cover stories for their time in the United States. They conversed in English, to each other and anyone they met, and read American newspapers and magazines to improve their English and familiarity with current American events and culture.

Erik knew of two operations set up by the Abwehr. The first was Operation Magpie, wherein two operatives in Maine gathered intelligence on American factories, shipyards, testing facilities, and whether Nazi propaganda was having any effect on the populace. Operation Pastorius was the other, to which Erik was assigned, a clandestine mission aimed at sabotaging key economic targets within the United States. The gravity of the task ahead hung heavy in the air, heightening the tension in the room as each operative mentally prepared for their first objective.

In the dimly lit room, a worn oak table served as the epicenter of the clandestine gathering. Spread across its surface was an intricate map of Manhattan, its web of intersecting lines breathing life into the sprawling of New York City. The map's focal point was the iconic Grand Central Terminal, marked with a fervent, fiery red circle.

Eight individuals, with faces cloaked in secrecy and eyes gleaming with purpose, surrounded the table, united by their enigmatic pursuits for the Reich. Among them stood Erik, absorbing every detail about the group so he could plan their downfall from within.

As a hushed anticipation filled the room, George Dasch, the group's leader, stepped forward, the wooden pointer clutched tightly in his hand, trembling with anticipation. His eyes and the end of the pointer fixed on the heart of Grand Central Terminal.

In a gravelly voice, Dasch said, "Tomorrow, our first target will be the ten rotary converters at the M42 substation in Grand Central Terminal." One of the other men carefully arranged black and white photographs of the facility and cross-section diagrams of the terminal's labyrinthine corridors on the table.

"Basement M42 and its ten rotary converters," Dasch continued. "A bucket of sand could take out a single one, but disabling all of them will cripple the Northeastern Rail Network." As his words hung in the air, the assembled group nodded in silent understanding, their anticipation of the task ahead palpable. Each was eager to delve deeper into the intricacies of the operation, their minds reveling in the thrill of their clandestine duties.

The atmosphere in the room crackled with tension as Dasch spun a web of deception and intrigue, tapping out a rhythm on the table that mirrored the chaotic pulse of the city streets. His gaze bore into Heinck, Thiel, and Burger as he issued commands. "I need you in position, ready to move when we leave the terminal." Sizing up Heinck, he asked, "Have you secured the cars yet?"

Heinck nodded, his voice steady. "I've taken care of everything. We have secured the lease for each vehicle tomorrow for twelve hours."

"Have you scouted the area around Grand Central Terminal over the past few days? The streets are a labyrinth, especially if we're being pursued by the authorities." He circled a section of the map with a pointer.

Heinck added. "The taxis will allow us to blend in, and we can elude the FBI. We've been practicing all week. We'll be waiting for you on 42nd Street."

Dasch placed a diagram of Grand Central Terminal on the table and tapped the upper right-hand corner with his pointer. "Kerling and I will retrieve the suitcases of sand from here, at the Cab and Baggage, and then proceed to M42."

Dasch looked at Haupt and Quirin and drew everyone's

attention to the black and white photographs as Haupt took over. The images depicted a labyrinthine ventilation system, a key element of their diabolical plan. Haupt revealed the blueprints that would grant them access to the air ducts above Basement 42. The group leaned in, memorizing every detail of the scheme.

"How long will it take for the Zyklon B to take effect?" Dasch asked, his voice tinged with apprehension.

Quirin answered with grim certainty. "Once released, Zyklon B will claim its victims within five minutes, and it will take an additional two minutes to clear the area of the deadly gas. You will have a narrow window of opportunity." Quirin's eyes locked with Neubauer and Erik.

Dasch then took command, revealing incriminating photos that exposed the true intentions of their enigmatic plan. As the group absorbed the gravity of the situation, Dasch turned to Neubauer and Erik. "Neubauer and Erik, you get the prize." He paused for a moment. "The rotary converters located in Basement 42."

As he was bestowing upon them the crucial task of locating the rotary converters in Basement 42, Erik's mind raced, calculating the potential ramifications and intricacies of the mission. As the meeting drew to a close, the operatives dispersed, each armed with newfound knowledge.

Erik lingered by the table, feeling the weight of responsibility settling upon his shoulders like an ominous cloak. As the door of the apartment shut behind those who'd left, Neubauer and Dasch approached him and offered reassurance. Erik's resolve deepened, not bolstered by their support, but by his determination to stop their plot. The coming hours and days would be fraught with peril and uncertainty, but Erik was ready for the battle of wits and courage for the sake of tomorrow. But first, he needed to be fitted for a suit.

CHAPTER 20

RUNNING FAST WHILE REMAINING STILL

"Getting stuck behind enemy lines is one of the hazards of being a spy. When it happens, you can either hide in the shadows and wait to get killed; or, you can march into the open and take your enemy head on. It's a game of high-risk, high-reward. Play it right and you might survive."

— Michael Weston, *Burn Notice*, "Hard Out"

NEW YORK CITY, NEW YORK.

As the first rays of sun pierced the concrete jungle, New York City teemed with life, oblivious to the impending danger that lurked within. Two enigmatic figures, clad in sleek black suits, emerged from the throng of commuters, their movements as stealthy as a pair of panthers stalking their prey. The city's rhythm hummed around them, but they remained singularly focused on their clandestine mission. Erik and Neubauer, shrouded in the guise of ordinary businessmen, navigated the bustling streets with the practiced ease of seasoned operatives.

Grand Central Terminal loomed ahead, a majestic labyrinth of steel and stone obscured by the morning rush. Inside, the symphony of clattering trains and echoing footsteps masked their measured advance. Every step they took reverberated with an undercurrent of tension, for they were fully aware of the grave risks that accompanied their presence.

The FBI, relentless in their pursuit, had been closing in on the German cell for months. The hollow murmur of distant chatter in the terminal betrayed the presence of FBI agents. The second German team, also a pair disguised as businessmen, headed to the luggage clerks. The FBI lay in wait, ready to pounce on them as they retrieved their belongings. As the spies were arrested, they yelled out in German, drawing the attention of everyone in the terminal. With the bait taken, the trap was sprung.

Erik and Neubauer swiftly located the concealed elevator entrance that would transport them to the depths of Basement M42. Erik pressed the button with a flick of his hand, and the doors slowly creaked open. As the two men stepped inside, the heavy doors closed behind them, enveloping them in a dimly lit elevator. There was a moment of silence between them, their eyes reflecting a mix of determination and apprehension, each for their own reasons. The descent seemed to drag on endlessly, each passing story adding to the mounting sense of urgency. Erik's mind raced with the intricate plan, anticipating the best moment to tear it all down.

As they descended, their anxiety coiled tighter. Down in the level just above Basement M42, Haupt and Quirin would unleash havoc—eliminating anyone in their path and deploying the deadly Zyklon B through the ventilation system, ensuring a lethal end to all within the targeted area. Their task was executed with cold precision, and they made a swift escape by getting into one of the three getaway cars that were manned by Heinck, Thiel, and Burger. The first part of the mission was a success.

Erik lamented the lives lost, but he couldn't be in two places at once, and protecting the generators was his primary goal.

Losing them would have far greater ramifications. It would delay the United States from entering the war, causing roughly eighty percent of troop and materiel movements in the northeast to be halted.

It was up to Erik and Neubauer to complete the mission. As they descended further into the dark, the stakes grew higher. The entire operation would take thirty minutes, tops.

Before the elevator lurched to a halt, the noxious fumes of Zyklon, which snuffed out life in mere minutes, filled Basement M42. Haupt and Quirin swiftly purged the deadly air, allowing Erik and Neubauer to emerge safely as the hum of machinery echoed off the stone walls. As they advanced through the grim scene of death, the glow of the overhead fluorescents showed the effects of Zyklon B.

A rich, ghastly sick stench of excrement, vomit, menstrual fluid, and fecal matter consumed the basement. Corpses were sprawled around the room, their skin discolored pink with red and green spots. Some foamed at the mouth, and many bled from their ears and noses.

They continued on… every moment pregnant with the weight of anticipation as they neared the rotary converters. The room was vast, filled with an intricate network of generators, transformers, and buzzing electrical equipment. The dull glow of the machinery cast eerie shadows on the walls. They got to the first of ten rotary converters that awaited them, surrounded by a labyrinth of generators and transformers. With a sense of grim purpose, Neubauer opened his suitcase and extracted a heavy bag of sand. As he reached for a knife, a wicked grin twisted his features, signaling the beginning of their dangerous task.

"What is it?" Neubauer asked as he dug a cup into the sand.

Erik gestured for Neubauer to keep silent, his hand tightening around the grip of his Luger. A low, ominous hum vibrated through the air, distinct and foreboding. It wasn't the sound of the rotary converters.

Unbeknownst to Neubauer and Erik the elevator had ascended and now was descending. Haupt, Quirin, and other members of the team had been compromised. Neubauer continued to ramble on, boasting about the accolades they would receive from Hitler and the glory of being heroes of the Reich. Erik moved slowly and deliberately, positioning himself behind Neubauer, who smiled and nodded in self-righteous satisfaction as he continued his grandiosity.

"Would you like to be the one who throws the sand first?" Neubauer raised the cup.

"No, I want to be known for something else," Erik replied.

Neubauer's expression shifted to uncertainty. "For what?"

"For being the one who stopped it." Neubauer's eyes widened in shock and realization just as Erik squeezed the trigger. Neubauer's body was driven forward by the bullet as a mist of blood, flesh, and bone fragments sprayed from his head.

Erik swiftly liberated Neubauer's Luger and concealed a paperclip underneath his shirt cuff before making his way to the elevator. The ding announcing the arrival of the elevator jolted him, as he expected it to simply be waiting for him. He suddenly felt like a cornered beast, as the elevator was the only way out of the basement.

The doors creaked open, and twenty FBI agents, armed to the teeth with Thompson submachine guns, shotguns, and pistols, stood before him, evoking a surge of adrenaline as he tightened his grip on his weapons. With lethal precision, Erik's Luger discharged, killing two agents in a barrage of muzzle flashes. Erik's only chance of escape lay in fleeing deeper into the basement, leaving them to navigate the maze of equipment.

Steeling himself, Erik dashed behind a rotary converter as the agents unleashed a hail of gunfire in his direction, forcing them to navigate the labyrinthine passages of the basement. Rounding the rotary converter, Erik and an FBI agent came face to face, each raising their weapons in a tense standoff. Two shots rang out before the agent could retaliate, and Erik swiftly maneuvered to evade their pursuit, the metallic ping of bullets against metal echoing around him. Suddenly, another agent emerged from behind a second rotary converter, leveling a shotgun at Erik with an ominous glint in his eyes. As the shotgun erupted, Erik slid and dodged the lethal projectiles before swiftly dispatching the agent with a well-aimed shot to the head.

Continuing his desperate flight between two rotary converters, Erik found himself caught in a relentless barrage of bullets from an FBI agent armed with a submachine gun. He ducked behind one of the machines until he heard the agent reloading, then capitalized on the moment, eliminating the threat with a single shot to the chest.

As Erik attempted to regain his bearings, a bear of an agent collided with him, momentarily dazing him. Another agent appeared opposite the bear, brandishing a revolver and cutting off his escape.

Erik's options were down to getting shot or giving up. "Wait, don't shoot," he said. "I have information. There are three getaway cars. I also know about plans to sabotage the hydroelectric plants at Niagara Falls, the Aluminum Company of America's plants in Illinois, Tennessee, and New York, and locks on the Ohio River."

That saved him. They handcuffed him and headed to the elevator. He had a new dilemma to weasel out of.

Erik soon stood in the elevator, bound in handcuffs and surrounded by four FBI agents. His eyes darted around the elevator, waiting for the right moment. Once the elevator reached the ground floor of Grand Central Terminal, he would have to run like hell to survive. Erik's mind spun with a whirlwind of strategy and calculated movements. He had to be quick, or he wouldn't make it. He took a deep breath and prepared to make his move.

As the elevator moved upward, the FBI agents seemed complacent in their victory. In a fluid explosion of motion, Erik sprang into action, utilizing his mastery of martial arts to his advantage. He only had one chance, so he made it count. He delivered every strike with precision and swiftness to vulnerable targets.

The two agents in front of him fell first. Erik raised his right leg and kicked down at an agent's ankle with a sickening sound of shattering bone. The man cried out in pain and collapsed to the ground, unable to stand, and a downward kick to the head rendered him unconscious. Erik then executed a series of rapid, well-placed kicks with both bound knee thrusts against the second agent, targeting pressure points until the man collapsed. He surged back into the agent behind him to the left, smashing the man into the wall, and kicked the fourth agent in the groin. As the man doubled over in pain, Erik pushed back into the agent behind him and brought both feet up to strike the bent man in the head, knocking him out. He then flung his own head back, striking the agent behind him in the nose, following up with an elbow to the temple. As Erik stepped forward, the man fell to the ground. It was all over in less than thirty seconds.

Erik searched the men for a key and freed himself from his handcuffs before the elevator door opened.

Erik strolled down a corridor with no other FBI agents around. The sound of footsteps and a distant hum of conversation revealed that people were headed in his direction. Could it be more FBI agents, or workers? It might be another team coming to pick up the prisoner—him. He had one advantage. They didn't know his face, so he could hide in plain sight. However, once past them, he would need to be quick. Once they get to the elevator and realize what happened, they would lock down the entire terminal. He melted into the crowd, leaving behind the chaos he had created. He took a deep breath and blended into the surroundings, his heart racing and adrenaline pumping through his blood, with all his senses heightened.

There were several exits from Grand Central Terminal, making it easy to escape. He might have had trouble getting out in the twenty-first century, but without hand-held radios in 1940, the agents discovering the mess left in the elevator had no way to contact those watching the exits before he was gone.

Erik emerged amidst throngs of people on the bustling sidewalks and streets swarming with cars and made his way down East 42nd Street. He did not know if he was being chased, but the adrenaline coursing through his veins fueled every stride as he maneuvered through the maze of people on the sidewalk, weaving through cars and pedestrians alike. He slipped effortlessly through the throng, the rhythmic sound of his footsteps echoing along with the cacophony of the city.

At the farm, he was taught there was no shame in retreating because rule one was *to never get caught.* He faced a more powerful enemy, both in weapons and manpower, so he kept moving. Erik's path led him down the bustling East 43rd Street. Risking a glance over his shoulder, he found uniformed police officers and FBI agents struggling through the crowds, hindered by the urban congestion. They looked lost, and likely didn't even have a description of his appearance. Erik turned down West 42nd Street with a swift but unassuming pace, blending into the city as he navigated the grid of asphalt and concrete.

With each step he took, Erik felt more secure with his escape. He adapted to the changing landscape of Bryant Park, keeping a brisk pace to stay ahead of the pursuit. The park might offer a place to hide and catch his breath. He took to the footpaths, searching for any opportunities that lay ahead. He was well past exhausted and hoped he could finally slow down.

The tranquil beauty of Bryant Park offered a place where Erik could momentarily put aside the chase. He slowed as he caught his breath, his chest heaving. On a park bench beneath the verdant canopy, an elderly man sat on a bench as the dappled sunlight passed through the trees, his eyes scanning the pathways as he fed a small flock of pigeons. After emerging from the shadows of the trees, Erik quietly sat down next to him, eager for a chance to rest.

The old man spoke softly but firmly. "Erik, why were you running?"

Erik was startled and stood up.

In response, the man patted the bench. "It's okay, I'm not a threat."

Erik hesitated, then said, "I was just in a hurry."

The old man shook his head. "No, Erik, you were running for a reason."

"How do you know my name?"

The man leaned over so only Erik could hear his words. "I can see past, present, and future simultaneously. My vision warning me of the future."

Erik gave him a sidelong glance.

"War cannot be avoided until the physical cause for its recurrence is removed. Erik, my friend, I understand that time travel has left you in a precarious situation."

Erik was about to ask a question, but the man raised his hand to silence him.

"I have devoted my life to understanding the mysteries of the universe, and I believe I can help you return to 1948."

Erik would have dismissed the man as addled from age, but he seemed to know too much. He decided to trust his gut, even if it meant leaving his fate in the hands of a stranger.

The man pointed at Erik. "You're wondering who I am?" The man lowered his voice to make sure no one else heard him. "I'm Nikola Tesla."

Erik hesitated for a moment before responding, "But how?"

"There are things better left unsaid." Tesla waved a dismissive hand before continuing. "Erik, I have spent a lifetime exploring the mysteries of the universe, delving into realms that most cannot fathom. Time is like a symphony, and I have studied its melodies. I have seen glimpses of the extraordinary, and I believe you possess the potential to restore the timeline. You can align your existence with the precise coordinates of 1948 and return home."

Erik stood up, shaking his head. "You believe I possess the potential to restore the timeline? You are aware I already have, not just once," he held up two fingers, "but twice."

Tesla rose from the bench, stepped toward Erik, and replied, "Indeed, but I need to correct you. The third time was this morning. The fabric of time is fragile, and any alteration can have profound consequences. That is why we must be meticulous in our approach. I will ensure that your presence in 1948 is as unobtrusive as possible, leaving the course of history undisturbed."

Erik noticed a man staring in their direction. Tesla introduced him as George Scherff, his driver and assistant. Deciding to trust the old scientist, Erik followed Tesla to his car. Their shared understanding grew as the shadows lengthened and the distant hum of the city's activity slowed. Once in the car, George proceeded to the New Yorker Hotel, where Tesla was living.

Tesla's eyes held a mixture of intrigue and camaraderie as he glanced at Erik, and he remarked with a faint smile, "You have a knack for finding yourself in extraordinary situations."

Erik's lips twisted into a rueful grin. "It's a gift and a curse."

Tesla's gaze was knowing. "But it's also a testament to your resilience and adaptability."

The journey ahead held both peril and promise, but together, they were determined to navigate the enigma of time and return Erik to the year 1948. However, while they had embarked on a journey that held the promise of unraveling the mysteries of time itself, Erik wasn't yet aware of the significance of their meeting and the challenges that lay ahead.

CHAPTER 21

THEY WILL FIND ME OR KILL ME

"When you live in the shadows, you learn to see in the dark."
— *The Bourne Ultimatum*

Nikola Tesla and Erik huddled together in the dimly lit corner of a secluded restaurant; their faces concealed by shadows. The world was embroiled in the throes of yet another devastating war, but amidst the chaos, these two men harbored a mission of paramount importance that transcended any conflict between nations. The soft chimes of Tesla's pocket watch accented their conversation as they continued their meal. The men shared a general intellectual curiosity and interest in learning new things.

Furthermore, they appreciated the value of culture, history, the sciences, and the arts. Erik noticed, for each topic, Tesla used a soft-spoken and assuring voice to make sure he had Erik's attention. In addition, he would often use poems as illustrations for his stories while using a keen sense of humor. They were not ordinary men; they were driven by an unwavering determination to undertake tasks that most mortals could not even fathom.

Tesla, a brilliant and visionary inventor, had poured every ounce of his being into the creation of a revolutionary technology. The fruits of his labor had culminated in a device of unparalleled power—a time machine. Erik, a seasoned government operative endowed with exceptional skills, had been handpicked for the perilous mission of rectifying the timeline in the Battle of Britain, and along the way stumbled into diverting the cataclysmic destruction of the M42 generators, thus preserving the sanctity of the continuum.

As they savored their dinner, an undercurrent of urgency permeated the air, lending an edge to their conversation. Their discourse revolved around the imminent completion of Tesla's time machine and the pressing matter of Erik's return to 1948.

"We've come a long way, Nikola," Erik replied. "But once I go back to 1948, everything will be as I remembered it." He shook his head. "I really hate traveling in time and fixing the timeline." Tesla nodded gravely. "Indeed, Erik. You have succeeded so mankind can avert disaster. By correcting those mistakes, you have reshaped the future for the better."

"Nikola, time travel is a paradoxical thing. I've had to travel in the past to correct it to avoid a disastrous future. Me being in the present, correcting the timeline becomes the past, so a better future can occur. As with a flash of lightning, it all happens at once. One could say I am a thread in the eye of the needle that keeps the timeline in check."

Tesla nodded. Erik asked about time travel and Tesla explained his solutions simply and quickly, without using complicating mathematical terms. "My theory is if you can create a warp bubble, one can travel vast distances in space rapidly. This is done by first creating the warp bubble, then creating a contraction in space in front of the device and an expansion of space behind. But there's a different way of doing this."

Tesla continued explaining quantum pairing. That he can create two quantum bubbles. One in the point of origin, and one in the distant point to which one wants to travel.

"What is it called... a what again?"

"A quantum bubble." Tesla explained he had that proven quantum pairing, when two molecules move in the same way. If he affected the state of one molecule, he would also affect the state of the other through quantum pairing. Erik nodded, even though he didn't fully understand. Nikola resumed explaining that quantum pairing can happen over vast distances, and whatever happens to one molecule happens to the other.

Nikola took a sip of Dewar's Scotch Whiskey, a wonderful brown fluid which sparkled in many iridescent colors, before he began again. "Now, if you're creating a communication device and you can watch what's happening with those molecules, you've just granted a way of communicating that cannot be intercepted or decoded. But if I can create a quantum bubble in this time and a second quantum bubble in another, the singularity between the two only needs to be a pinprick."

He nodded at Erik to make sure he understood before continuing. "Think of the fabric of the universe being very elastic. Okay?"

"Okay."

"So, this creates a shape like an hourglass. I turn the hourglass this way," He gestured his hands as to symbolize it was vertical, 'going from one point to another.' He pointed as if there was an imaginary hourglass as he pointed to the top and bottom. "As I put pressure on this bubble, the molecules travel through and reform in the second bubble. Now, this works perfectly for traveling distances through space, but it can also be applied to time travel. So, if my quantum bubble is in another time, when I put pressure on the first bubble and push that person into the past, their own time is always going to try to pull them back."

"To 1948?"

Nikola nodded.

"Why?" Erik asked.

"Because nature's always trying to correct the imbalance." His high, broad forehead was deeply lined in concentration as he described his theory. "When we apply pressure, there's a reaction. When we relieve the pressure, there's an opposite reaction. In your case, your neutral state is the future, in 1948. It will always try to pull you back toward 1948 if you travel in the past. If you are in the future, it will always try to pull you toward the past, or your present, okay? "Doesn't matter where you go in quantum pairing, it'll be the same thing. That's why, in my opinion, if you don't get to your original time, in your case 1948, within one hundred and eighty days, you will never be able to get back."

Tesla emphasized that if he squeezed this bubble, Erik's norm would always try to pull him back. He leaned forward to look Erik in the eye and said, "Getting there is the hard part. Getting back is the easy part, unless you go over the one hundred and eighty days. The hard part is controlling how far you returned to neutral." He paused and took another sip. "Have you ever heard of the Phoenix Theory?"

"No."

From under protruding eyebrows Tesla's deep, steel gray, soft, yet piercing eyes seemed to read Erik's innermost thoughts. "Phoenix Theory gives us a mathematical approach. We're determining if you are in a warp field, where you are going. So, if I create a warp field, you're suspended from my current time and space, but you take your normal time and space with you within that bubble. Okay?"

Erik nodded.

"So, Phoenix Theory gives me a mathematical formula to figure out how to move that bubble to where you want to go." As he waxed enthusiastic about fields to conquer and achievements to attain, his face glowed with almost ethereal radiance, and Erik continued to listen, transported from the commonplaces of today to imaginative realms of the future. "You need navigation within time and space, okay? So, within space, you need a point of origin. In addition, you need two points of reference. Say that's up and down, two points of reference, or right and left, and one point of reference as far as distance is concerned."

He finished his drink before continuing. "You also need to reference time. In your case, 1948. I believed in the power of frequencies. For example, if I have a railroad track and I send you a mile down the track to hit the track with a hammer, I will feel it here." Erik nodded. "And you'll feel it there. But the frequency from the impact would be much higher at the point of origin. The frequency I was observing a mile down the track would always be lower. Now, let's replace that. This is the center of the universe."

He placed the saltshaker in the center of the table. "Everything is expanding out from the center of the universe. And now, as things travel farther and farther from that center, their frequency drops. The atoms are not as energetic, they don't vibrate as much, and they don't spend as well. So, even though thirty seconds have passed, our frequency has changed. Our distance from the center of the galaxy has changed our energy, the Earth has moved, and our sun, our entire galaxy, has moved farther away from the center. So, if you're moving into the past, that makes it far more difficult to predict where you need to be because you could materialize in space.

"However, using quantum displacement, the theory I just told you about with the two warp bubbles, right? You can simultaneously disappear here and reappear at my target at the same moment. What this allows is for me to achieve time travel with the singularity, for which I need only to create a pinprick in spacetime. When I met Einstein, he told me the secrets of the universe will never be opened with a sledgehammer, but a single pin prick could do it. That leads me to believe he believed in time travel."

After dinner, George picked them up, and they left the restaurant. The car blended into the busy streets of 1940's New York. Nikola glanced at Erik; his voice full of determination. "Erik, next week will be the time. You'll travel to 1948, and the events you corrected in the timeline, people will never know they transpired. The world will be grateful someday, even if they never know why."

Erik was going home in a week, and he saw Tesla's time machine as a shimmering beacon of hope. Erik was anxious about his return as the hours turned into days. Nikola worked tirelessly to perfect the time machine. Little did they know that their clandestine rendezvous and their audacious endeavor were thrusting the timeline into a maelstrom of uncertainty, and the future hung precariously in the balance.

CHAPTER 22

THE TROUBLE WITH KNOWING

"I could see past, present and future simultaneously."

— Nikola Tesla

Deep in the heart of the North American Aerospace Defense Command, or NORAD, approximately fifty Air Force radar analysts nervously monitoring an inflow of strategic information, stationed at various tracking and communication consoles on the main floor. Some of them focused on the Missile Defense Alarm System, or MIDAS. MIDAS consisted of nine early-warning satellites providing limited notice of Soviet intercontinental ballistic missile launches. For and ICBM launch, there would be twelve minutes from warning to impact. But for a launch from a submarine, there would be only six minutes warning.

Each individual was occupied monitoring a small screen in front of them. Ten large screens overhead showed the world and the world's armed forces. Hovering above the main floor was a balcony, where the NORAD Commander General John K. Gerhart and the Deputy Commander Air Marshal C. Roy Slemon sat. Gerhart had several phones on his console, which connected to different locations and individuals. The most important phone was the red one, which linked Gerhart to the White House to brief the President on the current status of military affairs.

Just above the screens was a display with the numbers one through five in descending order. The current state of defense readiness condition was DEFCON 4, exercise term Double Take, which meant an increased intelligence watch and strengthened security measures.

Gerhart was stunned for a split second, but kept his composure, as he jerked up and focused on one of the screens on the right, representing the Eastern Bloc of the Warsaw Pact countries. At that moment, several symbols extended from East German to Hungary. One of the analysts, whose job is to watch that section, declared on the loud speaker, "We have Soviet troops massing on the border of West Germany and Austria. Confidence is high. I repeat, confidence is high."

Gerhart turned to Slemon. "Alert NATO to increase their force readiness and have SAC ready to mobilize in fifteen minutes." He took a deep breath and declared, "We're at DEFCON 3."

Slemon immediately picked up a phone and made several calls, advising a scramble of all alert aircraft and heightened readiness for ground forces.

Several more symbols lit up throughout East Germany, indicating more troop movements from the Soviet Second and Third Tank Guards and the Soviet First Guards Tank Army. The Soviet Central Group in Czechoslovakia was mobilizing. In addition, the Soviet Northern Group Forces were mobilizing in Poland.

NATO's response was to mobilize the First West German Corps, First Netherlands Corps, First British Corps, First Belgian Corps, and the Sixth West German Mechanized Division.

Slemon explained to Gerhart the Soviets were deploying their troops for a military exercise known as Seven Days to the River

Rhine. It was designed for the Warsaw Pact countries to game out a seven-day nuclear war between NATO and Warsaw Pact forces. In total, the Soviets could muster one hundred and seventy-five divisions of their own with sixty-two satellite divisions. NATO could only muster thirty-five divisions. In addition to striking several key targets in the United States, the Soviets would target several cities in Western Europe.

In the event of World War Three, two 500-kiloton bombs would be dropped on Vienna, while a single 500-kiloton bomb would be dropped on Vicenza, Verona, Padua, and several Italian bases. The goal of Hungary was to capture Vienna as soon as possible. It was planned that nuclear weapons would be used to destroy Stuttgart, Munich, and Nuremberg in West Germany. Afterward, Czechoslovakian and Hungarian forces would occupy those cities. Lastly, Roskilde and Esbjerg would be the first two cities in Denmark to become nuclear targets.

Suddenly, eight red outlines submarines closed on the eastern coast of the United States. They triggered the Sound Surveillance System, a submarine detection system based on passive sonar.

"Eight Soviet nuclear subs have crossed the sonar nets of the eastern coast of the United States." There was a moment of silence as the analysts studied the reports coming in. "Clarification, eight Hotel II class submarines have crossed the sonar nets of the eastern coast of the United States. Confidence is high. I repeat, confidence is high."

"Still think this is just an exercise?" Gerhart asked.

Slemon shook his head and advised Gerhart that the Hotel II class submarine was armed with the D-4 missile system, carrying three R-21 missiles. Each had a two to three-point-five megaton warhead.

Gerhart pinched the bridge of his nose then announced, "Gentlemen, we're at DEFCON 2." Several more symbols lit up, indicating Soviet forces, approximately seven divisions, massing at the Turkish northern border.

Gerhart picked up the red phone, pressed several numbers, and composed himself. "Mr. President, we've got eight nuclear subs closing on the United States' eastern coastline. We have calculated approximately twenty-two Soviet divisions mobilizing on the West German border, twenty-one divisions mobilizing on the Turkish, Iraqi, and Iranian borders, and approximately fifty divisions mobilizing in the Eastern Bloc countries. We're monitoring their subs, and our bombers are on alert. Yes, sir…"

Gerhart's face drained of blood as he turned to Slemon. "Yes, sir… Understood, sir… Yes, sir." He hung up the phone and whispered to Slemon. "The president has authorized me to go to DEF-CON 1 once we get a Soviet launch detection."

Slemon nodded.

An analyst declared over the intercom, "We have a Soviet submarine launch detection, and we have Soviet launch detections from Kozelsk, Derazhnya, Pervomaysk, Tatishchevo, Kapustin Yar, and Kostroma. Repeat, we have a Soviet submarine launch detection, and we have Soviet launch detections from Kozelsk, Derazhnya, Pervomaysk, Tatishchevo, Kapustin Yar, and Kostroma."

Slemon announced so all could hear, "BMEWS has confirmed a massive attack. Missile warning. No malfunction. Confidence is high. This is *not* an exercise."

He turned to face Gerhart. "Sir, MIDAS 2 is tracking three hundred inbound Soviet ICBMs and 24 R-21 missiles. Estimated impact: twenty-three minutes for the ICBMs and six minutes for the R-21s."

Without hesitation, Gerhart declared. "Flush the 52s up and to their assigned targets, give the sub commanders authorization to launch their missiles, and get the boys in the silos authorization to launch their missiles. We are at DEFCON 1."

***

Two missile operators quietly held a conversation in a ten by twenty compartment, isolated from the ground above. They were at their respective launch consoles, twelve feet apart, which were identical to each other.

In front of the operators were control panels with high-frequency transmitters, circuit breakers, and other buttons and switches. One of the most important panels was labeled as *Missile Group Status Board*, which showed the status of ten Atlas D ICBMs tipped with nuclear warheads. Both had a phone that was linked with the Strategic Air Command. In between the consoles, mounted on the wall, was a bright red tin box with bold white stenciled letters that read, *ENTRY RESTRICTED TO MCCC AND DMCCC ON DUTY*, referring to the Missile Combat Crew Commander and the Deputy Missile Combat Crew Commander. Two combination locks sealed the box, with each combination only known by one of the operators. They were one of fifteen squadrons of their missile wing, each controlling ten ICBMs, for a total of one hundred and fifty silos spread out over hundreds of miles of rural countryside, hiding in plain sight.

A message projected through the loudspeaker. "Raven, this is Eagle with a Red Dash Alpha message. Break. Break. Red Dash Alpha."

Both men leaped out of their chairs, retrieved a red three-ring binder labeled *Emergency Action Message Book*, and turned to a page titled *RED DASH ALPHA-EXECUTIVE ORDER*.

The MCCC was alarmed by alert as he grabbed a grease pencil and declared, "Stand by to copy message."

The DMCCC replied. "Standing by."

The message continued an audio transmission of a thirty-five-letter code. "November Oscar Tango Alpha Delta Romeo

India Lima Lima Tango Romeo Alpha Charlie Kilo India November Golf India November Bravo Oscar Uniform November Delta Sierra Oscar Victor India Echo Tango India Charlie Bravo Mike Sierra."

After ensuring the code matched, the operators proceeded to a red safe containing the documents for the missile launch.

"Stand by to authenticate," the MCCC said in a commanding tone.

"I agree with authentication also, sir," the DMCCC acknowledged.

On the red safe were several paper envelopes with two letters written on them. Embedded within the thirty-five-letter code that was sent to the field by HQ was a seven-letter subcode. The first two letters of the sub-code indicated which envelope had to be opened. Enclosed was a piece of plastic, called a "cookie", with five letters written on it. The missile operators authenticated the launch order by matching the cookie to the remaining five digits in the sub-code. The message also included a six-letter code which enabled the missiles to be launched once the operators received confirmation.

They entered the code into another system, opening butterfly valves on the oxidizer lines of the ICBMs' engines. After the missiles were unlocked, they could be launched at their assigned targets. The message also included instructions to launch immediately.

"Enter launch code," the MCCC ordered.

"Entering launch code," The DMCCC replied as he punched the keys on the keyboard.

Within seconds, the loudspeaker declared, "Launch order confirmed. Target selection: complete. Time on target sequence: complete. Yield selection: complete. Begin countdown. T-minus sixty."

In order to launch, the two operators inserted their respective keys into their control panels into a slot marked *OFF, SET, LAUNCH.*

"On my mark, rotate launch keys to Set," the MCCC ordered. Within two seconds of each other, the keys had to be turned and held for five seconds before they had to be turned again.

"Roger."

"Three… two… one…mark."

"T-minus fifty." Every ten seconds, the countdown was announced to the missile operators. "T-minus forty… T-minus thirty… T-minus twenty"

"On my mark…rotate launch keys to Launch."

"Roger."

The speaker began counting down by the second, "T-minus ten… T-minus nine… T-minus eight… T-minus seven… T-minus six… T-minus five… T-minus four… T-minus three… T-minus two… T-minus one… Launch!"

The operators turned their keys, and the launch sequence of their fifteen missiles began. The ICBMs' batteries charged up completely, then the missiles disconnected themselves from their power sources within the silos. As the silo doors opened, an alarm sounded inside the control room. The guidance system of the ICBMs configured to control the missiles and input all data necessary to guide them to their targets. In moments, the main engines ignited, filling the bottoms of the silos with roaring flames. Pyrotechnic bolts released the supports holding the ICBMs in place, and the metal behemoths lurched free, soaring into the skies, the trails of smoke they left behind heralding the coming apocalypse.

The missile operators, like everyone else on the planet, waited in silence for whatever was to come next. For those above ground, the end didn't come in the form of loud explosions, nor even millions of voices whimpering, or even terror. It was like life was suddenly silenced.

***

Erik took a deep breath and stared with fascinated horror as he stared at Tesla. "This isn't real."

Tesla calmly stared back and replied, "Let me warn you now: What you saw could be a prediction of the future, but not at all forthcoming."

"Forthcoming?"

Tesla nodded. "I can see past, present, and future simultaneously, and I might go on to add that this vision is serving as a warning of the future."

Erik stepped out of the chamber. Shadows engulfed him as he tried to calm his nerves.

Tesla motioned him to come closer.

"I know the future," Erik said, pointing back at the temporal chamber. "I can tell you for certain, that was not it. That was not it!"

Tesla calmly replied, "From this vision, it seems man has destroyed the world. Those who survived this tragic event are but shadows and dust." Tesla looked gloomy and he tilted his head down. "Shadows and dust."

"But this can't be," Erik argued. "We came close, but President Kennedy brought us through one crisis after another. We made it through. This never happened."

Tesla gave a blank stare. "Who?"

"John F. Kennedy? He was elected in 1960." Erik waited for a response, but his argument fell on deaf ears.

Tesla shook his head. "When I looked into the future before, I saw a man named Richard Nixon as president in 1960. I also saw a small group of islands, an untouched paradise, with deserted white-sand beaches and beautiful sunsets. The islands were laden with coral reefs, surrounded by clear water, and were teeming with wildlife, both above and below the surface. Then I heard several deep roars, one after another, as motors stuttered into life, followed by a huge belch of thick, black smoke from exhaust pipes. I saw a group of olive-green boats. They were small and fast, and appeared to be scouting. They were armed with torpedoes and machine guns. There was a man on one of the boats who seemed like he had an important future, but that future would not come to pass."

Erik shook his head and breathed out a long, frustrated breath. "Dammit," he muttered. "One mission. I agreed to one mission. I feel like I'm chasing my own tail. Every time I fix something, there's a new problem. Are you telling me there's another break in the timeline I have to fix?"

"Yes, there is. You need to put right what went wrong, and once the timeline is corrected, you will be able to go home."

"I don't even know where that place is or what I would be doing."

"Wait," Tesla urged as he explored the memory of his vision. "What seemed like a grain of sand grew larger over time. It was eight black circles with bold-black lettering. *Todd City.*"

It took a minute for Erik to rack his brain for anything and everything that dealt with Todd City. Then, a flood of information consumed him, and he shook his head in disbelief.

Tesla cupped Erik's shoulder to offer some kind of support. "What is Todd City? Does it have to deal with this man named Kennedy?"

Erik nodded. "Kennedy was stationed there, in the Solomon Islands. He was a lieutenant in the US Navy, assigned to PT 109, one of the boats you mentioned, most likely."

Erik rubbed his chin as he closed his eyes and contemplated. He pointed at Tesla. "You said you could see past, present, and future simultaneously, correct?"

Tesla nodded.

Erik didn't understand that, but it was all he had to go on. "I know for a fact he didn't die in combat, so they must have sent someone back to kill him."

"They?"

"Somebody. I don't know who." Erik dismissed the issue with a wave of his hand and moved on. "Are you able to speak to FDR directly?"

Tesla nodded.

"Tell him you need a khaki tropical uniform with the rank of lieutenant commander and the tan shoes that go with khakis." Tesla nodded as George wrote down Erik's measurements.

They sat down, Erik rubbing his fingers through his hair. Tesla asked, "Erik, is there someone special back where you come from?"

Erik nodded.

"You miss her?"

"Yes, she's what has kept me going through all this. But for now, I have to focus on the task at hand."

"That must be hard," George said.

Tilting his head up, Erik replied, "It is. Trust me, this is not the first time I've had to do something like this." Erik took a long, slow breath. "The first time I traveled in time, I had to prevent the Nazis from using rockets armed with atomic warheads."

"When was that?" George asked.

"1944." Erik paused for a moment, remembering that year. "On our way back, we stopped at London and I took my wife's picture." Erik pulled out an old, torn, and faded picture of Jamie. As he stared at it, he thought out loud, "She was young there, like she is now. She wasn't smiling… just a little sad… I always wondered what she was thinking at that second." Erik closed his eyes and imagined reaching toward her. His fingertips tracing the contour of her chin, her cheeks, then combing his fingers through her hair.

Erik opened his eyes and shook his head to clear the thought. He stared into their eyes and stated, "The future is not set. There is a way to change it, and I will stop them. They attempt to alter history for their own ends, and they think no one can stop them." Erik stood up. "Not again! I must fix things, or the future I know will never exist."

Tesla bobbed his head as if he were deep in thought. Then he cupped both of Erik's shoulders and stared at him. "It just might work. All I need is five days, and I will send you forward in time."

"But to when?" Erik asked.

Tesla closed his eyes, again searching his memory. He then pointed to George and made a scribbling motion. "August first, 1943."

George nodded as he noted the date.

Erik looked at Tesla. "How will I get back to 1948?"

Tesla motioned for Erik to walk with him, "I will get you back." Tesla turned to George, "Remember his face. This is the man who was searching for a way back home, but he became a hero for the future."

Erik just nodded as Tesla continued, "Time for dinner, and I want you to meet a good friend of mine. His name is Samuel Clemens." Erik was speechless as he turned to George, who mouthed, *He's dead.* Tesla continued, "Samuel is a great writer."

Erik considered the veritable army of scientists and technicians, with the resources of the entire US government, it took to send him back in time from 2008. He found himself putting his faith in a man who thought Mark Twain was still alive, with a plan based on *visions* the man had of the future. If Erik hadn't seen a vision with the strange machine, he'd write the man off as a lunatic and find another way home. But he had. Someone once said the difference between genius and insanity is success and failure. Erik had five days to wait before he found out which applied to this self-proclaimed Nikola Tesla.

CHAPTER 23

WAKE UP. EAT. REPEAT.

"The only way to outrun your past is to confront it head-on."
— *The Bourne Ultimatum*

Every day, Tesla was busy working. He explained all the science behind his machine, But Erik didn't understand it. Instead, he spent the last five days focused on preparing to go back in time and planning a way to keep Kennedy alive. Sometimes time travel felt like he stole a ride on a passing star. He knew where he was going though, and what to expect. When he stepped into the chamber, the walls would emit that same electronic, bee-like humming which grew louder by the second. Then a blinding, bluish-white light would appear as he was transported back through years of light. Future and past would merge into one.

"Sir, here is your breakfast, and another orange juice," the server said in a gentle voice, breaking Erik from his thoughts and back into the present.

Kellogg's Diner was filled with people, locals mainly, since it was the neighborhood's staple since 1929. The entire place was busy with activity, which Erik didn't mind, but he wasn't able to get a corner table because it was blocked off for somebody, with bodyguards preventing anyone from going back there and to keep prying eyes from looking. However, he felt pretty secure, because it appeared to be a recent high school graduate talking about easily passing the entrance exam to the United States Naval Academy and wanting to become a pilot. But only being sixteen, he was too young to enter that year. Thus, the Navy sent him to the Admiral Farragut Academy, a prep school for the Naval Academy.

While eating, Erik glanced up as George barged through the front door, his eyes dancing around the room to find him. He advised the hostess who he was looking for as he pointed and waved in Erik's direction. George detached himself, strolled over, and slid into the booth, eying Erik's bacon.

As George reached for a piece of bacon, Erik squinted and said in a deep, menacing voice, "Really?" He turned his fork in a stabbing position, and George withdrew his hand to his side of the table.

"Mr. Tesla has everything ready." George leaned forward, "I cannot believe you are going to be time traveling."

Erik saw and felt George's glow of admiration for him and his majestic achievement. He took a deep breath, paused, and looked up. Erik peered sharply, resentfully, into the man's innocent, naive eyes and said very quietly, "We met for a reason. I just don't want to share that reason with everyone else."

At that moment, a man in a three-piece suit walked by. Erik took his last bite and bowed his head, clearing his mind of all regrets. He prepared himself for what was about to happen or could happen and focused his attention on the preserving the timeline… again. He settled himself more comfortably into the bench, rested his hands on the table, and mumbled to himself.

"Erik?" George asked as he gave Erik an inquisitive glance. "What are you doing?"

Erik slowly exhaled as he replied, "Praying."

"Praying?" Erik nodded as George asked for an explanation.

"I'm reciting the Shepard's Prayer." Erik paused for a moment. "Dear Lord, please don't let me fuck up."

"You call that a prayer?"

"Yep."

Before Erik could grab his check and leave, a young man sitting behind him got his attention. "Sir, I just wanted to say that's an interesting prayer." An older man across from him, presumably his father, rolled his eyes as if to say he was sorry.

Erik motioned that it was okay. He had no intention of becoming emotionally involved with any person from the past who he might never see again.

"Sir, you said the prayer is called the Shepard's Prayer?"

Erik nodded.

"That's my last name. Alan Bartlett Shepard Jr."

Erik put two and two together. In front of him was a young man who was going to be one of the first seven astronauts. Erik extended his hand to shake hands with Alan.

"Nice to meet you, sir."

Erik grinned. "Alan, it was a pleasure meeting you." He pointed to make his next point. "You made a good choice by joining the Navy and wanting to become a pilot. I think you will do great. Oh, one other thing, if…" Erik leaned closer and whispered, "When you become a pilot and some gentleman asks you about being an astronaut…"

"What's an astronaut?" Alan asked.

"It's like a pilot on steroids," Erik explained. "They will tell you it's a hazardous undertaking. In fact, they will say it's extremely hazardous. Do you know what you should say?"

"Yes?"

Erik nodded.

"Count me in," Alan grinned.

"Keep what I said to you under your hat, no matter who it is."

"Including my father?"

Erik nodded and finished by saying. "Lastly, use the Shepard's Prayer when you don't want to mess up on a critical job. Trust me, it's a great prayer." Both Erik and Alan exchanged their goodbyes.

After paying for the check, George advised Erik they were heading back to Tesla's Lab in Shoreham, New York. On the way out, Erik stared out the window, upward at the buildings of the city and his surroundings. He closed his eyes and envisioned a city laying desolated as silence drifted through the streets. Abandoned cars, still bumper to bumper, as they were left before a nuclear war. Their weathered rusty frames caging skeletons of their passengers. That city would be like so many other cities across the nation and other continents, with tens of thousands of people killed and the stench of death wafting within the ruins.

Those who survived the nightmare would only have their hope, which would be all but bleak. There would have been no time for evacuation before the ICBMs struck. The world would be left in a dreary, deserted state, with disorder that could be seen everywhere. Erik could only imagine, from the skies, all the devastation that would be wrought. If he survived that nuclear holocaust, he would be wandering alone in the city, drifting from street to empty street, reminiscing of the dead and wondering why he was left alive while the city, like so many others, were lying in state in a black shroud.

"You awake?" George asked as he elbowed Erik gently.

Erik nodded, and his eyes adjusted to his surroundings. It was hard to believe he was there five days earlier, seeing what the future could be. There were between five to six weathered brick buildings scattered on Tesla's property of two hundred acres, containing Tesla's other experiments. As before, George turned the wheel and headed to 46 East Houston Street, which was the address of the main building of several thousand square feet. George told Erik the famous architect Stanford White, who was friends with Tesla, designed the lab building made of red brick.

As before, the Tesla Tower was an intimidating sight. It stood 187 feet tall, made from wood pillars. Atop the tower perched a fifty-five-ton dome made from a conductive metal, with the diameter of sixty-seven and a half feet. Most people who saw it described it as a giant mushroom. However, what Erik, like others, didn't know was that beneath it stretched an iron root system that penetrated more than three-hundred feet into the Earth's crust.

Upon entering, Erik was welcomed by Dorothy Skerrit, one of Tesla's secretaries, who advised Erik that Tesla was waiting for them in the basement. George led the way through the laboratory, which had an Italian Renaissance style. Intricate mechanical mechanisms, glass blowing equipment, and other strange machines cluttered the tables. One went off as Erik walked by, and he had a difficult time trying to turn the thing off. George motioned for him not to bother.

They passed a complete machine shop, including eight lathes, X-ray devices, and many varieties of Tesla's high frequency coils. Erik slowed down as George pointed out a radio-controlled boat within an exhibit case with at least a thousand bulbs and tubes. George informed Erik there was also an instrument room, electrical generators and transformers, a library, and Tesla's office.

Getting in the elevator leading to the lower chamber, George struck up a conversation. "I have your uniform fitted and pressed for you."

Erik nodded in appreciation.

"Do you think you can save this person named Kennedy?"

Erik shrugged. "It's true, you know. I travel back in time to preserve the timeline. However, if I don't, the world is going be in the biggest shit storm anyone has seen."

"I don't want to add more pressure here, but am sure you are the best person on the planet to handle this situation."

Stepping out of the elevator, Erik turned to George. "You better believe it."

George was shocked by Erik's boldness.

"I was and still am a CIA Paramilitary Operations Officer, and the attitude comes with the job. Where is the uniform?"

George handed the uniform over and waited for Erik to change. Afterward, they continued down several hallways, as Erik expressed, "It seems like I always have to clean up people's messes when it comes to the past." They came upon an iron door, and beyond that, another room.

The space, like a vast catacomb, so immense it swallowed one whole from the mere size. Erik approximated it was nearly two stories tall, two hundred yards long, and fifty yards across. The room was carved out of the bedrock of the Earth's crust. There was enough light to see where to walk, while other areas were in darkness. Erik noticed long, rubber-like cylinders that were thick as tree trunks with supports holding them down, branching out like the root system of an oak tree. The cylinders merged into a single focal point as they approached a large compartment which looked like an oversized phone booth. That had a single black door in the center of it. It was the entrance to the time machine.

"This still reminds me of a dream," Erik stated.

Hovering over a control panel, Tesla lifted his head and replied, "It is not a dream. It is a simple feat of scientific electrical engineering, only expensive… Blind, faint-hearted, doubting world."

Then, he looked down at the control panel as he was thinking out loud. "Coils are at peak and levels are one hundred percent." Tesla chuckled, "We may dim half the lights in New York City and New Jersey." He walked from around the control panel and approached Erik. "I'm ready." With a grin, he continued, "Erik, are you ready?"

Erik nodded.

"There is one other thing I forgot to bring up." Tesla picked up a rubber band, placed each end around his index fingers, and began to stretch it as he explained. "Every time you travel back in time, you are very elastic. When you go to another place in time, you create pressure from your own time, 1948, trying to pull you back. Because nature is trying to correct the unbalance, two things may happen. One, you make it there with no problem. Or, you could end up like hamburger meat."

Erik's expression went blank.

"Don't worry. I don't see that happening."

Erik took a deep sigh and replied, "Why am I the only person doing this?" Erik stared at Tesla. "I wish I didn't know about any of this, or Project Pegasus. I wish I never joined the agency. I was like everybody else in the world. The world would just be over, and there would be no time to be sorry about anything. Oh, Jesus!"

"Erik, it's a huge burden for anyone to bear. But you were sent here for a reason, and that secret is something you still have to find." Erik tried to get a word in, but Tesla kept on talking. "I have to believe that there have been mysteries from the beginning of time." He pointed at Erik's chest. "There are answers you and I are not wise enough to see." Then Tesla pointed to the sky, "But, someone else is."

They embraced. Erik stepped into the machine, and that was the last time they saw each other.

CHAPTER 24

TOMORROWS START HERE

"The scientific man does not aim at an immediate result. He does not expect that his advanced ideas will be readily taken up. His work is like that of the planter—or the future. His duty is to lay the foundation for those who are to come, and point the way."
—Nikola Tesla

RENDOVA ISLAND, SOLOMON ISLANDS, SOUTH PACIFIC, 1 AUGUST 1943

As the nightmare started, it took a turn to a weird beginning. Erik took a quick glance around and was amazed at what he saw. The ground, a concaved circular shape, was blackened. It was three feet deep and ten feet wide. Either Erik was in a large bomb crater or Tesla's machine made one on the Earth's surface. This was Erik's third time traveling in time, and he thought to himself that, given enough time, he could get used to anything, even correcting the timeline… again. Once again, Erik found himself in a lonely place where his emotions were under strain, but all he had to do was relax, trust in his abilities, and focus on the mission.

He climbed the wall of the crater and stopped at the edge, then peeked around. Not a soul was around. He heard people speaking English and let out a deep sigh of relief as he climbed out and dusted himself off. The humidity was as thick as the London fog, which made the temperature seem hotter than it was, and heat engulfed him as if he were in a sauna. There was a slight breeze in the air, with a hint of salt from the ocean. Erik tilted his head up at a deep blue sky filled with dozens of white, puffy, cotton-like cumulus clouds. He started walking, and as his eyes adjusted to his surroundings, everything came into focus.

Half a dozen PT boats were anchored along the shore, and a few were tied lengthways on a manmade pier, with another three boats anchored in the middle of the harbor. Their crews carried on their duties, loading, and unloading provisions and ammunition. The gunner mates were oiling and making adjustments to their machineguns, located on the starboard sides. Another machine gun was located at the sterns of the boats, and there was also a twenty-millimeter gun. Erik's eyes widen as he inhaled the strong, thick smell of diesel fuel, as he observed several of the boats being refueled. It wasn't a U-boat bunker, but it resembled one.

Erik paused for a moment as he observed one crew making last-minute adjustments as they secured a thirty-seven-millimeter anti-tank gun to the foredeck of one of the boats. He saw a young lieutenant crossing the gangway to address one of his crew. "Mr. Thom, make sure that gun is secure before we leave. I want to use it on the barges tonight."

"Aye aye, skipper."

Then, Erik's eyes focused on three bold, white numbers. It read *109*. The young, prideful lieutenant, who strolled like a man in a park without a care or worry, approached. Erik recognized John Kennedy. When close enough to recognize Erik's rank, John saluted him. Erik returned the gesture.

"Good afternoon, sir."

Erik nodded.

John looked over his shoulder at the anti-tank gun. "Sir, I know it's not regulation," he chose his next words carefully, "but I figured since the Army wasn't going to use it, I could put it to good use."

"Improvise, adapt, and overcome," Erik replied.

"Excuse me, sir?" John tilted his head, trying to comprehend what he said.

"Something I learned when I was in training."

Like a lightbulb going off above John's head, he gestured he understood.

"Lieutenant, can you point me in the direction of Commander Warfield's office?"

"Yes, sir." John motioned Erik to follow. "I'm on my way to the hospital, and we'll walk right by it." He extended his hand. "I'm John Kennedy."

Erik shook his hand. "Nice to meet you, Lieutenant Kennedy. I'm Lieutenant Commander Erik Foge."

"Sir, when did you get in?"

"Lieutenant Kennedy, I just got here." John looked baffled, because he never saw a boat pull up.

"I'm in Naval Intelligence. We don't make grand entrances. We just appear."

John nodded, yet still confused, but shrugged it off. "Sir, you are lucky you didn't come earlier."

Erik raised a curious eyebrow.

"In late June and early July, the 24th Naval Construction Battalion began building RON 9's base force." Like a tour guide, John used casual hand gestures as they walked. "They erected some huts and tents and a temporary pier, which you just saw, and an administrative office, which is where you are going to. In addition, they built a supply and minimal repair facilities."

Erik nodded as he observed and studied everyone who came into his field of vision.

John continued. "Sir, the real headache came when the boats

needed any major repairs or even torpedo reloading." He shook his head in disbelief as he explained. "We would have to go back to the base near Guadalcanal at Tulagi. Sir, that's a four-hundred-mile round trip."

Erik nodded as he glanced up to eight white-painted oil drum heads suspended between two palm trees with rope, with bold-black capital letters that read, *Todd City*.

John pointed to the structure where Commander Warfield's office was located. "Sir, it was a pleasure meeting and talking to you." Then, he snapped a salute.

"You too, Lieutenant Kennedy."

Erik strolled into the structure made of plywood, bamboo, and screening with a palm frond roof. He was greeted by an enlisted man, a radio operator who occupied one side of the room.

"Sir, how can I help you?"

Erik acknowledged him and stepped closer. "I'm Lieutenant Commander Foge, from HQ, and I have an urgent message for Commander Warfield." Erik emphasized these last words. "I would like to express that it is urgent I see the commander."

"One minute, sir." The enlisted men strolled into the office, and the men talked in a half whisper. Warfield glanced at Erik a few times. The enlisted man then approached Erik. "Sir, Commander Warfield will see you now."

They exchanged salutes and Warfield gestured for him to take a seat. "How can I help you?" He eyed Erik up and down as he leaned back in his chair. Then Warfield leaned forward as his eyes scrutinized Erik. "Who are you?"

"Lieutenant Commander Erik Foge, from Naval Intelligence."

Warfield gave an enigmatic expression as he steepled his fingers. "When did you come in?"

Erik knew when it came to situations like that, he had to give false information. "I just arrived." He also knew he would have to provide actual intelligence, which was why he came prepared. He pulled out a message that would have been sent and placed it on Warfield's desk.

DATE/TIME GROUP 312356
FROM: CTF 31
TO (ACTION) COMMTBROM (RENDOVE) APC 28:1
MAR RD REG
TO (INFO) COMSOPAC CTG 31.2 ATFC SOPAC
MOST SECRET

INDICATIONS EXPRESS MAY RUN TONIGHT ONE DASH TWO (1-2) AUGUST X ALSO HEAVY BARGE TRAFFIC RO BAIROKO OR SUNDAY IN-LET X WARFIELD OPERATE MAXIMUM NUMBER PETER TARES (PT) IN AREA BAKER (B) X KELLY OPERATE ALL AVAILABLE PETER TARES (PT) IN KULA GULF SOUTH OF LINE BAMBARDI DASH RICE X BURKE WITH SIX (6) DESTROYERS GOES UP SLOT ARRIVING NORTH OF KOLOMBANGA-RA AT ZERO ZERO THIRTY LOVE (003L) AUGUST SECOND (2ND) X IF KELLYS BOATS FORCED RE-TIRE TO LEVER DURING NIGHT ROUTE THEM CLOSE IN NEW GEORGIA SHORE X JAP AIR OUT TO GET PETER TARES (PT) X WARFIELD KELLY EACH ACKNOWLEDGE AND ADVISE NUMBER OF BOATS THEY WILL OPERATE TONIGHT X RICE ACKNOWLEDGE[5]

Warfield gave Erik a look of uneasy puzzlement as he glanced over the top of the paper. "What is this?"

"Your orders for tonight." Erik was using a shot-gunning

---

5. Dovan, Robert J. (1961). PT 109 John F.Kennedy in WW II. 78-79

technique which mind readers often used. He was going to throw a bunch of information at Warfield and watch his reaction, then make it so he couldn't say no. "There will be three to four destroyers headed to Vila. If our sources are correct, they are due there at midnight to put nine hundred men and supplies ashore." Erik peered into Warfield's eyes as if he were touching his soul. "Headquarters is expecting your reply by fifteen hundred hours." Warfield was about to reply, but Erik raised his hand. "We believe the Japs might be able to intercept our communication. When you send your message, it needs to be cryptic." He looked coldly into Warfield's eyes. "And don't mention I'm here, or our surprise attack will fail."

Warfield's facial muscles twitched nervously as he swallowed a lump in his throat.

"Do we have an understanding, commander?"

Warfield nodded.

Erik leaned back in his chair and rubbed his chin. "I need to go out on one of your boats tonight as an observer."

"Lieutenant Brantingham is one of my best officers. I will make it happen."

"I would prefer going out with a junior officer. I met a young lieutenant on my way here. His name was," Erik paused to sell the act, "Lieutenant Kennedy."

"Lieutenant Kennedy has not been here that long, but I have to admit he was able to fix up the 109 in a week. That was impressive work."

Erik nodded in agreement.

"Would you like to consider another skipper?"

Erik gave a deadpan look and Warfield dispatched one of the ensigns to get Kennedy.

"He will do, and he mentioned he was going to the hospital. You might check there first."

Warfield and Erik continued their conversation, talking of

missing home and their wives. The screen door creaked open and smacked closed with a cracking sound. They both heard a calm, thick Harvard accent as the ensign advised the lieutenant to go in.

Erik got up and turned to face John as Warfield made the introductions. "Lieutenant Kennedy, this is Lieutenant Commander Foge, from Naval Intelligence. He will be an observer on your boat."

"Yes, sir."

Erik stared at him with complete apathy.

John looked at Erik. "Sir, I wasn't expecting this."

"Neither was I, until now," Warfield explained.

Erik addressed Kennedy in an authoritarian tone. "It's called orders. Lieutenant Kennedy, you don't have a say in the matter, and this is non-negotiable." He paused for a moment and asked, "Are we clear?"

John snapped a salute as he faced Erik. "Yes, sir."

Warfield stood up, dismissed both of them, and headed to the radio operator to reply to the order that Erik gave him.

John turned to Erik. "Sir, may I speak freely?"

Erik nodded.

"My men are superstitious. They believe it's bad luck if we have too many men on board."

Erik stopped and faced John. "Lieutenant Kennedy, are you superstitious?"

It appeared he didn't want to respond.

"Lieutenant, answer me."

John shook his head.

"Are you sure?"

"Yes, sir."

Even though Erik was not superstitious, he knew most Navy men were, and he had to show he was like the others. "When you go into battle, you need to know that things could go wrong, and anything could happen to you."

The color drained from John's face. "Lieutenant Kennedy, this is war. The Japs will not cooperate or be forgiving. If you hesitate, everything is going to go south for you and your crew." Erik motioned John to walk with him. John listened with rapt attention, as if he were making mental notes every time Erik spoke.

"So, when the shit hits the fan, you think, 'This is it.'" Kennedy nodded, but his eyes widened as Erik pointed his finger at him. "You'll have two choices. Either you accept death or you work to survive."

Kennedy butted in. "Sir, it sounds like you are talking from experience."

Erik nodded.

"Sir, can you share a story when you had to experience that?"

Erik shook his head.

"Sir, why not?"

Erik glanced at him as if to say the conversation was over. "I was in Europe during the blitz. That's all I can say." He then motioned to John to continue walking to the boat, picking up where he left off. "You must encourage yourself and or your crew to work for survival. Weigh out the pros and cons, but remain focused and have a positive mental attitude. You, as the skipper of your boat, need to solve one problem at a time. Then you solve the next problem, and so on." Erik stopped and faced John with a grin and an elaborate hand gesture. "When you solve enough problems, you and your crew get to go home."

"Sir, I don't know what you have been through, but thank you for your words of encouragement."

Men yelling Condition Red and the moaning of the air-raid siren drifting through the island broke the calm. Japanese bombers approached, engines roaring and their bombs whistling downward to their targets. Erik and John ran, but the loose sand made it hard to get traction and slowed them down. Men scrambled in different directions like pool balls being hit by a cue ball. The anti-aircraft crews prepared to fire their batteries. The bombs turned every tree and structure into a mass of flames and debris. Men clawed out of the man-made ditches and ran for shelter. Erik followed John as he ran toward his boat, feeling he was being toyed with, like an ant trying to avoid being stepped on by a man's boot.

Once the pier was near, Erik felt he was on the verge of safety. The men on the boats were scrambling to get them launched as others were yelling aircraft descriptions and preparing their anti-aircraft weapons to fire. Then, a near-deafening explosion erupted in orange flames, and thick, black, choking smoke spewed from PT 164 and PT 117. Erik peered upward and saw two dive-bombers making their attack approach, skimming just above the ocean like pelicans.

One of the crews hit its target, and the dive-bomber burst into flames, leaving a trail of black smoke from one of its engines. The pilot tried hopelessly to pull his aircraft out of the deadly crash. As Erik and John jumped on board, the dive-bomber smashed into the ocean within several feet of the pier. A massive wave, tall like a tree, rose above and crashed on the deck of PT 109. The boat's machine guns repeatedly burped, spewing a hail of shells at the other aircraft.

John scrambled to the cockpit and thrust the boat in high gear as he yelled, "Cast off!" Suddenly, PT 109 throttled off, and with a deafening roar and whoosh of spray, it swung about and drove at full speed toward the open ocean.

Erik struggled to stand and walk along the starboard side. One of the gunner's mates, trying to unjam a gun, repeatedly yelled, "Clear that gun! Get down, you two!"

Erik dropped to the deck beside the starboard torpedo tube. A

Japanese Zero approached just above the ocean with its machine guns blazing, and splashes of bullets penetrated the water, inching toward the boat. Erik felt the boat zigzagging through the chaos. The water was a conflagration of boats as the other skippers attempted to do the same thing. Zeros flew above them, and dive bombers continued their attack.

As fast as they came, the planes broke off, and the attack was over in twenty minutes.

Erik got to his feet and braced himself as he approached John.

Somebody cupped his shoulder from behind. "Sir, are you okay?"

Erik nodded.

The sailor faced John. "Skipper, it looks like the Japs are flying away."

John picked up his binoculars. "Yes, they are." He lowered them. "It appears they are flying to the northwest." John turned to the other man, who could be his XO. "Damage report?"

"We have taken no damage, and the hull is intact." He turned to face one of the machineguns. "One of Marney's fifty-calibers got jammed in the attack, but he's fixing it now." John turned to Erik. "Sir, this is my executive officer, Ensign Leonard Thom."

Leonard and Erik exchanged salutes.

"Mr. Thom, this is Lieutenant Commander Erik Foge, from Naval Intelligence."

"Sir, we see a lot of action out here." Lenny faced Erik as he adjusted his cap. "Sir, I'm sure you don't see much action since you are probably stationed in headquarters most of the time." "Mr. Thom—"

Lenny cut in and asked Erik to address him as Lenny.

"Mr. Thom," Erik gave a cold stare into his eyes and uttered in a calm, firm voice, "I actually have seen more action than anyone of this boat or the flotilla."

Lenny looked like he was a deer facing oncoming headlights. Then he turned to John, who was also speechless, and back at Erik. "Sir, did you say more?"

Erik nodded.

"Sir, you mean like top-secret missions behind enemy lines?"

John subtlety shook his head at Lenny to stop with the questions.

However, Lenny was desperate for information, and he continued, trying to fill in the blanks to sound educated.

However, Erik gave a blank, emotionless stare and walked away.

"Lenny, you went too far." Lenny tried to get a word in, but John raised his hand. "Lieutenant Commander Foge is going to be an observer on our boat, and I don't know what it is about him." John paused and pondered for a moment. "When I was walking with him a few minutes ago, he was insightful. That five-minute conversation with him showed me he could find a problem, take it apart, and fix it. Not only that, he was in Europe during the blitz."

Lenny pointed in Erik's direction. "What is he doing there?"

John shrugged.

Lenny continued. "I never heard of anyone being in both theaters of war."

John raised his hand to advise Lenny to lower his voice. "Go back to your duties. Let me see what I can find out."

John, like the other skippers, brought his boat in. Erik stood at the bow and took slow, deep breaths. Every time he traveled through time to correct the timeline, it was a lot like going on a blind date. Erik knew his objective, but he never knew what the situation would be. Posing as an intelligence officer, he knew people will act a certain way, as Lenny did. Still, Erik would be open to new friends and new challenges—like the food—and the worse part, new unseen enemies. Once again, he was dealing with an enemy he did not know. They could be from ONE or the Phoenix Group, and they will be very resourceful and trained in martial arts. However, Erik had one advantage: they wouldn't know about his presence. To describe that type of assassin would be like the Antlion. It waited patiently, hiding in plain sight, waiting for its target. Once the target was in striking distance, it launched its attack. After that, it disappeared, never to be seen again.

Erik's senses were raised as he heard creaking wood slowly growing louder as an individual neared. "What is it, Mr. Thom?"

Lenny was caught speechless as Erik turned to face him.

"Well, lieutenant?"

"Sir, I would like to apologize for my behavior."

Erik nodded.

"Sir, may I speak freely?"

Erik nodded again.

"Sir, I always wondered what it is like to work for Naval Intelligence." He gathered his thoughts as he chuckled a little. "I bet you have an interesting job, and—"

"Mr. Thom, don't worry about it. My wife was the same way when she learned what I did for a living. So, maybe I should thank you." Erik knew he needed to convince Lenny to work with him. It was always a good idea to offer a token of friendship and show they were in it together.

"Sir, for what?"

"Making me remember what I'm doing."

Lenny tilted his head, trying to comprehend what Erik was saying.

"Striving to put right what once went wrong and hoping one day I can go home."

Lenny smiled. "Sir, you have an interesting way of saying things."

After docking the boat, John walked up toward Erik and

Lenny and motioned that he would like them to accompany him as the crew prepared the boat for action. They walked on the deck as the crews of the other boats prepared them for a patrol. The skippers and XOs were headed in the same direction as John.

"John," a voice declared as a man approached him with a smile and a hand extended. "How are you?"

"Good. When did you get here?"

"A few days ago." The man turned to Lenny and shook his hand. "Lenny, welcome to your new home."

"Thank you, sir."

Then he faced Erik and snapped a salute. "Sir, I'm Lieutenant Cluster. Nice to meet you." He extended a handshake. "Commander Warfield advised me that your presence is requested. He's waiting for you in operations." He faced Lenny and John. "Your presence is also requested."

"What's up?" John asked as everyone followed Cluster to a jeep and climbed in.

"Briefing. Something big, I think." He turned to John as he drove. "John, you are going to be assigned to Brantingham's group for the time being."

"Squadron commander?"

Cluster nodded. "A damn good one. One of the best we have." He parked the jeep. "This way, gentlemen." Erik and the others followed Cluster to a structure similar to Warfield's office. "This is it." Cluster turned to face John. "I'm going to be leaving for a special assignment. I will see you in a few days. Good luck." Then he turned to face Erik, saluted him, and went on his wayImmediately entering operations, they removed their caps and took their seats with the other skippers and XOs. Warfield glanced at Erik and motioned for him to join him in front, near an enlarged map of several islands.

"We have fifteen boats available for tonight," Warfield stated as he looked around to make sure everyone was present.

The room went quiet as he announced, "I received a message from Lieutenant Commander Foge, from Naval Intelligence." He nodded in Erik's direction as everyone faced forward.

Erik glanced around the room before he started to speak. "Gentlemen, there is a strong chance the express will run tonight. Up to six destroyers and heavy barge traffic." He went to the map and pointed to a position located on Kolombangara Island. "Their mission is to land troops and supplies here." He used his index finger to circle a small dot that was labeled *Vila*.

Warfield cut in. "My instructions are to use every available patrol boat." He looked at each squadron commander and emphasized. "Each of your boats has radar, and you're to coordinate your attack with your other boats."

Next, he told each squadron commander where they would patrol. He finally came to John's squadron. "Brantingham, your group will be further up the Blackett Straight, across from Vanga Vanga." He paused for a moment. "This should be enough to stop any traffic. Boat captains, man your boats and get with your squadron commanders for your rendezvous point."

Following this, each of the groups formed up for detailed instructions from their squadron commander. Brantingham's group consisted of Lieutenant Liebenow, call sign OAK 21, on PT 157; Lieutenant Lowrey, call sign OAK 36, on PT 162; Lieutenant Kennedy, call sign OAK 14, on PT 109; and lastly, Lieutenant Brantingham, call sign OAK 27, on PT 159.

As Erik approached the group, he heard the last of the Brantingham's briefing. "Visibility is going to be poor tonight, so be there for each other. Be careful of those Jap destroyers and have your fish ready when you attack them. When you call to the other boats, use your assigned radio call number." The junior officers nodded. "For those of you who weren't supposed to go out tonight, you have sixty minutes to get ready. Any questions?"

The silence was a clear sign everyone understood.

"Dismissed."

Brantingham approached Erik. "Sir, the commander advised me that you are going to be an observer on Lieutenant Kennedy's boat."

Erik nodded.

"Sir, I feel it would be best if you were on my boat since I'm the commanding officer of the squadron."

"Thank you for addressing that matter, and it's been noted. Anything else, lieutenant?"

"Sir, would you reconsider?"

"Lieutenant, this is not a matter of discussion," Erik said firmly. "Is that understood?"

"Yes, sir." Brantingham snapped a salute, then looked at John. "Good hunting, John."

"You too, sir." John motioned to Lenny to get back to the boat and get it ready. Then he faced Erik and said, "Sir, I'm not asking what your orders are, but they must be extremely important."

"They are, Lieutenant Kennedy." Erik leaned forward so only John could hear. "There's a lot at stake if they are not carried out. I'm willing to give my life if I have to." Erik motioned him to start walking.

"Sir, for the most part, we are informal out here. You can call me John."

Erik pondered for a moment and agreed that when they talked with each other, they would go on first name basis.

"How long have you been in the Navy, and were you always stationed in the Pacific?"

"Ten years." Erik rubbed his chin. "I was stationed at several locations. First in Virginia for a while, then I visited some of our allies in Europe."

"England?"

Erik nodded.

"My father was the US ambassador. I lived there with him and witnessed the Luftwaffe's bombings first-hand."

"So was I."

John turned his head from side to side.

"It was a scary time." Erik glanced at him and assumed his next question would be why he was there and shook his head. John's eyes motioned he would like to know more, so Erik gave in. "What I can tell you is that I prevented Operation Sealion, which was the German's planned invasion of England."

John mouthed the word *damn*. "My father supported Prime Minister Neville Chamberlain's policy of appeasement during the late 1930s." Erik smirked and shook his head. "If we knew then what Hitler's intentions were, things would have turned out differently.""You have no idea how true that is." Erik raised his finger to emphasize his point. "It would have if the English listened to some of the German generals in May 1938."

"May 1938?" John struggled to find words.

Erik nodded. "General Oster and Beck warned the British government that Hitler was going to start a war and urged resistance toward him. They also asked the British government to help overthrow Hitler." Erik paused. "They ignored the messages, and the rest is history."

"How do you know such things?" he asked.

"In my line of work, I have been exposed to a lot of things. However, I cannot and never will be allowed to tell anyone what I have seen or done."

"Hey, John." Both Erik and John's eyes focused on an officer approaching them. John assured Erik he was a good friend. His name was George Ross, but his friends called him Barney. The lieutenant snapped a salute to Erik and continued his conversation. "Sir, I'm without an assignment since my boat was destroyed. I could give you an extra hand."

"The Lieutenant Commander is going to be on board—"Erik cut in, "John, you can station him on the thirty-seven-millimeter."

John nodded.

Then Erik turned to Barney. "Lieutenant, can you fire a thirty-seven-millimeter anti-tank gun?"

"Sir, I'm a quick learner."

"Good." Erik replied. "Mr. Ross, here are a few basic things you need to know. The gun's elevation can be plus fifteen degrees." Both Barney and John gave incredulous looks at each other and then at Erik as he continued. "You will have a good field of fire since the traverse is sixty degrees, and the maximum firing range is around four miles." Erik started walking and turned. "Mr. Ross, I forgot to mention the shells only weigh approximately one and a half pounds." Then. he headed to the boat.

"John, who is that?"

"Lieutenant Commander Erik Foge, from naval intelligence."

"And he knows about anti-tank guns?"

John shrugged.

Barney added, "He is more than meets the eye."

John nodded in agreement.

CHAPTER 25

NOT KNOWING HOW NEAR OR HOW FAR

"We demand rigidly defined areas of doubt and uncertainty!"
— Douglas Adams, *The Hitchhiker's Guide to the Galaxy*

SOUTH PACIFIC OCEAN

As John and Barney boarded the boat, Erik, Lenny, and two others were adjusting the anti-tank gun. Lenny addressed John as he strolled toward the gun. "We can say we have class on our boat with this little beauty."

John grinned.

"Sir, what about the mounting?"

John pointed to a rope and advised them to lash it against the planks, and that they would bolt the gun on later.

"Yes, Sir."

The officers huddled, and John stated they were to monitor regular channels and maintain radio silence. Then John and Barney went to the cockpit. At the same time, Lenny and Erik continued to overlook the securing of the anti-tank gun. One of the enlisted men spoke freely to Lenny once they realized their skipper wasn't near. "Sir, can you tell me why we have an anti-tank gun on the bow?"

"I believe the skipper would put a tank on the bow if he could."

The enlisted men shook their heads as they continued working.

"These types of guns are on M3 Stuart tanks," Erik added, and all three stared at him. "It's true. They were used in the North African Campaign when we fought the German tanks."

"Then the skipper made a wise choice when he got this gun." Lenny smiled and nodded like the others. "I bet our tanks kicked some ass when we went up against those Nazi tanks."

Erik let out a deep sigh and walked away. The remainder of the crew was huddled around John as he addressed them. "Men, again we go out tonight and meet our enemy. May God be with us, so one day we can be reunited with our families and loved ones. As you already know, we have two guests onboard." John glanced to his right. "This is Lieutenant Ross. He was the executive officer for PT 166." Then he looked over his shoulder and pointed in Erik's direction. "Next to Lieutenant Thom is Lieutenant Commander Foge, from Naval Intelligence."

He faced the crew again and saw their nervousness. "Men, I know you are superstitious about having visitors on board, but we have a crew of fourteen, not the unlucky thirteen." He let those words sink in. "So, let's make this patrol successful and uneventful. Most of all, be on your best behavior. We leave in two hours."

"The skipper sure knows how to motivate the men," Lenny said, and Erik nodded. "Sir, may I ask a question?"

Erik motioned for him to continue.

"Why didn't you answer my question?"

Erik glanced at Lenny. "Which one?"

Lenny nodded toward the 37mm gun.

"What I am going to tell you, you need to keep it to yourself."

Lenny nodded in agreement.

Erik explained the 37mm would be effective against wooden barges, but it wouldn't be against a destroyer, nor was it against German tanks.

Lenny was intrigued and wanted to know more.

Erik summed it up the best way he could. "America was blissfully ignorant when it came to tank warfare. At first, there was foggy unawareness, which transitioned into painful reality." Erik continued to explain, which Lenny tried to understand. Erik explained the most feared German anti-tank gun was able to penetrate 110mm armor at a range of 2100 yards away. However, the frontal armor on the M3 Stuart tanks was 51mm thick.

Lenny, with blood draining from his face, went back to the gun, and Erik headed to John and Ross. Both gentlemen were staring at the navigational charts while John motioned to Erik. He would give him a tour of the boat and meet the crew.

John faced the starboard side, where Charles Harris was positioned, and then he looked on his port side where Harold Marney was stationed. Both men were manning the fifty-calibers. John acknowledged Barney again, who was lookout and gunner for the 37mm. They strolled up to the bow.

Lenny approached them. "Skipper, do you think the ropes will hold the 37mm?"

"It will have to do for tonight. We will pin it down tomorrow." Lenny went below deck as John asked how things were going, and they advised that they would make the gun secure enough until they got back to port. John pointed to his left, to Raymond Albert, and to his right, to William Johnston. A man appeared from the forward hatch and headed in Erik's and John's direction.

"Skipper, with your permission, I would like to serve sandwiches and coffee to the men before we go out, so everyone will have something in their stomachs."

"What kind of sandwiches?" Erik inquired.

"Sir, peanut butter and jelly."

Erik gave a dissatisfaction look.

"Sir, I could just put jelly on yours."

"Do you have any butter?"

"Sir, I believe I do. Would you prefer that over peanut butter?"

Erik nodded.

"Sir, then I will make you a butter and jelly sandwich." Then the man disappeared under the boat, closing the hatch behind him.

"That's our quartermaster, cook, and signalman, Edgar Mauer." John turned to Erik, "You don't like peanut butter?"

Erik shook his head.

"But you have had a PBJ sandwich before?"

Erik shook his head again.

"Every kid has eaten one or tried one."

"My wife said the same thing."

John asked, "Would you ever try one?"

Erik shook his head.

Another enlisted man approached John. "Skipper, OAK 27 wishes to communicate with you."

John nodded and motioned he would be back shortly.

"Sir, is this the first time on a PT Boat?"

Erik nodded at the enlisted man, who introduced himself as Radioman Second Class John Maguire.

Then John reappeared, and Maguire disappeared under the hatch. Mauer advised the coffee and sandwiches would be out shortly and advised John that he should get below deck because there was some commotion going on. Erik followed John below and heard two individuals talking.

"Harris, will you take care of my things if I die?" A voice trembled.

"Kirksey, are you nuts?" Harris replied.

Harris headed to the coffee pot and saw John and Erik. In a quarter whisper, he asked, "Skipper, can you spare a minute?"

John nodded.

"You better talk to Kirksey." Harris explained the man was convinced that he was going to die. Kirksey has been having premonitions of death. This was going to hamper things for the crew morale and effect Kirksey's duties. John motioned Harris to go on deck and keep it to himself, then motioned Erik to join him. Kirksey was sitting at a table. He was pale, with his facial muscles twitching nervously and eyes darting manically.

John poured himself a cup of coffee and motioned the coffee pot to Kirksey. "Join me?"

Kirksey's voice lacked confidence, as the blood continued to drain from his face and sweat beaded on his forehead. "Thank you, sir." Kirksey's hand trembled as it reached for a coffee cup. "Maybe I do need a cup." John poured him one and Kirksey sipped between words.

"Skipper. I don't know what's the matter with me." He took a deep breath as he rubbed his fingers through his hair. "I have this awful feeling I'm not coming back."

John placed his coffee down and replied, "There isn't a man on this boat, including myself and Lieutenant Commander Foge, who hasn't had that thought."

John tried to get a few more words out, but Kirksey blurted out, "You don't understand, Lieutenant Kennedy." He raised his hand so he could finish his thought. "I don't think it." Kirksey slammed his fist against the table. "I know it." He leaned forward. "Sir, did you ever have a feeling something's going to happen before it happens?" Both Erik and John nodded. "It's like someone, or maybe even God, put a cold hand on my heart."

John took a deep breath. "Kirksey, listen to me." He tried to put it delicately, but Erik knew there was no easy way to put it. "It could happen. You could die. That's war. Try to remember the odds are on our side."

"Yes, sir, but shouldn't I worry?"

John shook his head. "You'd be a fool if you didn't."

"Skipper, then what can a man do," Kirksey tossed his hands up, "except pray?"

John straightened his posture. "Do your job and do it well, like every man on this boat." He glanced at Erik. "Do you have anything to add?"

Erik leaned forward and looked into Kirksey's eyes, "What's your name, sailor?"

"Andy, sir,"

"Can I call you Andy?"

Kirksey nodded.

"I know at times you feel like you are burned out, and you just want to quit, right?"

Andy nodded as he took a sip of coffee.

"Whenever you feel that way, think of these words to motivate you to keep focused. "Ask not what your country can do for you. Ask what you can do for your country."

Andy drank the last of his coffee, stood up, and smiled. "Lieutenant Kennedy, thank you." Then he looked at Erik. "Sir, what you just said gave me new inspiration, and I will remember it when I lose focus." Andy saluted and added before he left. "Thank you, sir."

Mauer walked in and placed more coffee and some sandwiches on the table.

John faced Erik. "Wow, that phrase was powerful."

Erik took a bite of his sandwich and shrugged.

"In all seriousness, where did you come up with that?"

"I made it up."

"Have you ever thought about getting into politics after the war?"

Erik shook his head. "If you get into politics, maybe if you become president, you should use that line in a speech."

"Can you write that down?"

Erik nodded as John's attention was pulled away by another member of the crew approaching him. "Skipper, the fish are ready for tonight."

"Let's hope they don't run cold[6]. Is anything else, Starkey?"

"The XO needs you topside."

John nodded, and Starkey disappeared as both John and Erik finished their sandwiches. John gestured to Erik to follow him to the engine room. The two men operating the compartment were Machinist's Mates First Class Gerard Zinswer and Patrick "Pappy" McMahon. Short waves accompanied the introductions since both men were checking and adjusting the engines before going out.

"Skipper, be easy on her. We need to conserve our fuel, and the batteries are not like they used to be." Pappy complained about the same issues on his boat as anyone who worked on engines on a naval vessel. And like any other, he got the same response from his skipper: a nod, a grin, and a familiar, "Anything else?"

"The auxiliary generator is still having issues."

"When we get back, I will see if I can get a new one."

Erik and John climbed out of the hatch. Lenny advised that Brantingham said they were heading out in ten minutes. John nodded, took the conn, and looked for the signalman on Brantingham's boat as he grabbed Erik's attention. "We will finish our conversation later."

Erik just nodded, keeping to himself as he stared at the horizon. The palm trees, with their huge, lime green, pinwheel-like palm frowns, transformed into silhouettes as the sun's golden rays slowly faded. The clouds were highlighted by the sun, with a touch

---

6. A torpedo "running coldly" was defective in some matter.

of amber and a hint of cinnamon. Their color gradually became muted as the sun sank behind the horizon.

Barney's voice drifted over Erik's shoulder. "Sir, haven't you had enough action for one day?"

Erik glanced at Barney and chuckled as he shook his head.

"Sir, if you ask my opinion, it's not safe on that island." Barney was looking for a response that would never come. "I'd rather have a boat under me."

Erik shrugged.

"Sir, you don't talk much." Barney was trying to get Erik to open up and study him, which Erik already knew. "Are all you guys in intelligence like this?"

Erik smirked and replied, "I have to admit, there's something about working for naval intelligence that intrigues and thrills everyone."

As Erik headed to the bow, Barney leaned over to John. "I heard guys like him are called spooks or are a part of JANIS."

John gave an awkward expression, as if he had a lemon in his mouth.

"An Army-Navy-OSS joint project." Barney pointed at Erik, but John motioned to keep his hand down. "How do you think he knows about the gun on your boat?"

John shrugged.

"I wonder why he's out here?"

John shook his head. "Barney, don't push him. He requested to be on my boat." He stared directly into Barney's eyes. "Don't fuck this up for me."

"Okay, John, but there is something about him."

The tranquil and quiet Rendova Harbor transitioned into a thundering roar of fifteen PT Boats starting their forty-five engines. Thick, choking black smoke drifted upward from the stern of each boat as each division of the flotilla went to their assigned locations, with Division B headed to Vanga Vanga. PT 109, like the other boats, had their torpedo tubes filled and ready, its guns were ready for action, engines growling, and the American flag dancing in the wind.

Barney tapped Erik's shoulder. "I just wondered if you want to talk and get to know each other since we are stuck on this boat." He looked at Erik for an encouraging nod before continuing. "Did you know John's nickname is Shafty?"

Erik shook his head.

"It's because he constantly uses the word shafted, as in, 'I've been shafted', or screwed."

Erik just nodded.

"Lenny told me that you knew about this kind of gun and where it was used."

"I do."

"Can you explain that to me how a naval officer, like yourself, knows about anti-tank guns?"

"I read." Erik knew the man was trying to be friendly, but everyone was on alert for enemy ships. Radio silence would only be broken if enemy ships were spotted. PT 109 was to get radar, like OAK 27, the next month, but until then, all the boats wait patiently for their orders. "It is like looking into an abyss," Erik replied.

Barney nodded as he looked through the binoculars, magnifying the void.

Under a starless and moonless night, PT 109 and the other boats were spread out like a picket line across the Blackett Strait. It was an overwhelmingly dark night, like a black hole in space. The blackness consumed everything, making it difficult to see ships.

Erik overheard nights like that could have a disorienting effect, even on experienced sailors. "Barney, do you have the time?"

He shook his head.

"Want some coffee?" Erik asked.

"Love some."

Erik began to leave, but Barney's voice stopped him. "I just want it black."

Erik nodded.

As Erik neared the helm, Mauer advised Kennedy that during the afternoon confusion, he forgot to turn in the muster sheet to base. Even though Erik knew that should have been a bad thing, it was actually a good thing, because his name would not go on record as being on PT 109.

Mauer faced John and said in a half-whisper, "Message from OAK 27. Sir, reduce speed to six knots. Muffle all engines." Then he went back to looking for any additional messages.

John repeated and directed the order to Lenny, who, in return, told the engine room, "When are we going to get radar?" Lenny asked John, who advised they would get it the next month. Nobody believed that until they saw it.

Lenny started a conversation, "Did you know," he tilted his head toward John, "John was in England when the Nazis were bombing it?"

Erik nodded.

John added, "So, was Erik."

Erik always had to be prepared to answer a question that he was not expecting. When that happened, the best thing was to nod and deflect. "John, I know you said your father was the ambassador at that time. Did you ever meet Churchill?"

Lenny focused on John.

Erik asked Mauer if there was any coffee below and went below. Erik never acquired a taste for coffee, but needed some to keep him awake. A few moments later, he climbed on to the upper deck and stepped into the middle of a conversation.

"Mauer, can you still see them at one-five-nine?" John asked for an update.

Ross replied, "No, Sir. It appears they just vanished."

John wasn't pleased and shook his head. "She was off the port beam about ten minutes ago."

"Thank you," Ross replied as Erik handed him his coffee and glanced at his watch. "Nearly two-thirty." He took a sip. "Erik, if you want to take a nap, I can stay up for a few hours."

The worse part being in such a situation was the strain of allowing history to take its course. Of course, no matter how bad they describe things in the history books, it is always worse experiencing it.

IN THE MIDDLE OF NOWHERE IS WHERE WE ARE

"Don't get lost in what's happening right now—looking ahead will prepare you for what's next!"

—Adrian Griffin, *Buzz to Brilliance*

It was a moonless night on the vast expanse of the Pacific Ocean as the young and charismatic Kennedy stood aboard his boat with his crew, the vessel swiftly gliding in the current. The crew of PT-109 believed it was a formidable patrol boat, and they were entrusted with the crucial task of protecting American interests and doing their part to win the war. Erik knew John was a man of great ambition with a burning desire to make a difference. His spirit was reflected in his confident posture and intelligent gaze.

As the salty sea breeze brushed against his face, he felt an overwhelming sense of duty and responsibility. Erik knew it was on that fateful night that PT-109 would embark on a patrol mission, so he continued to wait and let history take its course. The waters were dark and treacherous, filled with lurking dangers that only added to the suspense of the mission. Kennedy and his crew were well aware an encounter with the enemy was always a possibility, but nothing could have prepared them for the events that were about to unfold.

As PT-109 glided through the shimmering water, the crew's senses were heightened, scanning the horizon for any signs of danger.

"Skipper?" Maguire called out, as John focused on him. "I am getting some exchanges from other boats."

"Who, and what are they saying?"

"I'm not certain." He cupped the headphones so he could listen better. "They are saying things like they are being chased and have fired fish." John stood up and got everyone's attention. "General quarters. General quarters." Everyone was ready for action as Erik headed to the anti-tank gun. "Advise OAK 31 and OAK 36 it will be best if we reverse our direction. We have a better chance of rejoining the others if we return to the vicinity where we were scattered at first."

"Skipper, OAK 31 and OAK 36 are in agreement," Lenny stated. John turned the wheel until PT 109 was headed to the southeast, going thirty knots, where they encountered heavy mist.

Once John thought he was in the area, he ordered one engine to idle to reduce noise. In the quiet, water lapped against the bow and a slight breeze drifted over the boat. Erik and Ross stood on the foredeck, by the thirty-seven-millimeter gun, prepared to fire. John was at the helm, scanning his surroundings, with Maguire to his right. Lenny was outside the cockpit, and Mauer was behind it, on the left, lying on the deck. Albert was acting as lookout at amidships. Harris and Kirksey were off duty, trying to get some sleep on the deck. Harris was between the day room canopy and starboard torpedo tube, and Kirksey was lying aft on the same side. Zinser was at the aft gun turret. In the engine room, McMahon was on duty, while Johnston was starting to get some sleep on the starboard side by the engine-room hatch.

The air, thick with foreboding, draped the men, and their ears were attuned for the distant hum of the other boats' engines. Then, with alarming swiftness, the stillness was shattered by a thunderous shout by Marney. "Ship at two o'clock!"

From that, terror spread across PT 109 as the crew hurled across the decks, preparing to fire their guns. Panic and desperation seized their hearts as they grappled with the sudden peril that engulfed them. Emerging from the darkness, a foreboding silhouette loomed through the mist—a Japanese destroyer. Its form was menacing and relentless, clearly an imminent threat. Surrounded by the boundless sea, the crew realized their vulnerability as the enemy approached, and time decelerated to a nerve-wracking crawl.

"Lenny, is that one of ours?" John yelled.

Lenny rubbed his eyes as others tried to identify the ship which was closing fast. John's eyes enlarge in horror as he realized a Japanese destroyer was heading right toward them. Suddenly, the boat experienced a tremendous jolt as the Japanese destroyer began to tear it into two like a hot knife in butter. The stress on the plywood hull splintered it. The impact knocked John's hands free of the wheel, throwing him against the rear wall of the cockpit. Others fell to the deck or were tossed into the ocean. Erik lurched into the day-room canopy, hitting his head and falling unconscious.

The boat's forward compartment remained afloat, while the sheer weight of the engines dragged the stern under. The impact threw McMahon sideways, to lay against the auxiliary generator, and tossed Johnston into the ocean. Mauer and Maguire were still on deck, calling for their friends. In the darkness, small patches of fire and debris floated on the surface. Among the wreckage, John, Lenny, Johnston, Zinser, Ross, and Albert were able to swim back on their own. John swam out and helped his crew back to the ship. Once everyone was on board, he did a head count and realized that both Marney and Kirksey were missing and possibly killed. They looked in the distance, neither seeing or hearing other boats.

"John, should we fire the flare gun?" Lenny asked.

"No, we'll attract the attention of the Japanese, either on that ship or the islands."

"How long do you think we have until it sinks or capsizes?"

John took a deep breath and tried to guess, but he couldn't even do that. "I don't know, Lenny." He glanced at Ross, who was attending to Erik as he bled from his forehead, but he couldn't do much without a first aid kit. "How is he?"

"Well, he is alive. I just don't know when he will regain consciousness."

The night wore on, each passing minute feeling like an eternity. Exhaustion tugged at their weary bodies, and hope threatened to fade. Kennedy knew their only chance of survival was to abandon ship and swim toward the safety of a nearby island. They would have to wait till morning so they could see where they were going. Until then, in the moonless night, the crew of PT 109 drifted quietly through the black abyss, their senses heightened by the eerie silence that surrounded them. The stars above shone dimly, as if aware of the grave danger lurking beneath the surface and around them.

CHAPTER 27

LESSONS LEARNED WHILE IMPROVISING THE UNKNOWN

"To succeed, planning alone is insufficient. One must improvise as well."
— Isaac Asimov, Foundation

The sun beat down like someone holding a magnifying glass, and a biting saltwater breeze carried a sense of urgency as it ruffled the hair of the stranded crew aboard the sinking PT 109. John, Erik, Ross, and Lenny huddled around a map spread out on the deck, their faces etched with determination and concern. John's gaze flickered over the map, tracing the path to a group of small islands in the distance. "Those islands," he began, his voice low but firm as he looked westward, "are about three and a half miles away."

He drew everyone's attention to the map as he guided his finger along the group of small islands in the shape of an anchor, extending from the southeastern tip of Gizo.

Ross leaned in; his brow furrowed. "What's the distance between those two points?"

John calculated quickly, his finger marking the length on the map. "The anchor is four or five miles long."

Lenny shifted his weight and turned to Erik. "Do you think the Japanese have any outposts on those islands?"

Erik shook his head. "The latest intelligence reports suggest these islands are clear of enemy outposts."

John glanced at Erik, a flicker of doubt in his eyes. "How recent is this intel?"

Erik hesitated. "Close to a month old."

"It's a risk," John mused, his jaw clenched. "But staying here is an even greater danger."

Erik's gaze swept over the group. "The reef near those islands borders Ferguson Passage," he said, tapping a spot on the map. "We could signal for help from PT boats passing by Rendova at night."

The rest of the officers nodded in agreement, their eyes reflecting a mix of anxiety and resolve.

John checked his watch, the numbers blurry in the dimming light. It was well past one o'clock. Gathering the men around him, he spoke with authority. "Men, I have decided, we're abandoning the boat and heading for land before nightfall."

A ripple of tension spread through the group. No one wanted to risk swimming to shore, but the alternative was clear. Remaining on the sinking vessel was not an option. "The officers and I agreed on the eastern island group as our destination," John continued, noting the reluctance in their expressions. "Plum Pudding Island," John declared, his voice cutting through the air. "That is where we're swimming to."

A murmur of uncertainty arose among the crew as they exchanged uneasy glances. One of the crew cleared his throat, breaking the uneasy silence. "But some of us aren't strong swimmers, Lieutenant Kennedy."

John met their gazes, his eyes steady. "Lieutenant Commander Foge reported Naru as safe, but that was a month ago. We cannot take chances." John looked into everyone's eyes. "Plum Pudding Island is too small for all of us, but it's less likely to host a Japanese outpost."

Lenny shuffled his feet, anxiety evident in his stance. "What if we're spotted?"

John's jaw tightened. "We move quickly. Every hour we delay is a risk."

Erik placed a hand on Lenny's shoulder, offering a reassuring nod. "If we stick together, we will make it."

The sun continued to slowly move, casting shadows across the deck of the adrift vessel, a silent witness to the crew's taut nerves and unspoken fears. With a final, resolute nod, John took the lead, determination blazing in his eyes.

The sun continued to beat down mercilessly on the group of men huddled around the bow of PT 109 as it bobbed in the vast expanse of the South Pacific. The salty tang of the sea mingled with the acrid scent of burned flesh from McMahon's injuries, a stark reminder of the perils they faced. John's gaze swept over his crew, faces etched with doubt and fear in equal measure, knowing some of the men were better swimmers than others. It would be difficult to keep the group together on the long swim. Erik pointed out to John that one of the two-by-eight planks they had placed under the anti-tank gun was still floating by the bow at the end of its rope, suggesting the plank could solve the problem of separation.

"Listen up," John said. "It's our time to leave. I will take McMahon, and the rest of you can swim together on this plank." He pointed to the piece of wood. Then John looked at Lenny. "Thom will be in charge." Next, John glanced at Erik. "Is that okay?"

"It's your boat and your crew." Erik's voice cut through the tense atmosphere, practicality grounding their desperate situation. "Remove your shoes and tie them around the plank so you can kick better."

Ross and a few others took the boat's battle lantern, a square gray flashlight, wrapped it in a kapok to keep it afloat, then tied it to the plank. Erik ordered Maguire to throw the secret radio code book overboard.

An anxious voice broke the uneasy silence. "Will we ever get out of this?"

The question hung in the air, laden with uncertainty and fear. John's response was firm and unwavering. "We'll do it," he declared, his voice a beacon of reassurance amid the chaos and determination hardening his gaze. The moment of truth arrived, the air thick with anticipation and fear. "It can be done," John continued, looking at everyone. "Prepare yourselves. We leave at once."

With a final glance at their stricken PT 109, a symbol of their shattered past, they cut the two-by-eight loose from the bow and, buoyed by their kapoks, grouped themselves about the plank, four on one side and four on the other. A ninth man, often Thom, helped Erik on each end, pushing and pulling at the plank. The men on the sides each threw an arm over the plank and paddled with the other. Each stroke took them closer to the refuge they desperately sought. Clinging to hope, they battled against the currents, fighting for their lives. John knew with a heavy heart, still pulsating with adrenaline, he would need to lead his crew through the unforgiving waters.

The distant crash of waves served as a grim reminder of the ever-present danger that surrounded them. Shadows danced on the surface of the water, the play of light and shadow mirroring the uncertainty that gripped their hearts. Then a sudden disturbance in the water broke the monotony of their struggle. A sleek shape cut through the waves, a dark shadow gliding beneath the surface with deadly intent. A collective gasp escaped the men as realization dawned on them.

Sharks, drawn by the scent of blood and the thrashing of limbs, circled ominously, their cold, unblinking eyes fixated on the vulnerable prey before them. Panic threatened to engulf them, but

John's voice rang out, cutting through the chaos. "Stay together! Keep kicking!" His words were a lifeline in the swirling sea of fear and uncertainty, anchoring them in the face of impending danger. The men rallied, their movements becoming more frantic as they redoubled their efforts to outpace the circling predators. Adrenaline surged through their veins, lending strength to their weary bodies as they fought for survival against nature's most ruthless predators. As if fear of the sharks and the exhaustion of the struggle to shore weren't enough, the crew were burdened with anticipation, wondering when the Japanese would show up and capture them.

"Hey!" Zinser called out. "Kicking speeds us up *and* scares the sharks."

"Great," Lenny muttered between gasps. "So shut up and keep kicking."

As they pressed on through the treacherous crossing, the men tapped into depths of courage and resolve they never knew they possessed, honed in the crucible of imminent peril. Each stroke propelled them closer to safety, their bond a bastion against the lurking dangers beneath the waves. With the sun sinking beneath the horizon, casting a fiery glow over the water, they edged ever nearer to their coveted refuge. Despite their exhaustion, the men arrived at the distant shore undeterred, their countenances a mosaic of relief and gratitude. It had taken them a grueling four hours to traverse the treacherous three and a half miles of Blackett Strait from the capsized hull of PT 109 to the enigmatic southeastern rim of Plum Pudding Island.

Seated beside Erik, John surveyed the vast expanse of ocean before them. The waves caressed the shoreline with a rhythmic melody, and a profound sense of achievement pulsating through their very beings. As the crew congregated on the sandy beach, an unspoken camaraderie enveloped them, a shared aura of triumph cementing their unity in a moment of silent acknowledgement. The perils ahead remained daunting, but in that fleeting instant, they found solace in the realization they had stared into the abyss and emerged fortified on the other side.

Opting for much-needed respite before sustenance, Erik veered off, disappearing into the depths of the island, his mission weighing heavily on his mind. Observing Erik's departure with a quizzical glance, John endeavored to catch up before he vanished into the shadows.

A rustling behind Erik signaled John's approach, prompting him to pause momentarily before resuming his path forward.

"Where are you headed?" John asked, to which Erik merely gestured ahead. "You should rest," John advised, but Erik's mission remained paramount.

"I must attend to something first," he replied cryptically, brushing off John's attempts to glean more insight into his purpose.

"You're a true enigma," John quipped, prompting a wry grin from Erik.

"My wife thinks the same. Rest assured; I shall return shortly."

Delving deeper into Plum Pudding Island, Erik meticulously scrutinized every detail of his surroundings. Surveying the oval expanse of green terrain bordered by a ring of pristine sand, he marveled at the kaleidoscope of Pacific hues blending seamlessly from sapphire depths to minty shallows. The symphony of rustling palms intermingled with unfamiliar, towering trees. Their lengthy needles shrouded a canopy of branches, which cast a shadowed tapestry over the ground below.

While the absence of footprints initially signaled solitude, Erik remained vigilant, aware that a skilled assassin could effortlessly conceal their tracks. The faint fragrance of sweet decay enveloped his senses with each advancing step, and the ground underfoot was carpeted with a mosaic of withered needles and decaying leaves. Coral fragments peeked out from beneath an array of white-flowering shrubs, hinting at the island's clandestine mysteries waiting to be unraveled.

Returning to the shore, Erik's keen eye caught sight of nautilus shells and kauri relics scattered along the sandy expanse. Hermit crabs scuttled about, the larger ones tantalizing with the promise of sustenance. A cacophony of avian inhabitants dotted the skyline, from shore-dwelling waddlers to aerial acrobats, their presence portending a potential food source. Yet, caution dictated an inconspicuous approach, lest their presence be betrayed by telltale flames or smoke.

By nightfall, Erik found refuge beneath a dense bush, eschewing the comfort of a fire as he sought a fitful reprieve. Stirred from a troubled slumber by the restless dance of trees in the ocean breeze, Erik resigned to settle back, attuned to the perpetual melody of nature's nocturnal symphony.

***

The sun beat down mercilessly on Plum Pudding Island, in the Solomon Islands, deep in the South Pacific, where the survivors of PT 109 huddled under the shade of the tree canopy. The men were unprepared for the horrors of survival in the savage arena, and they would be tested to the limits of their endurance. Hiding behind scrubs and fallen trees, Erik scanned the horizon, his eyes narrowed in suspicion.

John quietly crouched next to Erik, wiping sweat from his brow, his gaze fixed on the shimmering blue expanse of the ocean. "Any sign of rescue yet, Erik?" John's voice was tinged with hope, but his eyes betrayed his worry.

Erik shook his head grimly.

"Have you seen any japs?"

"Not yet, but that doesn't mean they aren't out there."

Distant voices carried on the salty breeze, making the men tense up. They exchanged anxious glances, their hands instinctively reaching for their weapons. The sub-machine gun was gone, and the few remaining sidearms were in dubious condition. Erik scanned the shoreline, his eyes enlarged, and motioned everyone to high alert.

The threat of a Japanese barge loomed over them like a dark cloud. The men knew they had to stay vigilant, for danger could come at any moment. They couldn't afford to let their guard down, not even for a second. Everyone laid quietly and tried to blend into the foliage and shadows. The motorized Japanese barge chugged up Blackett Strait only a couple hundred yards away. Erik and John knew if they spotted any trace of swimmers or the encampment, they would send a shore patrol.

"Do you think this is a regular patrol?" John asked.

Erik shrugged and replied without looking back. "The question we should ask is whether the Japs would head in for a routine reconnaissance of the islands."

"If they do, what should we do if we are challenged by superior firepower?" John asked.

"Run, hide, and pray you're not found."

John just nodded.

"Set up a two-hour watch, with two men, to be on a lookout for any friendly boats and the Japs. Have them crouch on the beach with one man looking in either direction. Starting now."

"Yes, sir."

Erik looked at John. "Since fresh water will be scarce, when it rains, have the men try to drink water from the plant leaves, but make sure the leaves are clean so they won't be swallowing anything they wouldn't want to."

Night fell, and some of the men gathered around in a small

circle. The pale moonlight cast shadows on their weary faces. "Too bad you don't have some of your chocolate bars. They would taste really good." Lenny chuckled, a hint of mischief in his eyes. John rolled his own, a sheepish grin playing on his lips. Laughter bubbled up from their midst, a brief respite from the constant fear that gripped their hearts.

A distant rumble shattered the lighthearted moment, the sound of an approaching engine cutting through the night. Erik grabbed a sharpened stick, which he carved earlier that day, and scanned the darkness for any sign of movement. The men tensed, bracing themselves for whatever danger lay ahead, and grabbed branches for weapons. Adrenaline surged through their veins as they prepared to drive their makeshift weapons forward with a relentless force to push the Japs back into the sea.

The men on watch waved it off. It was just their imaginations playing tricks on them.

By the end of day three, with only a couple of hours of daylight left, their hopes of rescue before another night were fading. Earlier, another barge passed slowly, but it did not turn.

The men had thrown themselves on their stomachs and crawled up to the bushes bordering the sand, ducking under several trees. A Japanese officer looked through his binoculars, searching for any activity on the island. Tensely, the men watched through the bushes. At the last minute, the barge changed direction, and a deep sigh consumed all the men on the island. If the Japanese had come by only a few minutes earlier, they would have caught Kennedy and his men helpless in the water as they were trying to catch something to eat. They could have shot them or taken them prisoner, to be tortured.

The days were filled with endless toil and danger, but they faced each challenge with courage and determination, refusing to be beaten down by the harsh realities of their situation, at least for the time being. As they scoured the island for food and water, things looked grim, since there was nothing to be found. Yet, through it all, they clung to the flicker of hope that burned within them, refusing to let despair consume their souls. For as long as they drew breath, the survivors of PT 109 would continue to fight, to endure, and to hold on to the fragile thread of hope that bound them together in the crucible of war.

On the fourth day, Lenny, Erik, and John sat on the powdery white beach, their shadows stretching long under the midday sun. The scorching heat pressed down on them, making their uniforms stick to their skin. Mauer hadn't provided them with a proper meal—it was coconuts again that day—since late Sunday afternoon, and the men could feel the gnawing hunger in their bellies.

As they huddled together, John's voice cut through the air. He spoke of their dwindling supplies of coconuts and the need to move to Olasana Island after Ross's return. Erik listened intently as John described Olasana's location, nestled just two miles inward from Plum Pudding Island to the southwest. Sheltered under a palm tree, Erik and John strategized, while Lenny gathered the rest of the crew to share the upcoming plans. The vast expanse of the ocean stretched out before them, a constant reminder of their isolation in the midst of the war.

John's thoughts raced as he considered their dire situation. Their only hope lay in being rescued, but uncertainty gnawed at him. He scanned the horizon, always on edge, knowing that danger could appear at any moment. Suddenly, a frantic wave from Lenny sent shivers down their spines.

Ross ran toward them with urgency in his eyes. The men sprang to their feet, their hearts pounding in anticipation. As Ross reached them, his breath came in ragged gasps. He relayed news of a potential threat lurking nearby, a shadow in the water that didn't belong.

John's jaw clenched, his mind racing with possibilities as he issued swift commands to his men.

As they prepared to defend themselves, a low moan filled the air, a sound that seemed to reverberate off the waves. The tension was palpable as the men readied themselves, their eyes scanning the ocean. They spotted a Japanese barge with three or four men on it. A few minutes passed, as did the barge, and the men prepared to leave Plum Pudding Island.

John stared out at the endless blue horizon, beads of sweat trailing down his brow. "This war is brutal. Makes you wonder about a lot of things."

Erik, his gaze distant and thoughtful, murmured, "War has a way of stripping away the facade of civilization, revealing the raw essence of humanity."

John turned sharply to Erik; his curiosity piqued. "You speak like someone who's seen it all. What's your story, Erik?"

Erik offered a cryptic smile, his eyes holding secrets untold. "We all carry our pasts, don't we? Some are just heavier than others, and mine is pretty damn heavy."

John furrowed his brow, sensing the enigma surrounding Erik. "Are you really who you say you are?" John stared at Erik closely. "How did you end up here?"

Erik's gaze flickered toward the horizon, a whisper of a breeze stirring the leaves above them. "Fate. It brings us to places we never expected."

John's eyes widened in disbelief, his mind struggling to comprehend Erik's words. "Fate? Do you actually believe what you are saying?"

Erik chuckled softly, a sound like the rustle of leaves in the wind. "To the uninitiated, perhaps. But truth is often stranger than fiction, wouldn't you agree?"

"You talk in riddles."

Erik's voice cut through John's soul. "Be wary, John. Not everything is as it seems."

Confusion and fear played across John's face as Erik stood calmly, his gaze never fading as he continued, "War is a beast that knows no mercy. Sometimes, it devours even those seeking salvation. We'll make it out of here, John. Together." Erik's nod was a silent vow, a promise unspoken yet understood. Then he got up and walked away.

Another hour passed, and the men dragged the plank into the water, John taking the strap of McMahon's kapok in his teeth and towing him along. The risky journey led them to leave the safety of one island for the uncertainty of another, suspected to be occupied by Japanese forces. Observing Olasana for several days had revealed no signs of activity, but the abundance of coconut palms hinted that there was food on the island. As they made the crossing, the current felt stronger among the islands, making their progress slow. After John and McMahon reached the shore of Olasana, the other men struggled to make their way closer, with Albert leaving the plank to swim ahead. Fear gripped them as they worried about their voices carrying to potential enemy ears.

The twelve survivors gathered in the trees behind the curved beach, gazing across the water at Naru Island, bordering Ferguson Passage. In hushed voices, they debated whether to explore Olasana, ultimately deciding to stay near the beach, given the risks involved. The men gathered coconuts for sustenance, but some, including John and McMahon, fell ill after consuming them. Ross, perhaps in jest, ate a live snail, finding it repulsive. Zinser attempted to dig for fresh water, only to injure his fingers on the unforgiving coral. Concerns about the Navy declaring them missing in action weighed heavily on their minds, especially on Zinser, who dreaded the impact it would have on his wife.

As darkness descended, weariness settled over the group, and for the first time in three nights, no one ventured into Ferguson Passage. Huddling together for warmth, the coolness of the night seeped through their damp clothing. The surf crashing against the reef grew louder, mingling with the eerie noises emanating from the jungle, stirring anxiety among the men. Unidentifiable sounds pricked their fears, heightening the tension of their situation. During the night, a shower passed over the island, and Erik, parched, ventured out to lick some leaves. In the darkness, he encountered a chilling sight—a shadowy figure standing before him. The suspense was palpable as Erik and the stranger regarded each other, a silent standoff that spoke volumes in its intensity. Erik considered the man could be a native of the islands.

"Beware. Someone is not who they say they are," the stranger said to Erik.

Erik looked around before he responded. "Who are you?"

"My name is not important. Remember my warning."

Eventually, the native retreated. The encounter left Erik with a lingering sense of unease. As the days passed, the fear of being discovered by the Japanese loomed larger, feeding the growing sense of dread within the group. Their time on these islands was running out, amplifying the urgency of their situation. Determined to secure their rescue, Erik understood the gravity of the task ahead—the need to confront and eliminate the threat lurking on Naru Island. Only by facing the danger head-on could he avert disaster. The clock was ticking, and Erik braced himself for the impending confrontation that would test his courage and resolve in the face of wartime peril.

Erik knew the longer they remained in the islands, the greater was the danger the Japanese would find them. They had no solution to their problem, and the fear of disaster was growing among many of them. However, Erik knew if he and John were able to go to Naru Island the next day, the recue would come, but he would need to face the assassin and kill him. Then and only then would the timeline be preserved.

John led Erik, Lenny, and Ross down the beach a short distance from the crew, their faces etched with grim determination. John ran a hand through his hair, his brow furrowed in deep thought. "What do we do now?"

They stood in silence, racking their brains for a solution, haunted by the relentless pursuit they had endured over the last five days. Navigating through Ferguson Passage under cover of darkness, switching islands, and maintaining a vigilant watch for enemy boats and planes had taken its toll on their already weary minds. John's voice broke the tense silence, revealing the inner turmoil plaguing him. "Is there anything more we can do to save ourselves?" The restlessness in John's tone did not escape Erik's notice.

Lenny interjected, refusing to accept the idea of idly waiting in the shadows. "We can't just sit around all day. Our morale is hanging by a thread. We need to show the men we are actively seeking a way out, even if it's just a desperate facade."

Erik's gaze drifted toward Naru Island, a glimmer of hope flickering in his eyes as he turned to John. "John, how far do you think Naru Island is?"

John's shoulders lifted in a hesitant shrug as he tried to recall the navigational chart. "Perhaps a half-mile swim. Why do you ask?"

Erik painted a picture of their potential escape route, his words laced with determination. "The far side of Naru faces Ferguson Passage. Although Allied vessels would not risk daylight operations, it's a risk worth considering."

John's inner conflict surfaced as he grappled with the idea of venturing to Naru Island, a territory he had not intended to explore. Yet, the possibility of salvation tugged at him, nudging him toward agreement. "Let's scout Naru, regardless."

Ross voiced his dissent, his tone tinged with concern. "John, that's a dangerous proposition." He turned to John, questioning the feasibility of their survival strategy. "How long can we keep this up? Evading the enemy, subsisting on coconuts and scraps. It's a losing battle."

"Ross, giving up is not an option. Our men look up to us to find solutions." Erik reassured him, his hand resting firmly on Ross's shoulder. "We must persevere for their sake."

With a nod of understanding, Ross yielded to their decision. They returned to the men, outlining their plan with resolve. John advised Erik on the importance of rest before their journey to Naru Island at first light.

CHAPTER 28

TIME KNOWS WHEN IT'S TIME

"No matter how fast light travels, it finds the darkness is always there first…"

— Terry Pratchett

John and Erik carefully navigated onto Naru Island's sun-drenched beach, their senses sharp and their hearts full of anticipation. As they caught their breath, Erik was still uncertain when John was to be killed, since nothing had happened in the past four days. But he got that warning from the native, which had him on alert.

John's gaze was fixed on the distant horizon where the sea met the sky. The ever-present roar of the crashing waves provided a haunting backdrop to their conversation. "I'm starting to believe the odds of being rescued are slim," he said, the tension in his voice palpable. "And even if we do make it back, what then? Our lives won't be the same."

Erik nodded; his eyes focused on John's. "We will make it through," he replied.

John shook his head in disbelief.

"I have been in more dire situations, and after everything I've been through, I knew I had to keep pushing through."

"How do you keep yourself motivated?"

"I once told my commanding officer it was a slap in the face when I saw other individuals had graduated from the Naval Academy, or had family members that were in the Navy, and they looked at me differently." Erik paused for a moment, remembering that day. "I told him, I just had to let it go and work harder to prove to myself and them that I could do the job. I knew I would never be accepted as an equal because I wasn't like them, and in their eyes, I wasn't as good as them. Then I told him that didn't mean I would give up."

John absorbed everything; amazed Erik finally opened up to him. "What did he say?"

Erik smirked. "He said that he wanted me to know he believed in me. If the world were going through hell, he'd only want one person in the goddamn world to fix it."

John nodded in Erik's direction.

"Damn straight." Erik placed a hand on John's arm, his touch offering a small measure of comfort. "We can't lose hope," he said firmly. "There's a chance, however small, that we'll make it out of this. And when we do, we'll face it together."

John squeezed Erik's hand, his eyes reflecting unwavering determination. "We'll make it back," he vowed. "And when we do, I'll make sure the world knows what we've endured."

Their words hung in the air, mingling with the salt-tinged breeze as they clung to the fragile hope that they would, against all odds, survive their ordeal on Naru Island and get back to the crew.

But before taking their next step, Erik laid down a serious directive for John. "You need to tell your story when we get out of here, but you have to leave me out of it."

John protested. "No way. You are a part of this."

"I know, and you know, and it's good enough for me that you'll remember. However, nobody else can know I was here." Erik's gaze was steel and uncompromising. "It's for my safety."

John said nothing more, but it was clear he wasn't yet convinced.

Erik's resolve was immovable. "If they ask about me, don't give in, don't tell them anything. Even though you know it's the wrong thing to say, say you don't know me, and never say my name." Erik waited for John to acknowledge. "Even if you want to believe there's a way to say I was here, act like I never was."

"But, why? Even if you are a spook, how could it hurt to say you were here with us?"

"I don't have time to explain it to you, but maybe one day I will." Erik looked into John's eyes. "Because of what I do for Naval Intelligence, I sometimes use false identities, as if I'm a man without a name."

"Like a man who doesn't exist?" John asked.

"You don't know what is at stake and who you're dealing with here."

"Explain it to me."

"I can't."

"Why not?"

"I don't have enough time to explain. John, I can try to explain it, but you would have to understand mechanical engineering, dimensional optics, chronography, temporal causality, and temporal paradox, then multiply that by infinity, take that to the depths of forever, and by the expression on your face, you don't have a glimpse of what I'm talking about."

"What in the hell are you talking about? Do you understand everything you just said?"

Erik nodded. "Things that I have experienced are so horrible that it has haunted my dreams for all time."

John finally accepted where Erik was coming from and suggested they get to work on exploring the island. Before they set off, Erik said that it would be best if he went first and John tailed behind, approximately twenty feet, just in case they meet some Japs, John could hide and not get caught.

As they delved deeper into the heart of Naru Island, they found themselves ensnared by its exquisite yet treacherous allure. Sunbeams pierced through the dense foliage, casting an eerie, ethereal glow upon the jungle floor. The atmosphere hung heavy with the oppressive weight of humidity, creating an almost suffocating presence. Birds frantically squawked in disarray, as if ensnared within an invisible trap. Glinting insects scuttled across the ground, while unseen creatures chorused in a cacophony of discordant sounds.

The untamed wilderness seemed an uncharted realm, a forbidding domain untouched by human presence. Pausing intermittently to wrestle aside encroaching vines and hanging branches, Erik and John ventured onward with caution, fully aware that peril lurked ominously in every shadow. Their surroundings demanded unwavering vigilance as they treaded deeper into the unknown.

Erik reached the crest of a small hill and motioned John to come forward. Their eyes were immediately drawn toward the remnants of a small Japanese vessel on the reef. The weathered wood and rusted metal spoke of a vessel long abandoned. Curiosity burned within them, urging them to explore further. With great care, they crept through the thick underbrush, aware of the potential dangers hidden in the island's untamed wilderness. Their excitement grew with every step they took, knowing that they were on the brink of discovery.

Among the sand and debris, a discreetly labeled Japanese box caught their eye. It was as if the island itself had guided them to that spot. With trembling hands, they opened the box and found a surprising cache of treats — traditional Japanese candies and snacks that had withstood the test of time. The taste of those rare delicacies elated their senses, heightening the atmosphere of their adventure. The mystery deepened when they stumbled upon several hidden tins of water and a one-man canoe hidden in the bushes. It was a lifeline in that remote place, carefully placed for those who dared to venture into the unknown.

They knew they had to rest before returning to the crew, but continued a little while longer to see if they could find any other supplies. Erik and John forged through the lush jungle of Naru Island. Erik led the way, using a stick as a machete, pushing a way through the dense foliage. The scorching sun beat down on them, casting an ominous mix of light and shadow on the forest floor, heightening their vulnerability.

Without warning, a deafening crack pierced the air, and a single shot reverberated through the jungle. Erik stumbled, tripping over an obscured root, and crashed to the ground. He had taken a shot just below his left shoulder. Acting on sheer instinct, he lay motionless, feigning death to evade the sniper's deadly aim.

Meanwhile, John's heart raced as he scrambled for cover within a nearby thicket of bushes, his senses roaring with urgency. An uncanny stillness settled over the forest, interrupted only by the faint sounds of wildlife in the distance. John's mind raced as he desperately formulated a plan to rescue his friend and himself from the perilous, unseen assailant. In the suffocating stillness, time seemed to lose its grip as John strained to pick up any hint of movement in his surroundings, every fiber of his being on high alert. The oppressive tension in the stifling air was nearly palpable, intensifying with every passing second.

Footsteps echoed through the jungle as a Japanese soldier cautiously approached Erik, scrutinizing the fallen man as he moved closer. The Japanese soldier had an Army marksman's patch on his uniform, a red star with five blunt points on a dark green background.

Erik laid motionless on the forest floor, his breath shallow and controlled as the heavy thud of the soldier's boots drew closer. Each step sent a shiver down his spine, the sound reverberating through the silent jungle. His heart pounded like thunder in his chest, the weight of impending danger pressing down on him.

As the soldier closed in, the tension thickened in the air, suffocating Erik's senses. His instincts screamed at him to remain still and bide his time. He could feel the soldier's oppressive presence looming over him, a dark and forbidding shadow.

Then, without warning, excruciating pain exploded through Erik's ribs as the soldier kicked him, testing the facade of death. Erik gritted his teeth and resisted the urge to cry out, keeping his eyes shut and waiting for his moment to strike. When the soldier bent down to inspect him, his eyes, once calm and unassuming, suddenly widened with realization, and a look of confusion crossed his face. He uttered a few futile words as he came to the shocking understanding that the man before him was not John Kennedy, his intended target.

With a surge of adrenaline, Erik's eyes snapped open, his senses fully alert. He seized the opportunity with lightning speed. With all his weight moving in a single, fluid attack, he swept his leg out, causing the soldier to land on his back. The man tries to fight back, but Erik landed a jackhammer punch to the soldier's chest. Before Erik could do another one, the soldier rolled out of the way and got to his feet. Erik stood in a mixed-martial-arts stance, his eyes darting around for anything he could use as a weapon.

The soldier stared at Erik, smirking as he shook his head. "An MMA stance?" the assassin stated with a mocking chuckle. "Looks like someone doesn't belong here."

"It seems neither do you."

They were both from the future, and each had their own objectives.

The assassin's eyes widened as he realized Erik's objective. "Who sent you back?"

"I came of my own free will. I want to preserve the timeline."

The assassin looked disinterested.

"It seems we have some professional differences to resolve."

Erik nodded. "Check."

Erik was ready, every muscle in his body coiled like a spring. The two adversaries circled each other like predators in a deadly dance of combat, their fates hanging in the balance. Adrenaline surged through Erik's veins, sharpening his senses and focusing his mind. Despite the fear of uncertainty clawing at his insides, Erik remained unwavering and composed. Each move revealed the mounting frustration in their eyes, a dawning realization that they had underestimated their opponent.

The assassin pulled out a Japanese Tanto dagger and waved the blade slowly back and forth in front of Erik. Sunlight glinted off the blade, flickering over Erik's face.

Erik carefully navigated the unforgiving jungle ground, his pulse thundering in his ears as he confronted the grim reality of his precarious situation. Surrounded by dense foliage, he pondered his next move with lethal precision, fully aware of the formidable enemy in front of him. Reacting with swift reflexes born from years of training, he scanned the hostile environment for any advantage. There, amidst the chaos and danger, lay a seemingly insignificant branch. In a split-second decision, Erik seized the makeshift weapon, assuming a defensive stance that silently promised his ruthless determination to survive the imminent face-off. He also eyed the rifle behind the assassin, but it was too far to reach.

The assassin smiled with confidence, knowing Erik could not get to the weapon, as he maneuvered like a piece on a chessboard waiting to strike.

Erik took a few quick steps to his left, as if in fear, placing himself to the right of the blade rather than directly in front of it.

A wicked grin spread across the assassin's face as he waved

the dagger back and forth, slowly teasing. The sunlight filtering through the tree canopy cast dappled shadows on the jungle floor, projecting an eerie glow on the scene. The assassin taunted, twirling the dagger expertly in the air.

The assassin lunged forward, lunging upward, downward, and side to side. Erik moved in a defensive posture, searching for an opportunity to counterattack. If he was not careful, the assassin would exploit any opening.

Leaves rustled underfoot as they circled in the silent dance of death. The assassin struck again, steel flashing as the dagger slashed through the air, missing by a hair's breadth. Erik dodged and fell to his knees. His movements were fluid and precise, a fighter born of necessity and survival, his instincts honed as he raised the branch and smashed it against the assassin's left knee. Then Erik unleashed a flurry of explosive punches to the man's gut and ribs. Suddenly the assassin countered with a shot to Erik's head. As he stumbled back a step, the assassin danced back to put distance between them.

An eerie silence fell over the jungle, broken only by the rustle of leaves and the distant call of a tropical bird. The two men faced each other, locked in a deadly dance of survival. The assassin moved with deadly precision. His movements were swift and silent, a lethal predator. Erik, his muscles tense and his mind focused, matched the assassin's every move with trained expertise. Without warning, the assassin struck, raining a flurry of blows down on Erik like a ninjitsu master. Erik staggered back, his breath coming in ragged gasps as he struggled to defend himself.

The assassin chuckled and gave a cold, mischievous grin. His voice was taunting and dripping with malice. "I don't know what agency you are with, but you fight like an undernourished child, so why don't you give up?"

"I would rather die a gruesome and horrible death trying to

preserve the timeline." Erik gritted his teeth, his jaw clenched in determination. With an inner strength, he launched himself at the assassin. Their movements became a blur of limbs as they seemed to move as one, mirroring each other with uncanny precision. Yet, the assassin's skill was exceptional, his strikes precise and deadly. Erik felt the sting of each blow like a branding iron on his skin, his vision swimming with pain. Erik stumbled back, his eyes widening in realization that he might fail his mission.

The assassin's grin was feral, his eyes gleaming with triumph. "Now there's a new timeline," he hissed, his voice a serpent's whisper. "ONE's will is inexorable, and you are but a pawn in the grand design."

Erik's heart pounded in his chest, his breathing ragged as he kneeled, defeated. The assassin picked up and raised his dagger, poised to strike the final blow. The jungle seemed to hold its breath, waiting for the inevitable. Then a low, guttural sound rose from Erik's throat, a sound of defiance and determination. "There must be a hundred reasons why you joined ONE, and you thought this would be a walk in a park. Right now, I can think of one thing to say."

"What's that?" the assassin hissed, his grip tightening on the hilt of the dagger, ready to strike at a moment's notice.

Erik replied, "Trust is good, control is better."

The assassin hesitated for a split second and realized Erik was looking over his shoulder. A rustle of leaves signaled John's stealthy approach; his trained eye locked on his target through the scope of the rifle. With a sudden realization dawning in his eyes, the assassin spun around, but it was too late, and the flash of the muzzle was the last thing he saw.

The sound of the rifle echoed through the jungle, a battle cry signaling victory, the end of one chapter, and the beginning of another. The conflict had been resolved, and the timeline restored to continue as it originally had. The jungle enveloped Erik in its verdant embrace. The challenge was over, and he had faced it with courage and tenacity.

John felt he was on the outside, looking through the lens of the scope at a mystery he was not able to comprehend. It was clear that Erik was a fighter, his friend, but no angel. Most importantly, Erik was the man who saved him. John kneeled beside him, his gaze searching his friend's face for any sign of injury, despair flooding through him at the sight of Erik's gunshot wound and battered face and body.

"How are you feeling?" John's voice was rough with emotion and adrenaline, as if the fight were still humming under his skin.

Erik nodded, a grim smile tugging at his lips, his eyes still locked on the defeated assassin. It was a shadow of the man in 1943, but known in the future, dead and defeated. Erik took a deep breath and slowly exhaled as he replied, "I'm alive."

John helped Erik to his feet and their eyes met, a silent understanding passing between them.

"You never saw any of this," Erik said between gasps of pain. "This never happened. Do you understand?"

John nodded, then asked, "Can you walk?"

Erik nodded, his jaw clenched in determination as he surveyed the dense undergrowth around them, every sense on high alert. The assassin's fate was sealed, but the threat of Japanese soldiers still loomed large. If they were shot or caught, it would again alter the timeline.

With that danger in mind, they moved as one through the jungle, synchronized and purposeful. Adrenaline coursed through their veins, their senses heightened to a razor's edge as they navigated the dense foliage, every shadow seeming to hold a potential threat. The jungle seemed to pulse with a malevolent energy, as if it sought to test their resolve at every turn. In time, they reached the beach.

A sudden rustle caused Erik to freeze, his muscles coiled in readiness as he scanned the surrounding terrain. Two men stood near the Japanese wreck. They appeared to be islanders, and noticing John and Erik, they took flight and paddled away from the wreck in a canoe, despite John's hails. However, Erik recognized one waving to him, as if to say *thank you.*

CHAPTER 29

ACCEPTING WHAT YOU CAN'T CHANGE

"Things didn't go exactly as planned, but I'm not dead,
so it's a win."

— Andy Weir, *The Martian*

The setting sun painted the sky in shades of orange and pink, casting a warm glow over the beach where Erik and John sat in exhausted silence. The rhythmic sound of waves lapping at the shore accompanied their heavy breathing as they processed the events that led them to that moment of respite.

John turned to Erik, his eyes filled with a mixture of determination and concern. "I'll take the canoe back to Olasana Island tonight," he said, his voice hoarse from the ordeal they had just been through. "I'll bring the candy and water to the other men and come back for you in the morning. Keep your wound clean as best you can."

Erik nodded weakly, grateful for John's unwavering support. The two men had faced insurmountable challenges together, and had forged a bond through hardship and camaraderie. John pushed the canoe into the water, paddled away into the dusk, and disappeared into the horizon, a lone figure against the backdrop of the vast ocean.

Alone on the beach, Erik let out a deep sigh, his body aching from the physical exertion and emotional toll of their ordeal. The cries of animals on the island mingled with the gentle rustle of palm trees, creating a symphony of sounds that soothed his weary soul. He made his way back to the scene of the fight, and it was as if the island itself were guiding him through the treacherous journey, testing his resilience and determination. Erik remained aware of his surroundings, watching for poisonous snakes slithering silently in the underbrush and other deadly animals.

He was challenged with every step, but he pushed forward with unwavering determination. He finally arrived, grabbed the dagger, and looked for anything edible. In time, he was able to find Indian Spinach and bananas, then headed back to the beach.

As he ate, the sun dipped below the horizon, casting long shadows across the sand. The dark and ominous blanket of night appeared like black granite with the Milky Way galaxy whirling like steam from hot tea over Naru Island, like so many times before he stared at so many horizons without boundaries.

Erik, a man running out of time, sat by the shore of Ferguson Passage, gazing at the horizon with a heavy heart. The weight of Tesla's theory pressed down on him, threatening to crush his hopes of ever reuniting with Jamie and Max in 1948. His eyes searched the darkness, straining to catch a glimpse of a US Navy ship he desperately needed to return home.

As waves crashed against the shore, a sense of impending doom filled the air. Erik's heart raced with each passing second, knowing time was slipping through his fingers like grains of sand. Would he ever get back to his family, or was he destined to be stranded in 1943? He placed his head down, closed his eyes, and allowed himself to drift into a restless sleep.

Images of Jamie and Max flashed before his mind's eye, but his dream turned into a nightmare. The screams and moans of dying men on the He-111 echoed in his ears. He saw the faces of the men in the bomber, their eyes hazed over and filled with hope and despair in equal measure. The night passed in a blur of fragmented visions and restless slumber, until the first light of dawn broke over the horizon, painting the sky in hues of gold and pink.

The morning sun rose over the horizon, casting a golden hue over the tranquil waters surrounding Naru. Kennedy strode across the sandy beach, the weight of their situation heavy on his shoulders. Two of the native islanders, Gasa and Kumana, walked beside him, their faces drawn with determination. "Erik," John called out, relief flooding his voice as he spotted his friend by the shore.

Erik turned, a flicker of hope crossing his face. "Welcome back."

"We've found a boat hidden here on Naru," John said, excitement lacing his words. "It might be our ticket out of here."

Even though he knew they were going to be rescued, Erik's eyes widened with disbelief. "A boat? That's incredible."

The islanders gathered around them, guiding Kennedy and the others to the hidden vessel with hushed whispers and gestures. Waves crashed against the shore as they approached the boat, its weathered wood a stark contrast against the azure waters. "How are we going to send a message for help?" John asked, his brows furrowed in thought.

Gasa's eyes gleamed with determination as he picked up a green coconut, swiftly carving a message into the husk with practiced precision. The scratching sound echoed in the quiet morning, each stroke spelling out their desperate plea for rescue. Gasa and Kumana left with the message: Nauro isl commander. Native knows pos'it. He can pilot. 12 alive, need small boat. Kennedy.

As they waited for a sign of hope on the horizon, John turned to Erik. "We need to take our chances out at sea. Will you be able to row?"

Erik nodded resolutely. "I'll do whatever it takes. if it gets me back to my wife and son."

Together, John and Erik launched the two-man canoe into the churning waters of Ferguson Passage, determined expressions etched on their faces. The sea roared around them, waves towering over the small vessel as they battled against the elements. The sound of water lapping against the canoe mingled with their grunts of effort, their muscles straining against the relentless onslaught. Just when it seemed like all was lost, with lungs burning and arms aching, they managed to steer the canoe back to shore, gasping for breath.

The next morning dawned with a glimmer of hope as eight islanders appeared at Naru, their faces bright with anticipation. Food and instructions in hand, they relayed Lt. A. Reginald Evans's message to John, their voices eager and urgent. "Come with us," one of the islanders urged, gesturing toward Evans's post. After a brief stop at Olasana to provide food and water to the crew, the islanders concealed John under a pile of palm fronds before paddling toward Gomu Island in Blackett Strait.

The rhythmic sound of paddles dipping into the water filled the air as they navigated the treacherous waters, their movements synchronized with practiced precision. John's heart raced with a mixture of fear and anticipation, the stakes higher than ever before. As Gasa and Kumana's message floated toward the horizon, a sense of urgency hung heavy in the air, driving John and Erik forward into the unknown. The distant cries of seabirds overhead mingled with the whispers of the wind, a haunting reminder of the vast expanse of sea that separated them from safety. With each stroke of the paddle, they drew closer to Evans's post, their fate hanging in the balance.

The islanders' voices murmured low amongst themselves, their eyes reflecting the flickering hope that burned within their hearts.

Closer and closer they drew to Gomu Island, the anticipation building with each passing moment. As they neared the shore, the sound of waves crashing against the rocks filled their ears, a symphony of danger and possibility. With a final push, the canoe glided onto the sandy shore, marking the beginning of a new chapter in their harrowing journey.

When the PT boats arrived at the rendezvous point, John stood up in the canoe, the cool night air whipping past him as he prepared to signal his presence. The sound of guns sent a shiver down his spine as he steadied himself. Four shots echoed through the night, breaking the silence, signaling the arrival of PT 157 and PT 171. As John raised the fallen assassin's rifle, his heart raced with anticipation. The weight of the weapon in his hands felt foreign, but there was no time for hesitation. With a deep breath, he aimed and fired. The recoil caught him off guard, throwing him off balance, and the world seemed to spin around him before he plunged into the cold embrace of the water.

Sputtering and gasping, John emerged from the water, his wet clothes clinging to him. He scrambled up the side of PT 157, his frustration evident as dripping strands of hair fell over his forehead. The crew looked on, a mix of concern and amusement evident on their faces as they watched the soaked lieutenant try to regain his composure.

The PT boats navigated the Blackett Strait with precision under John's guidance, gliding through the darkness like silent predators. As they approached Olasana Island in the early hours of the morning, John's voice rang out, cutting through the silence like a knife. "Men of PT 109, where are you?"

His urgency carried on the wind, a mixture of relief and anxiety evident in his tone. The men of PT 157 and PT 171 exchanged nervous glances, their hands instinctively moving to their weapons. Japanese patrols could be lurking nearby, adding to the tension of the moment, but Kennedy's determination was unwavering. His voice echoed across the water as he continued to call out for his stranded crew

Suddenly, a faint response carried on the breeze, a groggy voice calling back from the darkness. "Lieutenant Kennedy, is that you?"

The relief in the voice was palpable, and a small smile tugged at John's lips as he realized his men were safe. As the rescue unfolded, the men of PT 109 were helped aboard the waiting boats, their exhaustion evident in the way they leaned heavily on each other for support. The sound of their laughter mingled with the lapping of the waves as they were guided back to the safety of the US base at Rendova.

At five-thirty in the morning on August eighth, the sun rose on a new day, casting its golden light on the weary but relieved faces of the men of PT 109. John stood at the helm, his gaze fixed on the horizon, a sense of accomplishment blooming in his chest as he guided his crew back to safety.

Later, he glanced down at Erik, who was in a jeep that was bound for a hospital where his injuries would be treated. He nodded in friendship and mouthed, *thank you*. For Erik and the rest of the survivors of PT 109, the echoes of the night's events lingered in the air, a tale of resilience and camaraderie that would be told for years to come.

CHAPTER 30

CONNECTIONS BUT DON'T ASK WHY

"Isn't life a collection of weird quizzes with no answers to half the questions?"

— Pawan Mishra, *Coinman: An Untold Conspiracy*

As Erik's vision slowly adjusted to his blurred surroundings, he glanced to his left and realized he was in a field hospital. Then all his senses went into overdrive and he gasped. The moist air quietly suffocated Erik as he took a breath of relentless humidity mixed with the overwhelming smell of disinfectant and anesthetics. Nurses, doctors, and other medical staff worked together in perfect harmony, each endeavoring to preserve lives.

He was in a ward of some sort, with many occupied cots and mattresses lined up against the wall. Some of the cots had mosquito netting over them, but Erik had no idea why. Was it for whomever was dying next, or was it for those with the best chance of survival? Erik had a net over his, so he hoped it was the latter.

Wounded patients had their bodies and limbs wrapped in imbrued bandages. Others were getting new sterile gauze pads, while nurses rubbed hydrocortisone, antibiotics, and antiseptic ointments on their wounds. Erik felt a sharp pain, as if an icepick were being pushed into his left shoulder. It was the gunshot wound. He was one of the lucky ones.

A nurse approached Erik with a tray, soft eyes, and a smile. As she placed the tray by the bedside, she said in a caring tone, "Good morning, Commander, how are we feeling?" She helped him sit up, and then she administered a Penicillin G shot.

"I'm okay. Where am I?"

"Tulagi Island." She placed the syringe down and reached for a box labeled *Medical Item No. 9115500 – Morphine Tartrate, 5 Tubes*. She gestured to offer the morphine, and Erik nodded. As she prepared his upper arm with alcohol, she said, "The full effects of Morphine are not felt for twenty to thirty minutes after injection." Then she stuck him, and it felt like a bee sting. "You are not to be given another one within two hours."

As Erik nodded his understanding, he saw John headed in his direction.

"You are good to go. Get some rest," the nurse said before heading to tend her next patient.

"How are you feeling?" John asked as he tossed Erik a chocolate bar.

"I'm alive." Erik brought the candy to his brow in a mock salute as a way of showing gratitude.

From the corner of his eye, he noticed a man staring at him with brown eyes that were almost black. Erik glanced around for anything he could use as a weapon. Perhaps he was being paranoid, but the assassins of ONE were nothing if not patient and persistent, and he had been a target of theirs on at least four occasions that he knew about. He found a pencil that was left on a table near his bed, casually grabbed it, and positioned it in his hand as if it were a dagger. He looked up at John and asked as if he hadn't noticed anything, "How have you been?"

"Never better," John replied.

Erik and the stranger's eyes locked.

"Actually," John continued, "I have excellent news to share. I'm going to be assigned to command PT-59."

Erik nodded as he kept a watch on the dark-eyed man.

"I'm eager to get back into the fight, and I have to report to my new boat on September first."

Erik grinned at the news as he tried to focus on the staring stranger, but he had vanished.

John noticed Erik seemed preoccupied, and he waved his hand in front of Erik's face. "Erik, what's wrong?"

Erik dismissed the subject with a short sideways jerk of his hand as he glanced around the hospital ward. He has learned to live with the idea of people wanting him dead, while at the same time acting like everything was perfectly fine. "No, I'm fine. I just thought I recognized someone." The next few bunks over, a young man was being restrained by orderlies, nurses, and any other medical staff that were not busy while a doctor prepared a shot to sedate him.

"The Japs are all around us! Get them off me!" The man screamed.

Erik recognized the man's face and voice as more orderlies approached with restraints. He maneuvered to the man's bed, but was stopped short by a nurse. "Sir, please return to your bed." She got one of the orderly's attention; then stated in a firmer tone. "Sir, I am asking you to return to your bed."

"I know him, and I can calm him down." He looked into her eyes. "Let me talk to him."

An orderly took the nurse's place and demanded, "Sir, you need to go back to your bed." His words fell upon deaf ears. The orderly's tone became cold, hard, and scornful. "Sir, we know how to do our job! Go to your bed!" The orderly reached for Erik's wounded shoulder. His hand never got there.

Erik moved lightning quick, and suddenly the orderly's hand was trapped with Erik's fingers grinding into his palm. The orderly cried out in pain as he stumbled to the floor. Erik flashed a menacing look to persuade the man to let him see the patient. The orderly nodded, and Erik released him.

The orderly cleared space for Erik to see the man. Erik looked calmly into the frightened blue eyes of the young soldier. The man's young face was etched into Erik's memory from photos he'd seen since he was a child. Of all the hospital wards in the Pacific theater, what were the odds they'd end up only a few beds away from one another?

Erik smiled down at his grandfather, who was deathly pale, his face streaked with blood, dirt, and perspiration. "Arthur." Erik held his hand.

"They're all around us! They attacked us! They wiped us out! Hundreds dead!"

Erik cupped the soldier's shoulders to restrain him and stared deeply into his weary eyes. "I got them. They're all dead." Erik turned to face John and motioned for him to bring the chocolate bar. "We are safe." Erik's grandfather's eyes slowly become calm as John handed the chocolate to him. "Here, eat this." Some of the medical staff walked away while Erik continued. "Everything will be okay."

"I'm scared." Arthur gripped his arm. "I don't want to die."

Erik turned to a doctor and asked if his wounds were life threating. They shook their head. Erik asked if he needed surgery. They nodded, but said it would be minor.

Arthur screamed out again, "I don't want to die!"

Erik let out a deep sigh and pressed his forehead against his grandfather's. "You are not going to die; you have my word." He gave his grandfather a hug. "Let the doctors and nurses help you." Arthur's eyes said everything, as if to say he didn't trust them.

"If I were you, I would let them. I trust them."

"You would?"

"Yes, Arthur, I would." Erik paused. "You have to trust me, okay?"

Arthur nodded, but had a puzzled look on his face as he replied, "Excuse me, how did you know my name?"

"I overheard someone say it."

"What's your name?"

"Erik," he said, then nodded before turning around.

Arthur asked, "Erik, will I ever see you again?"

Erik's eyes begin to water. "You will. If not soon, you will see me in the future."

"Promise?"

"Promise."

"Are you okay?" John asked.

Erik nodded, as he headed to his bunk.

"Who was that guy?"

"I don't know. He just reminded me of my grandfather."

"Sounds like he was a good man."

Erik nodded.

John moved on. "I have put in that you should be awarded the Bronze Star for what you did."

Erik shook his head.

John protested. "You saved my life."

Erik agreed but continued shaking his head.

"Then give me one goddamn reason why not."

"I already told you why."

"Come on. Cut the bullshit."

"Fair enough." Erik nodded and locked eyes with John. "I don't want the fucking medal. Give it to someone who deserves it."

Tossing his hands up in the air, John blared. "You are impossible. You do remember that you saved my life?"

"It was the right thing to do."

"All the more reason you should get the medal."

Erik shook his head. "I told you: I was never on those islands. I was never on your boat. You never met me."

"God damn. Are you always this secretive?"

Erik grinned.

John pointed to his chest. "I bet your wife would agree with me."

Erik chuckled and nodded as he replied, "Why don't you ask her when you meet her? She might even say I'm mysterious."

"I can count on it. Maybe if I ask my father, he can find your secrets. Then we can have a conversation, since you can't seem to talk about anything."

Erik slowly raised his head and squinted into John's eyes. "I wouldn't recommend you do that." Erik's words dripped with ice. "I know who you are and what your father can do. You are not going find anyone in DC or anywhere else to get information on me. This isn't my first fucking rodeo, and you are not dealing with a student here. I'm the fucking professor."

John tried to avoid eye contact.

"Lieutenant Kennedy, look at me when I am talking."

John straightened his posture.

"Anytime the government has an operation that can't fail, they call me. So, extend me some fucking courtesy and leave my past alone. Do we have an understanding, Lieutenant?"

John gulped and replied firmly, "Yes, sir."

Erik nodded. "If you still want to be friends, I'm all for that."

"Do you think you will ever be able to tell me who you are?"

Erik sunk his head into the pillow as he stared at the ceiling. "John, I need some sleep."

"You're avoiding my question?"

"I'm not avoiding it. I'm just refusing to answer."

John gave a puzzled look.

Erik took a deep breath. "You need to listen to me very carefully. I know you are curious about what happened on the island, who I am, and why I was on your boat. Those are all great questions, and under any other circumstances, I would love to answer them." Erik paused to emphasize his next point. "However, some things are best left unknown."

"I do not like the unknown."

"I know, neither do I. My wife, bless her soul, always tells me I keep hiding the keys to all the places in my mind, so she won't know what I have seen or experienced. A good friend told me I was here for a reason. He didn't give me the reason, but whatever it is, it meant I was going to make a difference in this world." Erik paused. "His last words were that one man can make a difference."

John seemed to relent. "Erik, you are a very private person, and I respect that."

Erik nodded in appreciation.

"I bet if you look up the word private in the dictionary, your picture would be right next to it." John nudged Erik's shoulder jokingly, and they both grinned.

John's grin faded as he faced Erik. "I heard once you are better, you are going back to the States. Is that true?"

Erik nodded.

"Once you get back, what are you going to do?"

"Finish writing my book and spend as much time as I can with my wife and son."

John stood up and pointed at Erik with a chuckle. "Go straight home. No secret missions."

"That's the objective. I still need to cross over the Pacific. So, I can say I am going to try."

"Try?" John asked with an underlined tone curiosity.

"Yes, try. I just have to get home by a certain date."

John looked puzzled.

"When I travel, I'm a meticulous planner. I prefer arriving at my destination at a certain date and time."

"I'm sure you will do fine." John cupped Erik's shoulder. "Get some sleep. I'll look you up in DC when I get back."

Erik wrote down his personal information and handed to John, but gave him very specific instructions. "Do not try to call me, write me, or visit me until January of 1945. Understood?"

John looked perplexed, but seemed to have given up on questioning Erik's odd behavior and simply nodded. "Thanks again for saving my life." They embraced lightly and shook hands. John took a step then turned and faced Erik. "Also, from now on, since you saved my life, call me Jack."

Erik nodded, placed his head on his pillow, and closed his eyes. In the back of his mind, he knew that getting to Colorado Springs would be the easy part. But he had no documentation of who he was and would not be able to get near, much less enter, Hidden Meadow Apartments. One step closer to home, but one more hurdle to leap.

CHAPTER 31

MY LITTLE MYSTERY SOLVED

"Not every puzzle is intended to be solved. Some are in place to test your limits. Others are, in fact, not puzzles at all…"
— Vera Nazarian, *The Perpetual Calendar of Inspiration*

A doctor approached Erik as he slept and looked over his chart then gave him a little nudge. "Erik, it's Dr. Stein. I need you to wake up for me." He nudged Erik again, and Erik started coming to his senses and glanced up into the doctor's calm, relaxed eyes. "How are you feeling Erik?"

"I am alive, doc."

The doctor looked at Erik as if what he said was inappropriate. "I can see that, but I am asking how you are feeling."

Erik nodded as the doctor checked his vitals and wound. "I'm okay. A little sore, and wanting to go home."

"I will give you something for your pain, but only take it when you need it." He finished his examination. "You have gotten your wish; I'm releasing you in a few days, and you are going home."

Erik nodded in appreciation.

"Do you have questions?"

"What day is it?"

The doctor gave a puzzled look. "Friday."

"The date?"

"Thirteenth."

Erik nodded as he calculated the days since he was back. He only had eight days, according to Tesla's theory, before he was stuck permanently in time.

"Is everything okay?"

Erik looked around to see what things he needed to gather up.

"Erik!" The doctor snapped his fingers in front of him to grab his attention as he called two orderlies over. "I'm not releasing you."

Erik swung his legs over the bed as he sat upright.

"I'm giving you an order lay down."

Before the doctor continued, Erik stood up and stared him in the face. "Since, I got here, it has been most stressful and inconvenient." Erik paused for a moment and prepared to do whatever he needed to do next as the orderlies stood on either side of him. "I am leaving, and you can't stop me."

The doctor nodded. "You're correct. I won't, but they will." He motioned to the orderlies.

Over the doctor's shoulder, a Native American man approached. "The lieutenant commander needs to come with me," the man ordered.

The doctor turned to face the man, gave him a quick look over, and said, "Lance Corporal, the lieutenant commander is going nowhere."

The lance corporal handed over a document. "Sir, I have documentation from Major General Clayton B. Vogel, and he will be released to me now."

Lifting the paper in the air, the doctor muttered, "I will get to the bottom of this."

"Sir, I would like to inform you if you make a call to Major General Vogel regarding these orders, or anyone, you will be violating the Espionage Act." He reached out his hand to take the document. "Sir, release the lieutenant commander and forget this incident ever happened."

The doctor and the orderlies stormed off as the corporal turned to Erik. "Sir, do you need anything?"

Erik gestured to his clothes.

In return, the corporal gave him his clothes and waited for Erik's return. A few moments later, Erik returned and gestured to the lance corporal to lead the way.

"Sir, I will drive you to the airfield."

"Thank you."

After reaching a jeep and setting out from the hospital, Erik asked, "Why does Major General Vogel want to see me?" Not getting an answer, he quickly looked around the jeep for a weapon. Opening the glove compartment, Erik grabbed a screwdriver and held it like a knife as a slow, intense chill crept up his spine.

Looking at Erik at the corner of his eye, the lance corporal replied, "Running Wolf, I am not here to hurt you." The lance corporal felt the dull tip against his side as he continued. "Didn't I tell you Tawa has sent messengers during the time of the Red Star Kachina so they can help mankind change? And that you are one of the messengers?"

Erik tried to recall where he heard that before. The lance corporal pulled the jeep to the side, off the road, and stared into Erik's bewildered eyes.

"Also, you asked if I would ever see you again." He paused for a moment to see if Erik recalled before continuing. "I told you that you would see me, but not in the way you saw me the first time we met."

Erik shook his head in disbelief. "It can't be." The man stared at Erik as he slowly realized who he was talking to. "You warned me that I would learn horrible truths, and they would haunt my dreams for all time."

The man nodded.

"You're Eagle Eyes from the Hopi People?"

Eagle Eyes nodded.

"How did you become a Navajo code talker?"

"There are things better left not said."

"Great, more riddles and vague answers." Erik uttered, not enjoying being on the other side of that table for a change.

"Running Wolf, you have proven to me and my ancestors that you are intelligent, persistent, and, most of all, you have the ability to be a true survivor." Eagle Eyes raised his finger to emphasize his next words. "Even though you're misunderstood, you are compassionate, friendly, loyal, and perseverant to your friends and family."

"So, you knew I was coming and where to find me?"

"My ancestors said the Eagle, the Principal Messenger of the Creator since the creation of the world, gave a message of a wolf that had a gift to travel throughout time." Eagle Eyes maneuvered back on the road and continued to the airfield. Erik was overwhelmed with curiosity, eager to grasp on the rest of the story. "The Eagle said the wolf would be driven to correct history because somewhere in the past, our fates were attacked, resulting in an alternate timeline and events."

Erik was completely engrossed. "Well, that sounds like me."

Eagle Eyes nodded. They finally made it to the airfield, where ground crews were preparing a C-54 Skymaster to take off as the pilot and co-pilot stood around smoking.

Erik took a deep breath as he searched for an explanation, then shook his head and replied. "I never asked for this."

"Then why did you go back to 1944?" Eagle Eyes asked.

"To change the world to a better place and save lives."

"Why'd you want to travel in time again, to 1940 and 1943?"

"To correct the timeline—"

"To correct the timeline because somewhere in the past, the timeline skewed, and to put right where it was once wrong?"

Erik nodded. "I only changed one event to prevent another."

"Do you actually believe that is all you did? Change one event to correct another?"

"Yes."

"Running Wolf, despite your ego, I would like to say that you have achieved a lot more every time you traveled back in time. In addition, you have done more than correct the timeline." Eagle Eyes pointed to Erik's chest to get his point across. "You have educated others about history, and that touched their lives. Their lives touched others."

"Even Hitler?"

"Yes, even him." Eagle Eyes looked up to the sky. "The Creator is pleased with what you have done. He has plans for you."

Erik dismissed the idea as he shook his head. "I do not want any more. I want to go home to Jamie and Max."

Eagle Eyes cupped Erik's shoulder. "I understand." He leaned forward. "Remember your gift. Knowing historical events is both good and bad. And a curse."

"I cannot interfere."

Eagle Eyes nodded again.

"But how can my gift be any good if I cannot interfere." A puzzled look overcame Erik's face. "For example, say I knew there was going to be a train wreck. If I interfere, I could save lives."

Eagle Eyes disagreed. "The Creator does not want you to interfere with things like that."

"Then what good is my gift if I cannot use it?"

"It is forbidden for you to interfere in human history."

Erik rolled his eyes.

"However, I do know the Creator, and I know that you are here for a reason." Eagle Eyes raised his hand to Erik to let him finish. "I don't know when the reason will occur, but when it does, be prepared for it."

Erik nodded.

"Running Wolf, when that day arises, use your skills to get through the dark passage."

"I will."

The pilot motioned to Erik it was time to board. Erik and Eagle Eyes shook hands and embraced. Just before he entered the aircraft, Eagle Eyes grabbed his attention. "We've come far, you and I. I will not forget you. Running Wolf, I am Eagle Eyes." They stared into each other's eyes. "Do you see that I am your friend?" Erik nodded. "Can you see that you will always be my friend?"

Erik nodded one last time, raising his hand proudly above his head and held up two fingers in a V, which meant to some tribes in the western plains of North America that they could still fight. Eagle Eyes returned the gesture.

As Erik took his seat, the pilot and co-pilot went over their checklist in the cockpit. Then, without warning, several thundering roars pierced Erik's ears as each engine fired up. They stuttered, shooting sparks, then thick, black, choking smoke blasted out of the exhaust as each came alive. In time, each engine settled into a low rumble. Erik closed his eyes, knowing the flight would take nearly seventy-two hours, with a layover in Pearl Harbor, Hawaii, then on to Colorado Springs, and then finally back home.

CHAPTER 32

TO THE ENDS OF TWO PATHS

"Okay, enough self-pity. I'm not doomed. Things will just be harder than planned. I have all I need to survive."

— Andy Weir, *The Martian*

The C-54 Skymaster hovered effortlessly in the stratosphere. The sun released its last bright, blinding rays as they descended gracefully through the late afternoon sky. The aircraft's four engines droned steadily, carrying it and its cargo of one passenger over the vast expanse of open desert. From the window, Erik glanced out at the world below him, at the intermingling of earth and sky, as they made their final approach toward Peterson Army Air Force Base.

A gentle downward push on the yoke by the pilot nosed the Skymaster lower. The co-pilot informed him that he saw a silhouette emerging from the distant horizon, noting the possibility that it was a flock of birds. They soon confirmed it was a ballet of birds, their spread wings catching the light as they flew, feathers shining like gold dust in the sunlight, making it difficult to discern their direction of travel. As the silhouette of birds approached the aircraft, the pilot assumed that the flock would scatter or that he would have enough time to maneuver around them. Nevertheless, as they approached the aircraft, the birds merged together into one large, dense flock.

Judging where the flock would be, the pilot gradually began to loosen his grip on the yoke as he recalculated his course. As the aircraft climbed higher, its engines roared louder. The pilot made a sudden turn to the left and noticed that there were many birds approaching from all directions as he shifted courses.

The birds collided with the cockpit, engines, and fuselage with a series of dull thuds resonating throughout the airframe, resembling flak. A whirl of feathers and debris swirled around the shuddering aircraft, a chaotic scene unfolding in a matter of seconds. Three of the four engines erupted in flames, going dead with a sputter and whine. The pilot struggled to keep control of the aircraft as well as tame the burgeoning fires, while the co-pilot checked the Quick Reference List.

Erik was jolted in his seat by the violent shaking of the aircraft. A master alarm blared from within the cockpit as controlled panic swarmed through the cabin. The aircraft's forward momentum slowed, a chilling reminder of the calamity that had struck just moments earlier. During the struggle for control, the experienced pilot battled with the controls, his hands moving with muscle memory as the co-pilot assisted and advised of what was happening. As the damaged engines belched smoke, the altitude of the aircraft dropped at an alarming rate.

So close to the end of Erik's journey, the desolate land below rose rapidly, portending the danger that lay ahead.

Erik tightened his grip on his seat, his heart pounding in his chest as he braced himself for impact. The cacophonous sound of alarms filled the plane and deafened everyone inside. The world outside held its breath as the Skymaster descended, drawing ever closer to the vast desert. Suddenly, with a deafening crash that reverberated through the airframe, the aircraft struck the hard sand of the desert. Under the force of the impact, bushes snapped and splintered. The fuselage groaned as it absorbed the force of the impact. The Skymaster left a trail of destruction in its wake as it plowed through the coarse sand.

Erik was thrown around like a rag doll as chaos reigned inside the cabin. There was a cacophony of destruction as debris tumbled through the air within the aircraft, adding to the massive damage. Within moments, the Skymaster was ensconced deep in the desert and the violent descent came to an abrupt halt.

In the aftermath, there was a scene that could only be described as devastation. Plumes of smoke rose from the fires of the wreckage, mingling with the desert air. The once-mighty aircraft was twisted and fragmented, with one wing bent and battered and the other torn off.

As he looked out at the world around him, Erik realized how lucky he was to be alive. Trying to avoid the scattered debris in his path, he stumbled out of his seat and struggled to stay on his feet. As the smell of fuel filled his nostrils, his eyes became alert, and he was able to focus on the situation. He realized he was the only person in the aircraft who was alive, as the cockpit was separated from the remainder of the fuselage. In the aftermath of the crash, Erik emerged from the wreckage, dazed but alive.

Finally on solid ground, he ran as fast as he could. After feeling he was at a safe distance, he turned around and surveyed the wreckage of the plane. He was filled with grief for the two lost pilots. Erik bowed his head and closed his eyes in a moment of silent mourning. Turning away, unable to bear the sight of the destruction, he continued on his journey. He walked with heavy steps, thoughts of the tragedy still fresh in his mind, and silently vowed to never forget the people who had lost their lives that day. He promised himself to make the most of his own life in their memory.

In the vast expanse of the desert, the sun sank to the horizon, casting an amber hue across the arid landscape. Only the soft crunch of Erik's shoes on the sand beneath his feet broke the silence. He trudged forward, his steps measured and deliberate, his silhouette standing in stark contrast to the endless sand that surrounded him. His face was weathered, his eyes reflecting determination and fatigue. As the temperature dropped, he felt comforted by his uniform as he walked through the desert. The brim of the officer's cap cast a shadow over his face. Despite it being dusk, beads of sweat trickled down his forehead, a testament to the harsh environment he had to navigate through. He hoped to run into civilization if he continued south. There was nothing else he could do. He knew he had to stay on the path for as long as it took. The sun slowly faded over the horizon as he marched along, slowly disappearing into the distance.

As the sun dipped below the horizon, streaks of pink and orange spread across the canvas of the heavens. Erik left behind a trail of footsteps in the vast sea of sand. It was a lonely mark left behind by a single journey. There was purpose in his stride as he looked to the horizon with a fixed gaze, guiding his every step toward his distant goal.

Suddenly, Erik's skin got clammy, and he suffered painful muscle cramps in his arms and legs. His body got cold sweats. When he tried to shake it off, dizziness and lightheadedness consumed him. As he became more confused and his vision blurred, he stumbled on his own feet. Erik realized he was suffering from heat exhaustion. After what seemed like an eternity, Erik found himself enthralled by the sight of a road stretching away from him, a thin ribbon of asphalt cutting through the desolation of the desert. As he quickened his pace, the promise of civilization and safety beckoned to him from the distant horizon, and a sense of relief overcame him.

Erik's shoes struck the firm pavement with a satisfying thud. His eyes flicked in both directions, a surge of hope sweeping through him. Amidst the ancient sands of the desert, the road stood out as an oasis of modernity, offering a path forward. His determination grew stronger as he steadily continued down the road, the rhythmic sound of his shoes echoing in the quiet desert air. As night approached, the sky faded from an otherworldly glow of pink and purple to a single shade of black.

Each step took him closer to the end of his journey, as the road stretched out miles before him. There seemed to be no end to the lifeline that could offer safety but provided no guarantee of rescue. As Erik walked, his thoughts drifted to the comforts that were waiting for him at home, such as a soft bed, Max, and Jamie's love and comfort when she held him in her arms.

As the night deepened, Erik's surroundings changed as the darkness enveloped him. Stars appeared like pinholes against an inky canvas. Erik sat down with a deep sigh in his chest and shook his head, staring at the road stretching on, a solitary thread connecting him to the world beyond the desert. Beyond the horizon. He got up and started walking again, determined to make it to his destination.

Suddenly, just as the desert night settled, the distant hum of an engine that seemed to be coming from nowhere startled Erik. The sound grew louder, accompanied by the glimmer of headlights in the distance. As the car approached in the darkness, its headlights pierced through the night.

Erik rushed out to the middle of the road, waving his arms, but the driver blared his horn and swerved around him. Adrenaline coursed through Erik's body and his heart beat against his chest. The car's taillights broke through the darkness and its tires crunched against the road as it came to a halt, and Erik felt a rush of hope.

A passenger leaped from the car. The man yelled as he approached Erik. "Are you drunk, or are you just stupid?"

The sudden outburst took Erik aback, but he kept his composure. He tried to explain but couldn't get a word out.

The man shouted again, accusing Erik of irresponsibility, and demanding an apology. "We almost killed you!" the man declared, waiting for a reply that never came. "Are you going to answer me, you son of a bitch?" The man squinted as he moved closer. His eyes enlarged and his jaw dropped as he recognized Erik and ran toward him in a state of shock and confusion. "Erik? Is that you?"

Erik nodded in silence, still with a blank expression. The man suddenly hugged him, tears streaming down his face. "Oh, thank God you're alive!"

With a mixture of relief and excitement, Erik fell to his knees with a look of confusion on his face. The man yelled for his driver to assist him. Then he looked back at Erik and said, "I'm George Scherff. I was Tesla's assistant, and we met in 1940."

Erik nodded, sure that either the heat had addled his brain or he was having a death vision.

George stared at Erik's pale skin, his bloodshot eyes, and his pale complexion.

Erik's eyelids felt as if they were weighted with lead. He tried mumbling something through his cracked and scabby lips, but nothing came out. George reached out his hand and put it on Erik's shoulder, and said with a sympathetic voice, "You don't have to say anything. I know where you're headed. I'm here to help you."

The driver and George assisted Erik into the car's back seat. During the journey, Erik glanced out the window. They were once again on their way to Hidden Meadow Apartments. The desert's embrace slowly faded behind. George ordered the driver to hurry since Erik was slowly dying of heat stroke. George offered words of comfort as Erik drifted off. As the car raced past the desert, Erik's vision blurred. When they arrived at Hidden Meadow Apartments, Erik was barely conscious.

The car stopped at the entrance. Sentries stared at the vehicle apprehensively. In their crisply pressed uniforms, the guards studied the driver and George as they rolled down their windows. Their posture was rigid as they held their weapons at their sides. Their fingers hovered over the triggers as one approached the driver, who produced his ID, with George following suit.

"What about him?" the sentry asked, glancing at Erik.

"He's part of the project," George explained. "You know who I am now, and I'm sure you'll accept me vouching for him. You need to let us through, because he needs medical attention."

The sentry, equally determined, squared his shoulders and met George's gaze with unwavering resolve. "Sir, I'm following standard operating procedures. I won't let anyone pass without proper authorization."

George shook his head, his face a mask of frustration. Then he barked, his voice cutting through the air like a whip, "Let us through."

The sentry's rigid posture exhibited unwavering determination. "Sir, I cannot let anyone through these gates without identification. This is a restricted area."

George stepped out of the car and stepped right up to the sentry's face and yelled, "Get Major General Cochran Lane on the phone now!"

The sentry hesitated, not expecting such a demanding order.

There was no time for George to waste, so he stepped around the sentry and headed straight for the guard box. It was not long before the sentry caught up with him, but George held the telephone at arm's length and placed the call before the sentry and his partner could do anything to stop him. "Get me, Major General Lane," George demanded into the phone. The sentry, with beads of sweat forming on his brow, hovered over George.

Within moments, the general answered the call. "Yes, General

Lane. George Scherff here. I have one of the travelers who just returned, and he needs medical attention fast. I can't pass the gate. A Sergeant…" George glared at the sergeant with piercing eyes, and the sergeant gulped as he gave his last name, Weaver. "Sergeant Weaver said no one is allowed in without proper identification, but I tried to explain to him one of our travelers wouldn't have that since they are returning… Yes… In addition, he needs medical attention, and if we don't hurry, he could die… Yes… Maybe you can explain it to him."

George held out the phone, staring hard at Weaver. After contemplating the phone, Weaver shook his head.

George held the handset back to his ear. "Thank you, General." He then got in the car, and the sentry opened the gate and allowed them to pass. After driving for a few more minutes, they finally reached the hospital. Immediately after getting Erik out of the car, George and the driver rushed him inside and demanded that a doctor be called.

Erik was disoriented as he was placed on a gurney. A nurse examined him quickly as he was wheeled back. It was obvious they only had a few minutes to save Erik's life from his pale complexion, sunken, bloodshot eyes, extremely hot skin, and shallow breathing. He was wheeled to a vacant emergency room as the medical staff moved with purpose, their footsteps echoing the gravity of the situation. At that moment, the attending physician, Dr. Martinez, shouted orders to the nurses. His voice was both concerned and commanding at the same time. The nurses bustled around the room, gathering supplies and preparing equipment with great efficiency. I felt like they were running out of time, as Erik's condition was deteriorating.

Erik's clothes were quickly removed, his body slick with sweat. They swiftly inserted intravenous lines into his arms, delivering much-needed fluids to combat dehydration. The medical team worked with coordinated precision. A nurse monitored his vital signs, adjusting the IV drip as needed. Several team members applied cooling measures. Ice packs were placed under his arms, around his neck, and on his forehead.

The frigid touch contrasted starkly with his feverish skin. A fan whirred in the corner, sending refreshing air gusts across the room. Lastly, an individual ensured his oxygen levels remained stable, gently fitting an oxygen mask over his nose and mouth. A battle was being waged within his body. He was in and out of consciousness, unable to understand the flurry of activity surrounding him. The doctor and nurses all had a single goal in mind: saving his life.

A set of piercing eyes were fixed on Erik as Dr. Martinez leaned over, his gaze focused and determined. In a soothing tone, he spoke, and his words were a balm to Erik's disoriented mind. "Stay with us. You're in good hands. We're here to help."

As the minutes stretched on, Erik's body battled against the relentless heat that had brought him to the point of death. Slowly, his breathing steadied, his color returning from pallor to a healthier shade. The medical staff maintained a vigilant watch throughout the ordeal, their focus unwavering. A sigh of relief swept through the room as Erik's body temperature dropped and his skin, once fiery to the touch, felt less feverish. Amid this, his breathing became less labored, and he could focus his eyes more clearly.

The transformation took place over several hours, and it was truly amazing, as Erik's color had returned to a healthy hue. In addition, he could speak coherently once more. Dr. Martinez smiled, his eyes reflecting the satisfaction of a battle hard-fought and won.

"Welcome back," he said, his voice warm with genuine relief. Those were the first words Erik heard, and he offered a weak smile in return, gratitude evident in his gaze.

Following that, Dr. Martinez walked to the waiting room to inform George of Erik's condition. "Thanks, Doc," George whispered for saving his friend.

CHAPTER 33

EYE OF THE BEHOLDER'S AFTER VISIONS

"You have to believe that God or time or something was just waiting for your quantum leap to correct a mistake."

— Sam Becket, *Quantum Leap*

In a quiet corner of the hospital, under subdued lighting, Erik lay in a bed, still recovering from his ordeal and trying to find a moment of peace. He was grateful for the kindness and care of the nurses and the doctor and found solace because the pain he felt all over his body was better than the alternative. His hospital room door slowly opened, and George's head peeked in with a smile. "Now there's a sight for sore eyes."

"George, it's good to see you."

George walked in and stood by the window, lost in thought, but the keen mind he had was working overtime wondering how Erik had changed the future for the better. An empty chair was calling for George to engage in a conversation with Erik that defied the boundaries of time. A pair of wise and ageless eyes were George's gaze as he sat down.

"Erik, you timeless fuck, maybe you can work a little harder so we won't work as hard to bring you back."

"Where would be the fun in that?"

George stared at Erik as he leaned forward. "From water to the desert, how did the mission go?" He leaned back in the chair. "Were you successful?"

Erik took a deep breath as he nodded and replied. "I was, again."

"Erik, do you really think you can change the world all by yourself?"

"Sometimes it feels that way."

"Maybe God has given you a gift, dear boy," George said with a grin. "So, on a friendlier note, when was the last time you saw your wife and son?"

"Three months, two weeks, and this morning."

A knock came at the door, with an officer entering the room and staring at Erik. "Sir, my name is Lieutenant Burrows. I will be escorting you to the project location in ten minutes."

"Thank you, Lieutenant."

"Sir, I will be waiting outside." Erik nodded, and the lieutenant dismissed himself.

As Erik got ready, George said, "You know, Erik, I'm going to be very sad to see you go again. You've made a difference, preserving the timeline. Just knowing that you and I are going to be around to see 1948, that I'm part of Tesla's time machine project with the United States Government!" He pointed at Erik. "That you had a chance to travel through time."

Erik nodded.

"It's going to be hard waiting five years to talk to you about everything that's happened since you left." George stood up when Erik was ready and cupped his shoulder. "I'm really going to miss you."

"I'm going to miss you, too."

"When I see you again, we can talk about the World Series."

Erik shook his head. "Not a fan of baseball."

"Are you serious?"

Erik nodded.

"Did you know the defending champions, the St. Louis Cardinals, are facing the New York Yankees, as they did in the 1942 Series?"

Erik shrugged.

"The St. Louis Cardinals are favored to win."

Erik shook his head.

"How would you know? You said you don't follow baseball."

"Correct, but I can tell you this game saved my life."

Grinning ear to ear, George replied. "You going to put a large wager on the game?"

"You have no idea."

Once outside the room, the lieutenant led George and Erik down the long hallway, talking away. It seemed they had been best friends since grade school and had developed a close bond throughout the years, but it had been nearly three years since Erik and George met.

They finally got to the place where the time machine was kept and stood in front of the foot-wide, bright red line on the floor and the words, *DANGER: RADIATION. ONLY TRAVELERS AND AUTHORIZED PERSONNEL BEYOND THIS POINT.*

Their expressions were a mix of both sorrow and acceptance. The atmosphere was charged with bittersweet energy, a reminder that their time together was drawing to a close, and an unspoken understanding seemed to culminate in the poignant moment.

George faced Erik. "Now we know that the timeline is stable, what is our follow-up action."

Erik shook his head. "I don't believe anything is needed."

"And if the timeline is skewed?"

"Then you can seek my counsel."

"Erik, no one understands or will know the timeline of this war better than you."

"If you come to me, I'll run down the historical events and a synopsis of how to fix it." Erik paused for a moment. "I might even tell you what I think." Erik smirked.

"Erik, this isn't some science experiment where we can find another way if it didn't work." George rubbed his forehead. "If the timeline gets changed, then it will need to be fixed. If not, there could be a catastrophe on a global scale."

"I guess you could call it a huge cluster fuck, but I prefer calling it cause and effects of historical events." Erik stared into George's eyes. "If you have questions for me, you can be sure I will be there for you."

George knew there was no doubt that Erik carried the weight of his unique ability to fix the timeline at the expense of his own life. There had been no doubt in his mind that somebody like Erik existed. In the end, he came to understand that Erik was damn proficient at what he did, and he respected him for it.

Before Erik disappeared behind the door, George got his attention. "You and I both know you'll be called up again to preserve the timeline."

With those parting words, Erik stepped into the time machine. The room was consumed by a blueish-white light and Erik's form wavered. His presence faded like a distant memory.

The weight of the profound encounter left George with a sense of wonder and a newfound appreciation for the threads that weave the fabric of time and knowledge.

CHAPTER 34

THAT WAS NOW AND NOW THIS IS MY LIFE

"Life can only be understood backwards; but it must be lived forwards."

— Søren Kierkegaard

KENNEDY WARREN APARTMENTS, WASHINGTON DC, AUGUST 9, 1948

As the sun succumbed to the night, the pale-blue sky morphed into a glaucous hue. The half-moon gleamed on the clouds, accompanied by the stars, which slowly multiplied like raindrops on a sidewalk. Street lamps flickered to life, casting a radiant glow as headlights from passing cars sliced through the dusk.

Erik strolled down Connecticut Avenue as he approached the Kennedy Warren. He was pleased to see that everything was as he remembered, or at least it appeared to be. His eyes were drawn to the pale glow of lights flicking to life in the windows of the surrounding buildings. Having finally returned home, he was overjoyed. For the moment, he did not want to think about Project Pegasus. He also did not want to leave his family again.

There were even times when he considered relocating to Peoria, Arizona. There were many people who believed that there was nothing out there besides the hot sun and the desert, and they were right. While looking at the sky, he nodded, thinking that it would be a great idea to do that. How come? Because there was hardly anyone there, and he would be away from everything. Although history might change soon, at least there would not be any nuclear targets, at least not yet.

He was amused to see Jerry, the doorman of Kennedy Warren, across the street trying to entice a stray dog to come with him. Taking a glance over, Erik saw the streetlight above glinting green as the dog stood motionless, her eyes filled with apprehension. Once she had reached darting distance, the dog's eyes brightened, and she dashed across the street. Once she had reached leaping distance, she jumped up to Erik, who greeted her with gentle rubs on her back. Her tail wagged vigorously as she licked his face, and he positioned her better to carry her. Erik thought to himself, *Yes, you are welcome to stay with me.*

Jerry, on the other side of the street, waved to Erik. "Looks like you have a new friend Mr. Erik."

Erik grinned and nodded.

"What are you going to name her?"

"Esme."

Jerry smiled. "Mr. Erik, I am so glad you are home. Your wife and son are fine, and I am sure they will be excited to see you home."

Erik nodded in appreciation.

"How was your business trip?"

"You could say it kept me busy from time to time."

Jerry smiled, regardless of him not understanding what Erik truly meant. "I miss our talks about history."

"Me too."

"Mr. Erik, you said you fought in World War Two, right?" Again, Erik nodded. "What did you do?"

"Jerry, that's something we can discuss later. You could say I ensured the Germans lost their strategic advantage in certain battles." Erik knew Jerry would never believe him if he told him the truth, even if he could tell him the truth.

"Like, when the Germans lost the Battle of Britain?"

Erik gave a subtle nod. "Good night, Jerry."

As Erik reflected on the things he had experienced and the people he had met, he was left with gloomy thoughts. In the back of his mind, he knew he had to stop thinking about it. Having the knowledge that he was able to correct history through the power of his heart, faith, and skills, it might be a good idea to mix in a bit of luck as well. Despite all that, he almost didn't make it back home. Erik shook his head in disbelief and thought to himself, *Stop it. You need to focus on the here and now.*

He glanced up at the window in Max's bedroom and saw that Jamie was putting him to bed. Soon, she would be getting ready for bed, and he would be joining her. In Erik's opinion, that was an amazing thought, and he would cherish it for a very long time to come. There was a smirk on Erik's face as he gave Esme a skimpy ear massage.

He opened the door and looked around. He knew that most people wanted and lived a simple life, and they were averse to exploring any other option. Even though they could set a new path for themselves, they wouldn't. Erik remembered Eagle Eyes' prediction that some people, like Erik, would come along who would vanquish all the obstacles and challenges in life. There came a time in Erik's life when he realized that free will was a gift. Further, he was not aware of the power within it until he fought for it and realized how powerful it was.

ABOUT THE AUTHOR

Erik Foge holds a Bachelor's Degree in History, with an emphasis on Russian history and politics, from the University of Central Florida. His passion for history began at age thirteen when his parents sent him to Washington D.C. to learn about the United States and its governmental processes. The trip sparked Foge's interest in the federal government and the individuals within the Intelligence Community who are responsible for shaping the country's national policies. The characters in the *Project Pegasus Series* are drawn from his friendships and interactions with people from within the Intelligence Community at-large: the NRO; the NSA; the CIA; an Admiral and the Master Chief of the Sixth Fleet; Navy Seals, Astronaut John Glenn, and others.

www.ingramcontent.com/pod-product-compliance
Lightning Source LLC
Chambersburg PA
CBHW061114310726
48974CB00002B/536